Mack Bolan would continue his war at all costs

But there were moments, when he was reminded of the sacrifices he had made, reminded of the bitter cost of the course he had chosen.

Not that the Executioner would do it any differently if he had to do it over again. He had done what needed doing, and in that light he felt no regrets. There came a time in a man's life when he had to take a stand. When he either opposed the spread of evil, or he crawled into a hole and pretended it didn't exist.

Bolan had chosen to fight for what he believed. To confront those who wanted to make a cesspool of the world, those who were motivated purely by greed, hatred and fanaticism. Those who thought no more of snuffing out a human life than they did the life of a fly.

Someone had to do something. He had no choice.

DON PENDLETON's
MACK BOLAN®

WAR
LOAD

A GOLD EAGLE BOOK FROM
WORLDWIDE®

TORONTO • NEW YORK • LONDON
AMSTERDAM • PARIS • SYDNEY • HAMBURG
STOCKHOLM • ATHENS • TOKYO • MILAN
MADRID • WARSAW • BUDAPEST • AUCKLAND

First edition January 2002

ISBN 0-373-61482-9

Special thanks and acknowledgment to
David Robbins for his contribution to this work.

WAR LOAD

As long as it is realized and accepted that warriors must comprehend right and wrong, and strive to do right and avoid wrong, then the way of the warrior is alive.

—Taira Shigesuke,
Code of the Samurai

Why do I do what I do? Because it has to be done. Because it's right. If I turned my back on all evil in the world and did nothing, I'd be no better than those who have embraced evil.

—Mack Bolan

PROLOGUE

Six sleek helicopters dropped out of the inky night sky and leveled off above the glistening Pacific Ocean, nearly skimming the waves. Like predators swooping in for the kill, they flashed toward their objective with their running lights off.

"ETA in seven minutes, sir," the pilot of the lead chopper reported via his helmet com link.

Colonel Chen grunted in displeasure. A lean, wiry man with stern features, he pulled up his sleeve to check the glowing hands of his watch. "We will arrive two minutes later than projected," he said harshly.

"It couldn't be helped, sir," the pilot responded. "The storm."

"Tell that to the general," Chen snapped. He shifted in his cockpit seat to glance to the west at the roiling bank of clouds they had just passed through. Bad weather was the one contingency they hadn't anticipated. Storms at that time of year were rare. Now, thanks to a fluke of Nature, the success of their operation was in jeopardy. "He doesn't tolerate failure."

The pilot gestured at the speed indicator. "I'm pushing as fast as I can, sir."

The indicator was pegged at over 130 miles per hour, maximum speed for their modified McDonnell Douglas

Model 530MG. Chen couldn't fault the pilot. But the delay might prove costly, and the last thing he wanted was to incur the general's wrath. Few who did lived to tell the tale.

"In a way, sir, the storm has helped us," the pilot mentioned. "It has masked our approach. The Americans are less likely to detect us. We will be on top of them before they know it."

"I hope so, Captain," the colonel said sincerely. "Americans are not known for being stupid, and their technology is second to none."

The pilot grinned. "Perhaps we should thank them for our helicopters, sir."

Despite the seriousness of their situation, Chen smiled. Such sweet irony! he mused. Using illegally obtained American helicopters to attack an American warship and steal a revolutionary new weapon right out from under their noses! Only the general could have conceived of so bold a plan! Only the general possessed the brazen audacity to carry it out!

Chen turned to the four soldiers dressed in combat blacksuits who sat as rigid as statues behind him. "You heard, Sergeant Yatsen?"

"Yes, sir," the noncom crisply responded.

"You will have less time than anticipated."

"We will not let you down, sir," Yatsen declared. "Our strike teams have trained for weeks for this mission. We know the *Hampton* from bow to stern. More so, I should think, than most of her American crewmen."

Chen agreed. "Intel is always worth its weight in gold."

Yatsen nodded and remarked, "As Americans like to say, they will never know what hit them."

THE USS *HAMPTON* was dead in the water, but not through any fault of her twin D2G nuclear reactors. The Virginia-class guided-missile cruiser had come to a full stop in the North Pacific Ocean one hundred nautical miles east of Japan at the command of the officer in charge of the sensitive exercise they were engaged in.

Commodore John Hale gazed down from the bridge at the flurry of activity surrounding the quadruple launcher on the forward deck. His thick eyebrows knit. "Are we about ready, Captain?"

The *Hampton*'s senior officer, Captain Wallace Benson, turned toward the duty station. "Are we?" he repeated, striving mightily to quell the butterflies fluttering madly in his stomach. A lot was riding on the test they were about to conduct, and having a bigwig from the Navy's Department of Special Operations on board to personally oversee things only added to the tension. His crew was on edge, and Benson couldn't blame them.

"Sir! Launch control reports the first PPS-1 will be set to go in ninety seconds. Mark!"

"Very well," Benson said, his tone tinged with pride. His people were performing flawlessly. He could only hope the test went as well. "It's hard to believe the missile we're about to fire will hit a target anchored four thousand miles away, off Hawaii," he commented.

"Believe it," Hale replied. "The PPS-1 has unlimited range. Four thousand or forty thousand miles, it makes no difference."

Benson skeptically regarded his superior. "Are you telling me, sir, that thing can fly completely around the world?"

"Captain, the PPS-1 could fly to the sun and back if we needed it to." Hale was glued to the deck. "It's the stuff a military man's dreams are made of. Remember the profound impact the A-bomb had? The PPS-1 will have the same effect, possibly even more. If we succeed, we'll initiate a whole new era in warfare."

A low whistle escaped Benson.

"Exactly," Hale said. "The importance of our undertaking can't be stressed enough. The President himself is awaiting the outcome of what we do here tonight. For all intents and purposes, the United States will become invincible."

The butterflies swarming in Benson's gut redoubled their fluttering with a vengeance. He saw seamen scurry away from the quadruple launcher, and it spurred him into barking, "Launch control station, report!"

"Forty-two seconds, sir!"

Benson stared at the launcher, wondering what it was that made the PPS-1 so special. The commodore had been incredibly tight-lipped about the whole affair. All Benson had been able to gather was that the new missile's propulsion system was unlike anything ever seen. It was as advanced over conventional systems as lasers were over slingshots.

"Thirty seconds, sir!"

Commodore Hale stepped closer to the window. "I've devoted the last two years of my life to this project, Captain," he disclosed. "Two years of bucking the odds, of accomplishing what everyone claimed was impossible. This is the payoff. My whole career is on the line."

As if Benson didn't have enough to worry about.

"Give me a countdown commencing at ten seconds," he commanded.

The duty officer obliged. "Ten-nine-eight-seven—"

Hale pressed his palms against the window and leaned forward as if he intended to dive out.

"—six-five-four-three—"

Benson's pulse quickened. He barely heard the last part of the countdown. Then it happened; the missile shot from the launcher in a blur. One instant it was there. The next it was gone, streaking eastward at astonishing speed. Had he blinked, he would have missed it.

Benson had never seen the like. No cruise missile ever made was that fast. Something else was different, too. Normally, when a cruise missile was launched, it spewed enough smoke to cover one-third of the forward deck and continued to spew smoke as it climbed. But the PPS-1 did no such thing. Other than a telltale reddish glow emitted by the thrusters, there was nothing to indicate its engines had ignited.

Accustomed to the rumbling roar that always accompanied a launch, Captain Benson instead heard a high-pitched whine more reminiscent of a turbine than a turbojet engine. In a span of seconds, the red glow dwindled to a tiny red speck that vanished over the horizon at sea level.

"Good God!" Benson blurted. "How fast is that brainchild of yours?"

"Not mine alone," Hale said, sounding almost as awed as Benson. "And to answer your question, theoretically the PPS-1 can attain speeds in excess of thirty thousand miles per hour."

"Thirty *thousand?*" Benson was flabbergasted. He

performed quick mental calculations. "Why, at that rate, it will hit the target off Hawaii in—"

"In under ten minutes, yes," Hale finished for him. "I wasn't exaggerating when I told you a new era in warfare has begun. Think of the repercussions."

Benson was doing just that. With the aid of a satellite tracking system, the PPS-1's unlimited range enabled it to destroy targets anywhere on the planet. The implications were staggering. Conceivably, if trouble broke out in the Middle East, the United States could fire one of the new missiles from, say, Lake Michigan, and end the hostilities from half a world away. "I'll be damned," he breathed in amazement.

"Your men are preparing the second missile," Hale commented, his nose to the pane once again. "I commend their efficiency."

"Thank you, sir," Benson said. "I just hope the rest of the launches go as well as the first one."

As if on cue, the duty officer hollered, "Captain! Surface-search radar reports six unidentified aircraft approaching from the west! Range, five hundred yards and closing."

"Hail them," Benson directed. Given the *Hampton*'s proximity to Japan, he assumed the aircraft had to be Japanese. Perhaps a routine military flight that had blundered into the area. Which was understandable, since the Pentagon had insisted on keeping the test hush-hush, and the Japanese government had no idea what was taking place. "Find out who they are and what they're doing here."

"We've tried, sir. They don't answer." The duty officer touched a finger to his headset, then stiffened. "Sir! They are in attack formation!"

"There must be some mistake," Benson stated. No

one knew where they were. No enemy could possibly find them without obtaining the exact coordinates, and only a few people in the upper echelons of government were privy to the highly classified operation the *Hampton* was engaged in.

Even as Captain Benson spoke, half a dozen squat black locusts whisked out of the night and an explosion rocked his ship.

COLONEL CHEN TILTED in his nylon mesh seat as the pilot banked to avoid fireballs mushrooming skyward from the USS *Hampton*'s helicopter flight deck. The pair of Sikorsky SH-60 Seahawk helicopters that had been at rest on the deck were blazing wrecks. It had been essential they take out the American helicopters, and now that they had, his strike team concentrated on crippling the vessel's sophisticated armament and defensive systems.

The war loads on their helicopters consisted of 40 mm grenade launchers and 7.62 mm six-barrel miniguns. In addition, each chopper was fitted with a reinforced support tube fairing to which a special housing had been attached. At the moment the housings were empty, but if all went well, they wouldn't be for long.

Another blast reduced much of the *Hampton*'s mast to scrap metal. With the mast gone, so was the cruiser's surface-search radar capability. The TACAN antenna and the electronic warfare antenna were also in ruins. A third explosion shattered the air search radar.

Chen was extremely pleased at how swiftly they were crippling the craft. In rapid succession his black war birds took out the ship's gun director, as well as its pair of 127 mm Mk 45 gun mountings and the Phalanx close-in weapons systems mountings. The main gun mounts were next.

Columns of black smoke and searing flames were belching skyward from the *Hampton* forward and aft.

A black fury swung in close to a Standard-MR surface-to-air missile launcher and let fly with a series of grenades that mangled it beyond recognition. Other black helicopters were taking out the Harpoon surface-to-surface missile launchers and the ASROC launcher.

None of Chen's people, though, fired anywhere near the quadruple launcher nearest the bridge. They couldn't risk damaging their precious prize.

Everything was going exactly as projected. All of their meticulous planning had paid off. Weeks spent memorizing the USS *Hampton*'s schematics down to the finest detail had reaped devastating results. But Colonel Chen reminded himself not to become cocky. There was still much to do, and the Americans were bound to counterattack at any moment with what little hardware they had left.

One step remained before the retrieval process could begin.

"The bridge!" Chen snapped at the pilot, and their helicopter looped around and dipped level with the main deck, then flitted sideways like a giant hummingbird until it faced the command center head-on.

ON THE BRIDGE all was chaos. The systems had been incapacitated with lightning swiftness. Seconds ago Commodore Hale had bellowed something about the PPS-1s and rushed from the room, leaving Captain Benson to oversee countermeasures.

Benson couldn't believe how quickly his vessel had been stricken. It was impossible, he kept telling himself. Their attackers knew exactly where to strike, knew every gun emplacement and systems center. The men in the black choppers even knew where every antenna was located.

"Lieutenant Sturm!" Benson roared to be heard above the din. "Bring the Phalanx to bear! Order the gunners to fire at will!"

"The Phalanxes are out of commission, sir!" Sturm shouted.

"Both of them?" Benson said.

"Yes, sir. The 127s aren't responding, either."

Incredulous, Benson said softly, "How is this possible?" Never in his wildest imaginings would he have thought so much damage could be inflicted in so short a time. "It just can't be."

"Captain!" Sturm shouted, jabbing a finger at the forward window. "Look out there! Look!"

Benson spun, and his blood turned to ice. One of the black helicopters was poised in midair, squarely facing the bridge. Tinted glazing on the cockpit prevented him from seeing who was inside. "Evacuate the—" he began to yell, a microsecond before his world erupted in startling hues of scarlet and orange, and a deafening concussion lifted him off his feet and hurled him rearward as if he were a rag doll. He was dimly conscious of slamming into a console, of agony spiking his chest, of blood in his mouth.

Screams and wails rent air. Struggling to rise, Benson was enveloped in a choking cloud of smoke and dust. He staggered to the left, toward the companionway, he thought, but when he stepped clear of the smoke he was back near the ravaged window. The unmarked black helicopter was still out there, still hovering, about to unleash another salvo.

Benson screamed. Not in pain or fear, but in monumental frustration. His men were being slaughtered, his ship was being systemically neutralized and there was nothing he could do. The attackers were making a mockery of the best the Navy had. He yearned to retaliate, to give the raiders a taste of their own medicine, but all he could do was elevate his fists in impotent outrage and scream into the draft from the helicopter's rotor blades.

COLONEL CHEN SAW an American officer shake his fists at them, and he almost laughed aloud. He hated Americans. He despised them for their arrogance and their decadent imperialistic customs. They were a blight on humanity, an affront to the common good of the masses. Whether his government agreed or not, the only way to deal with Americans was to destroy them, to combat them as humankind would combat a plague of rats—with total extermination.

Chen's hatred was one of the reasons the general had selected him. All the men in the Red Brigade shared a similar view. One and all, they were devoted to bringing the United States to its knees by any and all means. One and all, they were fanatically loyal to the one person they believed capable of bringing their dream about—General Tsanghsien.

"Fire another grenade!" Chen directed, and felt a tingle of supreme satisfaction course through him as the American officer dissolved in a violent spray of flesh, bone and gore.

"Sir, Lieutenant Heshui reports all of the *Hampton*'s guns and launchers have been knocked out," the pilot relayed the good news.

"Excellent! Take her down! Sergeant Yatsen, be ready!"

The 530MG tilted and dropped, alighting with precision near the quadruple launcher being utilized for the PPS-1 test. The instant the nonretractable tubular landing gear touched the deck, Yatsen flung the door open and vaulted out. The three men in his squad were hard on his heels.

A second black helicopter dipped out of the darkness to land dangerously close to the first. Four more men in combat blacksuits jumped out and joined the noncom's crew at the dolly.

The remaining four choppers hovered overhead in a defensive posture, their miniguns swiveling from side to side, the gunners ready to cut loose at the slightest threat to the retrieval teams.

It was the moment Chen had dreaded most, the interval when his strike force was most vulnerable. They had drilled endlessly so they could complete the operation in the shortest time possible, but there were no guarantees they could finish before the Americans regrouped.

The procedure was simple. Since each helicopter could hold only one PPS-1 in the special housing fitted for that purpose, each helicopter had to take a turn at landing so a missile could be loaded. But it was no easy task. Not when the PPS-1 was twenty-one-feet long and weighed in excess of 2600 pounds. A special winch and hoist did most of the work, small comfort to the men who had to operate it and were exposed to enemy fire.

"All gunners, stay alert!" Chen barked. The first PPS-1 had been hauled to his helicopter, and Sergeant Yatsen was supervising the soldiers operating the hoist.

To Chen, they seemed to be moving at a snail's pace even though they were working as fast as was humanly possible. The minutes stretched into an eternity.

"Where are the Americans?" the pilot wondered aloud. "Why aren't they trying to stop us?"

"They will," Chen predicted. "Wait and see."

COMMODORE JOHN HALE sped along a corridor toward a door that opened onto the forward deck, an M-16 firmly grasped in both hands. Behind him were nine grim sailors, armed either with autorifles or pistols taken from the armory. They were all he could round up on the spur of the moment. Other crewmen were busy fighting fires and tending to the scores of wounded.

Hale paused at the door. He had suspected the reason for the attack within seconds of its onset, and he was determined to foil those responsible or perish in the attempt. Out of everyone on board, only he fully appreciated the terrible consequences if the PPS-1s fell into the wrong hands.

"Listen up!" Hale bellowed. "We mustn't let the classified hardware get off this vessel. No matter what the cost, we must stop whoever is in those choppers. Do you hear me?"

Several of the sailors nodded. One seaman said rather timidly, "Sir, why don't we wait for more of our boys?" He wagged his pistol. "Using peashooters against the firepower they're packing is downright crazy."

"No, Seaman. You have it backward," Hale said, setting him straight. "Allowing them to make off with just one of the missiles I brought on board is what's crazy. With it, they can destroy any city in the U.S.

from anywhere in the world.'' He pulled the M-16's charging handle all the way to the rear, then released it. Flicking the selector lever from safe to semi, he put his shoulder to the door. "Are you men with me?"

"Yes, sir," a tall sailor answered for the rest.

"Then let's do it!" Hale declared, and shoved. Out he charged, pressing the M-16 to his shoulder. A knot of men in black combat rigging and ski masks were loading a PPS-1 onto a chopper. He triggered several rounds, saw one of the marauders collapse, then darted to the right, seeking cover.

The sailors spilled onto the deck in his wake, unleashing a ragged volley.

Another hooded figure dropped.

"Pour it on, men!" Hale thundered. "Give 'em hell!"

"COLONEL! The Americans are counterattacking!" the pilot cried.

"I see them," Chen calmly replied.

In his headset he snapped, "Copter Four, you have a clear line of fire. Eliminate them! Now!"

The gunner in the designated chopper activated the 7.62 mm M-134 minigun mounted on its side. With a firing rate of up to four thousand rounds per minute, the M-134 was a devastating weapon. In a span of seconds, half the Americans who burst onto the deck had been chewed to ribbons and several others were grievously hurt.

Chen saw two men gain cover. Judging by the insignia one wore, he was a high-ranking officer. "Copter Three, their backs are to you. You know what to do."

The minigun on the third helicopter burped, and the

officer and the tall seaman at his side buckled, their torsos riddled.

More tense minutes ensued. The first PPS-1 was successfully loaded, and Chen's chopper rose to provide covering fire for the others. He expected another attempt by the *Hampton*'s crew to stop the theft, but none materialized. The only conclusion he could reach was that most of the officers had been slain and the chain of command had broken down.

Soon the second helicopter was loaded. The third. The fourth. As the fifth set down on the forward deck, Chen's headset crackled.

"This is the last one, sir."

"The last?" Colonel Chen echoed. "There should be six."

"Maybe the sixth one is still below, sir. Or our intelligence was faulty."

Chen knew better. "Very well. Load it so we can get out of here." He tried not to think of how the general might react. He told himself General Tsanghsien would understand about the storm, and forgive him. But his mouth went dry at the prospect of relaying the news. He almost wished one of the *Hampton*'s guns would flare to life and blow his chopper out of the sky. His lunacy faded when the final PPS-1 was snug in its housing.

"Assume formation!" Chen bawled.

Swiftly rising above the searing flames and acrid smoke, the six helicopters raced westward. Only when the *Hampton* was a glowing speck in the distance did Chen relax enough to smile and compliment his unit. "Well done. All went according to plan. Thanks to your efforts tonight, before long millions of Americans will die."

CHAPTER ONE

Heroin was being funneled into North America through Vancouver, Canada. That much the American authorities knew. They had also learned the head of the operation was a freewheeling entrepreneur by the name of Carl Merrill. Merrill's legitimate ventures in recent years had reaped millions, making him one of the wealthiest Canadians alive. But evidently that wasn't enough to suit him.

The Feds had approached their Canadian counterparts with the evidence they had uncovered, hoping to mount a joint operation that would put Merrill out of business, but to their surprise, they met with resistance. Hal Brognola, the director of the Justice Department's Sensitive Operations Group, finally came to the conclusion Merrill had contacts in high Canadian circles who were hindering efforts to bring him to bay.

Rather than spend years trying to go through official channels, Brognola sent in the one man he could depend on to remedy the situation swiftly and efficiently.

Mack Bolan was the best there was at what he did, and what he did was put a permanent end to piranhas like Merrill. The Executioner was all too willing to help. A man with a mission, he had devoted his life to making America safe again. To stopping the decay that

ate at her like a cancer. To ending the drug blight that
ravaged her cities and towns. He had pledged to eliminate any and every threat by the most direct means
possible.

Now, in a modified four-door Chevy sedan supplied
by the Feds, Mack Bolan cruised northward along Interstate Highway 5 toward the U.S.-Canadian border.
Lush Washington landscape hemmed the highway.
Ahead, no more than a quarter of a mile, was the point
of entry. He had deliberately picked late afternoon,
when traffic was heaviest, to cross over. He was less
likely to be stopped, less likely to have his vehicle
inspected. Not that he was worried. The Feds had done
an excellent job of concealing the tools of his trade.

Several lines had formed, and Bolan wheeled the
sedan to the end of the nearest. He wore loose-fitting
outdoor clothes he had bought at a sporting goods outlet in Seattle, including a vest favored by fishermen,
with enough pockets for dozens of hooks and sinkers.
He also wore a cap with a largemouth bass on the front,
framed by the motto Fishing Is My Life.

Taking out his wallet, Bolan unfolded a fake birth
certificate that identified him as one Mike Belasko,
from Tacoma. He also took out the car's registration
and an insurance certificate. All three had been supplied by Brognola's people. Before long it was his turn
to cross, and he braked as a young examiner leaned
down to greet him.

"Good afternoon, sir. Is this your first visit to Canada?"

"Heck, no," Bolan said, smiling good-naturedly. "If
I could, I'd move up here. It's a fisherman's paradise."

The examiner's quick, knowing eyes flicked around

the interior of the vehicle. "And what is the purpose of your visit?"

"To get away from the nag I married," **Bolan** quipped. Playing his part to perfection, he jerked a thumb at the fishing gear piled on the passenger side. "A few days of R and R are just what I need to recharge my batteries."

"Enjoy your stay." The man waved him on.

Once Bolan was out of sight of the checkpoint, he tossed the hat onto the floor and slid a map from the glove compartment. The route he was to follow had been highlighted in yellow. Highway 99 would take him into Vancouver. According to the timetable, he would arrive at his destination approximately forty-five minutes after sunset.

As he drove, Bolan mentally reviewed the file on Carl Merrill. A bachelor, Merrill lived at a walled-in estate in North Vancouver, an affluent suburb. Only thirty-nine, he regularly dated a harem of beauties. His other pet passions were expensive cars and fine food. Among the businesses he owned were a clothing chain, a restaurant, several apartment complexes and a string of curio shops on both sides of the border.

Intel on Merrill revealed he was protected around the clock by a bevy of private bodyguards. None had criminal records. Indeed, as far as the Feds were aware, none of Merrill's many employees were in any way involved in the illicit import and distribution of heroin. Which meant the smuggling operation had to be separate from Merrill's legitimate concerns.

It handicapped Bolan. He couldn't very well take down the bodyguards if they were simply law-abiding men doing a job. The same with the other employees in Merrill's far-flung organization.

Bolan's target was the top man himself, and only the top man. Merrill was the lynchpin in the whole illegal operation. If he was taken out of the picture, the heroin flow would stop. At least until the suppliers overseas found someone else to peddle their vile addictive wares.

The heroin Merrill was funneling originated as opium grown in Pakistan. It was processed into heroin in Burma, part of the Golden Triangle, and trans-shipped to ports around the world. According to the DEA, its purity averaged 68.8 percent, an extremely high level, which explained why Merrill's network had flourished into a major drug pipeline in a relatively short span of time.

It was a known fact that the higher the purity, the higher the abuse levels, with a subsequent spike in deaths attributed to overdoses. Dozens had already died using heroin smuggled in by Merrill; scores more would succumb unless he was stopped.

Vancouver's modern skyline appeared. Skyscrapers reared to the azure sky, among them a twenty-one story, glass-covered structure that gleamed like a bea-con in the spreading twilight.

The city bustled with a steady flow of traffic and pedestrians. The third exit was the one Bolan wanted. He took Cambie Street north, past Queen Elizabeth Park and city hall and over the span across False Creek. Once on the other side, he linked to Georgia Street, which hugged Burrard Inlet. He traveled around Lost Lagoon and on into Stanley Park, a peninsula of virgin evergreen forest.

Lions Gate Bridge connected the peninsula to the suburbs of North and West Vancouver. Two majestic snowcapped peaks towered thousands of feet into the air to the north.

Bolan soon came to Marine Drive and turned right, driving slowly, taking his time to await the descent of darkness. Out of habit, he repeatedly checked the rearview mirror to insure he wasn't being shadowed. When he came to Lions Heights, a section of ritzy estates, he turned left. Imposing homes lined both sides of the street, sprawling examples of the opulence money could buy.

Only a few of the estates were walled-in. Merrill's acreage was toward the rear of Lions Heights, nestled at the bottom of a pine-covered slope. An ornate wrought-iron gate was the only way in, manned by security men twenty-four hours a day.

Bolan drove to the next junction and pulled to the curb. Swiveling, he surveyed the high brick wall, then took a package from an inside vest pocket and removed a set of aerial reconnaissance photos. Taken from a small Cessna piloted by one of Brognola's people, they showed the layout of the property down to the smallest detail.

The main house was centrally situated. Flanking the circular drive was a helipad for Merrill's helicopter. West of it was a large heart-shaped pool. To the east stood the long garage housing Merrill's large collection of vintage cars. A few outbuildings dotted the northern third of the property, but it was primarily undisturbed woodland.

Vultures like Carl Merrill never ceased to anger Bolan. They had everything money could buy, yet their greed drove them to amass even more wealth by any means necessary. Merrill's facade of being a playboy bachelor hid the evil side of his nature, the side that

thought nothing of preying on innocents to further line
his bulging pockets.

The sun was long gone, and myriad stars filled the
firmament. Bolan turned the key and looped through a
maze of side streets until he came to a narrow thoroughfare. Heading north, he stayed on the lookout for
a side road on the left and wheeled onto it. The road
wound along the base of the pine-covered slope, a few
dozen yards from the wall bordering Merrill's property.
A cluster of trees offered a convenient stop to pull off,
and Bolan carefully threaded the sedan into them.

Cutting the engine and the lights, Bolan quietly got
out and opened the rear door. Sliding in, he faced the
back seat and slid his right hand underneath it, close
to the side panel. Pressing a small latch, he gripped the
top and bottom of the seat and lifted. It detached, revealing a concealed compartment.

Bolan pulled out his duffel bag, opened it and removed a combat blacksuit. Shedding his fishing garb,
he swiftly donned the blacksuit, along with other assorted items that might come in handy. A 9 mm Beretta
93-R fitted with a suppressor went snugly into a shoulder holster under his left arm. He also chose a .44 Desert Eagle, which he strapped to his right hip.

Bending, Bolan reached into the back of the compartment and tugged out a streamlined gun case. Inside
was a special rifle he had brought along just for the
occasion. Officially dubbed the SEU Light Tactical Rifle, it was a beauty, the perfect sniper weapon for urban
environments.

The rifle boasted a Remington 700 action, a detach-
able 4-round box magazine and a Shilen trigger adjusted for a 2.25-pound trigger pull weight. It was also

fitted with a Winchester Kreiger chrome moly match-grade barrel.

Only forty-one inches long and under eleven pounds in weight, including a new Leupold Vari-X III 4.5-14×50 mm Long Range Scope, it was a streamlined, compact work of art. In extensive testing at Stony Man Farm using moly-coated ammunition, Bolan had consistently achieved 0.5 MOA accuracy or better at ranges up to 500 yards. Without question, the SEU Light Tactical Rifle was one of the best on the market.

Removing the magazine, Bolan opened a box of ammo and loaded four rounds. He slung the rifle over his right shoulder, then smeared combat cosmetics on his cheeks and forehead to dampen their sheen in the starlight.

Easing from the car, the warrior left the back door open and catfooted through the trees toward the brick wall. Fifteen yards out, he crouched to look and listen. No electronic surveillance devices were present, which he chalked up to Merrill either wanting to keep a low profile or being too smug for his own good. Probably the latter.

Deeming it safe, Bolan sprinted to the wall. Glancing both ways, he took a step back, then hurtled upward with his arms extended. His fingers hooked the edge. In another moment he had coiled his whipcord-hard body and swung lithely up on top. From his vantage point the rear of the house was plainly visible. Many of the windows were lit, their curtains parted.

Unslinging the rifle, Bolan trained it on a particular third-floor window and peered through the scope. Adjusting the magnification factor to 4.5 gave him a field of view of over twenty feet, more than enough to locate his target with crystal clarity.

The Feds had pinpointed the room in question as Carl Merrill's bedroom. Bathed in the glow of a lamp was a mahogany dresser, part of a canopy bed, plush carpet and a strip of mirrored ceiling.

The room, though, was unoccupied.

Bolan lowered the scope to a large picture window on the ground floor. It was a living room, complete with a giant TV and a pool table. Two young women in skimpy dresses were on stools at a bar, sipping drinks. In the next room a heavyset man of fifty or so was on the telephone. Bolan recognized him from a photo—Roger Simmons, Merrill's right-hand man.

But there was still no sign of Merrill himself.

Bolan frowned and settled down to wait. He could lie there all night if need be and never so much as twitch a muscle, a legacy of his days as a sniper. Sooner or later the heroin kingpin would return. All he had to do was be patient.

A stiff breeze from the northwest rustled the trees. A dog howled off in the distance. Up on the slope the underbrush crackled to the passage of a deer or some other animal, while from the opposite direction came the buzz of city traffic and the occasional bleat of a horn.

Laughter from the vicinity of the pool stirred Bolan's interest. Two lovelies in thong bathing suits were frolicking in the deep end.

The minutes dragged by.

Bolan's interest perked again when headlights swept up the driveway from the gate. A car braked near the garage, and several men in dark suits entered the house. Bolan scanned the windows to see where they ended up—the room occupied by Roger Simmons. From the look of things, they were the bearers of bad news.

Whatever they told Simmons agitated him tremendously. He gestured angrily, then scooped up the phone again and furiously punched in a number.

Not long afterward, the crunch of footsteps drew Bolan's gaze to vague figures approaching from the east. Placing the tactical rifle in front of him, he straightened his legs and tucked his arms to his sides to minimize his silhouette.

Two guards in suits strode out of the night. Both carried flashlights neither had switched on. One guard also held a walkie-talkie. His jacket was open, and a shoulder rig was visible. Stifling a yawn, he halted and stared toward the house. "Talk about a boring job, eh?" he grumbled.

"Tell me about it, Frank," the other man said. "I should have listened to my mother and gone to computer school."

"Merrill pays well," Frank mentioned. "But I'm sick and tired of the same routine night in and night out."

"Security work isn't all it's cracked up to be, that's for sure," complained his skinny companion.

"We could make more money working at a fast-food place, Eddie."

Eddie nodded. "Maybe we should quit and go into business for ourselves. Call our firm Executive Protection. Set our own hours, our own pay."

"Now there's a thought," Frank said. "Of course, I'd have to check with Susie first. The last time I quit a job without telling her, she made me sleep on the couch for a month."

Bolan was only twelve feet from them but they hadn't noticed him. They were rank amateurs, green-as-grass rent-a-cops trained to cope with common burglars and muggers but who wouldn't stand a prayer against a seasoned professional. He could have slain both before they knew what hit them, with no one the wiser.

"I hear Simmons was on the warpath again today," Eddie remarked offhandedly.

"What did he do this time?" Frank inquired while palming a pack of cigarettes.

"He jumped all over George and Harry out at the front gate. Reamed them good for not opening it fast enough to suit him."

"Simmons is a bastard," Frank spit. "Why Merrill keeps him on is beyond me. The way Simmons treats him, if I were Merrill I'd have fired his sorry ass long ago."

"Strange, isn't it, how Merrill lets Simmons treat him like dirt? Something fishy is going on, but I'm not about to pry. Not with those guys in the dark suits always hanging around. They give me the creeps."

"Who the hell are they, anyway?" Frank wondered. "I've been here five months and I don't know a thing about them."

"Word is, they're business consultants."

"Yeah, right."

The duo moved on, Frank wagging the cigarettes. "Got a light?"

Eddie sighed. "How many times have you asked me that? You know I don't smoke. You know I never have matches. What happened to that lighter your wife gave you for your birthday?"

"I lost it."

"Typical. You'd lose your head if it wasn't attached."

Their banter gradually faded.

The pair had unwittingly given Bolan something to think about. If what they said was true, something strange was indeed going on. The men in the black suits had to be the three who were with Roger Simmons at that very moment. From the sound of things, they did pretty much as they pleased, even to the extent of treating Carl Merrill "like dirt," as Eddie put it.

Bolan's musing was interrupted by the faint *whump* of rotor blades. A helicopter was heading toward the estate from across English Bay. Floodlights kicked on, sweeping the sky. They illuminated a Bell executive model chopper with wedge windows. The pilot descended smoothly onto the helipad as security personnel rushed to meet it. Only one man climbed out.

Bolan swung the scope into position. At last his target had arrived. Carl Merrill, a briefcase in hand, ducked low to run out from under the spinning rotor blades and hastened around the front corner of the house.

The Executioner swept the windows, waiting for Merrill to reappear. The time had come. He could complete his mission. But a tiny voice in the back of his mind pricked his conscience, saying that he should hold off, investigate further and discover what the connection was between Merrill and Simmons.

A shadow flitted across Merrill's bedroom window. Tilting the rifle, Bolan saw Merrill toss the briefcase on the canopy bed. He centered the crosshairs on the playboy's head just as Merrill turned toward him. The handsome face from the recon photos filled the scope, a face twisted in anxiety.

Bolan lightly touched his forefinger to the trigger. One stroke was all it would take. But suddenly Merrill started and spun, and Roger Simmons stalked into view. Simmons grabbed Merrill by the shirtfront, shook him like a pit bull shaking a cat, then shoved the man so hard, Merrill fell against the bed.

The three men in black suits appeared. Their expressions, their posture, told Bolan they were ready to pounce on Merrill if he so much as lifted a finger against Simmons.

The soldier came to a decision and slid his finger from the trigger. Obviously, the Feds had missed a few important pieces of intel. Based on what he had just witnessed, they had it all wrong. Simmons was much more than an employee of Merrill's. Their exact relationship remained to be seen.

The heavyset man yanked Merrill to his feet, shook him a few more times, then wheeled and lumbered out, dogged by the trio in black. Merrill slumped onto the bed, his face buried in his hands. When he next looked up, tears streaked his cheeks. The alleged drug lord and notorious playboy was crying.

Bolan was about to swing down and go investigate when the pad of footsteps warned him the two guards had returned. Frank and Eddie were hurrying toward him. Figuring they had spotted him, he flattened, his right hand seeking the Beretta.

"—just forget it and keep going," Eddie was saying. "You can always buy another."

"Easy for you to say," Frank responded. "They're mine, not yours."

The pair came to where they had stopped earlier.

"It has to be here somewhere," Frank said, scouring the ground. "It must have fallen out when I took my hand from my pocket." He pivoted. "Ah! Here it is!" Elated, he scooped an object from the grass—his pack of cigarettes.

"Good. Can we go now?" Eddie said. "We'll be late making our sweep as it is."

"What's five minutes, more or less?" Frank said.

Just then the walkie-talkie crackled. "Jensen? Wilson? Are you guys still doing your perimeter check?"

Frank pressed the talk switch. "This is Jensen. We're about halfway done. It's quiet as can be, as usual."

"Listen up. Simmons just contacted me. Mr. Merrill and him are leaving in about five minutes for Harrison Hot Springs."

"This makes the third time in the past month."

"So? It's their business, not ours," the man at the other end said. "They'll be taking the stretch limo. The goons in black are going, too. Once they've left, Harry and I are thinking of getting a card game going. Do you two want in?"

"You bet I do," Frank said eagerly, and glanced at his partner, who nodded. "Eddie, too. Same stakes as usual?"

"You've got it. Be seeing you."

Frank chuckled. "This is turning into my lucky night. Last game we played, I cleaned up. And the best part was, I got to keep all the money I won because the wife didn't have any idea I had it."

Eddie was gazing toward the garage. "Why do you suppose they're going way out to the lake at this time of night?"

"Who cares? While they're away, we get to play."

"And why are they taking the limo instead of the helicopter?" Eddie said. "If I didn't know Mr. Merrill better, I'd swear they were up to no good."

"Carl Merrill?" Frank laughed. "He's as straitlaced

as a Mountie. His only vice is women. Come on. Let's hustle. I can't wait to rake in the dough.''

The instant they were beyond earshot, Bolan turned toward the road and rolled off the wall. Alighting with one arm thrust out to cushion his fall, he sped toward the stand of trees and slid into the back seat. The tactical rifle went back into the custom case, which he shoved into the hidden compartment. Before he did the same with the duffel, he rummaged inside and extracted a dark green trench coat.

Once the back of the seat was in place, Bolan hopped out, shrugged into the coat and jumped behind the wheel. Starting the car, he drove to the road and tromped on the gas. He had only a couple of minutes to reach the front of the estate. Tires squealing, he roared onto the thoroughfare doing thirty miles per hour over the speed limit.

The sign announcing Lions Heights hove out of the gloom. Bolan didn't slow until he came around the last curve and spied a long black limousine wheeling from Carl Merrill's estate. As he went past the wrought-iron gate, he saw the two guards sprinting toward the house to take part in the card game. They hadn't wasted any time.

The limo held to the speed limit. In order not to be detected, Bolan hung as far back as he could without losing sight of the vehicle's taillights. He fished the map from the glove compartment and switched on a pencil flashlight. Harrison Hot Springs, he discovered, was a fair-sized town seventy to eighty miles east of Vancouver.

Bolan looked for the limo to turn in that direction, but it continued due south into the pulsing heart of the city. Shadowing them became a challenge. Traffic was heavy, and he had to close the gap a few hundred feet. They complicated things by making more than a dozen sharp turns, often without using a turn signal.

On the map of the city the Feds had given him, each of Carl Merrill's business enterprises was marked with a yellow X. But the limo didn't head for any of them. Instead, it traveled to a seedy industrial district, to a run-down warehouse with a faded sign that advertised Di Stefano Brothers, Inc. When the limo stopped, Roger Simmons was the only one who got out. He was inside the warehouse less than a minute. When he emerged, two more hardmen in dark suits were at his side.

The stretch limo roared northward.

Bolan resumed shadowing it. Reaching under the front seat, he retrieved a special cellular phone. At the press of a button, a relay somewhere in Vancouver uplinked him to a Department of Defense satellite with direct access to Stony Man Farm in Virginia, the U.S. government's ultrasecret center for clandestine operations. A member of the communications staff answered. Bolan briefly filled her in on the status of his mission and asked to have the information relayed to Hal Brognola.

"Copy that. But be advised, sir, there will be a delay. Mr. Brognola is temporarily unavailable. At this moment he is in conference at the Oval Office." Almost as an afterthought, she mentioned, "Stony Man has been placed on full alert status."

Bolan thanked her and hung up.

The limo was now beyond the city limits and there were fewer cars. Bolan was able to follow at a comfortable distance.

Several minutes later Bolan glanced into the rearview mirror for the sixth time in as many minutes and an inner alarm blared. He hadn't been sure until that moment, but now he was. The hunter had apparently become the hunted.

Someone was tailing him.

CHAPTER TWO

Mack Bolan decided to let whoever was shadowing him make the first move. If he tried to shake his tail, he risked losing the limo, and above all else he had to keep Merrill and Simmons in sight.

Although his natural inclination was to go faster, the soldier maintained the same speed. Soon he noticed the headlights were gaining. Whoever was at the wheel was closing in.

Bolan dimmed the dashboard lights, then rolled down his window. Drawing the Desert Eagle, he held it in his lap ready for use and marked the other vehicle's progress as it came up to within three car lengths of the Chevy. Suddenly, it slanted into the passing lane and drew abreast of him. Automatically, he started to bring up the Desert Eagle.

Nothing happened, though. No shots were fired. Nor did the other car swerve to try to force him off the highway. Instead, it gained even more speed. A glance showed four men in dark suits who weren't even looking at him.

Racing by, the quartet rapidly overtook the stretch limo. From then on their sedan stayed glued to the limo's fender.

The only conclusion Bolan could reach was that they

were more of Merrill's—or was it Simmons's?—men, and for whatever reason they had left Vancouver late and had to catch up with their boss.

Another mile, and Bolan's cell phone chirped. He answered it, expecting the woman he had talked to earlier, but the crisp feminine voice didn't belong to any of the communications personnel. It was Barbara Price, Stony Man's mission controller and a good friend. An extremely special friend.

"This is a surprise. They have you manning the phones now?" Bolan quipped.

"Hardly. We need you back here ASAP," Price informed him. "Something big has gone down. Hal called a while ago and set up a meeting for tomorrow. He asked me to relay the message personally."

"I would hate to abort," Bolan said. Not after all the trouble he had gone to. Not when he was so close to capping the pipeline.

"There's no need at this point," Price replied. "But your window of opportunity is shrinking. I'm having Jack fly to Seattle to retrieve you. Do you think you can be there by 8:00 a.m.?"

"I can try," Bolan said. He wanted to ask about the nature of the emergency, but even though the line was presumably secure, it would be risky to discuss it. "Anything else?"

"As a matter of fact, yes. We did a check on the company you mentioned, Di Stefano Brothers, Incorporated. It's a trucking outfit. The owners are American, not Canadian. Gino and Luigi Di Stefano, brothers from Chicago, Illinois."

The names stirred Bolan's memory of the time he waged a one-man war against the Mafia. "Weren't they soldiers in the Capaci Family?"

"They were, but they branched out on their own after old man Capaci was nailed for extortion. The Drug Enforcement Administration has long suspected them of being involved in drug trafficking but has never been able to uncover evidence solid enough to hold up in court."

"The DEA was concentrating on our side of the border," Bolan reasoned aloud. "What if the Di Stefano brothers are smarter than your average mobster? What if they based their operation outside the country to avoid federal scrutiny?"

"We're thinking alike," Price said.

"Any idea how Carl Merrill fits into the equation?"

"Maybe. I just finished comparing the recent surveillance photo our people took of Roger Simmons to mug shots of the Di Stefano brothers. Guess what? Roger Simmons is none other than Luigi Di Stefano, the younger brother."

"You don't say," Bolan said thoughtfully. The pieces of the puzzle were beginning to fall into place.

"I also went down the list of Merrill's business ventures in the U.S. He has two stores in Chicago, a clothing outlet and a novelty shop. Curiouser and curiouser, wouldn't you say?"

"That's putting it mildly," Bolan replied. "You might be interested to know I'm not so sure Merrill's involvement is voluntary."

"Interesting. It wouldn't be the first time the Mob muscled into a legitimate business and turned it to their own criminal ends." Someone spoke to her in the background, and Price said, "I'm needed elsewhere. I have to go. Take care."

"Always." Bolan switched off the cellular phone and shoved it under the seat, then rolled up the window. The night had turned chill, and they had a long way to go before they reached their destination.

In order not to arouse suspicion, Bolan adopted a pattern of letting the limo gain ground on him whenever traffic was light enough to permit it. In due course they passed Deroche and eventually came to Agassiz.

When the two vehicles switched on their turn signals, Bolan floored the accelerator. They were only a quarter of a mile off, bearing north, by the time he reached the junction. A sign explained why. Harrison Hot Springs was up ahead. According to another sign, so was Sasquatch Provincial Park.

The road was hemmed by virgin forest. Campgrounds were spaced at regular intervals, their neon signs luring tourists with promises of low rates and fine accommodations. As Bolan rounded a curve, he came upon a campsite on the left that had gone the competition one step better. In front of the entrance, illuminated by a spotlight, stood an immense statue carved from a gigantic block of wood. Over seven feet tall, it had broad shoulders, a sloping brow and was covered with hair.

Bolan indulged in a rare smile. He had never given the existence of the Sasquatch, or bigfoot, much consideration, tending to lump the beast with the likes of leprechauns and fairies. From the look of things, though, the Sasquatch was a prime tourist attraction. Once they entered the town, he saw half a dozen businesses named after it.

Harrison Hot Springs was located at the south end of Harrison Lake, a popular resort community that catered to outdoors enthusiasts. The limousine drove right through without stopping, then traveled north along the east shore of the lake. The road was nearly deserted, compelling Bolan to drop far behind.

According to the odometer, they had gone over seven miles when a cluster of darkened buildings loomed on the left, surrounded by a security fence. The limo and the other car pulled up to a chain-link gate and stopped.

Bolan promptly wheeled to the side of the road and snatched binoculars from under the seat. A sign caught in the glare of the limo's headlights read Merrill Curio Enterprises. A lanky hardman slid from the limo, unfastened a padlock, pushed the gate wide, then moved aside so the vehicles could enter. After they had, he swung the gate shut again and reattached the lock.

To play it safe, Bolan executed a U-turn and drove several hundred yards to a pull-off overlooking the tranquil lake. He left the rifle in the hidden compartment and descended a steep slope to the water's edge. The Beretta and the Desert Eagle were more ideally suited for the close-in tactics that would soon be called for.

Bolan jogged toward the complex. Lights had flared to life in one of the taller buildings, and now a pair of floodlights kicked on, one by the front gate, another near a narrow pier that jutted fifty feet from shore.

The soldier was almost to the fence when a couple of triggermen ambled from the tall structure toward the pier. Flattening, he watched them scan the sky. In search of an aircraft, perhaps.

Angling to the right, Bolan sought a patch of dense shadow. The fence proved easy to scale. But then, the Di Stefano brothers couldn't electrify it or string barbed wire at the top without drawing unwanted attention from the local police.

Sliding the Beretta 93-R from its holster, Bolan crept toward the tall building. The limo and the car were parked close by. No guards had been posted, and no one challenged him as he made his way to a window and cautiously peeked over the sill. Blinds had been lowered but they were open a crack, just enough for him to observe without being observed.

Carl Merrill was slumped in a chair, the perfect picture of misery. A few feet away Luigi Di Stefano paced like a caged bear. Seven wise guys were ranged along a table that stretched from one side of the room to the other. On it were a variety of novelty items, Canadian curios sold in Merrill's shops; mugs and clocks imprinted with Canada's national symbol, the maple leaf; T-shirts bearing images of Vancouver's skyline; reproductions of the Canadian flag; hockey paraphernalia; and, at one end, a score of oversize plaster feet.

Bolan was puzzled until he glimpsed a shelf lined with miniature statues almost identical to the giant Sasquatch at the campground. The plaster feet were supposed to be casts of actual bigfoot tracks. They were sixteen to seventeen inches long and about three inches thick. As he looked on, one of Di Stefano's triggermen picked up one of the casts and stuck two or three fingers into a wide hole in the heel.

"It's hard to believe these things hold as much horse as they do," he commented, referring to heroin.

Another mafioso had pried the end off the handle to a hockey stick. "These babies hold even more," he said. "One stick will supply a small city for an entire month."

Luigi stopped pacing. "Put them down before you break them, you lunkheads. They're not easy to make." Stalking to the chair, he grabbed Merrill by the shirt.

"I should beat you silly, but Gino wants to deal with you personally. Too bad you didn't have the brains to leave well enough alone."

"I just can't take the pressure anymore."

"What pressure?" Luigi snapped. "We're doing all the work, taking all the chances. All you do is pull in the dough."

"That's not true," Merrill responded. "I'm just as much at risk as you are. And if you're caught, my business holdings will suffer, not yours. I stand to lose everything."

"We'll break out the violins later. After Gino gets here."

As if on cue, the muted drone of a plane wafted from the west. Bolan looked but couldn't spot it. Gliding to the rear of the building, he hunkered.

The two men on the pier had ignited flares and were waving them back and forth, signaling the pilot. The growl of the prop grew steadily louder, and a pale shape circled overhead. The aircraft was flying illegally, without lights.

A second later the rear door of the building opened. Luigi Di Stefano and several wise guys stood outside. "My brother is going to be pissed as hell," Luigi commented. "You guys take care of the shipment and don't bother us, hear?"

"Whatever you say, Mr. Di Stefano," one answered.

The pilot killed the plane's engine and glided in low over Harrison Lake. An amphibian, its pontoons splashed lightly down and it coasted, rapidly losing momentum. With a precision born of experience, it was brought to a stop right next to the pier, its propeller still spinning.

Luigi and the others hurried to meet it. Lines were

secured to the struts and three men disembarked, among them a heavyset figure who bore a striking resemblance to Luigi but was roughly ten years older.

Gino Di Stefano embraced his brother. While the triggermen scurried to unload the heroin, the Di Stefanos made a beeline for the building. As Luigi had predicted, his sibling wasn't in the best of moods. Not if the fierce scowl on Gino's swarthy face was any indication.

Bolan sidled to the window and reached it just as the brothers entered. Without any warning, Gino marched straight to Carl Merrill and savagely backhanded him across the face, tumbling Merrill to the floor. Shocked, the Canadian was beginning to rise when the older Di Stefano brutally kicked him in the ribs.

"So you think you're too good for us, eh?" Gino demanded roughly. "You want to end our lucrative relationship?"

Merrill managed to rise onto his hands and knees. "Please!" he whimpered. "Calm down and hear me out!"

Gino Di Stefano snorted like an enraged bull and kicked Merrill again, low down in the gut. Merrill folded, gasping and wheezing, his whole body quaking convulsively.

"All this time and you still don't get it, do you?" Gino said. Seizing Merrill by the chin, he yanked him to his feet. "It hasn't sunk into that thick skull of yours that *we* call the shots, not you. My brother and I can do any damn thing we please and there's not a damn thing you can do about it."

"But—" Merrill objected, and was rewarded with a jarring blow to the cheek.

"When will you learn, dimbulb?" Gino said. "Do as we tell you, or else."

Luigi was proudly watching his brother. "I tried to tell him, Gino. But he insisted on speaking to you personally. He told me he wouldn't cooperate if I didn't contact you."

"Is that a fact?" Gino said, and immediately kneed Carl Merrill in the groin. A strangled cry escaped their scapegoat, and Merrill collapsed in an anguished heap. "Sounds to me as if someone needs to be reminded of his proper place in the overall scheme of things."

"My sentiments exactly," Luigi declared.

Gino clamped his thick fingers on Merrill's throat. "I don't appreciate having to leave the Windy City." He slapped Merrill again. "Do you have any idea how much trouble it was for me to rendezvous with the ship at Barkley Sound and then be flown all the way here?" A rumbling growl accented how upset he was. "Hell, I don't even like to fly!"

Merrill was shoved backward, toward the door, just as the three soldiers who had accompanied Luigi to the pier returned carrying sealed containers.

The heroin, Bolan deduced. Their next step was to transfer the drug to the bigfoot casts, hockey sticks and whatever else they were using to smuggle it into the United States.

The Executioner had seen enough. Holding the Beretta in a two-handed grip, he padded to the corner to learn the whereabouts of the two men who had arrived with Gino. They were still on the pier, by the plane. A strapping man in an aviator's cap had to be the pilot. The other was a mafioso.

Squatting, Bolan edged toward a stack of pallets. He needed a sure shot. But he was only halfway there when the back door opened again and two triggermen hurried out, on their way to the plane for more heroin.

A rectangle of light slashed toward Bolan. Coiling, he sprang into high grass and lay rigid as the men clomped onto the pier. Neither had spotted him. Their neglect meant he could further reduce the odds before he went after the head honchos. Snaking the rest of the way to the pallets, he rose slowly.

Luigi's boys were talking to the pilot and the other hardman.

The landward end of the pier was only twelve feet away. Taking a gamble, Bolan darted to the left of it. Water lapped gently near his shoes as he unfurled and beheld Luigi's underlings climbing into the aircraft.

Bolan had to work swiftly. The pair would reappear at any moment. Jumping onto the pier, he centered the Beretta on the pilot's skull and smoothly stroked the trigger. At the chug of the sound suppressor, the man clutched his temple and oozed onto the boards. His buddy, who had been gazing off toward Harrison Hot Springs, heard the thud and turned. Before he could cry out, a 9 mm Parabellum round cored his cranium.

Breaking into a run, Bolan sought to reach the plane before either of the errand boys emerged. He wasn't anywhere near close enough when one did. Taking a hasty bead, Bolan fired at the selfsame instant the man hollered.

"Pete! Look—!" The slug drilled the hardman high in the chest and he fell back against the fuselage, the container he held slipping from fingers gone limp and sinking into the lake.

A head poked out. Bolan got off a shot but he was certain he missed. A yelp confirmed it. The goon commenced shouting at the top of his lungs for help as the snout of an autopistol spiked from the aircraft and gun-fire blistered the night.

Bolan dived, landing hard but not so hard he couldn't return fire. His rounds spanged off metal, causing the gunman to duck back inside.

Simultaneously, the door to the tall building was flung open and out rushed Luigi Di Stefano and four more triggermen, revolvers and pistols in hand.

"What the hell is going on?" Luigi bellowed.

"It's a hit, boss!" the gunner in the aircraft cried. "He's on the pier!"

Luigi's group cut loose as Bolan flung himself to the left, rolling to the edge—and over it. An agile flip landed him on the near pontoon, the float rocking under his weight. He would have pitched headfirst into the lake if he hadn't grabbed a strut.

The guy in the plane leaned out. "Did you nail him?" he shouted.

Only six feet away, Bolan leveled the Beretta. "No, they didn't," he said, and when the dumbfounded gun-man twisted toward him, he added a third nostril to the man's face. Swiveling, Bolan edged along the float to-ward the rear of the aircraft. He hoped to reach shore before Luigi and company reached the pier, but as he eased down into the cold water, feet hammered the boards.

Drawing the Desert Eagle, Bolan slipped into the lake. An icy, clammy sensation spread up his legs and over his waist to just below his ribs. Moving to the pier, he ducked under it. There wasn't much space, no more than a foot or so, enough for him to keep his head and shoulders dry.

Up on the pier, Luigi cursed a blue streak. His rant

ended with, "Spread out, you idiots! Find the bastard who did this!"

The gunners scurried to obey. Up on shore, Gino Di Stefano had stepped outside, and his bellow carried like a foghorn. "What the hell is going on, Luigi?"

"It's a hit! Somebody just whacked Turnbull and three of our guys!" the younger brother replied.

"Did you get the bastard?"

"Not yet! But he has to be around here somewhere!"

Gino barked orders and more soldiers rushed to help.

"I don't see anyone, boss," declared a triggerman almost directly above the Executioner. "But I'm sure I saw him roll off right about here."

"Where could he have gotten to?" another wondered.

"Maybe we drilled him and he's at the bottom," someone suggested. "Or maybe he swam for it."

"Shut up and look!" Luigi directed. "Whoever he is, he won't get away with this. No one whacks my men without answering to me."

Bolan crept toward the other side of the pier. The water was freezing, and he involuntarily shivered. A cobweb brushed his forehead. He also felt something rub against his left ankle. A fish, perhaps.

Warily, Bolan looked out. A lone gunner was over by the building, but Gino had gone back inside. As for Luigi and the hardmen taking part in the search, they were scouring the lake to the east. His back to the pilings, Bolan waded toward shore. He wasn't worried about getting the various items he had brought along wet. The pockets in his combat webbing were watertight.

"Tony! Billy! Joe! Check the shore as far as the fence!" Luigi instructed several soldiers.

The men jogged right past Bolan without spotting him. Reaching dry land, he sank onto his elbows and crabbed toward a low boulder. Once safely behind it, he holstered the Desert Eagle, ejected the partially spent magazine in the Beretta and replaced it with a full one, then set the 93-R in front of him.

The warrior detached an M-67 fragmentation grenade from his webbing. Containing six and a half pounds of Composition B, it had an effective kill radius of over forty feet. He inserted a finger into the pull ring, jerked out the safety pin and rose high enough to see the pier.

Luigi Di Stefano and three wise guys were grouped together near the plane, and Luigi was going through the pilot's pockets.

Bolan whipped his right arm in a tight arc. As the grenade left his hand, he pressed against the ground and covered his head with his arms. The explosion seemed to shake the very ground. Stinging debris rained down, wood and body parts intermixed, and when he looked up, a ragged hole existed where Luigi and the gunners had been standing. Much of the plane was in ruin, too. Its fuel had ignited, and flames gushed from the ruptured tank.

The soldiers who had been sent to search the shore were racing back. One spied the flames and shouted for his companions to hit the dirt.

Bolan did likewise. A second after he lowered his face to the dank earth, the airplane went up. Hot air fanned him as a fireball roiled skyward, a prelude to another shower of debris. Someone screamed. A large section of wing crashed down a yard from him, followed seconds later by a miniature burning meteor that nearly singed his hair.

The scream rose to an hysterical screech.

Snatching the Beretta, Bolan levered onto his knees. One of the wise guys had been impaled by a twisted metal spear and was staggering toward the buildings, blood spurting from his mouth and nostrils. The other two were still prone, protecting themselves from the bits and pieces of sharp metal that continued to fall.

Rising, Bolan put the screamer out of his misery. A second gunner tried to bring a revolver to bear, but Bolan was quicker. That left the third man, who still had his head covered and didn't raise it until Bolan was almost on top of him.

"You!" The man stabbed for a pistol wedged under his belt.

Bolan let a 9 mm mangler teach the hardman the error of his ways. Then, pivoting, he sped toward the building Merrill was in—along with Gino Di Stefano and one last triggerman. To barrel in through the door would be foolhardy, so he sprinted to the left, along the wall to a window.

Gino and the last soldier were facing the back door. The Mob boss was holding Carl Merrill as a living shield.

Bolan ran to the front door and gingerly tried the knob. Slipping inside, he advanced along a narrow hall to the room where the heroin was packaged.

"Who can it be, boss?" the goon whispered nervously. "Someone from Santini's crew, maybe?"

"You moron," Gino responded. "Since when do wise guys use grenades?"

"The Mounties, then?"

"No. Those guys are straight-up. They walk right up

to your door and let you know they've come to arrest you.'' Gino firmed his grip on Merrill, who made no attempt to resist. ''It's a pro, that's for sure. But who hired him is anyone's guess.''

Bolan stepped into the open. The gunner either sensed him or caught movement out of the corner of an eye, and whirled. A single shot to the man's forehead crumpled him in his tracks, and the Executioner swung the Beretta toward the top dog.

Gino Di Stefano had spun. Holding Merrill at arm's length, he crouched and yelled, ''Who are you? Whatever they're paying you, I'll double it!''

''Let go of Merrill,'' Bolan ordered.

''You want him alive?'' Gino peered past the businessman's arm, and a sly grin quirked his fleshy features. ''Maybe we can strike a deal. I let you have him. In exchange, you let me walk out of here.''

''No deals,'' Bolan said. He stroked the trigger twice in swift succession, and Gino Di Stefano joined his brother in oblivion.

Merrill stared at the dead mobster, then rushed to Bolan, sank onto his knees and clasped the warrior's legs.

''Thank you! Thank you! Thank you! They were using me! Forcing me to help them smuggle drugs! They threatened my mother, my sister—''

The businessman's joy was short-lived. Bolan touched the business end of the suppressor to Merrill's head and Merrill froze, blinking in fear and confusion. ''As soon as I leave, get on the phone to the police.''

''I will! Honest to God, I will!''

''I'm giving you the benefit of the doubt. But if I find you've lied, or if you involve yourself in illegal activities, I'll be back.''

Merrill's Adam's apple bobbed. "Mister, all I want is to have my own life back! Please, tell me who you are."

The Executioner did no such thing. He was already in motion, sprinting down the hallway and out into the night.

CHAPTER THREE

Stony Man Farm was one of the best-kept secrets in the United States, if not the world. Few people in the upper echelons of government knew of its existence, and one of those was the President. In times of national emergency, the best and brightest America had to offer were mobilized at Stony Man to deal with each crisis. The latest was no exception.

Located in the scenic Blue Ridge Mountains, the Farm's name derived from Stony Man Mountain, one of the highest peaks in the region. Situated along Skyline Drive in a heavily forested region, Stony Man appeared to be just what its name implied: a rustic, isolated farmhouse, with a few outbuildings nearby. No one would guess from looking that the old farmhouse housed one of the most sophisticated clandestine operations on the planet.

The War Room was on the basement level. When Mack Bolan arrived, a number of familiar faces were on hand awaiting the arrival of Hal Brognola. The Executioner nodded at several of them and took a seat on Barbara Price's left. She swiveled toward him, her honey-blond hair framing her alert, intelligent eyes.

"Did I hear correctly? You let the target live? Don't tell me you're going soft in your old age?"

"It'll all be in the report. The short and sweet is that the Mob was playing him for a patsy."

Price's face clouded. "We're all played for patsies at one time or another, aren't we?" she said philosophically.

Bolan knew she was referring to her former husband, whose many affairs had destroyed their marriage. "Only if we let ourselves be," he responded.

"Too true."

Across from them sat Aaron Kurtzman, Stony Man's computer specialist. "Do either of you have any clue what's in the wind?" he inquired.

"All I know is that it's really big," Price replied. "When I talked to Hal on the phone, he mentioned the President is pulling his hair out on this one."

"That must hurt," joked the oldest man at the table. Yakov Katzenelenbogen was Stony Man's tactical adviser.

Bolan scanned the others: John Kissinger, their resident weapons smith; Akira Tokaido, a brilliant young man of Japanese descent; Huntington Wethers, a tall black, former professor of cybernetics at Berkeley; and finally, the ace pilot who had picked him up in Seattle and whisked them both to the Farm in an F-111, lean, lanky Jack Grimaldi, dressed, as always, in a blue flight suit.

Kissinger leaned across the table. "How did that tac rifle work out? Was it everything you hoped it would be?"

"I never had the chance to find out," Bolan said. "Cowboy" Kissinger, as they called him, was always eager to hear how new hardware performed in the field.

"No? Well, I'm sure you'll get another."

At that juncture the door opened to admit the hulking

form of Hal Brognola. Without comment he walked to his chair and sagged into it as if on the verge of exhaustion. Placing a briefcase on the table, he opened it and took out a manila folder. "I've just come from the Oval Office. The President was up all night weighing his options, and he's decided to give us first crack."

Katzenelenbogen cleared his throat. "But first crack at what, Hal?"

Brognola wearily rubbed his eyes. "Imagine the worse scenario you can conceive, multiply it by five, and you'll have some idea of what we're up against. There are threats, and there are threats. The latest is in a league by itself."

Bolan, like everyone else, waited for the big Fed to elaborate. "Approximately eighteen hours ago, six unmarked and heavily armed helicopters attacked the USS *Hampton,* a guided-missile cruiser, about one hundred miles east of Japan. Thirty-seven sailors lost their lives, another twenty-eight were wounded. All of the vessel's communications systems were knocked out, but thanks to a resourceful ensign who rigged a makeshift antenna, word was relayed to Washington."

"Word of what?" Kurtzman prodded when Brognola fell silent.

"Have any of you heard of the PPS-1?" the big Fed asked glumly. Their blank expressions were his answer. "No? I'm not surprised. It's as classified as Stony Man. Information is on a need-to-know basis, and as of this moment, all of you have a need to know." He flipped the folder open. "PPS-1 is an acronym for the Plasma Propulsion System Multiple Delivery Missile, a major breakthrough in weapons technology."

"Plasma propulsion?" Kissinger interrupted. "It must be fast as hell."

"Faster," Brognola said. "The PPS-1 incorporates a radical new system that utilizes Teflon fuel. It's top speed is theorized at over thirty thousand miles per hour."

"Did I just hear right?" Kurtzman said.

"There's more," Brognola said. "Imagine a bolt of lightning in a metal housing, and you have the PPS-1. No known defense system can counter it."

"What about a satellite, Hal?" Akira Tokaido asked.

"By the time a satellite could acquire a target lock and an intercept could be launched, the missile would impact its target. Not only that, the Teflon fuel gives the PPS-1 unlimited range. Consider that last tidbit carefully. It means the PPS-1 can be fired at any spot in the world from anywhere else in the world."

Brognola stopped as a smartly dressed woman in a black jacket and skirt entered carrying a tray laden with a pot of steaming coffee and disposable cups. She was one of the dozens of Stony Man support staff who handled the myriad ordinary tasks involved with running an operation of the Farm's scope and size.

"You told me to come right in, sir," the woman said, placing the tray at the big Fed's elbow.

"Thank you, Andrea," Hal responded. As she dutifully walked out, he poured a cup for himself, then arched his eyebrows. "Anyone else?"

"Not me, big guy," Jack Grimaldi said. "You know how caffeine makes me all jittery. Last time I had some, I couldn't sit still for a week."

The comment provoked grins. The pilot couldn't sit still anyway.

"I can use a gallon," Brognola said, and gulped half the cup. Sitting back, he rested his forearm on the arm of the chair. "As some of you have guessed by now, there must be a connection between the USS *Hampton* and the PPS-1. And there is. The *Hampton* was conducting the initial trials. She was scheduled to fire six PPS-1s from her classified position east of Japan at a mothballed destroyer anchored northwest of Hawaii. But she only launched one of the missiles before the choppers hit.''

"Have the attackers been identified?" Wethers asked.

"Not yet. They were wearing ski masks, and they took their fallen with them.'' Brognola swallowed more coffee. "From their general height and build, it's believed they were Oriental. Possibly Japanese, since they were last seen heading west toward Japan. But that's sheer speculation at this point.''

"Five of the PPS-1s went with them," Price surmised.

"Bingo.'' Brognola pushed the open folder toward her. "Pass this around. It's a photo of a PPS-1 along with the full report of the attack. For the trials, the missiles were fitted with conventional warheads. Our worry is they won't remain that way.''

"Good God!'' Kissinger exclaimed. "What if whoever took them decides to fit them with nukes?''

The full enormity of the menace struck everyone at the table with the force of a physical blow.

"Now you know about as much as I do,'' Brognola said. "The President has made retrieving the PPS-1s a top priority. The entire intelligence apparatus of the United States has been brought to bear on learning who stole the missiles and where they are.'' He glanced at Grimaldi. "As soon as we receive reliable intel, I want you ready to go. Whatever aircraft you'll need is yours. Speed and distance are crucial.''

Grimaldi unfolded his lean frame from his chair. "The F-111 will do. It's top speed is over sixteen hundred miles per hour, two hundred miles per hour better than the F-4. And its maximum range with internal fuel is close to three thousand miles."

Brognola nodded. "Have the F-111 refueled and on standby from this minute on. Be set to take off at a moment's notice."

"Will do, chief," the pilot said, and left the room.

The big Fed looked at Bolan. "I trust you have no objection to handling this one?"

Unlike the elite, government-sanctioned strike teams who operated out of Stony Man Farm, namely Able Team and Phoenix Force, Bolan had the option to decline a mission. His status was unique. While he had agreed to work with the government, he wasn't an official operative. He could do as he pleased. In this instance, as he invariably did when the stakes were so enormously high, he responded, "I'll be happy to."

"I knew I could count on you."

Brognola refilled his coffee cup. "Time to barnstorm. I'm opening this up for general discussion. I want to hear observations, comments, questions. Then we'll roll into high gear."

Kurtzman sat up straighter. "The thing that leaps out at me is the intelligence breach. The exact location of the test was classified, right? So how did the attackers know where to find the *Hampton?*"

"There has to be a leak somewhere," Katzenelenbogen said. "At the highest level of our government."

Brognola frowned. "I came to the same conclusion. The President gave me a list of everyone who had access to the information. After we're done here, I want background checks run on every name on that list. Not standard checks, either. Dig deeper than anyone has gone before. Verify every nitpicking detail. Look for red flags, anything that doesn't seem right. If a mole or a traitor is involved, we need to ferret him or her out.''

Price brought up a pertinent point. ''You haven't said what kind of helicopters were used in the attack.''

The big Fed's frown deepened. ''There's the kicker. Several of the survivors swear they were American made. From the descriptions they gave, we're leaning toward a McDonnell Douglas model, maybe the 500 series, but that's tentative at this point.''

Tokaido coughed. ''How's that possible, Hal?''

''Blame politics,'' Brognola said. ''The good-neighbor policy. We've sold some to allies all over the globe. Israel, Japan, South Korea and a dozen other countries all have variations on the basic model. Some have contracted to build their own based on our specs. In Japan, for instance, Kawasaki is licensed to meet the needs of the Japanese.'' His tone became tinged with resentment. ''That doesn't even take into account copters obtained illegally by our enemies. Iraq managed to get authorization to buy thirty 500Ds. They claimed they wanted them for civilian duties, like crop dusting.''

''And our government believed them?'' Wethers said in disbelief.

''Where money and munitions are concerned,'' Brognola answered, ''our policy can best be described as see no evil, hear no evil. So no one should be too surprised to learn Iraq converted them to military use.''

''Tracking down the ones involved in the attack will take some doing,'' Kissinger commented.

''Maybe, and maybe not. We're leaning toward the

belief these were sophisticated war birds, not basic models. If that's the case, the number manufactured drops dramatically. Which should make our job a little easier. I emphasize 'should.'"

"Something else interests me," Kurtzman stated. "How is it they were able to completely cripple the *Hampton*'s communications systems? A feat like that requires inside knowledge."

"Tending to validate the mole angle," Brognola said. "Whoever they were, they knew precisely where to strike to inflict the most damage. Almost as if they had a layout of the *Hampton* right in front of them."

"Information that's also highly classified," Price added. "Maybe we can trace our mole from that end."

"I love an optimist," the big Fed commented dryly.

Bolan, as usual, had said little. He usually left the barnstorming to the big brains. The tactical end was his specialty. But now he remarked, "We're not dealing with a two-bit terrorist organization here. These people were professionals in every sense of the word."

"Professionals with deep pockets," Brognola stated. "Think of how much money those choppers had to cost. That alone narrows the list of suspects considerably."

"It's their precision that intrigues me," Bolan said. "Even the best terrorists can't match a squad of highly trained soldiers."

Price turned. "What are you saying? That you think we're talking about a military operation?"

"Everything points to it," Bolan replied. "Their military hardware. Their efficiency. They took on a guided-missile cruiser and disabled her before she could get off a Mayday. The only American units who could do the same are elite groups like Delta Force or the SEALs.''

Brognola's brow knit. ''Few units in the world are in their class. We can eliminate the British and the French on general principle. Same with the Japanese. I'd be inclined to suspect rogue Russians, but the sailors at the scene insist the stature of their attackers was on the middling to small size.''

Kissinger lifted his hand. ''I have a question no one has brought up. How did the test go? Did the PPS-1 they fired hit its target?''

''Right on the money,'' Brognola stated. ''A bull's-eye from four thousand miles away.''

''We have to assume that whoever took them intends to use them,'' Katz interjected. ''But against whom? The U.S.?''

''That might be an unwarranted assumption,'' Kurtzman said. ''Maybe they only intend to use them to blackmail other countries into forking over a king's ransom. The mere threat is enough to make most governments cave in.''

''Relatively speaking, it would alleviate a lot of anxiety if that were all they were up to,'' Brognola said. ''But I agree with Katz. My gut instinct on this one is that they're not looking to open accounts in a Swiss bank. As the old saw goes, there's a method to their madness, and it's up to us to find out what that method is.''

''Just say the word,'' Tokaido offered.

''Consider it said,'' the big Fed responded. ''Katz, I want Aaron and you to work on the intel aspect. Look for the leak. Barbara, I'd like you and the others to trace all sales of McDonnell Douglas helicopters within, say, the past two years. That includes clones manufactured by other countries. Meanwhile, I'll work on the mole angle."

He smiled thinly at Bolan. "As for you, Striker, you get to twiddle your thumbs until we come up with something concrete."

The meeting broke up and everyone filed out, eager to get started. Almost everyone, at any rate. Hal Brognola lingered. After replacing the folder in his briefcase, he drained his cup, crushed it and tossed it at a nearby wastebasket. It bounced off the rim onto the floor. "We can't afford to do that," he said softly.

Bolan understood. "To blow it?"

"The threat is incalculable. In a worst-case scenario, let's say they convert the warheads. They'll have possession of five nuclear missiles able to strike anywhere in the world. If they do intend to use them against us, we're helpless. Millions could die. Major cities would be in ruin." Brognola wearily ran a hand across his face. "This is the stuff my nightmares are made of."

"They have to obtain those nukes somewhere," Bolan remarked.

"That they do. I'll have Katz look into who has been offering nuclear warheads on the black market." He stiffly stood. "I should have thought of it myself. Thanks."

"What are friends for?" Bolan rose and walked around the table. "Looks to me as if you need to catch forty winks. You won't be of any use to anyone if you're a zombie."

"All in due time. You think I'm bad off, you should see the President. He has bags under his eyes the size of Mount Rushmore." Brognola stretched. "I guess you're wondering why we're not using Phoenix Force on this one? Dealing with international crises is their specialty.''

''You must have your reasons,'' Bolan said. And the big Fed was one of the few people he trusted implicitly.

''Not so much mine as the President's. He's worried to death that word will leak. The repercussions would be horrendous. Mass panic, not just here but in other countries. Our allies would accuse us of being unforgivably careless. Strained relations will be strained even further. And if the PPS-1s are turned against us, or used against major civilian centers elsewhere, it will give whole new meaning to the phrase 'hell on earth.'''

''Are the media on to the story yet?''

''No, thank God. The USS *Hampton* has been diverted to the Philippines so the wounded can be ferried to a hospital and the dead can be temporarily put under wraps. In the interim, the ship is to stay well offshore.'' Brognola closed the briefcase. ''Containment is the best policy. To that end, the President has mandated a low profile. Instead of sending in an entire strike team, we're sending in you.'' His concern was transparent. ''But make no mistake. I'll be ready to back you up with all the firepower you'll need. I'm putting Phoenix Force and Able Team on standby. Say the word and they'll be there.''

''Just like the cavalry in the movies.'' Bolan didn't see any point in bringing up the fact that if he got in over his head, by the time help could be sent it would most likely be too late. Brognola knew it as well as he did.

''If anyone wants me, I'll be in the com center. I want to start the ball rolling on possible nuke suppliers.'' Briefcase under his arm, Brognola nodded and left.

The Executioner helped himself to a cup of coffee. If events ran true to form, the next several days promised to be a whirlwind of activity. Quiet moments would be few and far between.

Bolan sat on the edge of the table and contemplated the latest upheaval. On a scale of one to ten, it was over the top. If there was a lesson to be learned from all the technological breakthroughs being made, it was that with each advance came a concomitant hike in humankind's ability to destroy itself.

That was always the way. Mass destruction came into its own during World War I with trench warfare, poison gas and the first tanks. World War II eclipsed its predecessor a millionfold with the creation of the first atom bomb. Korea and Vietnam saw many more die, but largely by conventional means. It wasn't until the past couple of decades that technology had taken another quantum leap forward, to the point where global annihilation was an ever present possibility.

Where would it end? Bolan mused. Would the arms race continue to spiral higher and higher, until eventually someone somewhere invented a weapon that would render the human race as extinct as dinosaurs? It was food for thought.

Japan

CORPORAL SESSHU of the Hokkaido Prefecture Police Department would much rather be assigned to a police department in a major urban center like Tokyo or Osaka than to the small force on Japan's northernmost island of Hokkaido. Circumstance rather than design had dictated otherwise, and on a wet and dreary morning he found himself pedaling a bicycle along a rutted path some ten miles northwest of the small town of Asahigawa.

"The end of the earth" was how Corporal Sesshu had described Hokkaido in his last letter to his mother. He was a city boy at heart, and Hokkaido's rugged mountains and bleak, flat regions of volcanic ash, gravel and coarse sand were not to his liking.

But Corporal Sesshu didn't let his personal feeling stand in the way of doing his job as excellently as he knew how. His goal was to rise in rank to become a captain some day, or maybe higher.

The path Sesshu was following was flanked by sparse forest. Light rain had lent the trees a clean, pristine aspect, and produced a glistening sheen to his raincoat. Going around a sharp bend, he spied the shack he was seeking. It belonged to an old woman the locals had dubbed "the goat lady." "Eccentric," was how the sergeant had described her, "but mainly harmless."

Sesshu had wondered about that "mainly" part. Bringing the bike to a stop, he leaned it against a rickety fence that enclosed a yard filled with goats of all sizes and shades, and stepped to a narrow gate.

"I wouldn't open that, were I you, young man."

Out of the shack hobbled a wrinkled, wizened crone of a woman whose wisps of gray hair and hooked nose reminded Sesshu of a sketch he had once seen in a book on witches. He took a step back, then caught himself and said, "Excuse me, but are you Masami-san? And did you not send word you needed a policeman?"

"Who else would I be?" the woman said in the same condescending manner as before. "I am glad they have sent so brave an officer. But if you open that gate,

I will not be responsible for what my children do to you.''

Sesshu saw that several of the larger goats had moved toward the gate as if to keep him from entering. Of particular interest to him were their curved, pointed horns. ''You call these animals your children?''

''They are the only family I have. And I want you to stop the soldiers from flying low over my home and scaring them.''

''Soldiers?'' Sesshu scanned the desolate terrain.

The old woman tittered and pointed at a ridge several hundred feet to the west. ''There are soldiers on the other side of the mountain.'' Cackling, she petted one of her children, then hobbled back indoors.

Since Sesshu had already gone to so much trouble on the crone's behalf, he decided to humor her and investigate her claim. Trudging up the slope, he made a mental note to tell his mother all about the remarkable crazy woman. A few steps shy of the ridge he slipped on slick grass but recovered. Then he reached the crest and gazed down into the valley below—and suddenly the old crone didn't seem nearly so crazy.

CHAPTER FOUR

The Shadow Man was coming.

Kerri Tanaka paused in the middle of her morning kata to gaze out her apartment window at the Tokyo skyline, and smiled. The message from Washington had excited her like no other, and with good cause. She had a personal interest in her next assignment. Not in the mission itself, but in the person she was to assist.

The Shadow Man.

That was Tanaka's pet name for the grim American who once saved her life. The brooding, secretive dispenser of death who had stirred her in ways few ever had. In her mind's eye she saw, once again, his broad shoulders and powerful frame, his jet-black hair and piercing blue eyes. Eyes that seemed to smolder with inner fires. Eyes that bored into the depths of her being.

Tanaka had seen a side to the Shadow Man she never guessed existed. When they first met, he had been cold and aloof to deliberately keep her at an emotional distance. It was only after she had been captured by their enemies, only when her life had been in the gravest jeopardy, that the Shadow Man showed a softer side to his nature. He had risked his life to save hers. He had confronted a pack of killers in their lair and wreaked magnificent havoc.

Later, when Tanaka was recuperating in the hospital, the Shadow Man had paid her a visit. His guard had been down, and Tanaka had seen his concern. She flattered herself she had also seen something more—genuine caring. Unfortunately, duty called him away and they had gone their separate ways, as was so often the case in their line of work.

Once Tanaka recovered, she'd considered sending a discreet message to her superior in Washington. A short note, asking if it would be possible to be put in touch with the Shadow Man. But she had wisely refrained. Her superior would deem it childish. His razor-keen intellect would see right through her girlish facade, and he might choose to end her employment.

Tanaka could not allow that. As interested as she was in the Shadow Man, she loved her job too much to risk losing it. So she had done nothing, although for a while she had pined and moped, saddened by the injustices of life. She had just about come to terms with the inevitable when the message arrived.

Now the Shadow Man was returning. He was on a mission, and she was to help him, as she had before. Her linguistic skill and other abilities would be of great value, their superior had said.

The blare of a car horn on the street below roused Tanaka from her introspection. Giving a toss of her head, she resumed her kata, a daily ritual since she had been old enough to walk. Her father, a black belt in *shotokan* karate, had instilled in her his passion for the martial art. Now, at age twenty-six, she was extremely skilled and had bested men twice her size in hand-to-hand combat.

Pivoting on the ball of her left foot, Tanaka flicked

her right foot in a *yoku-geri*, a side kick, then adopted the *neko-ashi-dachi*, the cat stance, and paused again.

Her proficiency at unarmed combat was another of the reasons the man from Washington had hired her. She still vividly recalled their first meeting in Ankara, Turkey. At the time she had been with the diplomatic corps, assigned to the American Embassy there.

Two weeks earlier, on a frigid winter's night, three fanatical leftists had crashed a car into the embassy gate, gunned down the Marine guards and charged inside with the intention of massacring every American they saw. Another valiant Marine slew one but was shot in turn. It was at that point Tanaka blundered onto the scene. The sight of an intruder about to finish the stricken Marine had galvanized her into action. The fight had been short and furious, and when it was over, both leftists lay dead at her feet.

Her heroics had brought her to the attention of the gentleman from Washington. The ambassador had called her into his office to explain an important man was there to see her, with an eye to possible employment. He had ushered her into another room, and there sat the one who was to change the course of her life.

Tanaka had been impressed by his warmth and sincerity. He had quizzed her about her academic background and her mastery of languages.

"It says here you're fluent in Japanese and Cantonese. You also minored in Chinese studies." His thick finger had ranged over her personnel file. "You studied Turkish, too?"

"I wanted a change of pace, something different," Tanaka explained. "It paid off eventually. It landed me the job here."

"Something different?" the man from Washington

had repeated. "If you agree to work for me, Ms. Tanaka, I can promise you a change of pace unlike any other. It's not a desk job. There's no nine-to-five with weekends and holidays off. You'll get to travel a lot and see more of the world than you probably would otherwise."

"I love to travel." Tanaka's parents had taken her to Japan several times over the years, and once to Hong Kong. New sights, new people always intrigued her. "I love adventure, love excitement."

"Oh, there's plenty of that. But that's the upside." The big man had paused. "The downside is the job entails long hours. You'll be on call twenty-four hours a day. You'll never know when I might contact you with a special assignment." He became intensely somber. "There's something else you should know, something important. An element of danger is involved. Your life will be at constant risk. There may arise situations where you will be called on to defend yourself. Instances where you must kill or be killed, as you did when confronted by those terrorists. Does that bother you?"

"No."

"It's not something to be taken lightly. You've done it once, but can you do it again? Some people can't kill at all, you know. They're unable to bring themselves to end the existence of another human being. They might think they can, but when put to the test, they can't squeeze the trigger or bury the knife."

"I think I've demonstrated I have what it takes, sir," Tanaka replied confidently.

"Yes, you have. It's why I'm here. Why I am offering you a once-in-a-lifetime opportunity. Are you still interested?"

The job had been everything the big man said it would be. He hadn't lied, hadn't sugarcoated the peril. She had undergone standard training in Washington, then been assigned to the embassy in Tokyo, Japan. Not as a member of the embassy staff, although she worked closely with them in matters her superior had an interest in. Her official title was policy coordinator, but she had absolutely nothing to do with the political side of the spectrum. The policies she coordinated were those of her superior in Washington. She answered to him, and him alone.

To Hal Brognola.

And now Brognola had contacted her with a new assignment. Tanaka was to pack and meet the Shadow Man in less than two hours. He would instruct her in the exact nature of their mission. Brognola had hinted there was great urgency involved. Usually, with urgency came heightened danger. But that was fine by her.

All that mattered to Tanaka was seeing the Shadow Man again.

She couldn't wait.

MACK BOLAN LIKED Japan. The quiet reserve of its people, its scenic beauty, appealed to him. So did the martial underpinnings of Japanese society. Stemming from the days of the ancient shoguns, Japan had long been a warrior culture. On her shores flourished the steely discipline of the samurai, the devious and deadly arts of the ninja, the notorious blood code of the Yakuza.

First and foremost, Bolan was a warrior. He was quite like the samurai of old in his sense of duty, his loyalty to his country, his personal code of honor. So it was small wonder he admired the warrior creed that thrived under the polite veneer of contemporary Japan. Every aspect of their society was laced with it. Which explained why, with the possible exception of China, the martial arts had flowered there to a degree seen nowhere else.

As Jack Grimaldi winged the F-111 in a wide loop north of Tokyo, Bolan gazed out the cockpit at the sprawling metropolis. He could see Tokyo Bay, sprinkled with ships. At that altitude they resembled a child's toy boats.

"ETA in five minutes, Sarge," Grimaldi announced.

"Roger," Bolan acknowledged into his helmet headset. Since they couldn't very well land the fighter at a civilian airport, they were bound for the Kanto Plain, twenty-eight miles northwest of the city, and Yokota Air Force Base. The base provided airlift support to all Department of Defense agencies in the Pacific theater of operations. It was also the closet American installation to his destination.

"Want me to tag along on this one?" Grimaldi asked hopefully. "I haven't seen much action lately and could use another fix."

Bolan sympathized. His friend was forever ferrying Stony Many personnel to points all over the globe. If not Bolan, it was Phoenix Force or Able Team or some of the other undercover operatives in Brognola's worldwide network. "Sorry. It's your turn to twiddle your thumbs. Refuel and be ready to head out the moment I get back."

"You're no fun."

"Complain to Hal," Bolan said. "He wants a low profile, remember?" Which was why the big Fed had arranged a charter flight for the short hop from Tokyo to Sapporo, the capital of Hokkaido, and had his agent in Tokyo rent a car for the ride from Sapporo to Asahigawa.

"Tell the truth. The real reason you don't want me along is so you can have that babe you worked with before all to yourself." Grimaldi chuckled.

"If I didn't need you to fly this crate, I'd hit your eject button," Bolan remarked, which tickled Grimaldi no end. Bolan didn't find it at all funny. He preferred to work alone. Always had and always would. Brognola knew it and whenever possible tried to accommodate him, but the current crisis dictated differently.

"She's an asset, not a liability," Brognola had stressed shortly before he left Stony Man. "She speaks Japanese, she knows the country, the customs, better than anyone I have. She can handle herself. And you've worked with her before. What more could you want?"

"She's a kid," Bolan had halfheartedly groused.

"If by that you mean she's not as experienced as you are, you're right. But then, who is? And if you're referring to her age, I don't need to remind you she's a grown woman."

No, Bolan didn't need to be reminded. Kerri Tanaka was not only grown, but she was also beautiful. Intelligent. Vibrant. Devoted to her country, and to many of the same ideals he was devoted to. Making her all the more attractive, all the more alluring. Bolan liked her, liked her a lot, liked her more than he should, more than was wise.

As the F-111 made its final approach to the field at Yokota Air Force Base, Bolan came to a decision. Fate had thrown them together again, but he wouldn't let anything come of it. Their relationship would stay purely platonic. Come what may, he wasn't going to become personally involved.

Several figures were waiting by the hangar. As the jet coasted to a stop, Bolan saw a full bird colonel and a captain move to meet it. Behind them, beside a sporty red car, dressed in a prim three-piece outfit that did little to detract from her stunning looks, stood Kerri Tanaka.

"Gentlemen," the senior officer declared. "I'm Colonel Stewart. I've been ordered to act as your liaison during your stay at the base. If there is anything you require, anything at all, you have but to ask."

"I'm out of cigars," Jack Grimaldi said.

"This is Captain Jennings," Colonel Stewart announced, introducing his subordinate. "He'll oversee the refueling of your aircraft and any other needs you might have."

"Does he clean windshields and empty ashtrays?" Grimaldi asked good-naturedly, and both officers laughed.

Bolan turned toward the red car, but Kerri Tanaka was no longer beside it. She was an arm's length away, her shoulder-length hair lustrous in the sunlight, her dark eyes as frank and inviting as ever. "Ms. Tanaka," he said formally.

The woman offered her hand. Her fingers were warm, her grip strong "It is a pleasure to see you again, sir. By what name should I call you this time around?"

"Mike Belasko," Bolan said. He now had a passport and other documents to go with the phony driver's license.

"Our plane out of Tokyo is slated to leave in forty-five minutes," Tanaka informed him. "If we hurry, we can just make it." She gestured.

Slinging his duffel over his shoulder, Bolan walked toward the car.

The trunk was barely large enough for the duffel. Tanaka closed it for him and moved to the driver's side. Bolan had to tuck his knees almost to his chest to fit into the passenger seat, even with the seat adjusted all the way back.

"You are displeased," Tanaka said. "I can see it on your face."

"I had more room on the fighter," Bolan mentioned, not meaning to be unkind, but she winced as if she had been slapped.

"I'm sorry. In my defense, I wasn't given much time to prepare. Not enough to requisition a car. So I brought my own."

"This is yours?" Bolan said with some surprise. Cherry red hadn't seemed like her color. It hinted at a side to her he would rather not explore.

"You were expecting maybe a moped?" As if irritated, Tanaka peeled out of the parking area, whipping around the hangar so fast, Bolan had to brace himself against the door. "You'll be happy to know I'm not completely incompetent. I've verified our plane will be ready to go, and confirmed the rental car has been set aside. I've also arranged to have Corporal Sesshu meet us at Asahigawa and conduct us to the site."

"He's the officer who saw the helicopters?" Bolan recalled from the talk with Brognola prior to his departure. "I understand we have you to thank for unearthing the information."

"I was only doing my job. Corporal Sesshu reported it to his superior. Word was sent up the chain of command to the chief of police, who in turn passed it on to the prime minister's office. Since Japan has grown to depend on the U.S. in areas of national defense, a discreet inquiry was sent to the American ambassador asking if we knew anything about it. The ambassador let me know, as he does with all information that might be of interest to Mr. Brognola. And I relayed it to him. Quite simple, when you get right down to it.''

Bolan knew the rest. Brognola had informed the President, who asked the Japanese to let his own people handle it. As a personal favor to him, as a token of the ties of friendship that bound the two countries, the prime minister agreed.

"If you will permit me to be informal, I must admit it is a pleasure to see you again,'' Tanaka said out of the blue.

"How have you been?''

"I am fully recovered, thank you. I had to undergo a psych evaluation and counseling for a couple of months. Then they green flagged me to return to duty. Whatever happened to the man you were after? And his bodyguard, the one who hurt me?''

"Neither will ever hurt anyone ever again.''

They neared the base entrance. Tanaka braked at a stop sign, then shot down the highway as if she were taking part in the Indy 500. She shifted like a pro. As her leg pumped the clutch, the hem of her skirt slid up above her knees.

Bolan feigned an interest in the farmland for which the Kanto Plain was famed. "What has Brognola told you about the mission?''

"Very little. His message said you would explain all I need to know.''

The soldier filled her in along the way. It helped to pass the time, and to keep him focused. She interrupted a few times to ask questions. When he concluded, she was quiet for a full two minutes.

"May I ask you another question? A personal one?"

Bolan shifted toward her. He believed it wise to nip whatever she was feeling for him in the proverbial bud, so he responded, "You know better. Our personal lives have no bearing on the mission and it's best we keep it that way."

The woman's disappointment was plain. "I only wanted to ask how long you have been a secret agent."

Bolan had almost forgotten. When they first met, she had jumped to the conclusion he was some sort of spy. In reality, nothing could be further from the truth. He left the cloak-and-dagger stuff to the CIA. His job, plain and simple, was to ferret out and eliminate threats that couldn't be neutralized by any other means. It was a fine distinction but a crucial one. He had met people before who leaped to the same false assumption, and he never bothered to set them straight. But now, to lessen the sting of his rebuke, he said, "You have me all wrong."

She opened her mouth as if to ask him to explain, then closed it again and was quiet for the rest of the ride.

Tokyo International Airport was the largest in the entire Far East. Situated nine miles southeast of the city, it sprawled over hundreds of acres. Commercial flights took off as regular as clockwork to all parts of the world. So did small private and charter craft, from secondary runways.

Tanaka knew where to go. Her pass permitted them to park in a reserved lot by the hangars. As Bolan claimed his duffel, she removed a leather suitcase from the back seat. "Our pilot's name is Mr. Ieyasu. I've flown with him before. He is dependable and discreet."

"How long will it take?" Bolan asked. As he recollected, the Hokkaido capital was about five hundred miles north of Tokyo.

"It's close to eleven now. Depending on how long the tower makes us sit on the runway, and whether they make us wait to land at Sapporo, I'd say about four hours."

Mr. Ieyasu was a middle-aged, kindly fellow who bowed low to Bolan and gushed over Kerri Tanaka as if she were his long-lost daughter. His plane was a twin-engine prop model, similar to a Seneca III. He stored their bags in a special compartment and ushered them inside.

The aircraft seated four in addition to the pilot. Bolan squeezed into a seat in front. When Tanaka sidled past to sit behind him, he gestured at the seat next to his and said, "I won't bite. You can sit there if you want."

"Are you sure, Mr. Belasko? I wouldn't want to overstep myself again."

"Sit," Bolan commanded more curtly than he intended, and she complied. As Ieyasu performed an instrument check, Bolan leaned toward her. "Let's get a few things straight. I don't know what's gotten into that little head of yours, but whatever personal issues there are between us can wait to be settled until after the mission is over. Until then, we might as well make an effort to get along." He reached for the seat belt. "If I seem too harsh, it's only because I don't want anything to happen to you."

The woman smiled.

"What's so funny?"

"That's the most I've ever heard you say at one time." She brazenly placed her hand on his. "And you are right. In my excitement at seeing you, I let my personal feelings override my professional bearing. It will not happen again." She gave him an affectionate squeeze. "I thank you for your concern. From here on out, I only ask to be treated as you would any other operative."

"Good." Glad they had cleared the air, Bolan strapped himself in.

"Be advised, though, I intend to take you up on your promise."

"What promise?"

"The last time you were here, you visited me in the hospital. I offered to cook a meal for you, remember? You said you had to go, that you would take a rain check. When our mission is over, I'm taking you up on it."

Bolan remembered all to well. Going to the hospital had been a mistake. He had done it out of common courtesy, because he liked her, not out of a desire to kindle a relationship of any kind.

He realized Kerri Tanaka was smitten by him. He viewed it as a schoolgirl-crush kind of thing. He had saved her life, and she had let her gratitude and affection get away from her. That was why he had told Brognola she was still a kid. Although he had to admit that in every other aspect she was very much a mature woman.

Tanaka was yet another example of why Bolan insisted on working alone. It wasn't that he disliked people. He wasn't a misanthrope. In the rarefied arena of lethal conflict in which he routinely operated, emotional attachments were more of a curse than a blessing. He kept people at a distance for their own protection, as well as his own.

Barbara Price understood. It was why they had never grown closer, why they limited their sharing to brief, stolen moments, and then went their own ways again. A young woman like Tanaka could never understand, Bolan told himself.

Ieyasu was taxing toward the runway and speaking into his headset to the tower.

"He's requesting permission to take off," Tanaka translated. She had buckled in and was smoothing her skirt. "Tell me, Mr. Belasko—"

"Mike," Bolan said.

Her full red lips twitched upward. "What will you do, Mike, if the men Corporal Sesshu saw are the men you are after? There are dozens of them and only the two of us."

"My primary objective is to find the missiles," Bolan said. "My secondary objective is to find whoever is behind their theft and deal with them accordingly." He looked at her. "Under no circumstances are you to put yourself at risk. I'll handle the rough stuff."

"I see," Tanaka responded, her lighthearted mood fading. "Then perhaps I should tell you what my orders are. I am to stick by you at all times. I am to assist you in every possible way. Including, if necessary, in the exercise of lethal force. He was quite specific on that point."

"He was, was he?" Bolan said testily, without mentioning Brognola by name.

"Why are you angry? He only has the best interests of our country at heart, does he not?"

The soldier couldn't argue with that. "Still, I'd

rather you didn't put yourself in danger if you can help it. I can't watch both my back and yours."

"You won't have to. You do what needs doing and I'll watch both our backs. What more could you want?"

Bolan recalled Brognola using the exact same words about her. At the moment, he'd like to take the both of them and drop them from the top of Tokyo Tower.

"We'll work well together," the woman said confidently. "You'll see."

CHAPTER FIVE

Washington, D.C.

Hal Brognola tiredly rubbed his eyes, then stacked the confidential reports he had been reading for the past several hours and slid them into a desk drawer so his visitors wouldn't see them when they arrived. He couldn't let on why he had arranged the meeting.

The big Fed had spent the better part of a day going over the list of those with access to information about the test of the PPS-1s. He had eliminated those whose loyalty was beyond reproach: the President, the vice president and a few others. He had also eliminated those who knew of the test but had no inkling where it was to be held, which included the second-tier workers involved in the design and construction of the missiles. Likewise scratched were those who knew where the test was being conducted but had no idea what the test involved, which consisted of the majority of military personnel privy to the intel. Not even the sailors on the USS *Hampton* had known what was going on.

A knock on the door signaled the time had come. Adjusting his tie, Brognola called out, "It's open."

Agent Sherman poked her head in. "Sir, there are

three people here to see you. They say you're expecting them.''

"Show them in," Brognola said. Rising, he moved around his desk and smiled in welcome. "Come in, come in," he urged. "I'm glad you could make it. Have a seat."

Into the office walked a pair of women, one in uniform, and a gray-haired man in an expensive suit. The woman in the Navy uniform was in her thirties, the other woman and the man both in their late fifties. Brognola shook hands with each of them, and they sank into the three chairs he had set in front of his desk just for the occasion. "I'm glad you could make it," he said, sitting on the edge of his broad mahogany desk. "I look forward to working together."

The woman in the chair on the right made a sniffing noise. "I really don't see why this is necessary, Mr. Brognola. As I told the President, I have no expertise in criminal law." Much older than she looked, she was tall and spindly, with green eyes and an aristocratic air. A thick gold necklace, a gold watch and gold rings showed she wasn't a typical civil servant.

"This is our chief executive's idea, not mine," Brognola said glibly. The truth be known, he was the one who had broached the plan, and the commander-in-chief had approved it. "Given the nature of the current crisis, he felt it best to appoint the three of you as special liaisons between the Justice Department, the White House and the Pentagon."

"But why us?" asked the same woman. "Surely someone in law enforcement would be of more use to you?"

"Before we get to that, let me see if I remember who is who." Brognola had seen their photos in their personnel files, and gone over their records with a magnifying glass, but he didn't want them to suspect how much he really knew. "You're Mrs. Harkness, correct?" he said to the woman who had complained.

"Mrs. Abigail Harkness, yes," she replied stiffly. "A deputy director for White House communications."

"I understand you've been on the White House staff for pretty near twenty years," Brognola mentioned. "That's quite an accomplishment."

"What can I say? I'm good at my job," Mrs. Harkness said. "To survive the staff purges that take place every four years when a new president is elected, I'd have to be, wouldn't I?"

No modesty on her side of the family, Brognola thought. "Effective immediately, you're my link to the White House." He smiled at the other woman, the one in the Navy uniform. "And you're Captain Bower, isn't it? You're attached to Admiral Thomas's staff, as I recall."

"Yes, sir," Bowers responded. She had a moon face, pleasant but not remarkable, and soft brown eyes. Her uniform was clean enough to use as a tablecloth, her hair cropped just below her ears. "As his adjutant."

And Admiral Thomas, as Brognola had found out, was responsible for arranging the classified test of the PPS-1s on the USS *Hampton.* "Until further notice, you're to be my link to the Pentagon."

That left the tall, distinguished gray-haired gentleman. "Ladies, in case you aren't aware, this is Bill Grant, coordinator for the PPS-1 project. He was in on it from the very beginning. And now he'll be my liaison in that regard."

"All well and good," Grant said. "But I'm a bit

fuzzy on your position here at Justice. No one I asked seems to know exactly what you do. Wouldn't this more rightfully fall under the jurisdiction of the NSA?''

''My official title doesn't matter. I'm familiar with sensitive operations,'' Brognola said, ''and I'm sure you'd agree the PPS-1 falls under the sensitive ops umbrella. It's the President's hope that by working together we can keep abreast of all current developments in our respective spheres of influence, which will help him formulate policy.'' Brognola neglected to add the other reason. He couldn't very well tell them to their face that he was one hundred percent convinced that one of them was a traitor, and if it was the last thing he ever did, he was going to expose the traitor and see that he or she never left prison.

It was the least he could do for all the valiant seamen who lost their lives on the *Hampton*. And something told him more carnage was yet to come.

Japan

THE CAPITAL of Hokkaido was unique. Established in 1871, Sapporo was patterned after Western cities and had a distinct Western atmosphere. Located not far from Oturu Bay, it was bursting at the seams with over a million people, and was a major manufacturing and cultural center.

''Too bad we won't have any time to ourselves,'' Kerri Tanaka commented as their pilot brought them in for a landing at Chitose Airport. ''They say the botanical gardens here are second to none, and I've always wanted to visit the Josankei hot springs.''

Bolan was thinking of their destination. ''This base we're going to. When was it last used?''

"It's not a base, per se. It's an old airstrip built during World War II and abandoned after Japan surrendered. The Japanese government had all but forgotten it was there until Corporal Sesshu submitted his report. Based on what he observed, whoever took it over did their best to disguise the fact."

Bolan expected as much. It was additional proof that whoever they were up against shouldn't be taken lightly. A lot of forethought and planning had gone into the theft of the PPS-1s. The sheer scope of the operation required resources far beyond what most terrorists could muster.

Kerri Tanaka thanked Ieyasu, then whisked them through the airport. All she had to do was show her papers and they were treated like visiting royalty. No one questioned them or tried to examine their bags. The keys to their car were waiting at the rental counter, and out front, in the parking lot, sat a brand-new hatchback. They placed their bags in the rear, and Tanaka once again climbed behind the wheel.

Bolan wasn't anticipating trouble. No one knew who they were or why they were there. So when he noticed two men in a beige sedan in the next row of parked cars, he didn't think much of it. Only after Tanaka pulled out and the sedan leaped into motion did warning bells jangle in his mind. Gripping the rearview mirror, he twisted it so he could see if they were being followed.

"What's wrong?" Tanaka asked.

"I don't know yet."

The beige sedan hung back a few car lengths. When Tanaka turned right at the exit, it did, too. When she turned left several blocks later, once more the sedan mimicked her.

"We've picked up a tail," Bolan announced. Reaching clear across the back seat, he snagged the strap to his duffel.

"How can that be? We've cooperated fully with the Japanese government. They have no reason to tail us."

"Who said it was the government?" Lowering the duffel to the seat, Bolan opened it and removed a shoulder holster and his Beretta.

"Who else can it be? Mr. Brognola and a few others are the only ones who know of our mission."

"At the American end." Bolan threaded a suppressor onto the 93-R. "How many at your end, would you say?"

"Myself, the ambassador, the prime minister and select members of his staff—"

"In other words, too damn many," Bolan cut her off. For a mission that was supposed to be cloaked in the utmost secrecy, they might as well have broadcast it with skywriting. He made sure the Beretta's magazine was full, then slid out of his jacket so he could slip on the shoulder rig.

"Do we run or fight?" Tanaka asked.

"Neither, just yet. There are too many civilians around. We'll wait until we're out of the city."

Traffic was heavy. Tanaka expertly negotiated a maze of byways congested with cars and pedestrians. After they had gone over a mile, she bobbed her head toward the rear. "Would you get my suitcase and open it for me?"

Hauling it into the back seat, Bolan worked the zipper. Inside were neatly folded blouses, skirts and dresses, a large cosmetics case and a black leather jacket with silver studs. Like her sports car, it hinted there was a side to her she had yet to reveal.

"What I need is in the cosmetics case," Tanaka said.

Bolan pressed on the two brass buttons, and the locks snapped open. The case had an upper section and a lower. Filling the top tray were tubes of lipstick, nail polish, eye shadow, blush and more. Lifting it, Bolan discovered a Colt Mark IV Mustang .380 stainless-steel autopistol in a clip-on holster. Owing to a barrel length of only two and a half inches, the pistol was compact and easy to conceal. Beside it were several preloaded magazines and a box of ammunition. Under the Mustang, in a black sheath, was a Tanto knife with a five-inch blade. "Are these what you're after?"

Tanaka hooked the holster on the right side of her belt, under her jacket. The dagger went up her left sleeve, attached by two strips of Velcro.

Fishing the Desert Eagle from the duffel, Bolan chambered a round and tucked it under his belt.

The beige sedan was still back there, pacing them. Presently the buildings and the traffic thinned. Farmland unfolded into the distance. The Ishikari Plain, like the Kanto Plain near Tokyo, was an agricultural oasis.

"Say when," Tanaka said, accelerating.

"Soon." There was still too much traffic to suit Bolan. A running firefight was bound to result in civilian casualties, and he didn't want any innocents caught in the cross fire. "Look for a side road, somewhere we can lure them in close."

"Don't tell me you plan to try and take them alive?"

"I doubt they'll give us the opportunity. I just want them close enough to take down without endangering anyone else." Bolan thrust his right arm deep into the duffel and groped about until he found a pair of pocket binoculars. Unsnapping the case, he pressed the flexible eyecups to his eyes and adjusted the central focusing drive.

The sedan came into sharp focus. So did the two men. Both wore black jackets with hoods. The driver still had his hood up and his face was shrouded in shadow, but the man on the passenger side had lowered his hood and was watching them through binoculars.

"Damn," Bolan said.

"What's the matter?"

"They know we're on to them." Now that the mystery men were blown, Bolan figured they would speed up to overtake the hatchback. But they held to the same pace, the man with the binoculars showing no alarm whatsoever. "Something isn't right."

"You mean something other than having two possible hit men on our tail?" Tanaka asked.

"It's almost as if they don't care whether we know they're there," Bolan said, shifting around. Almost immediately he spotted a brown four-door sedan parked just off the highway less than fifty yards ahead. In the front seat were two hooded figures. "It's an ambush!" he shouted, pointing.

Tanaka took one look and punched the gas pedal. As the hatchback bolted forward like a Thoroughbred out of the starting gate, she swerved into the other lane to avoid a slow-moving pickup in front of them.

One of the men in the brown sedan gestured and their vehicle lurched across the road, blocking it. An oncoming car had to veer to escape a collision. The driver of the sedan instantly poked an autopistol out his window.

"Hang on!" Tanaka cried, spinning the steering wheel. The hatchback sloughed wildly toward the right side, and for a moment Bolan thought she would lose control and crash into a roadside fruit stand. But she downshifted smoothly, corrected the wheel and flew past the brown sedan doing over sixty.

Slugs spanged off the side. The rear window splintered. Bolan rolled down his own window and leaned out as the brown sedan whipped in pursuit. Farther back, the beige sedan was racing to join the fray. The gunner on the passenger side leaned out, an assault rifle against his right shoulder.

Adopting a two-handed grip, Bolan sighted on the brown sedan's windshield and emptied half his clip. As holes punched the glass, the driver slanted sharply to the left, off the road, and the sedan slammed into an elderly couple with the brutal impact of a battering ram. The husband was sent cartwheeling. The woman disappeared under the front end. With a bounce the sedan ground over her, and in its wake left a gory mound of pulped flesh and bones. A child standing nearby screamed in horror.

Bolan ducked into the hatchback. "Find that side road!" he commanded, plunging his arm into the duffel. The Beretta and the Desert Eagle weren't enough. He needed something with greater range.

Tanaka whipped around a van and gained speed but not enough to shake off their pursuers. She frantically looked right and left for a turnoff.

The brown sedan slanted onto the highway just as the beige car caught up. Side by side they sped forward, heedless of oncoming traffic. Horns blared stridently as other vehicles ran off the road to avoid a collision.

Bolan found what he wanted at the bottom of the duffel. He had to use both hands to pull the two sections out, then placed them in his lap to assemble them.

"An M-16?" Tanaka asked.

For ease of transport the soldier had broken the autorifle down into the upper and lower receiver groups. Fingers flying, he began to reassemble the two halves. A slug struck the rear window. Another ricocheted off the roof.

Tanaka worked the wheel like a madwoman, her body as taut as a bowstring. "If only they had waited another half an hour to spring their trap! We wouldn't have so much traffic to contend with."

"Which is exactly why they didn't wait," Bolan said, enlightening her. "They're counting on it to slow us so they can nail us." Taking a cartridge from the magazine, he used the nose to depress the selector lever detent plunger so the plunger snapped into a notch on the selector lever shaft.

More rounds thudded into the hatchback, some dangerously near the gas tank. Bolan worked as rapidly as he could. He almost dropped the upper half of the rifle when Tanaka swerved again. Inserting the action spring and buffer assembly into the stock, he pushed the open end of the spring into the receiver extension until the buffer retainer snapped into place.

"Hang on!" Tanaka abruptly warned.

Centrifugal force pushed Bolan against the door as the car knifed onto a secondary road. A tree hove before them and was missed by inches, and then they were speeding along a straight stretch. He continued to work, oblivious to all else. Placing the charging handle in the groove in the top of the receiver, he seated the lugs in their grooves, then slid the charging handle halfway forward.

"Here they come!"

A glance revealed the sedans were beginning to gain.

Bolan inserted the bolt carrier group with the bolt in the unlocked position. Then he pushed on the charging handle and the bolt carrier group until they were both properly seated.

Angry hornets buzzed past the soldier's window. The gunner with the assault rifle was spraying lead fast and furious.

Bolan was almost done. Placing the upper and lower sections of the rifle together, he reseated the receiver pivot pin. Another few seconds, and he flicked the selector lever to semiauto fire, slapped the magazine back in and bent out the window. "Hold her steady!" he instructed.

Wind tore at the soldier as he tucked the M-16 to his shoulder. Since both the beige and brown sedans were less than three hundred yards away, he didn't adjust the sights. It wasn't necessary. Battle sights on the M-16 enabled a shooter to hit targets within that range with exceptional accuracy. There wasn't much of a crosswind, either, so he didn't need to compensate for windage. All he had to do was aim, hold his body steady and stroke the trigger.

The gunner with the assault rifle was ejecting a spent magazine. He looked up at the instant Bolan fired. His face seemed to break apart at the seams as scarlet laced his neck and shoulders.

Bolan swung the M-16 toward the guy leaning out the other car, but the man ducked back inside and dropped below the dash. The driver, however, was in plain sight. Bolan fired two short, controlled bursts, and at the second, the brown sedan careened wildly, first to one side of the road, then to the other. Suddenly it went completely out of control and spun like a top. It left the road and hurled up over a ditch. Two wheels became airborne. With a tremendous rending of metal and glass, the vehicle flipped onto its side and slid to a stop amid a mushrooming cloud of dirt and dust.

The beige car never slowed. The driver poked out his window, a pistol clutched in his left hand, and banged off several rounds.

Bolan sighted down the M-16. Just as he was applying pressure to the trigger, Tanaka came to a turn. He had to grip the edge of the roof to keep from being thrown out.

Tanaka almost lost control. The hatchback canted toward the same ditch that upended the brown sedan. At the last moment she pounded the brakes, slowing drastically. She prevented them from sharing the sedan's fate but they came to a complete stop.

Within seconds the brown sedan roared up beside them.

"Get down!" Bolan ordered. Rather than follow his own advice, he dived out the window, landed on his right shoulder and rolled up into a crouch. The driver was peppering the hatchback, after Tanaka.

Darting to the front fender, Bolan heaved upward and automatically centered the M-16's sights on the driver's torso. The man saw him and tried to turn, but a 5.56 mm hailstorm churned the windshield and the man's chest into ruin. Engine growling, the brown sedan coasted a few dozen feet and stopped.

Tanaka rose, holding the Mustang. Shoving her door open, she slid out. "Is he dead?"

"I'll find out." Replacing the magazine, Bolan cautiously advanced.

Both triggermen were sprawled across the seat, the driver on top of the gunner, both oozing crimson by the quart. Neither was breathing. Their faces were partially covered by their black hoods.

Leaning in, Bolan tugged on one and studied the distinctly Oriental features underneath.

"They're Chinese," Tanaka said at his elbow.

"That they are," Bolan agreed. A pistol lay beside the dead man's leg. Snatching it, he held the gun in the sunlight.

"Do you know what make it is?"

"A Chinese Tokarev, Model 51." Bolan tossed it onto the seat in the widening pool of blood.

"I don't get it," Tanaka said. "Why would the Chinese send a hit squad after us? How did they know who we were?"

Of more importance to Bolan was their connection, if any, to the theft of the plasma missiles. "Let's see if the driver of the other car survived," he suggested.

They turned and drove back. Bolan got out, motioned for Tanaka to stay put and stalked close enough to verify the driver was a candidate for the morgue. As for the gunner with the assault rifle, his face was shredded. The weapon itself had fallen and lay beside the road forty feet away.

Another Chinese model, Bolan learned when he hunkered next to it. A Type 68.

Returning to the hatchback, Bolan opened the driver's door. "I'll drive from here on out. Slide over."

The woman looked at him. "What wrong? Wasn't I competent enough for you?"

"You did fine," Bolan said. "But one of us needs to make a few phone calls to explain this mess. And since you're the one who knows the American ambassador and has contacts in high places in the Japanese government, I figured that should be your job." He paused. "You *were* assigned to be my contact, weren't you?"

The barb tinged Tanaka's cheeks a bright shade of pink. "Yes. Of course. Forgive me for being so defensive."

"Just don't make a habit of it."

Bolan slid in and placed the M-16 on the back seat. Wheeling the hatchback around, he headed for the main road at over eighty miles per hour. They had lost a lot of time, and a lot of daylight. The windshield was intact but had enough holes to qualify as a sieve. The rear window and one on the driver's side were gone, the others spiderwebbed with thin cracks.

Tanaka took a cellular phone from her purse. "The ambassador isn't going to like this. He promised the prime minister we would conduct a low-key investigation. The prime minister might change his mind about letting us handle it and order in Japanese agents."

All the more reason, Bolan mused, for them to reach the site without delay. At the junction he wheeled left, heading north again. While Tanaka was occupied making calls, he crossed the Ishikari Plain, driving through Iwamizawa without stopping.

When they came to Bibai, the soldier pulled into a gas station. They had over half a tank left, but he opted to top off the tank in case another hit squad was waiting somewhere along the way.

Climbing out to stretch his legs, Bolan walked to a strip of grass between the gas station and a shopping center. Soon they would be in densely mountainous country. From what Brognola had said, the airstrip they planned to check was in a remote, sparsely populated area, and had once been used as a jump-off point for Japanese aircraft attacking China during World War II.

A car door slammed. Tanaka ambled toward him, no trace of their harrowing clash evident on her lovely face or in the lively spring of her step. "I'm glad that's over with. The ambassador bent my ear, demanding to know every little detail. He said he would get back to me if the prime minister has any questions he can't answer."

"What about the police?"

"The chief has taken personal charge of the cleanup. So far the casualty count stands at one civilian dead, seven more hurt. Two are in critical condition."

"Did you relay word to Brognola?"

Tanaka gestured at a flock of sparrows frolicking in a neatly trimmed hedge. "Do birds fly? I authorized the transmission of my field report. He should have it shortly."

"I bet it will make his day."

CHAPTER SIX

Washington, D.C.

Hal Brognola had a secret passion. It wasn't wine or women or gambling or any of the usual vices. It was high-tech hardware. Specifically, high-tech hardware that had a bearing on his job.

In the old days, before the dawn of the satellite era and the advent of the computer age, highly sensitive intel was either encrypted and sent by teletype, relayed by courier or sent by code over a select broadcast frequency. No method was infallible. Encrypted systems could be tapped into. Couriers could be bribed or slain. Codes could be broken. And all three required precious time to be sent from their point of origin to their destination, particularly when that journey was halfway around the globe. A message sent from Japan would take hours to reach Washington.

But not nowadays. Satellite uplinks and computerization had resulted in near instantaneous flash-burst transmissions.

The latest update from Tokyo was deposited on Brognola's desk at the Justice Department by Agent Sherman eleven minutes and twenty-three seconds after it was sent. Brognola read Kerri Tanaka's report avidly, then sat back and rubbed his aching head. He didn't like it when the enemy was one step ahead of him. The hit-squad attack was an unforeseen development. One that added mystifying pieces to the overall puzzle. For starters, how had the four killers known whom to hit? Other than the team at Stony Man Farm, all of whom Brognola trusted implicitly, the only other person who knew he had sent someone to Japan was the President himself.

Had the chief executive mentioned it to someone else? It was, Brognola had to admit, entirely possible.

No two presidents were alike. Some were as tight-lipped as they came. Others, with less experience, were more inclined to make offhand remarks they shouldn't. They didn't realize that the slightest slip of the tongue could reveal a wealth of information to America's enemies.

Brognola made a mental note to make a few tactful inquiries. On the face of things, unless the President had let the information slip, the attack tended to clear his three prime suspects of wrongdoing. Abigail Harkness, Captain Bower and Bill Grant couldn't possibly have known about Bolan or Kerri Tanaka.

The big Fed also had to consider the likelihood of the leak being at Tanaka's end. Either someone high in the Japanese government or someone who somehow had uncovered the fact she answered directly to him.

Then there was the most startling news of all.

Brognola read the pertinent line again, out loud. "All four men were Chinese." A whole new can of worms had been opened, one with immensely sinister implications. He couldn't see the Chinese government risking a major international incident and the outbreak of World War III by stealing the PPS-1s. But then again, the

Chinese Communists were notoriously unpredictable. If they thought they could get away with it, and if they thought it would give them a decided edge militarily, they just might take the gamble.

Brognola's only recourse was to await further word. The Japanese had promised to let him know if and when the four dead men were identified. In the meantime, he would set the U.S. intelligence apparatus to work to see if there was any hint at all the Chinese were involved.

As for Mack Bolan, the man Hal Brognola was proud to call friend, the man who had bailed America's fat out of the fire more times than the big Fed cared to count, all he could do was pray Bolan made it through alive. Because now that their enemies were on to him, Bolan's job had become vastly more difficult and that much more dangerous.

The latest killing field might well be the Executioner's last.

Japan

ASAHIGAWA WAS a quaint, sleepy town nestled deep in the mountains. As Mack Bolan navigated its narrow streets under Kerri Tanaka's guidance, many of the passersby gave the bullet-riddled hatchback curious stares. "We need another car," he commented. "This one is too conspicuous."

Tanaka was consulting directions she had jotted down in a notepad. "Corporal Sesshu is bound to know if there is a place where we can rent one." She pointed at an intersection. "Take a right, then left at the next block, and we're there."

The Asahigawa police station was a plain two-story

building. A police car was parked in front, along with a dozen bicycles in a long bike rack.

As Bolan climbed out, a pair of short, stocky men in flowing clothes came out of the station and strode by him without a sideways glance. They had bushy beards parted in the center and skin much paler than most Japanese.

Tanaka openly gaped, then came around the car and breathed in awe, "Ainu! I never thought I'd actually see any. There are so few left. Seeing them is like seeing history come alive." She grinned sheepishly. "You've got to understand. My parents were second-generation Americans, but our roots are in Japan. I spent my childhood learning all I could about our ancestors. We came here several times when I was small, and I always wanted to return. When Mr. Brognola offered me the chance, I was on cloud nine."

"Do you plan to stay permanently?"

"Goodness, no. As much as I enjoy it here, I'm an American girl at heart. When I tire of all the cloak-and-dagger stuff, I'll go back to San Francisco. Maybe buy myself a cute little cottage overlooking the bay and spend my waning years puttering in my flower garden."

"You have it all worked out," Bolan said.

"What are your plans for the future?"

Only then did it hit Bolan they were doing exactly what he insisted they shouldn't do; they were discussing personal matters. But he saw no harm in answering her question. "I don't have any plans. I take each day as it comes and never look ahead."

The woman did a double-take. "How sad. Surely you must intend to settle down eventually, maybe marry and have a bunch of kids?"

Yearnings Bolan had long suppressed churned within him. Like most men, he'd once entertained the desire to have a family and a home. But his dream had been dashed on the hard rocks of merciless reality. The deaths of those who meant the most to him had forever changed his life. He was committed to the never-ending war, to purging the world of those who preyed on the weak and helpless.

There were moments, though, when his old feelings resurfaced. Whenever the soldier saw a loving family at a city park, or two lovebirds walking hand in hand or a father playing with his children, he was reminded of the sacrifices he had made, reminded of the bitter cost of the course he had chosen.

Not that Bolan would do it any differently if he had it to do over again. He had done what needed doing, and in that light he felt no regrets. There came a time in a man's life when he had to take a stand. When he either opposed the spread of evil, or he crawled into a hole and pretended it didn't exist.

Bolan had chosen to fight for what he believed, to confront those who wanted to make a cesspool of the world, those who were motivated purely by greed and hatred and fanaticism. Those who thought no more of snuffing out a human life than they did the life of a fly.

Someone had to do the job. If not for warriors like him, if not for dedicated soldiers like those on Able Team and Phoenix Force and others like them everywhere in the world, the plague of wickedness would engulf the earth.

So whenever Bolan felt his old feelings stir, whenever he began to long for a normal life, for a loving wife and children, he thought of all the families who were able to go to bed at night safe and happy because he and others like him were holding the forces of darkness at perpetual bay.

"Mike?" Tanaka said. "Are you all right?"

Bolan shoved his private thoughts back over the inner wall he had long ago erected to contain them. "I'm fine."

"You never answered me."

"Some things are just not meant to be," Bolan summed up his sentiments, and was spared from having to go into detail by a young policeman who stepped from the station and addressed them in Japanese. From his polished buttons to his waxed shoes, he radiated efficiency.

Tanaka answered, then translated. "This is Corporal Sesshu. He has been waiting for us, as he was instructed, and saw us from the window."

Bolan was somewhat surprised when the officer thrust out an arm. Shaking hands wasn't customary in Japan. "Pleased to meet you."

"And I, you, sir," Sesshu responded with only a trace of an accent.

Bolan knew many Japanese were required to take English as a second language, and the young policeman had mastered it. "We understand you were the one who reported seeing the helicopters."

"Thank the goat lady. She filed a complaint and I went to investigate." Sesshu bowed toward Tanaka. "My orders, Tanaka-san, are to be of whatever service I can to you and your friend. I am to accompany you and put myself at your disposal."

The sun, Bolan observed, was well on its downward arc. "Can we reach the site before nightfall?"

Sesshu stood with his hands clasped behind him, his

back as straight as an ironing board, almost as if he were on a parade ground. ''No, sir. The path is quite steep and rugged. On foot it would take us until two in the morning. On bicycles we can be there by nine or ten if we try hard.'' He nodded at the rack.

''Bicycles?'' Bolan said. He couldn't remember the last time he had ridden a bike. What concerned him most, though, was his duffel. He couldn't leave it behind, but its extra weight would hinder him.

''Is there a problem, sir?'' Sesshu was quick to inquire. ''Where we are going, there are no roads. The only one who lives up there is the goat lady. A hermit, I think you would call her.''

''Bikes it is, then,'' Bolan said.

''Would either of you care for a bite to eat before we leave?'' the young officer asked. ''Otherwise, unless the goat lady is kind enough to feed us, which I doubt, we will have to go without until we return.''

''Thanks, but I'm not hungry.'' Bolan wanted to reach the site without delay. He could go for long periods without food when he had to.

''Well, I am,'' Tanaka said. ''I haven't had a thing all day.''

Bolan elected to compromise. ''How about if we buy something to take with us?'' It would waste less time, and they would have something to tide them through the night.

''There is a small market four blocks away,'' the policeman volunteered. ''I can show you.'' He started to walk off.

Bolan turned to the hatchback. ''We'll drive. It's faster.''

They piled in. The soldier drove, Tanaka next to him, Sesshu in the back seat. The duffel was open, the

M-16 on the floor in case Bolan needed it in a hurry. The corporal screwed up his face as if it were a cobra about to bite him, and nervously cleared his throat. "Forgive my impertinence, but you do realize, I trust, special permits are needed to carry and transport firearms in Japan."

Tanaka took her papers from her purse. "These should satisfy you."

The young man scanned them, his eyes widening. "This one is signed by the prime minister! It says, in effect, you can do whatever you please. And all law-enforcement agencies in the country are required to assist you to the best of their ability." Whistling softly, Sesshu looked up. "Who *are* you?"

"I trust that's a rhetorical question?" Tanaka rejoined. "All you need know is that our assignment involves recovering military hardware stolen from the United States."

"And that the men who stole it will kill you without batting an eye if you get in their way," Bolan mentioned. The corporal had a right to know what they were getting into.

"Oh, my," Sesshu said, impressed. "I suspected this was important but I had no real idea." He grinned. "It will boost my career if we succeed. Why, I could make sergeant before the year is out. Wait until I tell my mother!"

Bolan and Tanaka swapped glances. "I'm afraid your mother must remain ignorant of our mission," she told Sesshu. "Our activities must be cloaked in the utmost secrecy."

The corporal chuckled. "Oh, never fear. Our operation is very hush-hush, as you Americans would say.

If you do not want me to tell my mother, I assuredly won't.''

Bolan's estimation of the younger man dropped a few notches. The Japanese were renowned for the respect and devotion they showed their parents, but Sesshu's ties to his mother's apron strings weren't typical. The good corporal sounded like a momma's boy. A momma's boy interested in furthering his career. The combination might cause trouble later on.

By the time they reached the market, Bolan noticed something else. Sesshu couldn't keep his eyes off Kerri Tanaka. Whenever she wasn't looking, he stole admiring glances, acting for all the world like a love-struck puppy.

''If you will excuse me,'' the corporal said as they moved down an aisle crammed with fruits and vegetables, ''I will get some bottled water.''

Bolan took advantage of his absence to comment, ''I'd like to have him draw a map of how to reach the airstrip so we can go on alone.''

''Why would we want him to do that when he can take us there in person?'' Tanaka was perplexed. ''If we refuse to take him along, it will shame him. He will lose face. We simply can't.''

Bolan sighed. For a woman who was raised in America, she was more Japanese than she imagined.

Fifteen minutes later they were back at the police station. Bolan broke the M-16 down into sections, stored it in the duffel after removing his spare clothes and everything else nonessential and slung the big bag across his back. Climbing onto a bike, he nodded to Sesshu, who smiled sweetly at Tanaka and pedaled northward. Bolan was content to bring up the rear, at least for a while.

Once beyond the town limits, the policeman led them to a narrow path that wound up into the mountains. The farther they traveled, the steeper the trail became. Occasionally they passed small homes perched precariously on adjoining slopes, but after the first few miles there was no habitation whatsoever.

Bolan began to think they would make better time on foot. Then they crested a rise and the path ran more or less level for the next two miles, until they came to the steepest slope yet.

Sesshu stopped and mopped his brow. "We have come about halfway," he announced. "The hardest part is just ahead." Removing a backpack he had procured from the police station, he handed each of them a bottle of water.

Bolan wasn't all that winded or thirsty so he settled for a few sips. The officer gulped half of his, while Tanaka filled her palm and cooled her face and neck.

Sesshu was mesmerized by the drops trickling under her blouse. "Pardon my curiosity, Tanaka-san, but how is it you hold so esteemed a position in the councils of your government?"

Tanaka's mirth pealed on the breeze. "Oh, I wouldn't say that, Corporal. I'm no more than a glorified errand girl. And I got where I am through a lot of hard work and a little luck."

"But, so sorry, you are a woman."

"So?"

"So wouldn't you rather have a house and a family and spend your days tending your husband and children as women are supposed to do?"

"Supposed to do?" Tanaka's features acquired a flinty cast. "Oh. I see. A woman's place is in the home, is that it?"

"Assuredly," Sesshu said with a blissful smile, blind to the blunder he had committed. "My mother gave the best years of her life to my father and their children and she has always been supremely happy. She told me so many times."

"Marry her, then, why don't you."

Bolan smothered the laughter that burst into his throat, and swallowed more water.

"Marry my own mother?" Corporal Sesshu said. "I am not familiar with that expression. What does it mean?"

"That you have a lot to learn about women in general and American women in particular," Tanaka said. "Some of us value our careers as highly as we do our families. Sure, I hope to marry one day. But it won't be until I'm damn good and ready. And until I find the right man." She looked at Bolan.

Still ignorant of his oversight, Sesshu asked hopefully, "What kind of man would that be?"

"One who has been weaned."

At last it sank in. "Perhaps we should continue on," Sesshu suggested, hurriedly straddling his bicycle.

The terrain grew rougher. The trail twisted and bent with no seeming rhyme or reason. Intermittent dips and holes posed a constant threat, more so when the sun started to dip below the horizon and gathering twilight made them harder to spot. A stiff wind fanned the pines and the high grass, growing cooler as the twilight deepened.

The corporal rode as if pursued by a demon, seldom slackening his pace even when the condition of the path called for it.

Tanaka was unusually quiet. Not once did she glance

at Bolan, in contrast to the many times she had done so before they stopped.

The soldier paid little attention to either of them. They were entering enemy territory, and his senses were primed. He was always scouring the forest, the peaks, always seeking sign of movement or anything out of the ordinary.

Darkness claimed Hokkaido, and the corporal halted to pass out flashlights.

"How much farther?" Bolan asked.

"Less than a mile, I should think, sir. It is difficult to tell. I have only been up here once before."

"Don't use your flashlight unless I say so," Bolan said. The beams would be visible a long way off, advertising their presence. Lowering the kickstand, he hauled his bike to one side. "We're going the rest of the way on foot."

"But it will take twice as long, sir," the corporal objected.

"And be twice as safe," Bolan rebutted. "I'll take the point from here on out. If I stop, you stop. No talking unless I do. Keep an eye on our back trail in case they had someone watching it."

Kerri had parked her bike and produced the Mustang. "I won't shoot unless you give the word."

Sesshu fidgeted. "You two sound as if you are going to war."

"We just might be," Bolan said, opening the duffel. He pulled out the two halves of the M-16 and commenced assembling it. At Stony Man he regularly practiced the procedure blindfolded, so putting the sections together under the wan glow of starlight was a cakewalk.

"No one said anything about this to me," Sesshu said.

"If you want to wait here, be my guest." Bolan hoped the younger man accepted. Sesshu would be out of his league in a firefight.

"My orders, sir, are to accompany you to the goat woman's residence, and that is exactly what I will do."

Tanaka faced the mountain. "Shouldn't we be able to see her place from here? She must own a lamp or a lantern."

"With her there is no telling," Sesshu answered. "She shuns civilization and all its trappings. Her shack has no electricity, no running water. My sergeant tells me she has been wearing the same dress for twenty years."

Before they left town, Tanaka had taken a black sweatsuit from her suitcase, bundled it up and strapped it to the rack on the back of her bike. Now she removed it, unfolded the cotton pants and shirt and moved a few feet away. "Give me a minute to change and I'll be ready to go." She went to remove her jacket.

"Wouldn't you rather go off into the trees, Tanaka-san?" the corporal asked.

"And get all scratched up stumbling around in the dark? I don't think so. If I embarrass you, turn around."

The young officer politely obliged her, saying, "For an American woman you are uncommonly uninhibited."

"What can I say? I was heavy into sports as a girl. The swim team, track, soccer, you name it. It taught me not to be ashamed of my body."

Moments later she announced, "I'm ready when you are."

The Executioner stuffed spare magazines into his pockets, closed the duffel and slung it across his back once again. Taking the lead, he padded up the path. He probed the woodland but registered only normal sounds and sights. After a while the path leveled, and they jogged for over a quarter of a mile.

A pungent scent brought Bolan up short. A sickly sweet scent, unlike any other. A scent he had smelled on countless battlegrounds. An odor no one ever forgot. He crept around the next bend. Ahead was the silhouette of a fence and a shack. The sickly stench was wafting from the old woman's place.

The others had halted. Bolan crooked an arm and the three of them crept to the dilapidated fence. On the other side lay dozens of ravaged four-legged forms, some piled in broken heaps.

"The goats! They're all dead!" the corporal whispered, aghast. "She called them her children." He grabbed for the gate. "Where is she?"

Before Bolan could answer, a low moan—or was it the wind?—issued from the shack.

CHAPTER SEVEN

Off the Coast of China

In the Yellow Sea off the coast of China lay one of many of islands that bordered China's four-thousand-mile shoreline.

Hakka Island was larger than most. In ancient times a fishing village flourished on its southern side, but their descendants were forcibly relocated and the village torn down decades ago to make room for a supply depot for the fledgling Chinese navy. Later, after the navy consolidated operations at the port of Tsingtao—since renamed Qingdao—Hakka Island was relegated to a minor cog in the Communist military machine. It became a storage facility for outdated arms and munitions.

Still later, when a unique situation arose, China's leaders put the island to a new use. A top general had become a thorn in their sides. A general who refused to abide by their edicts. A general who advocated war with the West. A man who became famous for an offhand comment at a Party fete, a comment quoted in newspapers all across the country: "America is an eagle whose wings have been clipped. China is a sleeping dragon waiting to be awakened. Soon, very soon, the dragon will rise from its lair and devour the eagle, and the whole world will be ours.''

In a day and age when the Chinese leadership was trying to convince the Western powers to be as generous with their money as they were with their secrets, the general's warmongering didn't sit well. But he was too widely liked and respected to be made a martyr, so the Chinese leaders did the next best thing. They exiled him to Hakka Island.

Now, standing in front of an enormous warehouse that had been emptied to make room for his new acquisitions, General Soong Tsanghsien grinned. Being exiled was the best thing that ever happened to him. The witless pencil-pushers who ran the Party had done him the greatest favor they possibly could.

Hands clasped behind his broad back, General Tsanghsien strutted into the warehouse. At six feet three inches tall, he towered over the soldiers assembled to greet him. Raven-black hair, trimmed short, framed his hawkish, handsome face. His eyes, unlike the majority of his countrymen, were a striking green. "Jade Eyes," his troops had nicknamed him, and he took it as the highest of compliments. Jade was not only a precious stone, long venerated in China, but it was also one of the strongest.

Striding to the mammoth dolly that supported the PPS-1 missiles, the general placed his hand on the smooth metal nose cone of the foremost, and his grin widened. Like a man in love, he feasted his eyes on the long, glistening body, on the gleaming rear stabilizer fins, on the vanes and the thrust ring. A remarkable engine of destruction, he thought, and it was his, all his, to do with as he pleased. The same with the other four.

Moving down the row, he placed his hand on each of the PPS-1s, then he pivoted toward the soldiers and their commanding officer. "Colonel Chen, I salute you. You and your men have done a fine job." He snapped a crisp salute, which Colonel Chen returned with a smile.

"But how is it again, Colonel, that you are one short?" General Tsanghsien inquired.

Chen's smile evaporated. "Sir, as I made clear in my report, we were delayed by a storm front. Our pilots did the best they could, but the delay was unavoidable."

The general walked closer, pleased at the fear that crept into his subordinate's eyes. "Remember when I told you there are two types of men in this world? Those who do, and those who make excuses?"

Beads of sweat broke out on Chen's forehead. "Sir, the forecast we were given led us to believe the skies would be clear."

Tsanghsien surveyed the assembled troops in their combat blacksuits. "As all of you know, I am a student of the great Sun Tzu. His writings on the arts of warfare have withstood the test of the ages." The general paused. "One particular verse comes to mind. 'The reason an enlightened prince and wise general conquer their enemies whenever they move and their achievements far exceed those of ordinary men is foreknowledge.'"

"A wise saying, sir," Chen said.

"And one that will be your salvation," the general responded. Raising his right hand, he snapped his fingers.

Into the warehouse marched four soldiers in standard uniforms, their rifles at right shoulder arms. Between them scuttled a skinny man in civilian clothes, a cheap suit and shoes, whose eyes were as big around as walnuts and who continually wrung his hands. The quartet halted near the general and stood at attention.

"Mr. Li," General Tsanghsien said, wagging a finger for the nervous civilian to venture nearer. "Thank you for coming."

"G-General," Li stuttered, gazing anxiously at the elite commandos in black. "This is quite a surprise."

"That I sent for you on such short notice?" the general draped his steely arm across the frailer man's slim shoulders. "Why should it surprise you? You are my staff meteorologist, are you not? When I saw you on that station in Beijing, saw all the awards you had garnered, I knew you were the person I needed. There are too few meteorologists in the army. And none of your caliber."

"You did hire me to be your weatherman, yes," Li said. "I would very much like to talk to you about that sometime, if I may. The only reason I agreed to come with you was because you mentioned I would be greatly rewarded for my services."

"And you thought I meant monetary reward?" Tsanghsien said. "Have you forgotten the founding principles of our illustrious nation? We do not worship wealth as the capitalists do."

"No, of course not. It's just that—"

"The reward I alluded to was much more valuable than money," Tsanghsien broke in. The man's petty concerns were of no consequence to him. Results were what counted. "It was the privilege to go on living."

"General?"

"Life is not an inherent right, Mr. Li. It is a privilege granted those of us who make worthwhile contributions to our great country.'' Tsanghsien indicated the PPS-1s. ''Tell me. How many missiles do you see?''

''Sir?''

''Count them, Mr. Li. I trust you can do that much without the aid of your fingers and toes.''

''Five, General. There are five missiles.''

''Excellent. The problem is that there are supposed to be six. The plan I meticulously worked out calls for six, and I was counting on six. But now I must go to the trouble of revising my strategy. A small matter, you might assume. But as Sun Tzu wrote, 'When officers are valiant and their troops ineffective, an army is doomed to distress.'''

''I'm not quite sure I understand,'' Li said.

The general placed his right hand on the pistol at his hip. ''You are ineffective. Your incompetence cost me a weapon I sorely need—''

''You can't blame me for the storm!'' Li had the audacity to interrupt. ''I told you the prevailing patterns were unstable. I warned you there might be pockets of severe weather.''

''You didn't warn me forcefully enough.'' So saying, Tsanghsien stepped back, drew his pistol and pointed it at the petrified meteorologist's head. ''Thank you for teaching me an important lesson.''

''Sir?'' Li bleated.

''Never trust a weatherman.'' The general fired three times into Li's forehead at near point-blank range. Jolted backward, Li sagged to the concrete floor, his mouth agape, the echoes of the shots booming off the warehouse walls.

The general shoved the pistol into his holster and faced his elite unit. ''Colonel Chen, you will see that the body is disposed of. Have it chopped into pieces and the pieces tossed into the sea.''

The colonel couldn't take his eyes off the corpse. ''Yes, sir!''

''Now then, on to more-important matters.'' The general stared out the hangar at flatbed trucks lined up on the asphalt. ''Will the convoy be ready to depart on schedule?''

''Without fail, sir,'' Chen said.

''Forty men will go with us. No more, no less. Pick the best we have. The rest will remain to welcome anyone who shows up looking for the missiles.'' The general saw a rivulet of blood seeping toward his polished boots and stepped to one side so as not to soil them. ''Speaking of which, has there been any word from the reception committee at the airstrip on Hokkaido?''

''Not yet, sir, but we know the two American operatives are on their way.''

''I trust they will be suitably surprised,'' he said, and laughed.

THE RICKETY GATE CREAKED as Bolan slowly opened it and slipped into the slaughter zone. Dead goats were everywhere, their bodies and the ground around them chewed to bits. Stepping over a ram, he sidled to the shack. It, too, was riddled. The plank door swung inward at his touch. Flicking on his flashlight, he verified the goat woman had shared the fate of her flock. There were more holes in the ceiling than anywhere else, which gave him a clue to what had happened. Switching off the flashlight, he rejoined the others.

''The woman?'' Tanaka asked.

''Beyond our help.''

Corporal Sesshu had turned his back to the blood-bath and was stooped over, a hand pressed to his stomach. "How could they do that? Kill a harmless old lady and her pets?" He shuddered. "And what did they use? Why type of weapon rips living creatures to pieces like that?"

"A minigun, would be my guess," Bolan answered. "Fired from a helicopter."

The corporal was incredulous. "A small gun did that?"

"The name is misleading," Bolan clarified. "Miniguns are electrically operated multiple-barrel systems that fire up to three thousand rounds a minute. There's nothing small about them. They're three feet long and weigh sixty to seventy pounds."

"The men responsible for this outrage must be taken into custody," the corporal declared, and marched toward a ridge to the west.

Tanaka stepped in front of him. "What do you think you're doing? Your orders are to help us, not go off on your own and get yourself killed. Show us where the airstrip is and we'll take it from there."

"Follow me," Sesshu said, continuing on.

Bolan fell into step behind them, scanning the sky although the choppers were long gone. The scent of putrid flesh told him the woman had been dead a good long while, twenty-four hours or more, murdered in her bed by a helicopter hovering directly over her shack. Small consolation, but he doubted she knew what hit her.

The slope steepened. Sesshu stomped up it like a mad bull, declaring, "That poor old woman was no threat to anyone. Why did they slay her?"

Out of the mouths of amateurs, Bolan reflected. The

policeman had a point. Why did they kill her? She certainly posed no threat. Not unless they learned she had reported them to the police. Or had they used her and her animals for target practice?

As they neared the crest, the warrior darted past Tanaka and Sesshu. "That's far enough. I'll let you know if the coast is clear." To forestall an argument, he sprinted to the rim and dropped onto his belly. Wind plucked at his jacket as he gazed into the valley below. It was mired in murk; not a single light shone anywhere. The only evidence of the airstrip consisted of long, squat shapes half a mile below, shapes that might be hangars.

Bolan glanced at his companions. Every instinct he possessed urged him to leave them there and go on alone. But Tanaka's linguistic skills in Japanese and Chinese might be of use if they took prisoners or found documents. Sesshu was another matter. In a fight the young policeman would be more of a liability than an asset, yet Sesshu wouldn't stand for being left out. Or would he?

The soldier hastened back down. "There's no activity. If the airstrip is still occupied, they're lying low. Kerri will come with me. Corporal, I'd like for you to head back and let your superiors know about the goat woman. Have them send a burial detail."

"You want to send me on a paltry errand when we are about to engage the culprits?" Sesshu's chin jutted forward. "The American expression, I believe, is that you are trying to get rid of me. And I will not stand for it."

Bolan refused to give up. "The old woman needs to be buried before her body deteriorates even more. The ground is too hard for us to do it with sticks and rocks.''

"Be that as it may," Sesshu said, "I am not leaving until our job here is done. Those were my instructions and I will abide by them.''

Bolan glanced at Tanaka for support. She had disagreed about the corporal in town, but now he hoped she would back him up. He should have known better.

"If Corporal Sesshu insists on accompanying us, we owe it to him to let him come along.''

"Suit yourselves. You're to stay twenty to thirty feet behind me at all times and only come up when I signal.'' Bolan turned but an unexpected question by the corporal gave him pause.

"You are a soldier, are you not? Or you were at one time.''

"What makes you say that?''

"You give orders as if you were born to command. There is something about you, Belasko-san. The way you hold yourself, your bearing. You are a lot like my sergeant.''

Tanaka chortled. "You must have one tough sergeant, Corporal.''

Bolan moved toward the crest. "Remember, twenty to thirty feet behind me at all times. And don't so much as sneeze.''

"Yes, Belasko-san,'' Sesshu said.

Once over the ridge, Bolan glided down into thick forest, exercising all the stealth at his command. Pine needles layered the ground, cushioning his footsteps. Treading on them was like treading on spongy carpet. Less welcome were the twigs and dead branches scattered willy-nilly. Avoiding them was a challenge but he succeeded. The same couldn't be said of the other two. One or the other was as clumsy as a cow, and every so often a sharp crack resulted. Bolan could guess who was to blame.

The sounds didn't carry far, though. Funneled by the narrow valley, the wind howled out of the west, rustling the trees and the undergrowth. It worked as much against them as it did in their favor. Noises made by their enemies would be drowned out.

Bolan angled toward the squat shapes, alert for a perimeter fence. He counted three hangars and two smaller structures running from west to east. Beyond them reared a water tower sagging at one end. The airstrip itself paralleled the buildings.

A hundred yards out the warrior squatted to reconnoiter. The absence of light, of movement, of life of any kind, tended to convince him the men he was after were long gone. He had anticipated as much ever since discovering the hit men were Chinese. There was no love lost between the two countries. If the Chinese had been engaged in an illicit operation on Japanese soil, they wouldn't stick around once they had what they were after.

The way Bolan saw it, the airstrip had served a double purpose. As a handy spot to conceal the choppers until the attack on the USS *Hampton,* and later, as a ferrying point to briefly conceal the missiles before moving them on to wherever the strike force was based.

But there was only one way to know for sure.

Bolan stalked to the nearest hangar. Constructed of corrugated tin, it was pitted with rust and other signs of decades of neglect. The only windows were on the sides.

Quickly stepping from the rear toward the front, Bolan ducked and peered inside. The interior was pitch-black. He had a flashlight in his front pocket, but using it would give him away so he went on, to the corner.

Both huge doors were closed. Bolan was about to slip over to them when a faint sound from off to the east froze him in place. Unsure what caused it, he waited awhile, raking the night for traces of the black-suited commandos. When the sound wasn't repeated, he dashed to the large metal handle on the nearest door and tugged. It swung outward without so much as a creak, proving the hangars had been in use recently.

Darting inside, Bolan ducked to the right and leveled the M-16. As his eyes adjusted to the inky murk he realized the hangar was empty. Going back out, he headed for the next and was stunned to see Kerri Tanaka and Corporal Sesshu already in front of it, looking around in confusion.

Tanaka spied him first, and waved.

Bolan was in no mood for niceties. Jogging over, he brusquely demanded, "What the hell are you doing? I told the two of you to stay behind me and wait for my signal."

"It is my fault, sir," Corporal Sesshu said. "We lost sight of you when I tripped over a rock and dropped my gun. Tanaka-san graciously helped me find it."

"I didn't want to use our flashlights so it took a while," she explained.

"Have you found anything of importance, sir?" the young policeman asked blithely.

"Not yet. Stay here while I check inside." Bolan pulled on the handle and entered. As before, the hangar was deserted. But he did spot a glistening puddle of fluid. Sinking onto a knee, he dipped the tip of a finger into it, raised the finger to his nose and sniffed. Engine oil, fresh as could be. The helicopters had been there, all right.

The next hangar was also empty. Bolan hated to think they had come all that way for nothing, but whoever they were up against was once again one step ahead of them.

The last two buildings were a barracks and what had once been the airstrip's HQ. Venturing into the former, the soldier discovered someone had gone to a lot of trouble to tidy up the place. The floor had been swept, and a piece of cardboard had been taped over a large hole in a window. The only furniture was an old chair and a three-legged stool missing part of one leg.

That left the command post. To reach it they had to cross an open space. Tanaka was on Bolan's right, Sesshu on his left. Midway there the young policeman suddenly stopped and called out, "Who's there?" Bolan instantly crouched, the M-16 wedged to his shoulder.

Sesshu was staring up at the water tower, which reared stark against the sky approximately sixty yards farther east.

Bolan looked but saw no one.

The corporal kept walking. "In the name of the Hokkaido Prefecture Police Department, I order you to show yourself!"

"Get back here!" Bolan warned, unsure whether the corporal really had seen someone or it was a trick of the shadows.

Tanaka had stopped. "Sesshu-san! Don't!" she urged.

But the young patrolman wouldn't listen to either of them. His pistol extended, he hollered, "You there!

Don't try to hide! Didn't you hear me? In the name of the Hokkaido Prefecture Police, I order you to—''

High on the tower, at the base of the water tank, muzzle-flashes flared. Simultaneously autofire ratcheted the night. The soil around the corporal erupted in geysers. Sesshu was punched backward, his torso and head skewered by slugs. He tottered drunkenly, made a feeble attempt to get off a shot, then caved at the knees.

Bolan was in motion before the firing ceased. He hurled himself at Tanaka, wrapped an arm around her waist and propelled her toward the headquarters building. They were fifteen yards from it when the sniper trained his weapon on them and ribbons of earth spewed across their legs. Zagging to the right, Bolan reached cover and let go.

To Tanaka's credit she hadn't panicked. Her back to the wall, she coolly regarded the disjointed figure of the slain policeman and said softly, ''I'm sorry. I should have listened to you. Losing face is better than losing one's life.''

''Our problem now is for us to stay alive,'' Bolan stressed. They were safe so long as they stayed put, but the prospect of being pinned down until daylight didn't appeal to him. ''I'll try to flush the shooter out. Do what you can to cover me.''

''Just give the word.''

''Now,'' Bolan responded and broke into the open, weaving like a madman toward the bottom of the tower. Behind him Tanaka opened up on the sniper, emptying her pistol in a cadence of well-spaced shots. Up on top a vague form rose into sight but was driven back down by her searing lead.

As soon as the Mustang went empty, the sniper rose again, only in a different spot.

Bolan danced to the right to avoid a swarm of sizzling hornets. It was only a guess, but he suspected the gunner was using the same type of weapon as the members of the hit squad—a Type 68 assault rifle. Not exactly ideal for sniping at night, but the gunner had the advantage of higher ground.

Another ten feet brought Bolan to the support beams. A ladder led up to the platform and the tank. Slipping underneath, he strained his ears and heard the sniper moving about, searching for him. When the steps stopped, he unleashed several short, controlled bursts at where he believed the man was standing. A yelp rewarded his effort, then there was a thump and something fell from the platform into the high grass. The assault rifle, he supposed, but he wasn't taking anything for granted.

The sniper began shouting in Chinese, his voice strangled by pain. Either that, or he was putting on a great act.

Bolan aimed at the spot the voice was coming from, but rapidly approaching footsteps spun him around.

It was Tanaka, bent at the waist, zigging back and forth. Darting past the ladder, she halted. "I thought you could use some help," she whispered.

"You should have stayed where you were."

"I saw his rifle drop. He's hurt. He keeps calling for help and asking 'Where are they?' over and over." She nodded at the ladder. "Shouldn't we go up after him?"

"And have our heads shot off if he has another gun?" Bolan moved deeper into the shadows, pulling her along. "We'll wait for him to come to us. If he's as hurt as badly as you say, he won't stay up there forever."

They hunkered. The wind chose that moment to gust nonstop, whipping dust from the runway. A hangar door they hadn't closed started banging like a kettle drum.

The sniper fell quiet.

Bolan tried to tell whether the man was moving around but couldn't. Seconds later Tanaka's fingers constricted on his hand, and when he glanced at her, she gestured toward the ladder. It was jiggling ever so slightly, as it would if someone were descending.

Bolan trained his M-16 on the highest rung visible and soon a foot appeared, then a pair of legs. The man groaned.

Tanaka looked expectantly at the soldier but he shook his head. They wouldn't show themselves until he was positive it wasn't a ruse.

Rung by rung the sniper slowly lowered himself. He was using one hand. The other was splayed across his sternum, and twice he suffered coughing fits that nearly dislodged him. At the bottom he took a single halting step and collapsed onto his hands and knees, panting as if he had just run a marathon.

Bolan nudged Tanaka and slunk forward, his sights fixed on the sniper's spine. They were almost on top of him when the man sank onto his side. His chin and throat were stained dark, and his eyelids were fluttering. He muttered some more.

"It's the same thing," Tanaka translated. "'Where are they? Where are they?' Think he's referring to us?"

The soldier was about to say he didn't know when

the rhythmic beating of rotor blades eclipsed the sound of the whipping wind. He whirled, knowing what he would see before he saw it.

A black helicopter was streaking toward them.

CHAPTER EIGHT

The war bird flashed in over the airstrip, the fuselage tilted, the cockpit lower to the ground than the tail. Painted entirely in black, it bore no markings and had no running lights, just like those that attacked the USS *Hampton*.

Of special interest to Mack Bolan was the minigun mounted on the aircraft's side. Throwing himself at his companion, he swept them both around the base of the water tower, seeking cover before the minigun operator opened fire.

They didn't make it.

The air was suddenly abuzz with 7.62 mm lead. Rounds ripped into the soil, spurting dirt upward. Rounds pinged off the tower supports, ricocheting every which way and heightening the peril. Just when it seemed they would be riddled, the helicopter banked and veered to the left to clear the tower.

Digging in his heels, Bolan reversed direction. Their only hope was to reach the buildings. The tower offered scant protection, while the woods were too far off. Pushing Tanaka toward the command post, he shouted, "Run like hell!"

The chopper was looping in a tight, controlled arc. Bolan recognized it as a McDonnell Douglas, exactly as Brognola had speculated. One of the later 500 models, a streamlined state-of-the-art killing machine with precision maneuverability and devastating firepower. No wonder the USS *Hampton* had been crippled so quickly and effectively.

They had covered half of the sixty yards when the helicopter sliced toward the water tower again, where the pilot mistakenly believed them to be.

"Down!" Bolan said, and dived, catching Tanaka across the hips and pulling her with him.

The copter hovered at the north end of the tower, a giant hornet poised to drive its stinger into prey.

"We're sitting ducks in the open," she whispered. "If they see us, you go one way and I'll go another. One of us is bound to make it out."

"We'll stick together," Bolan said. For all they knew, the Chinese had more nasty surprises waiting to be sprung, and he wanted her close to keep her safe. The irony didn't escape him. Here he was, doing exactly what he shouldn't need to do; protecting her at the risk of his own life.

As if she could read his thoughts, Tanaka whispered, "I can take care of myself. Don't worry about me. Worry about that damn chopper."

The weight of the duffel bag on his lower back reminded Bolan he had a means of dealing with the war bird if he could elude it long enough to attach what he needed to the M-16.

"It's moving!" Tanaka declared.

That it was, toward the far side of the water tower. The very second it was out of sight, Bolan sprang to his feet. So did his companion, and the two of them raced for the HQ, Bolan repeatedly glancing back to keep tabs on the whirlybird. They were still ten yards shy of their goal when the McDonnell Douglas swung around the south end of the tower. The pilot or copilot had to have spotted them almost immediately because the chopper dipped and was after them in a heartbeat.

The cough of the minigun galvanized Bolan into grabbing Tanaka's wrist and cutting to the left. Barely had he done so than the ground they just occupied was pulverized by a sustained burst.

Bolan changed direction, back toward the command post. They gained the rear corner and dashed around it, only to hear the wood being shredded. Without slowing, Bolan sprinted to the opposite corner and on around to the front of the building. Yanking on the door, he ran inside, crouched against the wall and peeked out the window, careful to only expose one eye.

Tanaka molded herself to his back.

The helicopter was rising up over the roof, the swish of its rotors like the ominous hiss of a serpent. It dropped into sight, the aircraft swiveling from side to side as the pilot tried to locate them. At a yell from the gunner, a thickset figure in a black combat suit and a black helmet, the war bird steadied.

Bolan guessed what was about to transpire and hugged the floor. Tanaka pressed against him just as the window was reduced to fragments by a leaden firestorm. Glass rained to the floor, tinkling onto Bolan's head and arms.

An old desk and a chair were next to be shot to bits as the gunner raked the room from right to left and back again. The rear wall thudded to multiple impacts, holes mushrooming like measles. A dusty coatrack that had been there since World War II was reduced to kindling.

The soldier felt Tanaka's fingers wrap around his

arm, felt her flinch as the minigun's rounds came closer and closer. Just when it seemed they were next to be obliterated, the firing ceased and the chopper rose up into the air.

Bolan waited a good long while before he looked out. The aircraft appeared to be gone, but he made no attempt to stand.

"What are we waiting for?" the woman whispered. "We should get out of here while the getting is good."

"And waltz right into their sights?" Bolan shook his head. "They could be anywhere. We'll wait them out." He leaned his M-16 against the wall and unslung the duffel. "Besides, I have something that can turn the tables."

"This is the second time today you've saved my life," Tanaka commented. "I never could have evaded them on my own."

"Practice makes perfect." Bolan opened the duffel and roved his hand over the contents until he found the article he needed.

"What is that thing?"

"A grenade launcher," Bolan said. Specifically, it was an M-203 breech-loaded, pump action 40 mm grenade launcher.

"Next you'll tell me you have a bazooka or a tank in that magic bag of yours."

Bolan placed the M-16 in his lap next to the launcher and pressed the barrel latch. "This packs enough of a wallop to do the job."

Outside all was still except for periodic gusts of wind. Tanaka sat with her back to the wall, her arms draped over her knees. "You do this kind of stuff a lot, don't you?"

"Define 'stuff.'"

"Missions like this. Missions a lot more dangerous than most. Stuff I wouldn't care to deal with on a regular basis."

"Didn't you tell me once you liked excitement and adventure?"

"I like sneaking into an apartment to plant a bug, or getting the goods on a suspected terrorist, or arranging a safehouse when Mr. Brognola needs one. That sort of thing. I don't like being shot at by helicopters. Or, for that matter, having shoot-outs with Chinese hit men." She paused. "We live in quite different worlds, you and I, Mike."

Bolan caught the sadness in her tone and elected not to say anything. Now that it had sunk in, maybe she would stop trying to make their relationship more personal than it had any right being. His refusal to let her draw close to him was as much for her benefit as it was for his own.

"You know—" Tanaka whispered.

The soldier lunged, clamping a hand over her mouth. He had heard the scrape of footsteps to the east. They grew louder, the shuffling, shambling gait of someone dragging his or her feet. Brushing his lips against her ear, he breathed, "The sniper."

She gave an odd little quiver, then raised the Mustang.

Wagging a finger, Bolan quietly slid the M-16 to the floor and palmed the Beretta. Tucked at the waist, he moved to the door, which had been reduced to tatters by the minigun and now hung from one hinge. In a few moments the sniper materialized, limping painfully, an arm across his bloody chest, his legs teetering with every step. He had a pistol in a holster but hadn't drawn it. His hood was down, and he was forlornly gazing at the sky, in search of his friends in the helicopter.

Bolan aimed at the man's head. But as he curled his finger to the trigger, the sniper staggered off toward the airstrip.

The Executioner let him go. The man wouldn't last much longer and posed no threat. And if the chopper was out there somewhere waiting for them to show themselves, killing him would give their position away.

Backpedaling, Bolan replaced the Beretta and was reaching for his M-16 when he heard voices. Out on the airstrip two men in combat blacksuits had rushed up to the sniper, who was on his knees. One of them slipped an arm under the sniper's shoulder and started to haul him toward the command post. The other man flanked them.

A single grenade could take out all three.

Bolan shifted to search the duffel, then registered movement much closer to the building—only a few steps from the window. A fourth Chinese was coming from the west. They set eyes on one another at practically the same split second. Both brought their weapons to bear, but Bolan was a hair faster. His burst slammed the Chinese backward.

The man supporting the sniper let go. Both commandos trained their assault rifles on the headquarters and took up where the chopper had left off, charging as they fired.

Amid flying shards of glass and wood, Bolan hunched over the duffel and hunted for the right grenade. He had brought several different kinds along, among them an M-397 airburst grenade and an M-433 armor-piercing grenade. But the one he wanted, the one he found and fed into the launcher, was an M-576 buckshot grenade, a short, black grenade ideal for close-range combat. He aimed a couple of yards in front of the charging Chinese and fired.

Tanaka was rising as Bolan spun from the window. Again he tackled her, landing on her chest and covering her body with his. The crump of the blast shook the entire building. The door and part of the front wall blew inward, showering tiny metal shards all over. When he heaved upright and looked out, ravaged torsos and severed limbs littered the blast radius.

Bolan yanked his companion upright. "Head for the forest. Don't stop. Don't look back. We have maybe thirty seconds before the chopper arrives." She bolted out into the night, and he followed, the duffel in his left hand.

His estimate was off by fifteen seconds.

They were only a few feet past the rear of the HQ when the aircraft whisked in from the north, nearly skimming the airstrip. It came to where the commandos had fallen, hovered briefly as the pilot confirmed they were dead, then sheared up and over the command post, a modern dragon out for blood. Only instead of breathing fire, it spit lead.

Bolan looked back and saw slugs stitch a path toward them. He shoved Tanaka to the left and bounded to the right an instant before the autofire cleaved the space between them.

The woman glanced at him, and Bolan motioned for her to keep going. Then he spun, dropped the duffel and jammed the M-16 to his shoulder. The helicopter was banking to give the gunner a clearer shot. It gave him a clearer shot, too. He triggered a short burst and had the satisfaction of seeing the gunner recoil from the impact.

Either the man was wearing body armor or the wounds were minor, because without missing a beat he gripped the minigun anew, about to let loose with another withering deluge.

Bolan shifted his attention to the cockpit. His next burst forced the pilot to swiftly gain altitude and bought him time to pick up the duffel and run after Tanaka. She was close enough to the undergrowth to reach cover before the copter opened up on them again. The same couldn't be said for him.

The chopper swooped out of the gloom, the minigun chattering. Bolan tore to the right, to the left, always a step ahead of the deadly hail.

The soldier covered another ten yards without being hit. Luck more than anything else had spared him so far, but no one's luck held forever. He was speeding flat-out when a score of rounds ripped into the duffel and tore it from his hand. He didn't dare stop, didn't dare go back for it. The helicopter was too close. He bounded on toward the woods, dirt kicking up all around, and when he was close enough, he flung his arms in front of him and levered into a forward roll that ended in a patch of weeds.

Bolan lay flat, catching his breath, as the chopper cleared the treetops with inches to spare. Twisting, he looked for the duffel but it was lost in the tall grass. To go after it invited another aerial onslaught, and the next time the outcome might be different.

The helicopter looped northward. Bolan glimpsed it high over the water tower, rising into the gloom. Whether it was leaving or a prelude to another strafing run, he couldn't say, so he remained where he was. Five minutes elapsed. Ten minutes.

Cautiously standing, Bolan went in search of Tanaka. She had entered the forest about fifteen feet east of him, so she had to be nearby. But when he whispered her name, there was no response. He tried several more times, louder each time, and she still didn't answer.

Kerri Tanaka had disappeared.

Washington, D.C.

THE E-MAIL FROM Stony Man Farm to Hal Brognola was routed through a string of proxy servers to prevent it from being traced to its source. Barbara Price had typed a single word: "Bingo!" An attachment was included.

Brognola moved his mouse, double-clicked on the icon and said aloud, "I'll be damned."

The team at Stony Man had struck paydirt. According to a complicated paper trail, a German aviation dealer had placed an order with McDonnell Douglas for two Model 300Cs, seventy Model 500Es, ten Model 500Ds and, finally, six 530MGs. All were listed on the bill of lading as being intended for agricultural use.

Amazingly, no red flags were raised at the State Department and the deal was allowed to go through.

The German, though, didn't exist, and the company he supposedly owned was a shell operation set up by the North Koreans. The choppers were duly shipped and immediately relayed to North Korea.

Even though the helicopters weren't fitted with military ordnance, it hadn't taken much to modify them. According to the CIA, every last helicopter was now in use by the North Korean military.

It was a damn clever coup on their part.

But that wasn't all. Owing to intel gleaned from sources in China, a dozen helicopters from the McDonnell Douglas shipment were transshipped from North Korea to Qingdao. Where they went from there was anyone's guess.

Brognola drummed his fingers on his desk, deep in thought. He still refused to believe the Chinese government was behind the theft. And if it wasn't a sanctioned operation, it had to be someone working behind the government's back, someone with a lot of clout, someone who wasn't afraid of how the government would react.

It had to be a rogue, Brognola figured. A renegade who wouldn't think twice about unleashing the plasma missiles on the U.S. or anywhere else. He intended to have Price and her crew research a list of possible candidates. There couldn't be all that many, not with the Chinese leadership so prone to snuff out dissent.

Opening the top drawer, Brognola took out a note pad and scribbled, "Who? Where?" and "What next?" It was the last question that worried him the most. To help answer it, he had invited Bill Grant, the coordinator for the PPS-1 project, to pay a return visit. Glancing at his watch, he minimized his e-mail.

Right on time, there was a knock. "Come on in," Brognola said, standing. He had instructed his staff to have Grant brought directly to his office.

The tall, gray-haired scientist sauntered in and shook

the big Fed's hand. "I received your message this morning." He gazed at the empty chairs. "Am I the only one invited? What about Mrs. Harkness and Captain Bower? I was under the impression we were working together."

"It's your expertise I'm most interested in at the moment, not theirs. Have a seat. This won't take long."

"I must confess," Grant said as he made himself comfortable, "coming here makes me somewhat nervous."

"Why would that be?"

"From what I've been able to gather, you wield a lot of power, a lot of influence. You're one of the top men at the Justice Department. You have the ear of the President, and I feel as if I'm out of my depth."

"Unless you did something wrong, you have no need to worry. And I can assure you that you're not part of any criminal investigation." Brognola was sincere. He had eliminated Grant as a source of the leaks. The scientist couldn't possibly have known about Bolan and Tanaka being sent to Hokkaido. Harkness and Bower were another story.

Brognola had established that the President had indeed made a slip of the tongue at a White House meeting concerning the PPS-1s six hours before the Chinese hit squad struck. Abigail Harkness and Captain Bower both attended but not Bill Grant. According to Brognola's sources, at one point the chief of staff had asked the President how soon they would have someone on the scene, and the commander in chief had casually replied that some of their best people were due in Hokkaido before the day was out.

"So what can I do for you, Mr. Brognola?" Bill Grant asked.

The big Fed leaned back. "I'm working under the assumption that whoever stole the missiles plans to fit them with nuclear warheads. You know the design schematics of the PPS-1 better than almost anyone, so I need you to tell me what's involved. They can't just take any old nuke and slap it on, I gather."

"Oh, no," Grant said. "But we did develop the PPS-1 with ease of retrofitting in mind. In other words, there isn't a warhead exclusive to the PPS-1. You could take a nuclear warhead from a conventional ICBM, if you wanted, and it would work."

Brognola needed to be clear on the full implications. "So you're saying the thieves could use a nuclear warhead off virtually any missile?"

"Not quite, no. Certain variables are involved. System mechanics, size, those sorts of things," Grant said. "Older warheads, for instance, would be too big. Others simply couldn't interface with the PPS-1's systems."

"Be more specific."

"Any warhead manufactured within, say, the past two decades would fall within our design parameters."

"By any country?" Brognola asked, dreading the response.

"Ah. I see what you're getting at." Grant was warming to the topic. "Compatibility is the key. Without getting too technical, let me use an analogy. If you were souping up a hot rod, you wouldn't use just any old carburetor. You would use one designed to fit your particular engine."

"How many countries have warheads that can be fitted onto the PPS-1?"

"England, France, Israel, maybe India," Grant said without hesitation. "But if I'd stolen the missiles, I would try to obtain Russian warheads."

"Why from Russia?"

"Because their warheads aren't as technologically sophisticated as some of the others, yet they're still sophisticated enough."

"You've lost me," Brognola admitted.

"The Russians always take the simplest approach, cutting corners wherever they can. Remember their space station? How basic it was compared to ours? Their warheads are the same way. Fitting one to a PPS-1 would take a minimum of know-how."

"Five nuclear missiles in the hands of fanatics," Brognola said quietly, more to himself than to his visitor.

"More than that, I'm afraid."

"Come again?"

"Have you forgotten? The official title for the PPS-1 is the Plasma Propulsion System Multiple Delivery System. Multiple, as in many. Up to five nuclear warheads can be fitted onto each PPS-1. Once the missile reaches a predesignated position, the nose cone breaks apart. Miniaturized thrusters engage and deliver the individual warheads to their detonation points."

The blood in Brognola's veins ran cold. "So you're saying that whoever stole them can strike twenty-five targets, not just five?"

"Within a limited range, yes. The nose cone thrusters are conventional, not plasma driven. Basically, we designed the PPS-1s with the capability to take out any large military installation or city on the planet,'' Grant said proudly.

"Be specific again."

"Well, as you're probably aware, a single nuclear warhead wouldn't completely destroy most major cities. Devastate them, sure, but not wipe them off the face of the Earth. Depending on the yield, it'd take two, possibly even three warheads." Grant had the clinical air of a college professor lecturing a class. "That's where the PPS-1s come in. The onboard computer is programmed to guide the missile to the exact geographic center of a given target. Once there, the nose cone disengages and the five nuclear warhead components separate."

"And their individual thrusters ignite," Brognola said when the scientist paused.

"Precisely. One warhead impacts at geographic ground zero. The others strike peripheral points. All timed to go off simultaneously, of course."

"Of course."

"Any city, any army or navy or air force base in the world, would be obliterated in a span of seconds," Grant stated. "There would be nothing left. No buildings, no people, nothing."

Brognola envisioned a PPS-1 targeted at Los Angeles or Washington, D.C., and couldn't repress a slight shudder.

Grant was smiling. "The PPS-1 is the ultimate nuclear delivery system. It's virtually infallible, and its destructive potential is unsurpassed. All of us involved in the program outdid ourselves. Especially in light of the continental doomsday scenario, as we dubbed it.''

"The what?"

"The ability to cripple an entire continent." Grant gestured excitedly. "Picture this. Instead of striking individual targets, all the PPS-1s are launched at the geographic center of a given continent. Europe, perhaps. Or Asia. Five or six missiles, it wouldn't matter. Not when all the warheads are programmed to go off at once. We're talking twenty-five to thirty nuclear warheads, with yields of anywhere from ten to thirty megatons apiece."

"Damn," Brognola breathed.

"It could well precipitate a nuclear winter, although the computer projections were distressingly vague on the full extent."

Brognola was appalled no one had brought up the doomsday scenario before. Maybe it was because the President wanted it kept hush-hush, or the chief executive and his advisers weren't looking that far ahead. They were primarily concerned with recovering the missiles *before* they could be used. "Tell me something."

"Certainly," Grant said cheerfully.

"How bad would it be if the stolen missiles were triggered over the center of the United States?"

"Funny you should ask. We ran that very scenario through the computers, just for the hell of it."

"And?"

"As best I can remember, millions would die. Radiation would contaminate our nation's heartland— Kansas, Nebraska, the Dakotas, parts of Illinois and several other states—for generations to come. Our breadbasket would be gone. The blast would knock out electrical power from coast to coast, disrupting all essential services. Our military would be nullified.''

"Dear God.''

Grant's eyebrows pinched together. "I don't see why you're so alarmed. The odds of that happening are astronomical.''

Brognola wanted to reach out and shake the man until his teeth rattled. "But what if whoever stole the PPS-1s had that in mind from the beginning?'' he asked angrily. "What if they have access to multiple warheads? What if they're able to fit nukes onto the missiles and launch all five at our heartland, just as you've described?''

Bill Grant blanched. "Well, then, in that case, the United States of America would effectively cease to exist.''

CHAPTER NINE

Japan

The Executioner was stumped. Kerri Tanaka hadn't been out of his sight for long. She couldn't have gone all that far. Yet although he scoured the woods for over an hour, he found no trace of her.

Nor had there been any sign of more blacksuited commandos or the helicopter, convincing Bolan the Chinese were gone. Even so, he never let down his guard as he warily prowled the dense forest in ever widening circles, calling Tanaka's name again and again, to no avail.

The soldier halted. Continuing to search would be a waste of time. He decided to wait until daylight. It was already close to midnight; another five and half hours wouldn't make much of a difference. In case Tanaka returned, he hiked back to the spot where he had last seen her.

To the north the airstrip lay quiet under the stars.

Bolan reached into his pocket for the flashlight. While he was biding his time, he might as well hunt for the duffel. Flicking it on, he swung the beam to the right, then to the left—and found out he wasn't alone. In a twinkling he leveled the M-16.

Twenty feet away stood an elderly man in flowing clothes. He had a long, bushy beard, parted in the middle, and wore a peculiar headdress. Short in stature, he had a stocky build and pale skin.

An Ainu, Bolan realized, and slowly lowered his rifle. The man had made no threatening moves. After staring a bit, the oldster beckoned and turned, clearly expecting Bolan to follow.

The soldier wondered if the aborigines had anything to do with Tanaka's disappearance. He doubted he was in danger, but he stayed frosty as they wound through the woodland. Twice the old man looked back to insure he was still there. Their course eventually led them out of the trees onto a boulder-strewn slope and over it into a rocky ravine. There, sheltered from the wind, were half a dozen crude grass huts. They had no doors, no windows. Small fires glowed in each, and around the fires more Ainu were huddled. Men, women and children.

The old man clapped his hands, and everyone gathered to greet them. The women, Bolan saw, had tattoos on their faces, lines that mimicked the beards of their men. All the Ainu had the same short, stocky builds. Grinning and giggling, they examined him from head to toe, fascinated by the alien in their midst.

No weapons were evident. Not even knives.

Bolan looked quizzically at the old man, who motioned toward a darkened grass hut. Resting a hand on the Beretta, Bolan moved to the opening. After a few seconds he made out the outline of a prone body dressed in black. A whiff of perfume let him know it wasn't one of the Chinese.

"Kerri?" Bolan said, slipping within and kneeling beside her. Resorting to the flashlight, he spied a discolored gash on her temple, caked with dry blood. She was alive but unconscious. When he rolled her onto her back she groaned.

The old man entered but came no farther than the doorway. He spoke a few words in an unfamiliar language.

"Do you speak English?" Bolan asked. A blank expression was his reply. To make the elder understand Tanaka needed water, Bolan held his hand to his mouth and mimed drinking and swallowing.

Smiling, the Ainu backed out, returning moments later with a bulging goatskin. Bolan bowed slightly in gratitude, and when he looked up, the old man was gone. He opened the goatskin, cupped his right hand and out flowed milk.

Tanaka's lips were parted. Bending, Bolan let some of the milk trickle between them. She stirred and mumbled. Another trickle caused her to cough, and suddenly her eyes snapped wide and she started to sit up, only to cry out and clasp a hand to her head.

"You'd better lie still," Bolan advised, gently gripping her shoulder.

"Mike?" She clasped his wrist and sank back down. "What happened? The last thing I remember is running into the trees and turning to see if you were all right."

"You must have been hit by a stray round, a ricochet, maybe," Bolan said. "It only creased you. You're lucky to be alive."

Tanaka gingerly touched the wound. "I am, aren't I? Another couple of inches to the left and it would have been all over." She squinted at the grass roof. "Wait a minute. Where are we? This isn't the airfield."

"We're at an Ainu village. An old man brought me."

The very next second the elder stepped back into the hut. Tanaka talked to him in Japanese, and the old man responded in kind. Their conversation lasted minutes, ending when the elder bowed and departed once more.

"What was that all about?" Bolan asked.

"He's the one who found me and brought me here. They heard the shooting and the explosions, and he had gone to investigate."

"That was nice of him."

"They usually shun strangers. But he remembered us from Asahigawa. He was one of the two Ainu we saw leaving the police station."

Bolan stared out the doorway. Everyone was gone, dispersed to their huts. "Did he say what he was doing there?"

"He and his brother went to report the bad men, as he called them, to the police."

"Bad men?"

"The Chinese. It seems the Ainu have been encamped here about a month. They were here when the Chinese occupied the airstrip, and were curious about all the commotion. So they spied on the Chinese for a week or so, then the old man and his brother went down to introduce themselves. The Chinese fired on them. After holding a council, they decided to report the incident."

"Why didn't Corporal Sesshu mention it?"

Tanaka closed her eyes and said wearily, "They had just finished telling the desk sergeant when we arrived, and we left for the goat woman's not long after. Odds are no one relayed the information to Sesshu before we took off." She licked her lips. "I could use more of that milk, if you don't mind."

Cradling her head in his lap, Bolan carefully tipped

the goatskin to her mouth. She gulped greedily, spilling some down her chin, which Bolan wiped off with his sleeve.

"Thank you," she said, turning so her cheek was cushioned by his thigh. "I don't feel so good. I keep having bouts of dizziness."

"You might have a concussion," Bolan speculated. "You need to rest. We'll spend the night here and leave for Asahigawa in the morning."

"What about the PPS-1s? Didn't you say recovering them is a top priority?"

"It is, but they're no longer in Japan. We'll call Brognola from town and fill him in. The next step is his. He has to track down where the missiles went from here. Once he does, I'll be on my way."

"Oh." Tanaka didn't sound particularly overjoyed at the news.

"We might as well get some sleep," Bolan suggested. The hut, though, was as barren as the ground outside. And while he was used to sleeping under combat conditions, he doubted very much that she was. "Want me to ask the old man for a blanket?"

"No. The Ainu are a poor people. If they own any, I wouldn't think of depriving them." The woman wriggled onto her side and patted the earth in front of her. "We'll have to make the best of it. Do what we can to keep each other warm."

Bolan laid the M-16 between them and reclined on his back, his head propped in his hands. "I'm warm enough, thank you."

"I'm not. One second I'm hot, the next I'm freezing." Wrapping her arms across her bosom, she shivered.

Suspicious she was up to something, but spurred by

concern over her head wound, Bolan switched the M-16 to his other side and slid a little closer. "Body heat can help," he conceded.

Eagerly the woman snuggled up against him, her cheek on his shoulder. She sighed contentedly and placed a hand on his stomach.

Bolan closed his eyes. The feel of her body provoked notions he quickly suppressed. He lay still, hoping she would drift asleep right away, but after a couple of minutes he could tell by her shallow breathing she was still very much awake. When her fingers traced a small circle on his stomach, he glanced down.

"I have thought of you often since you left the last time," Tanaka whispered.

"Don't start."

"I know. You don't want our relationship to become personal. But it already is. I have made no secret of my affection for you."

"It's best this way," Bolan said. "I won't be in Japan much longer, and there's no telling when I'll get back this way again, if ever."

"So by denying your passion, you think to protect me from myself?"

The blunt question put Bolan on the defensive. "I don't want your feelings hurt. It could never work out, Kerri. We both work for Hal Brognola, but we live in two different worlds."

"Let me worry about my feelings. In case you haven't noticed, I'm a grown woman."

Bolan closed his eyes again. Of course he had noticed. It was part of the problem. He couldn't let himself notice things like that.

"And another thing. You've jumped to the conclusion I expect some type of long-term relationship. But nothing could be further from the truth. My philosophy is to take one day at a time. If it works out between us, fine. If not, well, that's life."

Bolan pretended to be more interested in going to sleep than he was in her, but she slid higher and her warm lips lightly brushed his chin.

"You try to be a man of steel. You try to deny your feelings. Yet I can see that you care. A woman always knows."

"Maybe I do," Bolan conceded, breaking his silence, "but if I don't want to take it any further, you should respect my wishes and let it drop."

"You expect a woman to deny her innermost feelings?" Tanaka said, and lightly laughed. "You are so versed in the arts of war but you know so little of the female heart."

If she only knew, Bolan thought. Images of April and Barbara Price and other women he had been attracted to floated before him, and the pain was worse than a physical wound. "Try to get some sleep," he said sternly.

"Without a good-night kiss?"

Bolan looked at her. "Has anyone ever told you that you're a stubborn little minx? Why can't you take no for an answer?"

"Because while your mouth is saying no, your eyes are saying yes." With that, she slid higher still and hungrily molded her mouth to his.

The sensation was exquisite. Her full lips, her velvet tongue. Bolan returned the kiss without meaning to, an automatic reaction, and once he savored the sweet taste of her, he craved more. But as she rubbed her hand up over his chest, he gripped her wrist and reluctantly pulled back. "That's enough. If you can't behave, I'll go find a goat to keep you warm."

Her eyes were hooded with desire, her mouth parted in invitation. "You can't deny me forever."

"Just for tonight will do," Bolan said. Then he would be gone, and it would be a cold day in hell before he agreed to work with her again.

Rather sorrowfully, Tanaka rested her head on his chest. "You must lead a very lonely life, Mike. I don't see how you stand it."

"I do what I have to," Bolan said. Thankfully she didn't press the issue or pester him with questions. In due length she dozed off, and he stared at her in the darkness, at her cherry lips and her smooth skin, at the rise and fall of her sweatshirt, and his throat went dry with need. Tearing his gaze from her, he pillowed his head on his arm and tried to fall asleep.

It took a while.

Off the Coast of China

THE FERRIES WERE READY to go. On each sat a flatbed truck, the plasma missiles on the truck beds covered with enormous sheets of canvas. Twenty soldiers were to accompany each truck, twenty of the best soldiers in the Chinese army. Per orders from their commanding officer, they had traded their combat blacksuits for standard Chinese uniforms.

General Tsanghsien did not want to draw any undue attention to their convoy once they reached the mainland. To all intents and purposes, it must appear to be a normal military operation. The Party elite could not learn what he was up to, or in their misguided stupidity they might try to stop him. It was why he was ferrying the missiles from Hakka Island in the dead of night rather than in broad daylight.

Standing on a pier at the south end of the island, the general gave his base a last scrutiny and turned to descend a gangplank onto the second ferry. Sergeant Yatsen was at attention, awaiting him, and as he started down, the sergeant suddenly pointed.

"General! Here he comes."

Tsanghsien turned. Never one to tolerate tardiness, he demanded of the latecomer, "I trust you have a good excuse for delaying our departure?"

Colonel Chen saluted. "My utmost apologies, sir, but it couldn't be helped. I just got off the radio with Lieutenant Wun on Hokkaido."

"And?"

"I regret to report they have failed, General. The two Americans are still alive. The lieutenant reports all his men have been killed. He has camouflaged the helicopter and will rendezvous with the freighter two days from now."

The general straightened to his full height, and his eyes blazed with an inner light. "*All* his men were slain? Did he do exactly as I instructed them? Did he post a sniper on the water tower and wait to catch the Americans in the open?"

"Yes, sir," Chen said. "He is a competent officer or I would not have given him the assignment. He says that one of the Americans, a big man with dark hair, is quite formidable. Those were his exact words."

"Formidable," Tsanghsien repeated, rolling the syllables on the tip of his tongue.

"Lieutenant Wun is not prone to exaggeration, sir. He says the American fights like ten tigers."

The general smiled. The expression was an old one,

as old as China herself, and was the highest praise one fighting man could extend another. The last time he had heard it was when someone said the same about him. ''Perhaps Lieutenant Wun is right. The American disposed of the men we sent to stop him at Sapporo, and now the squad we left at the airfield. I am beginning to think fondly of this big man with dark hair.''

''Sir?'' Colonel Chen said. ''You think fondly of an enemy?''

''A true warrior, Colonel, always respects another. Even an enemy. And especially a formidable enemy. This American brings to mind a passage from Sun Tzu. 'For he wins his victories without erring.'''

''But at the expense of our own men, sir.''

The general glanced at Sergeant Yatsen and could tell he failed to comprehend, as well. ''Do either of you have any idea how many enemies I have destroyed in my rise to prominence?''

''Dozens, I would guess, sir,'' Chen said.

''You would be short by several hundred,'' the general replied. ''And out of all the men who have opposed me over the years, not one has been a man of merit. Not one has been a worthy adversary. I crushed them as easily as—'' A moth was flitting by, drawn toward a floodlight on shore, and with a lightning flick of his hand, the general caught it and crushed it in his palm. ''As easily as I did this insect.''

''That is as it should be, sir. You are China's greatest soldier. You are her hope, her salvation.''

''True, true,'' the general stated. ''But you miss my point.''

Sergeant Yatsen cleared his throat. ''I think I understand, sir. You're saying you have never met an enemy who was your equal.''

"No, Sergeant, I haven't." Tsanghsien rubbed his palm against a piling, removing what was left of the moth. "All my adversaries have been pathetic weaklings. They offered few challenges worthy of a man of my ability." He gazed out across the Yellow Sea in the direction of distant Japan. "Once, just once, I would like to be pitted against a foe worthy of my mettle. I wonder…"

"Sir?" Chen said when the general did not go on.

"Destiny, Colonel. The intertwining of lives like threads in a tapestry. Have you given Major Xinsi his orders?"

"Yes, sir. He knows what you want done. If the American shows up as you expect, he will be in for a surprise."

"Then let us be on our way." Pivoting, the general walked onto the ferry and over to the flatbed. He gave the command to get under way, which was relayed to the other ferry, and the two vessels pushed off.

He faced westward, toward the mainland, reviewing his plan and the steps he had implemented to carry it out. Was there anything he had overlooked? Any lapses in judgement? Had every possible precaution been taken and nothing left to chance?

The general had never told his trusted subordinates, but there were times when he was plagued by doubts. An unused sword soon grew dull, and his secret fear was that he would one day lose the edge that had brought him to the heights of power and influence. It was childish of him, he knew, but it couldn't be helped.

He thought of the American and a tingle ran through him. Wouldn't it be wonderful, he thought, if at long last a true adversary had arisen? Someone who would test his ability as it had never been tested before? Someone who truly was an equal?

The general sighed. The plain truth was he had no equals. He was one of a kind. His brilliance, his ability, were unique. In the entire course of human history, few men ever possessed his excellence of mind, body and character.

The general often wondered why fate had favored him, out of all of China's billions. He was partial to the idea great men were born great. That before they came into the world they were instilled with qualities that set them far above ordinary men.

Early on in life General Tsanghsien had learned how different he was. In athletic competitions he always surpassed his peers. He could run faster, jump higher and leap farther than anyone. His strength was that of three men, his stamina limitless.

In intellect he also had no rivals. He'd always achieved perfect scores on his tests, grasping the most difficult of concepts with elementary ease.

His character was flawless. His iron will and decisive nature made him an ideal leader, someone others looked up to. He had none of the false sentimentality of lesser men. Compassion, mercy and tolerance were flaws of the weak, traits he had removed from his character much as a surgeon removed afflicted organs.

A breeze fanned the general's face, and he breathed deep of the sea air. He would need all his ability, all his excellence of mind, body and character to carry out his grand plan. Since China's leaders refused to see things his way, he was taking it on himself to set the world right. He had embarked on a course destined to rid the earth of the vile harlot who tainted the planet.

He was going to destroy the United States of America.

Washington, D.C.

THE PACKET ARRIVED by special courier just as Hal Brognola was preparing to leave his office. He thanked the courier and took the packet to his desk. Out spilled dozens of high-resolution satellite-reconnaissance photographs taken within the past forty-eight hours.

Based on the assumption that whoever stole the PPS-1s intended to transport them to China, Brognola had submitted a request for relevant intel.

The photographs were labeled with latitudes and longitudes, as well as the times of day the shots were snapped. Brognola sorted them into three piles: those of western Hokkaido and the Sea of Japan, those of the Korea Strait and a few taken of the Yellow Sea.

He was particularly interested in the Korea Strait. Only a few hundred miles wide on average, it separated Japan from South Korea. In order to reach China by the most direct sea route from Hokkaido, a ship had to go through it.

One by one Brognola studied the prints. Most merited little interest. Photographs of a South Korean destroyer, several tankers and fishing boats were discarded. He examined eight or nine shots of freighters of various tonnages and nationalities. Then he slid the next photo off the pile and his eyes narrowed.

Brognola took a magnifying glass from his left-hand drawer. Holding it for maximum magnification, he was able to read the name of the vessel, another freighter called the *Pyongchang*. Ostensibly she was South Korean, but her position in the Korea Strait was such that she was much closer to the Japanese side than was warranted if she were en route to a South Korean port.

The next photo was also of the *Pyongchang* but taken much later in the day. She had cleared the strait and was plainly sailing westward into the Yellow Sea.

What piqued Brognola's interest even more were five large objects on the *Pyongchang*'s forward deck. Shrouded by canvas, each was over thirty-five feet long and fifteen feet wide. Part of that, Brognola guessed, was due to overlap from the canvas, which made the dimensions just about right for McDonnell Douglas 530MG helicopters.

Working rapidly, Brognola went through the rest of the Korea Strait pile but saw nothing of significance. Next he scanned the photos of western Hokkaido and the Sea of Japan. The fourth one showed the *Pyongchang* steaming south approximately fifty miles northwest of Hokkaido. It had been taken almost two days before the previous photos. The resolution wasn't as detailed, but with the aid of the magnifying glass Brognola could tell the canvas-covered objects weren't on the forward deck. Yet by the time the vessel reached the Korea Strait, they had been.

How was that possible?

Brognola put himself in the shoes of the party behind the theft. They'd needed to get the missiles out of Japan with as little delay as possible. Normal smuggling routes were out of the question. An aircraft big enough to hold the five PPS-1s was also big enough to be detected by the Japanese defense network. A ship was best, but if it came too close to shore it ran the same risk as an aircraft.

So what was the solution? Brognola smiled at the obvious answer.

The missiles had initially been airlifted from the USS *Hampton* by helicopter. It posed no problem for the same choppers to fly them out to sea and rendezvous with the *Pyongchang*. Her forward deck was more than wide enough for them to land on. Once they had, they were covered with canvas and transported—where?

Brognola turned to the last pile and anxiously skimmed them, hoping against hope there was another shot of the freighter. And there was. The last in the pile, the coordinates suggested that by then the freighter was well over halfway across the Yellow Sea.

Snatching up the telephone, Brognola punched in a special number. When Barbara Price answered, he said glibly, ''Chalk another one up for the old man.''

''You've found something?''

''I'm sending you a packet of photos. They show a freighter transporting the missiles. Analyze them. Run them through the computer. I want to know where that freighter wound up.''

''I already know.''

''What? You're psychic now?''

Price laughed. ''Better than that. We know who is behind it. Five will get you ten your freighter was bound for a place called Hakka Island.''

CHAPTER TEN

Hakka Island

The Yellow Sea was not as calm as the forecast claimed. High waves buffeted Mack Bolan's inflatable raft as he paddled toward the lights visible on Hakka Island. He was dressed for combat in a skintight black-suit, his face and neck smeared with camouflage cosmetics. Across his back was slung the M-16, the M-203 grenade launcher attached underneath its barrel. Under his left arm was the Beretta, while the Desert Eagle rode his right hip.

It was hard to believe that twenty-four hours ago Bolan had been snuggled next to Kerri Tanaka in the Ainu hut. A lot had happened since.

At first light the soldier and Tanaka had hastened to the airfield and he had reclaimed his duffel. The woman checked the bodies for identification but there was none. They immediately left for Asahigawa on their bicycles. Since it was mostly downhill, they made much better time than the night before. She reported Corporal Sesshu's death to the captain, who dispatched six policemen to recover the bodies and secure the airfield.

While she was occupied, Bolan put in a trans-Pacific

call to Hal Brognola, who asked them to return to Tokyo ASAP. Tanaka was to check in with the American
ambassador, while Bolan was to hook up with Jack
Grimaldi at Yokota Air Force Base. Another flight was
in order.

The Feds had learned the identity of the man behind
the theft of the PPS-1s. Intel was sketchy, but it provided enough background to give them some inkling
of the mastermind they were pitted against.

General Soong Tsanghsien was the youngest man to
ever attain that rank in China. At one time he had been
an up-and-coming star in the government hierarchy,
earning fame for his ruthless quelling of the Taiyuan
student protest and for his brutal tactics in dealing with
the Tibetan resistance.

The general had been at the top of his class at the
military academy. A master strategist, his thesis on the
application of *The Art of War* to modern warfare was
required reading for all new officers. A Chinese press
dispatch once mentioned he had memorized Sun Tzu's
writings and could quote them by the hour.

Of his personal life little was known. His father had
been a high-ranking officer; his mother died delivering
him. He had no brothers, no sisters. He was proficient
in Hung Gar kung fu, a certified marksman, and had
what was characterized as a commanding presence.

He also hated America with a passion that bordered
on fanaticism. Exactly why was a mystery. His hatred
went far beyond the intense dislike of capitalism so
common among Communists. Over the past decade he
went on public record again and again demanding
China go to war against the United States, a position
that put him out of favor with the Party elite. To silence
him they banished the general to Hakka Island.

But like all true fanatics, General Tsanghsien didn't let a minor setback like exile stop him. The evidence was conclusive. Tsanghsien was responsible for the attack on the USS *Hampton*. He now had the PPS-1s and undoubtedly planned to use them against the country he most despised.

Bolan's job was to see he didn't.

Another wave lifted the raft, and the soldier stroked his paddle smoothly, carrying the vessel up and over. He still had several hundred yards to cover to reach shore, and at the rate he was going it would take him another fifteen minutes. He was already half an hour behind schedule, but he had allowed enough leeway that he should be able to accomplish what he had to before daylight.

Floodlights lit up much of the installation. They revealed guard towers to the north and south and guards making regular rounds. Huge warehouses took up fully half the depot. A wide parade ground separated them from other buildings—barracks, an infirmary, the motor pool and more.

Bolan was bending into another wave when he spied a cluster of lights offshore, to the south. They were coming toward him at a fairly brisk clip, ten to fifteen knots or more. It had to be a boat of some kind, too small to be a freighter, too narrow to be a trawler. When a searchlight stabbed the darkness, he realized what it was and redoubled his efforts to reach the island.

A patrol boat was making its rounds.

Bolan saw the searchlight swing toward him, but the boat was still too far off for the beam to reach him. The motor grew steadily louder as he stroked and stroked, the inflatable raft making headway but nowhere near enough for him to gain dry land before the patrol boat went by.

A grenade could take the boat out but it would also signal a general alarm, and for Bolan to succeed, stealth was paramount. He gauged the distance, gauged the speed of the oncoming craft and flattened on the bottom of the raft, pulling the paddle in beside him.

The chug-chug-chug became a rumbling growl, so close Bolan thought he could reach out and touch the boat. He heard the swish of water against its sides, heard, too, muffled voices speaking in Chinese. The spotlight lanced the night, passing over the raft and illuminating a stretch of sea beyond it. He tensed for an outcry, his hand on the M-16, but none came. The growl faded and he raised his head.

The patrol boat was well past, its spotlight stabbing the darkness ahead of it.

Dipping the paddle into the briny deep, Bolan pumped his arms with renewed vigor. The closer he grew to shore, the smaller the waves became. Sailing the last twenty yards, he jumped out when the raft ground against the sand and hauled the raft out of the water.

It was time to lock and load. Bolan chambered a round into the M-16 and fed an orange M-433 armor-piercing antipersonnel grenade into the grenade launcher. He patted a black mesh pouch under his left arm, then bent and scaled a short slope ringed by boulders.

Bolan was on the north end of the island. The base occupied the southern two-thirds, its perimeter marked by a sentry tower and periodic floodlights. He started forward, probing the ground for possible mines.

The intel the Feds had on Hakka Island was skimpy.

They knew it was a storage depot for arms and munitions no longer in active use by the Chinese military, but that was about it. The number of personnel and the units they were from, as well as the base's defensive capability, were unknown factors.

The Feds hadn't known what Bolan would find when he got there. He had gone in cold, and had to rely on his own combat savvy and finely honed instincts to see him through. Which was fine by him. Surviving by his wits and experience were old hat. From the killing fields of Southeast Asia to the steaming jungles of South America, he had honed his lethal skills.

Intel was fine but he could get by without it.

Hakka Island's vegetation was spare, but its rocky terrain was pockmarked with clefts and gullies, more than adequate cover to enable him to get within sixty feet of the north sentry tower without being seen. Two sentries manned a floodlight, which they were sweeping over the ground to the west.

The warehouses were to Bolan's right, the other buildings to his left. He sidled westward, then froze when a pair of guards appeared. Like the tower sentries, they were fully alert, their rifles in their hands.

Something wasn't quite right, Bolan mused. Normally, guards at secure military installations were prone to be lax. They liked to chat and smoke on duty, victims of a sense of false security. But not the guards here. They acted as if they were expecting an attack at any moment. Or else expecting someone to try to infiltrate the base.

Bolan told himself it couldn't be. He was letting the incidents at Sapporo and on Hokkaido affect his judgment. There was no conceivable way the Chinese could have known he was going to pay them a visit. Brognola had assured him no one else knew except the President, and the President had promised not to let it slip.

Yet as Bolan watched the guards pass the sentry tower and bear to the south, he couldn't shake the nagging feeling that he was walking into a trap.

Shrugging it off, the soldier worked his way to a spot between two floodlights. The absence of a fence didn't strike him as unusual. The depot was on an island, after all, well within China's territorial waters, and civilians were banned under penalty of death. Easing from behind a bush, he snaked along a narrow belt of shadow.

The sentries in the tower turned their light to the north. Had they done so a couple of minutes ago, it would have caused problems, but now the Executioner's main worry was whether there were more patrols. He came to a stack of pallets and knelt beside them.

No sooner had he done so than another pair of soldiers appeared on the parade ground. They were heading toward a barracks and hadn't seen him.

Holding the M-16 at waist level, Bolan darted to the nearest warehouse and along it to the front. An office door was locked. A dozen yards to the left reared a huge metal door, chained and padlocked, that was wide enough to admit a diesel truck.

Bolan's primary goal was to find the plasma propulsion missiles. To gain entry, he opened a pocket in his webbing and took out a glass cutter and putty. Applying the latter to the pane, he held on to it, pressed the cutter against the glass and cut in a circle around his hand. He had to do it several times before the circle separated from the pane and he could lift it out. Next he slipped his hand inside and twisted the lock.

Once inside Bolan set the circle of glass on a desk and moved to an inner door. The warehouse was gigantic, able to fit a 747 with room to spare. Crates and boxes stenciled with Chinese writing were stacked to the ceiling. Bolan opened one of the crates and found cartons of old ammunition. If all the crates contained the same, there had to be tons of it.

Opening his black pouch, Bolan took out a one-kilo packet of C-4 plastic explosive and taped it to the inside of the crate. He added some detonation cord and rigged it to detonate when he gave the signal. Then he placed the lid back on and hurried out.

A check of the illuminated dials on his watch warned Bolan he had four hours until dawn. Not much time, considering there were nineteen more warehouses the same size as the first.

As he moved on, Bolan thought about the change in priorities. Instead of recovering the missiles, the President now wanted them destroyed.

Brognola had explained why. "You can't bring them out alone, and he doesn't want to provoke a major incident with the Chinese by sending in a full retrieval team. The Chinese government wouldn't think highly of having American forces invade their soil. So I've persuaded him our only alternative is to destroy the PPS-1s to keep them from being used against us."

"It seems a little extreme," Bolan commented.

"You wouldn't think so if you knew what they're capable of," Brognola responded. "You know me, you know I don't exaggerate. So believe me when I tell you the PPS-1s pose the greatest threat to our nation's security in recent memory." His voice had risen in urgency. "The missiles *must* be destroyed. No matter what it takes, you must stop General Tsanghsien."

"You make it sound like the end of the world."

"Would you settle for the end of the United States as we know it?"

Those words stayed with Bolan on the flight from Yokota in a Lockheed P-2H Neptune, a long-range aircraft usually assigned to long-range patrol duties. Jack Grimaldi had his choice of all the aircraft at the base and he had selected the Lockheed because, as Grimaldi phrased it, "She's fast, she has a range of almost three thousand miles, and I haven't flown one in a while."

Colonel Stewart had assigned Captain Jennings and a flight crew of six to accompany them. They had flown west to the coast and then zipped down through the Korea Strait. Once they reached the Yellow Sea, Grimaldi made a beeline for Hakka Island, kissing the waves all the way there to avoid Chinese radar. Once they spotted a flight of Shenyang J-6C fighters to the north, forcing Grimaldi to divert to the south to avoid being detected.

Originally they had hoped to arrive at the designated drop point north of Hakka Island by about midnight, but it was 1:00 a.m. by the time they got there. Grimaldi had cut speed, the bay door had been thrown open and the Executioner bailed out.

A parachute drop at night was always tricky. The choppy waves had made this one doubly so. All went well, though, and after Bolan inflated the raft, he'd headed for Tsanghsien's stronghold. Retrieval would be in twenty hours. He had until then to locate the PPS-1s and insure they no longer posed a threat to America.

The next two warehouses contained nothing but munitions. In each Bolan rigged more C-4. The fourth was empty. Darting to the fifth, he held the glass cutter and putty in his left hand. When he rounded the corner and

came on a pair of Chinese soldiers, it was hard to say
who was more surprised. But Bolan reacted first. He
kicked the man on the right in the groin, pivoted and
thrust the muzzle of the M-16 into the second soldier's
throat. It all happened so swiftly, the first man was
doubled over in agony and the second was gagging and
choking for breath before either could yell for help.

Bolan dropped the putty and the cutter and grabbed
for the Beretta. As it cleared leather, the man he had
kicked lashed out, slamming a boot against his shin.
Pain exploded up his leg, but it didn't keep him from
pointing the suppressor at the man's skull and trigger-
ing two shots.

The second soldier had no hankering to share his
friend's fate. Gripping his rifle in both hands, he swung
the stock at the Executioner's head.

Bolan ducked, jammed the Beretta against the man's
sternum and fired twice more. The impact drove the
soldier back against the building and his rifle clattered
noisily to the ground. Cocking his head, Bolan thought
he heard a shout, far off. Someone might have heard.
Quickly, he opened the door, shoved the putty and cutter into his pouch and dragged the bodies inside. He
was about to close the door and check if the missiles
were there when two more soldiers with their weapons
to the shoulders hustled around the corner of another
warehouse farther down.

Locking the door, Bolan backpedaled into a corner.
He trained the M-16 on the door, certain they would
spot the hole he had made and burst in. Their shadows
rippled across the glass, and he touched his finger to
the trigger. But the door never opened. He waited a
good two minutes before he glided over to find out
why.

The guards were gone.

Hurrying through the inner door, Bolan set eyes on another mountain of crates and assorted containers. He rigged another packet of C-4 and left before the two soldiers came back.

To reach the next warehouse entailed crossing an open space in plain view of the north tower. He watched the spotlight, and when it swung to the northwest he bolted from concealment. A shadow among shadows, he reached the next door and slid a hand into his pouch for the putty and the glass cutter.

Suddenly a brilliant beam of light spiked the night, catching him full in its glare.

Bolan spun and saw that the sentries in the south tower were to blame. As he jerked up his M-16 to shoot out their floodlight, dozens of soldiers pounded around warehouses to the right and to the left. Simultaneously a bullhorn boomed.

"Do not move, American! We have you surrounded! Resist and we will slay you where you stand!"

The man's English was atrocious, but there was no denying the soldiers had the firepower to carry out his threat. Dozens of SMGs and assault rifles were pointed at Bolan's chest.

"Lower your weapon! Now!"

The Executioner wasn't about to do any such thing.

Stony Man Farm, Virginia

BARBARA PRICE HAD TAKEN it on herself to acquire every satellite-recon photo taken within the past two weeks of Hakka Island and the adjacent coastline. Thanks to computer enhancement she had learned a lot more about the installation than they knew when Hal

Brognola sent in Bolan. And what she'd learned, she didn't like.

Far more troops were stationed there than was typical for a storage facility. Her best estimate was upward of two hundred, and the only way she could account for it was that they were troops loyal to General Tsanghsien and had been sent to the island with him. A wise move by the Chinese government, putting all their dissident eggs in one basket.

Price pegged the location of the command post, intel Bolan could have used. She also noticed a warehouse on the south side of the island had been emptied, its contents taken to other warehouses. In photo after photo, soldiers were seen moving crates and whatnot, sometimes using forklifts, at other times carrying it by hand.

Her hunch was that the good general had been making room for the PPS-1s. None of the photos actually showed the missiles arriving, but in a few of the later ones a lot of activity was apparent. Soldiers were constantly going in and out.

More intel Bolan could have used. Price didn't like it when he was sent in blind. The right intelligence often meant the difference between life and death, and in her opinion, in this instance he hadn't had enough.

"A hundred dollars for your thoughts."

Price looked up in surprise. She had been so absorbed in her work, she hadn't heard Kurtzman's wheelchair roll up. "Isn't it usually a penny, Aaron?"

"You're worth the extra money," Kurtzman said, and offered her a manila envelope. "These just arrived. The latest recon photos of Hakka Island and the nearby coast."

Price set them next to her keyboard. "I'm starting

to get eye strain from staring at this computer screen so long.''

"Why not take a break?" Kurtzman suggested. " I'll treat you to a coffee on Uncle Sam.''

"Is that where the hundred dollars was going to come from?''

"Why else do you think petty cash was invented?''

"I'll take a rain check. I owe it to Mack to see if this latest batch contains anything important.''

Kurtzman went to say something but wheeled his chair around instead. "You're a fine woman. Maybe one of these days you'll realize the fact and stop being so hard on yourself.''

Price watched him whisk out the door, then opened the manila folder and laid out the photographs. Nine this time, taken over a twelve-hour period. She scanned them, brought up the images on her screen and enlarged them where necessary. Right away she noticed something new, something that didn't bode well. Her anxiety mounted as she examined the rest.

Grabbing her phone, Price punched in Hal Brognola's number. He answered on the third ring, sounding tired to the bone. "We shouldn't have sent him in,'' she declared.

"Who? Striker?''

"They're not there,'' Price declared. "The damn things are no longer on the island.''

"Fill in the gaps. Take it nice and slow.''

"I've just gone over the latest satellite shots. Two ferries arrived at Hakka Island the day before he made the drop. They were gone the next morning. A photo of the coast taken about noon shows a pair of flatbed trucks heading west on a mountain highway. The trucks are covered with canvas.''

"The general is one step ahead of us again," Brognola growled.

"Striker was needlessly inserted into a hot zone. He has no hope of completing the mission and doesn't know it. Can we recall him?"

"Not an option, I'm afraid," Brognola said. "For better or for worse, he has to make it out on his own."

"He's been thrown to the wolves," Price said bitterly.

"Not intentionally. And he's survived tougher spots."

"Hal, he's up against almost a full battalion. One man against two hundred. There are limits, even for him."

"The best we can do is keep our fingers crossed and pray he makes it to the extraction point. I'll get on the horn to the President and see how he wants to proceed."

"They won't pull him out, will they?"

"I doubt it. We're in this one for the long haul. I have a feeling that if our mutual friend makes it off of Hakka Island alive, he'll be going from the frying pan into a blazing furnace."

Japan

KERRI TANAKA LAY in her warm bed in her Tokyo apartment and thought about how unfair life was.

The man she cared for more than any other had gone out of her life—again. She had opened her heart to him, but he had refused to open his to her. Her dream of growing closer had been shattered.

Tanaka relived their excursion to Hokkaido. She wanted to know where she had gone wrong. But after long consideration she decided she had never once overstepped herself or allowed her feelings to jeopardize their mission. Only in the Ainu hut had she bared her soul fully, and then only because the mission had essentially been over and circumstances had conspired to throw them together. She had taken it as a sign, as an omen, but he had been as aloof as ever.

What made her heartache all the more unbearable were the mixed signals Belasko gave. He had made it clear, in no uncertain terms, that a personal relationship between them was impossible. Yet the look in his eyes when he said it told her he liked her more than he was willing to admit. Perhaps even as much as she liked him.

Rolling over, she winced as pain pricked her temple. The doctors had examined her and given her a clean bill of health. The X rays showed no permanent damage, and she didn't have a concussion. She was fit for active duty but in no mood to go out into the field. She needed rest. A week would be nice, a week to herself, to visit the coast and walk along the beach and come to terms with Belasko's rejection.

Tanaka's eyes moistened. Being spurned hurt more than she had imagined. She wished now she had been more forceful, wished she had not let him talk her out of showing how deep her affection ran. She had meekly submitted to his will, and now she was paying for her timidity with her loneliness.

She wasn't a woman of the world. She wasn't someone who could wrap a man around her little finger. In her whole life she'd only had three lovers and two of those had been in college. Boys, really, as shy as her.

None could compare to Mike Belasko—or whatever his real name was. Tanaka would very much like to know, but it would have been improper for her to ask so she had refrained. Now he was gone from her life, and she would never find out.

Restless, she turned onto her back and stared at the ceiling. Her grandmother once told her that when a person wanted something badly enough and prayed for it with all her heart, the prayer would be answered. She hadn't prayed in many years. Now, though, she closed her eyes and yearned for that which she had been denied, yearned for it with every fiber of her being. She felt foolish doing so but she did it anyway.

Opening her eyes again, Tanaka stared bleakly out her window at the glittering city. Her heartache spread throughout her body, and she placed her face against the pillow. Maybe it was time she requested reassignment. She had been in Japan long enough. She would ask for a stateside position, bury herself in her work and, with time, forget all about Mike Belasko.

Or so she hoped.

Overcome by a floodtide of emotion, she started to give rein to her sorrow. Hot tears burned her cheeks, and she sobbed. Through sheer force of will she stopped. She refused to behave like a love-struck teenager. She was a grown woman and she would act like one. If that meant accepting Belasko was permanently gone from her life, so be it.

That was when the phone rang.

CHAPTER ELEVEN

Hakka Island

The Executioner literally had his back to the wall. Chinese soldiers were to the right of him, and more heavily armed men were to the left. They had him trapped against the front of a warehouse. He was outnumbered, outgunned.

"One last time, American!" the bullhorn boomed from the south sentry tower. "I am Major Xinsi. You will put your weapons down and surrender or you will perish. You have ten seconds to comply."

Bolan didn't need ten seconds. He had already guessed they wanted him alive. If not, they would have cut him down before he could blink. Now they thought they had him at their mercy, but it was the other way around. They wouldn't shoot unless he did, or they were given an express order by their major. That put him in control of the situation. Plus, he had an ace in the hole they were unaware of. By sparing him they had made the greatest mistake they could.

Whirling abruptly, Bolan threw himself at the warehouse door. He didn't use the putty and the cutter this time; he simply lowered his shoulders and slammed into it like a human battering ram, throwing all his strength and weight into breaking it down. At the crash of contact, glass rained and the thick wooden panel laced with fractures. But the stubborn lock held.

Stepping back, the Executioner pointed his M-16.

Some of the soldiers made as if to shoot but didn't, perhaps thanks to Major Xinsi, who was shouting shrilly in Chinese.

Bolan fired, reducing the wood around the lock to splinters. A swift kick sufficed to smash the door open, and he threw himself inside. Shoving his hand into a pocket, he yanked out the detonation device, a transmitter about the size of a calculator. He extended the antenna, pressed a yellow button to turn it on and, when the digital display lit up, entered a three-digit command code. All he had to do then was press a red button to activate the signal.

Flinging himself at the floor, Bolan covered his head with both hands. Seconds later an artificial earthquake struck Hakka Island.

In the four warehouses where he had rigged packets of plastique, four explosions were simultaneously detonated. The combined blast was loud but it was nothing compared to the secondary explosions set off when the munitions in the four warehouses went up, a thunderous series of detonations capped by a colossal upheaval of catastrophic proportions.

Bolan felt the floor heave against him as the office he was in quaked violently, the walls on the verge of collapse. Dust and bits of plaster pelted his back.

A concussive wave hit a second later. Hot wind spewed in through the shattered door, and everything in the room was blown about as if caught in a fierce gale. Furniture was upended. A chair smacked him in the shoulder. Something else clipped his right leg.

Outside, men screamed and cried out in mortal terror.

Bolan looked up just as two soldiers appeared. They were racing toward the doorway, but they never made it. A roiling fireball engulfed them, a roaring colossus that consumed them alive, igniting not just their clothes but their bodies, too. They burst into flame like Roman candles and screamed as they died, wailing in horrible agony as they melted like so much wax.

One of the walls cracked from top to bottom. A grating noise overhead drew Bolan's gaze to the ceiling. A slab the size of a coffin was breaking off. He rolled to the right as it dropped, and it crashed onto the floor inches from his arm. Chunks flew like shrapnel, several peppering him but doing no real harm.

More explosions rocked the island.

Bolan pushed upright and moved to the doorway, which tilted at an angle. Bodies littered the ground, some on fire, others thrashing and convulsing. Tendrils of smoke were drifting between the structures.

Springing from the office, Bolan hunched low, ready to spray anyone who posed a threat. But the few soldiers still on their feet were too dazed or too hurt to give any thought to him. Straightening, he stepped away from the building to survey the extent of the damage.

It was a spectacle he wouldn't soon forget.

Hakka Island was in ruins.

Gaping craters were all that remained of three of the four warehouses where C-4 had been rigged. Of the fourth, only part of a smoldering wall remained. Adjacent warehouses had been heavily damaged and many were in flames. So were some of the buildings on the other side of the parade ground. Flaming debris had set half a dozen on fire, and soldiers were scrambling to extinguish them before the entire depot burned to the ground.

The upper half of the south sentry tower was gone, the lower half was burning. Everywhere were wounded or dying men. Hanging over the widespread devastation was a dense bank of smoke, seething, acrid fog borne rapidly by the wind.

Within moments it shrouded Bolan. Under its welcome cover he angled to the right, seeking the next warehouse. His job wasn't done. He still had to ascertain whether the PPS-1s were at the depot.

The confusion and general turmoil worked to his advantage. The Chinese were too busy taking care of their own to come after him.

From then on Bolan didn't use the glass cutter; he broke out windows with the butt of his M-16. What with the roar of flames and the bedlam, the sound of glass breaking was lost in the din.

None of the next five warehouses contained the missiles. Three held munitions, though, and Bolan planted C-4 in each. As he emerged from the last, he smelled water. He took a few steps, looking for the source, and the smoke parted enough to afford him a glimpse of the sea and a long pier. A large number of troopers had congregated around it, the wounded being tended by medics.

Bolan headed west. He had only gone a dozen yards when the soldiers strode out of the wispy tendrils floating before him.

One of the men was bleeding from the neck and chest. The other two were supporting him. They had their rifles slung and stopped dead in astonishment. Neither made a move for his weapon.

Bolan had trained the M-16 on them, but he tilted the barrel up and motioned for them to keep going.

For a few moments the pair didn't move. Then the soldiers on the right whispered, and they hastened by.

As soon as the smoke enveloped them, Bolan ran to the left in case they tried to gun him down from behind. No shots rang out, and soon he came to yet another warehouse. He went through the same routine, planted more plastic explosive and was striding toward the outer office when voices warned him he wasn't alone.

Bolan dashed to the jamb. An officer and two soldiers were by a desk, the officer dialing a phone. Apparently the explosions had disrupted communications because after a minute the officer jammed the receiver down and pounded the desk in frustration. Rising, he shifted toward the entrance.

Bolan started to duck back, but at that instant one of the troopers glanced at the inner door and spotted him. The man yelled, turned, and extended an SMG, an older-model Type 49 submachine gun. The Executioner's reflexes were quicker. A burst from the autorifle shriveled the soldier like a withered plant.

The second it took for Bolan to chop the man down was all it took for the other soldier to whirl and cut loose with his own SMG.

Slugs thudded into the wall, tearing through the wood like hot knives through butter. Bolan skipped backward as chips zinged past his face. He thought the soldiers would try to keep him pinned down until reinforcements arrived, but the second man brashly charged in with the SMG chattering.

Bolan stroked the trigger. As the fool flopped like a headless chicken, the big American leaped to the doorway to eliminate the officer. But no one was there.

Racing to the outer door, he checked both ways, then sped westward. Shouts off in the smoke gave him some idea of where the officer had gone. The man was bellowing for assistance, and it wouldn't be long before more soldiers arrived.

The next warehouse was the last in the row. Bolan darted inside, found it crammed with ammunition and explosives and set up more C-4. When he emerged, the smoke was thicker than ever. To the east popping sounds punctuated the roar of flames, individual shells going up like firecrackers. He jogged a safe distance past the depot's perimeter and sought shelter in a cranny between boulders. Activating the detonator, he tapped in the code and pressed the red button.

The result was the end of the world, times two.

Another seething fireball boiled heavenward accompanied by a deafening din of cataclysmic proportions. The ground bucked and heaved as a titanic wave of pure force radiated outward from the epicenter. Buildings not caught in the primary blast radius were reduced to piles of broken debris. Men and machines were sent flying like rag dolls.

Bolan was hunched over with his forearms covering his head and his hands over his ears, yet the magnitude of the explosions was such that he winced in pain. His body was roughly buffeted, and the boulders shimmied and shook and came close to crushing him.

At long length the upheaval subsided enough for Bolan to lift his head and survey his handwork.

The devastation was staggering.

Flames hundreds of feet high licked the stars. Only a few warehouses remained standing, and they were severely damaged. Unending coils of smoke were blanketing the island. Screams and shrieks were raised in caterwauling chorus.

Over by the shoreline soldiers appeared. Many were wounded and being helped along by comrades. Limping, staggering, caked with soot and grime, they retreated onto the pier, getting as far from the conflagration as they could.

Bolan rose and plunged back into the smoke. His mission was to insure the PPS-1s were destroyed, and he wouldn't rest until they were. He had to hold his breath for long periods, filling his lungs when he came to pockets of air. The smoke stung his eyes terribly, but by squinting he minimized the discomfort.

Whole sections of buildings had collapsed and been scattered, as if tossed by a child having a temper tantrum. Smaller pieces, along with bodies and parts of bodies, were as common as blades of grass in a meadow.

Bolan could barely move without stepping on something. For him to reach the few warehouses that still stood took not only considerable effort but also considerable time. It was like running an obstacle course in heavy fog. He encountered no soldiers. Those still alive had vacated the immediate vicinity, most likely out of fear of more explosions.

At one point the swirling smoke parted enough for Bolan to see the north guard tower. The roof was burning, the guards gone, the floodlight cracked and glowing dully.

None of the remaining warehouses contained the plasma missiles. Two were empty, the third was filled with old rifles and pistols but no ammo, and the last harbored dilapidated vehicles, old jeeps and trucks and a halftrack.

The PPS-1s were nowhere to be found.

Bolan dismissed the idea they had gone up in the blasts. There hadn't been a shred of evidence they were anywhere on the island. So either they had never been there to begin with, or they had been taken off Hakka Island before he arrived. It was something for the Feds to figure out. He had done all he could.

Time to get out of there.

Bolan headed north. Gusty winds had begun to dissipate the smoke at that end, and he had to avail himself of natural cover until he reached the cove where he had cached the inflatable raft. Nosing the raft into the water, he hopped in and paddled around the point toward mainland China.

Years ago, when Hakka Island had been transformed from a rustic fishing village into a supply depot, the Chinese government had constructed on the mainland a modest airport eight miles inland as a relay point for equipment and personnel. Recently, due to a lack of military air traffic, it had been converted largely to civilian use. Jack Grimaldi was to touch down on one of the neglected runways at ten that night and pick up Bolan.

All Bolan had to do was reach it.

He was only a hundred yards out into the sea when a clarion siren pierced the night. A glance revealed the patrol boat he had seen earlier, now in pursuit. Its prow cleaved the surface smoothly as it passed the cove, its spotlight dancing across the waves toward his raft.

Bolan was sure the vessel hadn't been there when he started out. It had to have been lying close to shore, its crew riveted by the devastation. He stroked harder, choppy waves once again hampering his progress. The patrol boat would catch up in no time.

Shifting, Bolan saw figures scurry onto the forward deck, manning a small deck gun. They were going to blow him out of the water. He dipped the paddle in once, twice, three times. Suddenly a loud boom preceded a shrill whistling sound, and there was a giant splash less than twenty yards to the right of the raft. Their accuracy left a lot to be desired, but it wouldn't be long before they refined the range.

Bolan bore to the left, battling the wind. A wave tilted the raft's nose and it was slammed into a trough, drenching him from head to foot. He managed to keep afloat and pressed on.

The wail of the siren grew louder. Bolan glanced over a shoulder. Its props churning the water in its wake to froth, the patrol boat bore down on him with a vengeance. Again the deck gun pounded, and again a geyser erupted dangerously near the inflatable.

Soldiers rushed to line the bow, their SMGs and rifles raised, ready to open fire the moment they were close enough.

Bolan had no hope of eluding them unless he swam for it, and even then it wasn't a sure thing. In any event, as cold as the water was, he'd succumb to hypothermia long before he reached shore. So either he made a fight of it or he tried to outwit them.

He chose both.

Bolan stopped stroking and turned the raft so he faced the oncoming vessel. In order to convince them he was surrendering, he hiked his arms high. As he did, he palmed a grenade, jerked the pin and held the bomb close to his head so they wouldn't spot it.

The deck gun hammered a third time. Six yards from the raft the water spurted in a tremendous geyser, drenching Bolan even more. He saw the gunners prepare to fire again. Apparently they had no interest in taking him alive, and he was about to bend to the paddle when a shout from the bridge brought the flurry of activity at the gun to a stop.

An officer hurried onto the pitching deck. He shouted at the soldiers along the forward rail, who sighted down their weapons but held their fire.

Bolan couldn't let them get too close. Someone was bound to notice his clenched fist and guess what he was up to.

The officer moved to the bow and motioned, rasping a command in Chinese. It was plain he wanted the warrior to stand.

Bolan nodded, but when he tried to rise, a wave crested, carrying the raft with it and nearly pitching him onto his face. Sinking onto his knees, he shook his head to signify he couldn't comply.

Gesturing, the officer barked at several of his men, who hustled forward with a line they would toss over the side.

Bolan waited for the right instant, the raft rising and falling under him. Swells kept sweeping it onto foamy crests, putting him in clear sight of the soldiers, but seconds later he would dip into a trough, blocking their view. Along about the fifth or sixth time, as several soldiers were uncoiling the end of the rope, he made his move.

Another wave lifted the raft. Bolan tensed as he stared up into multiple gun muzzles and dozens of dark, hostile eyes. He felt the wave start to curl, felt the raft sliding into the next trough. Timing his throw to the split second, he hurled the grenade as the next wave reared before him, then flattened.

The officer shouted a warning but it was too late.

The grenade went off with the retort of a thunderclap, and soldiers screamed in anguish.

Autorounds crisscrossed the night, peppering the ocean. Bolan heard them hit on all sides as he scooped up the M-16. The raft surged toward the next crest, and he saw much of the forward rail was missing and a jagged gaping hole in the prow. Convulsing bodies littered the deck, among them that of the officer. Most of the soldiers not caught in the blast were scampering for cover, but a few others, braver than their fellows, had stayed at their posts and were trying to make the warrior pay for his ploy.

Leaden bees skimmed Bolan's ears as he returned fire, spraying half a dozen figures. He worked the grenade launcher, aiming at the bridge, as the raft dropped into a trough. Clutching the paddle, he turned the raft toward the mainland and headed westward. A few rounds were directed his way but they stopped, too, when he elevated the M-16 and shot out the spotlight. Blanketed by darkness, he slowly pulled away.

When next he glanced back, inky smoke billowed from the patrol boat.

Dawn was still forty or fifty minutes off. With a little luck Bolan could reach land before sunrise. But a problem presented itself. The hiss of the waves was matched by a rising hiss from the inflatable, and the bottom of the raft acquired a spongy feel. It was losing air fast. Setting down the paddle, he ran his fingers over every square inch until he located a series of small holes. Taking a repair kit from a pocket in the rim, he peeled off a self-adhesive patch and applied it to the first, pressing firmly to render the seal watertight. The rest of the holes received the same treatment. He couldn't be sure he found them all, but he had plugged

enough to give him a fair chance of reaching shore
without having to swim for it.

Soon a pink tinge banded the eastern horizon as
dawn crept across the surface of the sea. The faint light
revealed the coastline.

Bolan had been shown aerial photographs of the region. He knew where to make the safest landing—an
inlet situated along an isolated strip of winding coast
highway. The original plan, though, called for him to
make land at night, not when the sun was up. He
guessed it would take another half an hour. By then
fishing boats would be abroad. So would patrol boats
from installations farther up and down the Chinese
coast, much larger boats with much larger guns.

To complicate matters, the wind abated. The ocean
grew still. The waves that had plagued the Executioner
for hours dwindled to ripples.

Bolan stroked harder to reach land before he was
spotted. He had a quarter of a mile to go when the top
of a mast poked above the northern skyline. Soon after,
the outline of a fishing boat crawled out of the haze.
If they saw him, they gave no sign of it, but he didn't
feel entirely safe until he had coasted to a stop in the
shallow inlet, jumped out and dragged the raft up over
a rock-strewed beach into thick brush.

The soldier went prone. In a few minutes the fishing
boat sailed by. The crew was aft, preparing the nets.
No one glanced at the spot where he had come ashore.

Sitting up, Bolan pulled the plug on the raft. It de-
flated too slowly to suit him, so he helped it along by
pressing on the larger air bubbles. The whole thing
folded into a packet two feet square, which he buried.
He had no further use for it.

Bolan crossed the coast highway without seeing a

car or truck and struck off overland. He had all day to reach the airport but he maintained a brisk pace nonetheless, sticking to wooded ground where he could and tall grass where he couldn't. At 9:00 a.m. he stopped to nibble some of the rations he had brought along and take a few sips from his canteen.

The ground began to climb steeply. From a broad shelf Bolan was treated to a panoramic vista that included huge columns of smoke rising from a speck out on the ocean—Hakka Island. A number of vessels were steaming toward it from the south. Whether they were military or civilian was impossible to determine.

Half an hour later, as Bolan crossed a valley, the air droned to throaty growl of a flight of prop planes. Racing to a thicket, he crawled into it and peered up through the slender branches. Three older aircraft with military insignia were winging to the southeast, toward the island.

Soon the entire countryside would be on the alert. Bolan didn't waste a minute resuming his trek. The dense woodland and high grass gave way to cultivated farmland. To the southwest near a small pond grazed a pair of sturdy oxen. Beyond them was a large cluster of buildings, a collective, maybe. Workers were already abroad, stick figures trudging off into adjacent fields to toil for a pittance.

The airport was in the next valley. A barren ridge intervened, and Bolan was two-thirds of the way to the crest when the flight of observation planes returned. Sliding into a cleft, he watched as they ranged far and wide, evidently in search of him. They concentrated most of their energy on the ground he had already covered.

Bolan couldn't reach the crest without being spotted,

so he contented himself with waiting for the aerial hunt to taper off. By ten only one plane was left, and it soon winged off to the north. Rising, he caught sight of a column of trucks crawling along the coast highway from the other direction. More soldiers, dispatched to take up where the planes had left off.

The Chinese weren't fools. They knew he had made for the mainland, and they would pull out all the stops to apprehend him.

Bolan went up and over the ridge. A sheer incline dropped to shoulder-high brush through which he tramped for half an hour. A rutted dirt track brought him to a stop. That, and four wizened farmers in simple clothes and wide-brimmed hats, each carrying a large cane basket filled with grain. Their slim backs were bent by their burdens, but they were joking and laughing.

After the sun-bronzed quartet went around a bend, the soldier started across. He wasn't quite to the undergrowth when a startled bleat caused him to turn with the M-16 leveled. A boy no older than twelve was seated on a rock, fiddling with a sandal that had come off. Their eyes met.

Smiling, Bolan calmly lowered the autorifle. Never taking his gaze off the youngster, he backed into the trees, wheeled and bolted. He was sure the boy would cry for help, but no yell arose.

By two in the afternoon Bolan came within sight of the airport. Another concession to modernization, it had a two-story control tower and three runways. A chain-link fence surrounded it, but guards were conspicuously absent.

Shaded by a tree within a stone's throw of the runway Grimaldi would use, Bolan munched on crackers and sipped water and looked forward to sunset. The hours dragged. He saw six aircraft land, among them the prop flight that had sought him since dawn.

By seven that evening most of the airport staff had departed. By eight only three vehicles were left in the parking area. At nine, an hour before retrieval, Bolan scaled the fence and moved onto the runway.

Suddenly, to the east, radial piston engines whined. Bolan thought his friend would come in for a touch-and-go landing, but the Neptune's engines were cut when it was still distant, and it glided overhead at high altitude. Out of the night floated a lone parachutist. Seconds later the Neptune's engines resumed their whining, and the aircraft banked up into the clouds.

Not knowing what to make of the unforeseen development, Bolan moved to meet the new arrival. The parachute was identical to the one he had used when he dropped into the Pacific the night before. The black-suit was a carbon copy of his. He grabbed the lines to help collect the chute, and a pretty face smeared with combat cosmetics rotated toward him.

"I bet you're surprised to see me again," Kerri Tanaka said.

CHAPTER TWELVE

To say Bolan was surprised was an understatement. He had counted on being extracted, not for another operative to be inserted. For it to be Kerri Tanaka, of all people, the last person he wanted to work with again, left him riveted in rare disbelief.

"I have a lot to tell you if you'll give me a hand," the young woman said as she fought the wind for control of her chute.

Bolan hurried to help her. Between them they gathered the chute and trotted off the runway into the trees. He gave her a hand shedding the harness, and they hastily covered it with branches and leaves.

Acres away, over at the control tower, a spotlight had blinked on and was sweeping the night sky, but Grimaldi was too shrewd to be caught in its glare. The Neptune was well above the cloud ceiling, and when the sound of its engines faded, the spotlight was shut off.

By then Bolan and Tanaka were nowhere near the runway. He had her by the elbow and was none too gently propelling her in front of him. She didn't resist, nor did she complain when he spun her around and snapped, "This had better be good."

"I'm glad to see you again, too, Mike," she responded, rubbing her elbow. "Keep in mind, though, that if you break my arm I won't be of much use to you."

"Why?" Bolan demanded.

"Why me? Why here? Why now?" Tanaka said with a touch of irony. "Because the PPS-1s weren't on Hakka Island, which I guess you know by now. They're on flatbed trucks heading west across China even as we speak. Our job is to stop them by whatever means necessary."

"They could have told me that much with a packet drop," Bolan said.

"Yes, they could. But a packet of information can't teach you Chinese, can it? And you need someone fluent in the language if you're to have any hope of overtaking General Soong Tsanghsien."

"So they sent you." Bolan wished it had been someone else. Anyone else.

"Mr. Brognola phoned me personally," Tanaka stated. "He complimented us for how well we worked together on Hokkaido. He said that he didn't think you would mind if we worked together again."

If only he knew, Bolan thought, and sighed. What had been done, was done. He had to make the best of the curve ball he had been thrown.

"I'm well versed in Chinese dialects and culture," Tanaka reiterated. "I'm to translate and do whatever else you require. Anything at all. I'm at your complete command." She paused. "Professionally speaking, of course."

"There will be no more mention of Hokkaido," Bolan said flatly. "No more mention of what we talked about in the hut."

"None whatsoever."

She looked sincere and she sounded sincere, but Bolan couldn't shake the feeling she still had designs on him. "Did Brognola have any other messages to pass along?" he asked, changing the subject.

"He asked me to tell you he has no word yet on the leaky faucet, whatever that means. And they hope to have reliable information soon on a possible supplier for the nukes the general is after."

"How much of a lead does Tsanghsien's convoy have?"

"The latest intel I was given is that they were eight hundred miles inland. Satellite surveillance suggests they're not stopping at night. The general must be in an awful hurry to get where he's going." Tanaka unfastened a fanny pack. "I've brought along passports, maps, currency and everything else we'll need."

Bolan turned toward the airport. Their first order of business was to acquire transportation and clothing. "Come on," he said, and jogged toward the parking lot at the far end of the facility.

Tanaka unslung an M-16 from her left shoulder. "I've brought along a little extra firepower this time."

"Do you know how to use it?"

"I told you, remember? I've had all the standard basic courses, including small arms and this." She wagged her autorifle. "I may not be as good as you are, but I can hold my own if I have to."

"I hope so," Bolan said. Odds were, before they were done she would be put to the test, and if she came up short her life was forfeit.

At that hour the airport was deserted except for a small crew in the control tower and a janitor Bolan spied through a window in the administrative building, busily mopping the tiled floor.

Of the three vehicles in the parking lot, two were passenger cars, both too compact and cramped inside. Bolan opted for an older-model Jeep. It had a spare tire and a spare gas can and an overhead rack with three rectangular lights. It wasn't as fast as the cars, but it was vastly more rugged, which was exactly what they needed.

To the world at large, China liked to present an image of modern splendor. Paved streets were the norm in her urban centers, and a few new asphalt highways linked many of her major cities. But they were the exception, not the rule. Outside of the urban areas, the roadways were dirt-and-gravel ribbons pockmarked by holes and ruts. In the remote western mountains, it was a lot worse, with rockslides and washouts often closing roads for weeks at a stretch.

Bolan quietly opened the driver's door and leaned in. The keys were in the ignition. In America such carelessness would be unthinkable. In China, where the penalty for stealing an automobile was life in prison at hard labor, car theft was virtually unknown. Pocketing them, he headed for the admin building.

Tanaka had stepped to the passenger side and was about to climb in. "Wait for me," she whispered.

"You stay here," Bolan responded. "I won't be long."

The janitor was an elderly man with a bald pate and a beard down to his waist. He was humming to himself as he worked, and he never noticed the Executioner slip in the front door and pad down a hall toward a row of offices.

The first two contained nothing Bolan could use, but the third was a bonanza. Hanging on a coatrack in a corner was a hip-length green jacket. In a closet were two shirts and a pair of pants, all three much too small to fit him but they might fit his companion. He also helped himself to a folded towel on a shelf. With everything over his left arm, he crept toward the wide glass door.

The humming had stopped, and when Bolan reached the foyer he saw the bucket and mop but not the janitor. A sound to his left caused him to flatten against the wall. The janitor was over by the front window, gazing out at the parking lot. For a moment Bolan thought he might have spotted Tanaka, but he was only staring wistfully up at the stars. Presently the man returned to his bucket and dipped the mop into the soapy water.

The instant the janitor turned, Bolan sprinted outdoors. A glance at the control tower showed no one in sight, and he hurried to the Jeep. Tanaka was in the passenger seat, ready to go. Hopping in, he tossed the M-16 and his bundle into the back, pumped the clutch and shifted into neutral. "Slide over. You can steer while I get out and push."

"Push?"

Bolan nodded toward the tower. "We don't want them to hear when we start the engine, do we?" He slid out, leaving the door open.

"Oh. Sorry." Tanaka eased up over the stick and gripped the steering wheel. "Ready when you are."

Bracing one hand against the door frame and the other against the roof, Bolan dug in his soles and pushed. The Jeep lurched into motion, its tires crunching as Tanaka steered toward the road. Their arms brushed. Bolan glanced down to see if she had done it intentionally, but she was looking straight ahead.

The lot sloped gradually. Bit by bit the Jeep gained speed. When it was going over five miles per hour,

Bolan nudged the woman. "Slide back over. I'll take it from here." She promptly obeyed, and he gripped the edge of the roof and swung inside. They were rolling swiftly along when he cranked the engine, popped the clutch into second and shot through the open gate.

Tanaka unzipped the fanny pack and unfolded a map on her lap. Sticking a pencil flashlight between her lips and switching it on, she studied the map a minute and announced, "The road we need to take is eleven miles south of here. The quickest way to reach it is by the coast highway."

Bolan wasn't too keen on backtracking eight miles. He held the speedometer at sixty, farmland flashing past on either side. "Did you bring any explosives?"

"Afraid not. Why?"

"I'm running low on C-4. When we catch up to the missiles, we'll have to improvise."

"I'm beginning to think that's what you do best."

Bolan waited for her to say more, to make personal comments better left unsaid, but she bent to the map again. She either truly had learned her lesson or she was playing it cool. "How's your head?" he asked.

"Much better, thank you." She touched the bruise. The swelling had gone down, but the skin was still discolored. "It won't interfere with my work, if that's what is on your mind."

Was she rubbing it in? Bolan wondered. Trying to show she could be as professional and coldly impersonal as he was? "Did Brognola happen to mention how we're to get out of the country once our mission is completed?"

"No. I guess we'll have to do more improvising."

After that neither of them had a word to say until a

sign appeared on the right. "The coast highway is just ahead," she translated.

Bolan braked at a stop sign. They hadn't seen another car since leaving the airport, so he was instantly wary when he spotted headlights approaching from the south. He considered killing his own headlights and backing off the road, but whoever it was had undoubtedly spotted them. Turning right, he hunched low in the seat so the occupants of the oncoming vehicle wouldn't get a good look at his face.

Tanaka heeded his example. "Let's hope it's not the police. They have a habit of pulling over cars out this late."

So Bolan had heard. But it wasn't a police car. It was a military jeep with army markings and two soldiers in the front. It slowed, both soldiers staring intently. As soon as they went by, the driver zipped around in a U-turn and came after them, blinking his headlights on and off.

"He wants us to pull over," Tanaka stated the obvious.

"Use this," Bolan said, handing her the Beretta. The suppressor was already attached. "Go out the window the second I stop."

The woman never hesitated. "Do you want either of them alive for questioning?"

"It would be nice but it's not essential." Bolan tapped the brake pedal, taking much longer than he needed to bring their Jeep to a halt. She bailed while it was still in motion, diving headfirst into high grass.

The army jeep hung back a discreet distance. When it stopped, both soldiers climbed out, armed with SMGs. They cautiously advanced on either side, so preoccupied with Bolan they were on the ground spurting blood with Tanaka standing over them before they realized they had blundered.

Bolan got out. The driver, a lieutenant, was dead, but the other man, a private, was still breathing, a stain low on his shirt "Ask him why they stopped us."

Tanaka spoke in Chinese, and the private answered curtly. "He says we can rot in sewage before he will tell us a thing."

"Tell him I can persuade him to talk if I have to," Bolan said.

"Permit me," she stated, then shot the man in the knee.

Screaming, the soldier doubled over and clutched his ruined kneecap. When she pointed the Beretta at his other one, he couldn't speak fast enough.

"He claims they were under orders to stop anyone suspicious," she reported. "Ours was the first vehicle they'd encountered in hours."

"Under orders from whom?"

Tanaka posed the question. "All he knows is that his unit was put on alert and sent to patrol the coast road. They were told to be on the lookout for a tall, dark foreigner wanted in connection with the destruction of the Hakka Island munitions depot." She glanced up. "The entire depot?"

"I'll explain later." Bolan was curious about something else. "Has he heard any news of General Tsanghsien?"

"Only that the general is believed to have perished in the explosions." She listened as the man chattered on. "The public is being told a gas buildup was at fault. General Tsanghsien is being hailed as great hero and martyr. There's talk of the prime minister and the general secretary attending the general's funeral."

Politics at its worst, Bolan thought. The Chinese leadership believed Tsanghsien was dead, so they planned to capitalize on the tragedy to boost their own image in the eyes of the huddled masses.

It had also worked out well for the general. The government wouldn't launch a search if they assumed he was dead. Since they had no idea he had stolen the PPS-1s, Tsanghsien had a free hand to carry out his mad scheme.

"Anything else?" Bolan asked.

"That's all he knows," she said, and shot the private between the eyes. Holding out the Beretta, she commented, "Nice gun. It doesn't have much of a kick. Maybe I'll trade in my Mustang for one after we get back."

Hiding his surprise at her ruthlessness, Bolan accepted the pistol. There was something different about her, a harder, colder quality she hadn't demonstrated on Hokkaido. "Help me drag the bodies into the woods before someone else comes along."

Their next step was to toss the SMGs and pistols into the back of their Jeep. Bolan climbed into the military vehicle, and Tanaka followed as he searched for a place to ditch it. A dirt track leading down to the beach was made to order. He drove to the water's edge, killed the engine, and as he had done at the airport, put the shift in neutral and pushed the army jeep into the ocean. It sank swiftly, bubbles churning the surface.

Bolan let Tanaka drive the next leg. He had no qualms about trusting her; she had proved herself on Hokkaido. She kept her eyes on the highway and didn't interrupt once as he told her about Hakka Island, ending with, "My guess is that General Tsanghsien has a stronghold somewhere deep in the mountains. That's where he's taking the missiles."

"It makes sense," she agreed. "The outlying provinces haven't changed much since the days of the warlords. The people live pretty much as they did before the Communists took over, although now the state controls everything they do."

"It's too bad we can't get in touch with Brognola," Bolan commented. And, through Hal, the staff at Stony Man Farm. Their intel-gathering capability was second to none, and it would be nice if he had more information to go on before waltzing into the lion's den.

"I've been given a phone number to the American Embassy in Beijing," Kerri said. "But I was instructed not to use it unless we absolutely have to. The President still hopes to avoid an international incident if he can."

More politics, Bolan mused wryly.

"For better or worse, we're on our own out here," Tanaka said. "Just us against the general."

COLONEL CHEN HUNG UP the telephone and licked his dry lips. Once again he had to be the bearer of bad tidings, and once again he would rather have his fingernails ripped out with red-hot tongs.

Dawn was breaking as Chen walked from a small store in the middle of a sleepy hamlet and over to the flatbed trucks. They were being refueled and having their oil levels checked and their windshields cleaned. A squad of crack troops ringed them, a precaution that seemed unnecessary since the only other people on hand were the owner of the store, who had been roused out of sleep half an hour ago, and his son, busy pumping the gas.

General Tsanghsien was indulging in a favorite pastime of his—watching the sun rise. Despite being on the go for two days with little sleep and less food, he was as tireless as ever, his uniform as immaculate as if he had just had it cleaned and pressed. "You were able to get in touch with Major Xinsi?"

Chen snapped to attention. "Sir, I regret to inform you Major Xinsi is dead. Killed by the American."

The general turned, displaying no alarm. "Interesting. Who is in charge, then? Captain Hulan?"

"Sir, Captain Hulan is also dead."

"Captain Jing?"

Colonel Chen frowned. Jing had been a protége of his. "He, too, has been slain. I spoke with Lieutenant Anlu, currently senior surviving officer."

"Tell me everything he said," the general ordered. "Leave nothing out."

"As you predicted, sir, the American showed up at Hakka Island. He wasn't detected until after he infiltrated the depot, and by then he had planted a number of explosive charges. When he was confronted, he resisted and set off some of the charges. In the ensuing battle the depot was essentially destroyed."

"The entire depot?"

Chen saw a gleam come into his superior's eyes and girded himself for the worst. But to his amazement, the general smiled.

"What is the extent of the damage?"

"Fire has consumed much of the installation. Only three warehouses still stand, and they are badly damaged. Most of the munitions have been destroyed. The headquarters building, all the barracks and the infirmary have burned to the ground."

"The casualty count?"

"Of the 167 men we left behind, fifty-one are confirmed dead, thirty-four are missing and presumed dead and forty-nine were wounded. Of those, twenty-eight are in critical condition and are not expected to live." Chen couldn't accept the toll was so monumentally high. "How can one man, sir, have caused so much destruction? It's horrible."

"No, Colonel, it's marvelous."

"Sir?"

"I was right about him," the general said in rising excitement. "The American truly is a worthy adversary. He has proved it beyond my wildest expectations. I am reminded of Sun Tzu. 'Subtle and devious, the expert leaves no trace. Divinely mysterious, he is master of his enemy's fate.'"

"But the cost, sir." Chen mustered the courage to object. "All those lives. All those good men."

"They were soldiers and they died in the line of duty. What nobler fate can a military man ask for?" Tsanghsien hooked a thumb in his belt and gazed grandly at the golden orb perched on the rim of the world. "I must remember this dawn always. It is the greatest day of my life. In a while I will be tested as I have never been tested before, and I welcome the challenge with open arms."

"Tested, sir?"

"The American isn't done, Colonel. He will come after us. He will track us to our lair and strive to thwart me."

Chen glanced back down the road. "How can you be so certain, sir?"

"Because he and I share the same martial spirit. He can no more give up with a job half-done than I could. He comes to breathe life into me and I into him."

It was at moments like these that the colonel found himself questioning whether his commanding officer was indeed as brilliant as everyone thought—or insane. A fine line divided the two, and the general straddled it precariously.

"But do not fret, my friend," General Tsanghsien said. "I have everything well in hand." He quoted another passage from Sun Tzu "'The wise general in his deliberations considers both the factors in his favor and those against.' I will defeat this American and thereby increase my glory a thousandfold."

"I have complete faith in you, sir," Chen said.

"As well you should. You are intelligent enough to recognize greatness when you see it." Tsanghsien breathed deep of the crisp dawn air. "Was that all Lieutenant Anlu had to relay?"

"No, sir. Navy ships have arrived at the island to help out, and other troops are being sent in. General Gonjo is already on hand, overseeing—"

"Gonjo?" Tsanghsien growled. "That incompetent coward! For years he has pushed for peaceful relations with the United States. He's a closet capitalist if ever there was one. He would like nothing better than to have me dead."

"They already think you are, sir."

"Who does?"

"Practically the whole country. Lieutenant Anlu followed your orders to the letter and told no one you left Hakka Island before the American wreaked havoc. Word has gone out on radio and television that you perished."

"You don't say?" Tsanghsien said, and laughed. "This will work to our advantage. If the government learned what I am up to, they would try to stop me.

But now I can operate without fear of interference.'' He laughed louder. "Won't they be surprised when I reveal I am still alive? I will wait until I have brought America to her knees, a Phoenix rising from the ashes of his enemies. Poetic, is it not?''

Chen decided it was a rhetorical question and didn't answer.

"I wonder," Tsanghsien said, thoughtfully tapping his chin. "Will future generations read about me as we now read about Sun Tzu? A thousand years from now will the Chinese people look back and marvel at our accomplishment?''

Sergeant Yatsen approached and snapped a salute. "Sir! The fuel tanks are full. We're ready to go when you give the word.''

The general stared at the rising sun, as immobile as a statue. "I am at a cusp in my existence," he said softly. "Whether I become an entire chapter in history books yet to be written or a minor footnote at the bottom of a page depends on whether I overcome the challenges I face or am overcome by them." Shaking himself, he pivoted on a heel. "Colonel Chen, you will select four men to remain behind. This is the only gas station within a hundred miles. Eventually, my American nemesis will stop here. When he does, they are to do nothing.''

"Nothing, sir?''

"You heard correctly. They are to let him drive on. Then they are to contact me and follow him without being seen.''

Chen shifted his weight from one foot to the other. "Begging the general's pardon, sir, but wouldn't it be wiser, in light of the events at Hakka Island, to have them dispose of him?''

"And deprive me of the opportunity of meeting this marvel face to face?" General Tsanghsien snorted. "I should think not. But make no mistake. He will die. At a time and place of my choosing, in a manner that will have him pleading with his deity for the mercy I will never show." The general smiled grimly. "I look forward to holding his intestines in my hands and squishing them between my fingers as the light of life fades from his eyes."

CHAPTER THIRTEEN

The warmth of the morning sun on Mack Bolan's face roused him from sleep. Opening his eyes, he gazed at Kerri Tanaka without her being aware. Her raven hair and sparkling eyes were oddly contrasted by the combat cosmetics on her cheeks and forehead. She was undeniably beautiful, the skintight blacksuit accenting her shapely curves. Young, vibrant, attractive, she was everything most men wanted in a woman, and more.

Bolan tore his eyes from her, straightened and stretched. "It's been quiet, I take it?"

"Good morning," Kerri said cheerfully. "Quiet as a library. But traffic should pick up soon. The next town is only ten miles ahead."

"In that case we need to pull over," Bolan said.

Her mouth curled invitingly. "Oh?"

Reaching behind them, Bolan rummaged in the pile of clothing and weapons and snagged the towel he had taken from the airport. Bunching it, he twisted the rearview mirror and began to wipe off his own combat cosmetics. "We can't drive through a town looking like this."

Tanaka stifled a yawn. "It's called Minquan. According to the map, the road skirts it to the north. We shouldn't have any problem." She leaned forward. A break in the forest had appeared on the right, and she whisked the Jeep into it, braking inches short of a collision with a tree trunk. "One pit stop, made to order."

Bolan climbed out to stretch. He tossed her the towel as she came around the front of the vehicle. "Thanks for letting me get some rest. I'll spell you at the wheel." He pointed at her face. "Clean off the war paint, or the natives will think you're a loon."

"Just when I was getting used to looking like a zebra." She sighed.

Bolan brought out the hip-length green jacket and other garments. The jacket's sleeves were much too short, but it was the only one that would halfway fit him. The shirts would rip apart at the seams on a man his size.

Tanaka examined the rest of the clothes. "These are atrocious. They're for men. And the pants are way too short." She set them on the hood. "I have an idea. Why don't we stop at a shop at the next town and buy clothes that will fit? I have plenty of Chinese currency, courtesy of Uncle Sam."

"It's too dangerous." Bolan said. "Foreigners are bound to be noticed."

"Then I'll go in alone. I'm fluent in the language and can pass for a tourist." She thumped the grille. "We can't stay cooped up in this rattletrap forever. We'll need to stop for gas soon, and to eat now and then. With the right clothes we can get by without drawing too much attention."

There was no disputing her logic, but Bolan had reservations. He held out the jacket. "Wear this and a pair of pants. If anything goes wrong, try not to harm civilians if you can help it."

Nodding, she reached up and started to peel out of

her blacksuit. She did it so fast, she had stripped to her bra and panties before Bolan could avert his gaze. When he turned, the image of her alluring figure was seared into his brain. He didn't look back until she announced she was done.

The jacket fit loosely, and the pants were two sizes too small. "I look like I have the fashion sense of a hobo," Tanaka remarked.

"It will have to do."

Bolan adjusted the seat before he got in to allow more room for his legs, and so he could sit lower in the seat to disguise his height. Putting the Jeep in reverse, he backed out onto the road and bore westward. Tanaka, he observed, was in an unusually merry mood, more like her old self than she had been the previous night.

"Let's find out if there's anything more about you on the news," she said, switching on the radio. Music blared, string instruments and a flute. She tuned the dial, going from station to station, searching for a newscast. "Ah. Here we go."

The flat, clipped tones of the broadcaster droned on and on, all unintelligible to Bolan. He was more interested in a sedan coming toward them. As it passed, he looked the other way. He did the same with the next four vehicles they met.

More music warbled, and his companion lowered the volume. "Not one word about you," she informed him. "But there was a story on Hakka Island. A general by the name of Gonjo has taken charge and announced that a junior officer has been taken into custody for questioning in the mysterious disappearance of General Tsanghsien."

"They no longer think he's dead?"

"The news account didn't say. But the high muck-a-mucks in Beijing must suspect something."

Bolan digested the information as they neared the outskirts of Minquan. Traffic increased, although not nearly as much as he anticipated. As was customary in Chinese urban centers, most people preferred to get around by walking or on bicycles. Cars were a luxury few could afford. It didn't help that many Chinese streets were too narrow for vehicles, a legacy of bygone days.

Tanaka avidly read the signs bordering the roadway. "Take the next left," she urged, and after they did, she counted off three blocks. "Stop here," she declared.

Bolan pulled over. A narrow side street on the right was thronged with shops and pedestrians. Colorful banners etched with Chinese ideograms lined both sides. Under a red banner near the curb sat a white-haired man weaving a basket.

"The shop we need is only a few doors down," Tanaka said. "I won't be long." She gripped the door handle.

"Be careful. Take your Mustang. If you get into trouble, fire two shots into the air and I'll come on the run."

"Why, Mike," she said impishly, "I thought you didn't care." She slid out and blended into the throng.

Slouching in his seat, Bolan unfolded the map in front of him so no one could get a good look at his face. He didn't enjoy sitting there like a duck in a pond, never knowing when a hunter might come along and pick him off. Shucking the Beretta from its holster, he placed it between his legs.

The majority of the shoppers and townspeople who

filed past paid little attention to the Jeep. A few gazed inside but showed no undue interest.

Bolan looked for Tanaka to return any moment. He glanced down the side street and saw the old basket weaver staring at him. The old man smiled so he repaid the courtesy. When he peered up over the map again, two young policemen had sauntered into view.

The Executioner's hand dropped to the Beretta. The pair spelled trouble. They strutted toward him like peacocks, proud of their power and authority. Everyone in their path moved aside to let them pass. They were ten feet from the Jeep when one poked the other and pointed at it.

Bolan checked the rearview mirror. A car had pulled up behind him, leaving barely enough room for him to ease out.

The two young policemen halted, and the taller of the two leaned down and motioned for Bolan to get out. He debated making a run for it and coming back for Tanaka later. She was perfectly able to fend for herself for a while. But once they separated, they might find it hard to link up. And he needed her. Her linguistic skills were invaluable.

The policeman motioned again.

Out of the side street breezed Kerri Tanaka, her arms burdened with packages. She was almost to the Jeep when she realized the two cops were there. Smiling, she poured on the charm, gushing a string of Chinese. Whatever she said had an effect. The pair visibly relaxed. Placing the packages at her feet, she showed them the phony papers she had been provided, all the while happily babbling. It was one of the oldest tricks of the trade, distracting an enemy with friendly chatter.

Bolan didn't interfere. She knew what she was doing. When the policemen finally swaggered off, he shoved the passenger door open so she could throw the packages into the back seat and duck inside.

"Let's make ourselves scarce. I think they bought my bull, but there's no telling."

Bolan had to navigate a maze of side streets to reach the highway. He didn't feel completely safe until they had covered over a mile and the traffic thinned. As he drove, Tanaka filled him in.

"I told them you and I were on our way to Zhengzhou as part of a trade delegation, and we decided to stop in Minquan to buy souvenirs."

"What were they laughing at?"

"You. I mentioned that like most men, you couldn't read a map if your life depended on it. Told them we'd be lucky if we reached Zhengzhou before the trade meeting was over."

"Funny lady."

"I try."

They both smiled, and for a few moments Bolan forgot the vow he had made. He let his feelings show. He regretted it when she reached over and placed a warm palm on his forearm. "Better keep watch behind us," he directed, ending their lighthearted interlude.

The rest of the morning was spent on the go. Bolan advised Tanaka to take a nap, and she dozed from nine until shortly after noon. They were between towns, traveling along a lonely strip of bleak terrain, when she sat up and ran a hand through her hair. "Want me to relieve you?"

"I'm fine," Bolan answered.

"We need to stop if you want to change clothes. I also bought some food. Rations get real old real quick."

The scent had been tantalizing Bolan all morning. He slowed at a turnoff, a wide footpath overgrown with weeds. Downshifting, he drove far enough into the forest to be invisible from the highway and killed the engine. "Let's see what you've got."

She gathered up the packages and spread them out on the grass. The largest was for him. Inside was a blue cotton shirt and baggy pants typical of those worn by Chinese city dwellers. She had also bought him a pair of low-cut shoes and a wide-brimmed hat.

"I figured you can pull it down over your face when we're in public," she said as he tried it on for size.

"What about you?"

In the other package was a matching outfit, a green shirt and pants not much different in design than his. Sandals and a red bandana completed her attire. "Before we change, we should eat," Tanaka said. "I don't know about you, but I'm starving."

The food came in cardboard containers similar to those served at Chinese restaurants in the U.S. Bolan was given one crammed with noodles and another with millet awash in a sweet sauce. Leaning back against the front fender, he ate with relish. After two days without real food, the meal was positively delicious.

Seated cross-legged in a shaft of sunlight, Tanaka speared a ball of meat and popped it into her mouth. "Here we are, all alone in the middle of nowhere, enjoying a picnic, of sorts. Isn't it romantic?"

"No," Bolan stated, nipping her nonsense in the bud.

"Why do you keep denying we're attracted to each other?" she asked with disarming frankness. "Why do you insist on avoiding the inevitable?" Standing, she left her food on the ground and sashayed toward him, her hips swaying in alluring invitation.

"Sit back down," Bolan said, but she didn't listen. He saw the hunger in her eyes and felt a constriction in his throat.

"This time I won't take no for an answer. This time you'll have to slug me to stop me."

"Don't," Bolan said. But his heart wasn't in it and she realized as much. Kerri Tanaka boldly pressed her lush body against his, her arms looping around his neck. "You're making a mistake."

"I made the mistake on Hokkaido when I let you talk me out of following my heart." She lightly kissed his cheek, his neck. "I've had a lot of time to think since then. A lot of time to see that the only way I'll get through to you is by throwing myself at you like some shameless hussy."

"I'm not looking to tie myself down to any one woman."

"Who said anything about a long-lasting commitment?" Tanaka countered. "All that matters is this moment. The two of us, alone, here and now. If we don't quit playing mind games, we'll regret what we didn't do for the rest of our lives."

"You will, maybe—" Bolan began.

"Has anyone ever mentioned you talk too damn much?" she jested, and sculpted her hot mouth to his.

Bolan gripped her shoulders to push her back, but the exquisite feel of her breasts on his chest and her hips on his thighs stirred him to his core. His innermost need, so long denied, battered down his will, and his hands rose to cup her of their own accord. She was soft and yielding, a caldron of desire and passion no man could deny. Once his hunger had been given free rein, there was no stopping. He gently lowered her to the grass and melted into her.

For a while Bolan's universe consisted of the warm, willing woman under him. He became absorbed in their mutual need and mutual release. When, at long length, Kerri Tanaka cried out in the throes of ecstasy, he inwardly cried out with her.

Washington, D.C.

HAL BROGNOLA intently studied the image on his monitor as Barbara Price's voice came over the twin speakers beside the computer drive unit.

"What do you think?" she asked.

"If they ever have an ugliest-man-alive contest, this joker would win hands down," he replied. The man on the screen had a broad, brutish face. Glittering dark eyes brooded under a beetling brow framed by black, curly hair. A thick mustache adorned a cruel slash of a mouth. On the left cheek was a long, jagged scar, an old knife wound, perhaps, since part of the left nostril was missing. Whoever had sewn the nose back up botched the job, with the result it twisted to one side, adding to his ogre appearance.

"He'd also win the most-vicious-man-alive competition, hands down." She paused. "His name is Alexi Igra Smolensk. The Black Tiger, they call him in Russia. Not because he's black but because he's a kingpin in the Russian black market. You name it, he deals in it. Every illegal substance and armament known to man."

"I see where this is going already."

"We've been working on a list of possible suppliers for the nuclear warheads General Tsanghsien needs, and the Black Tiger is at the very top. When the Communist system broke down and the country went to hell, Smolensk feasted on the remains like a vulture on roadkill. He stole. He swindled. He supplied whatever anyone wanted—for the right price. His power and influence grew by leaps and bounds. He has scores of judges, politicians and military officers in his back pocket. The police can't lay a finger on him. He's untouchable.''

Brognola waited for her to get to the gist of her report.

''He's also the leading black market supplier of ill-gotten military hardware. The CIA has a report on file from a confidential source deep in Russia that Smolensk got his hands on a number of nuclear warheads thanks to some creative bookkeeping at an army base by a general Smolensk controls.''

''How many nukes are we talking about?''

''Estimates vary from as few as five to as many as— get this—forty.''

Brognola was staggered. That was more than most countries with nuclear capability possessed. Forty nukes in the hands of a degenerate who didn't care who ended up with them or to what use they were put. ''He still has them?''

''We believe so, yes. There's no evidence he's sold any. But bear in mind our sources aren't infallible.'' Papers rustled in the background, and Price went on. ''There are several reasons Smolensk is our prime candidate. He's well-known not just in Russia and neighboring countries, but throughout Europe and much of Asia. We've uncovered documents that prove he's had dealings in China.''

"So there's every chance General Tsanghsien is acquainted with him?" Brognola deduced.

"Exactly. And the fact Smolensk might have all the warheads Tsanghsien needs is a big factor in Smolensk's favor. The general doesn't need to hunt all over the place to acquire them."

"Smolensk sure sounds like our man. Do we have any clue to his current whereabouts? Better yet, do we have any idea where he might have the warheads stored?"

"Negative on both scores. The man would make Houdini proud. He pops up now and then, conducts a deal, then vanishes without a trace. Half the governments on the other of the globe would give anything to snare him, but he's always ten steps ahead of them."

"Keep at it," Brognola said. "I know it's a long shot, but if we can track him down before the deal goes through, we can put a major crimp in General Tsanghsien's plans."

"Speaking of the general, I have more to pass along."

"Good news or bad?"

"We think we know where he's headed. A check of old maps of China turned up an intriguing tidbit. Something you won't find on any of the new maps issued by the Chinese government." More papers rustled. "In the Bayan Har Mountains is an area called Tsanghsien Province. It's isolated, cut off from the rest of the world by high ranges on all sides. Only a few small towns to speak of, and an ancient fortress that overlooks Tsanghsien Lake."

"Let me guess," Brognola interrupted. "They named it Tsanghsien Fortress?"

"Close. In Chinese the name translates as 'the Heart

of Tsanghsien.' Tsanghsien Province is the ancestral homeland for a warrior clan by that name. General Tsanghsien's father was born there, as were his father's father and all the male ancestors for as far back as there are records. A family tradition, I suppose.''

"What about the general himself?"

"He was born in Beijing. Maybe his mother delivered early, and they just couldn't get her to Tsanghsien Province in time."

It was a piddling inconsistency, but the big Fed had learned long ago that piddling details often led to a wealth of valuable intel. "Check into it, would you?"

"His official biography mentions his mother died giving birth to him. You want more?"

"For centuries the Tsanghsien clan made it a point to have all male babies born in their home province," Brognola said. "You'd think the general's father would have wanted the same honor for his son. I'm surprised he took his pregnant wife to Beijing if there was any chance at all of things going wrong. Something doesn't fit."

Brognola checked his watch. He had a meeting with the President in forty-five minutes. "Anything else?"

"More satellite photos of Hakka Island came in. Our boy did some serious damage. The depot has been destroyed. They're saying the final fatality count could be well over one hundred. The Chinese government is demanding answers."

"So I've heard." Just that morning the President's chief of staff had told Brognola secret meetings had taken place at the highest levels of the Chinese government, and a general strongly opposed to Tsanghsien's policies had been appointed to oversee an investigation.

The President's advisers believed the Chinese leadership knew General Tsanghsien was still alive and they were laying the groundwork to have him ousted from the military and the Party. Brognola wasn't so sure. A man of Tsanghsien's stature had to be handled delicately. One slipup, and the Chinese government could have a revolt on its hands. Scores of army units were fiercely devoted to Tsanghsien and would storm the gates of Beijing if he ordered them to.

Brognola had also learned the Chinese were making quiet inquiries through their embassies in various Western nations, trying to learn the identity of the dark-haired foreigner responsible for the carnage at Hakka Island. He wasn't worried they would ID Bolan. Not when he had seen to it that all records of his friend's existence had been expunged from official files.

The most the Chinese might unearth was that an American had been involved. But it would be nothing more than hearsay, a rumor they couldn't prove.

Brognola realized Price was saying his name. "Sorry. What was that?"

"The latest photos show the convoy is still pushing west. Our best estimate is that it will reach Tsanghsien Province in twenty-six to thirty hours."

The big Fed thought of something. "We need to monitor all air traffic in a corridor from the Russian border to Tsanghsien's stronghold. A list of all airports would help. There can't be that many. Not as isolated as it is."

"I'll have them get right on it. Hmm."

"Something?"

"As far as we know, there's not a single airport anywhere in Tsanghsien Province. It's that backward. The only way in or out is by road, and that's over one of two passes. Both heavily guarded, I would imagine.''

"Train service?''

"Not to our knowledge, no. I'm looking at the old map, and there's a large lake near the fortress. One of the largest in China. An amphibian could land and take off with no trouble.''

"Tsanghsien Lake, by any chance?''

Price chuckled. "You're getting good at this. Yes, Tsanghsien Lake, fed by the Tsanghsien River.''

"Okay, then. Have our reconnaissance people concentrate on an air corridor between the Russian border and Tsanghsien Lake. If Alexi Smolensk and the general have struck a deal, that's how the nuclear warheads will be brought in.''

"Will do.''

Brognola broke the connection and sat back. He had new options to consider, new scenarios to work out. Foremost among them was sending in Phoenix Force. Bolan could use help penetrating the general's stronghold. Lots of help. But the President wasn't likely to approve inserting more American personnel onto Chinese soil. The chief executive had been against it all along, and he would be doubly so now that the Chinese were stirred up by the destruction of their depot.

Another option was to send in just one person. Jack Grimaldi would do. Grimaldi was a warrior in his own right, and could extract Bolan and Kerri Tanaka after the mission was over. But the only place for Grimaldi to set down was the lake, which was bound to be under constant watch. He might make it in, but making it out would be a whole different story.

The intercom buzzed, derailing his train of thought.

"Sir, there's a call for you on line two. A Captain Bower."

Brognola placed the receiver to his ear. "Captain Bower? What can I do for you?"

The female officer sounded somewhat edgy. "Sorry to bother you. I was wondering if there's been any word yet on the recovery status of the PPS-1s?"

"Nothing significant," Brognola lied. Only those with need-to-know were entitled to the information, and the captain wasn't one of them.

"You'll keep me posted, won't you? Admiral Thomas is quite upset about the whole affair, and as his adjutant it's my job to keep him abreast of the latest developments."

"If anything important comes up, you'll be one of the first people I call," Brognola assured her.

"Thank you, sir."

She hung up, leaving Brognola to ponder if she truly was looking out for the interests of the admiral, or whether she had been fishing for intel she could pass on to General Tsanghsien. A thorough background check by the FBI hadn't turned up any incriminating evidence against her, but Captain Bower just might be the traitor he was after.

CHAPTER FOURTEEN

China

A change came over Kerri Tanaka, a change that puzzled Bolan. Once they took up the chase again, she sat quietly on the passenger side, staring blankly out at the stark scenery. Where before she had gushed with enthusiasm and excitement, now she never spoke unless spoken to and avoided looking at him. He couldn't understand what had come over her.

As if the soldier didn't have enough on his mind. They needed to stop for fuel soon. He had poured the last of their spare gas into the tank hours ago, and now the gauge hovered shy of empty. They'd planned to stop back at Minquan, but things hadn't worked out.

"Keep your eyes peeled for a gas station," Bolan said. When she didn't respond, he glanced at her. "Did you hear me?"

"Yes," she replied in a whisper.

Bolan decided enough was enough. Her strange behavior was distracting him, and he couldn't afford a lapse in focus, not on a mission. "What's bothering you?"

"I'd rather not talk about it."

"You don't have any choice. I need you to be at

your best, not moping like a teenager.'' Bolan didn't mean to be unkind, but she flinched as if he had pricked her with a blade. ''Are you upset about what we did?''

''Heavens, no. It was wonderful. I just—'' She stopped and pointed. ''Pull over. There's a gas station.''

It wasn't much of one. A single old pump, a shack that looked as if a puff of wind would blow it down, and a portly man in grimy clothes who came around to Tanaka's side and made small talk for five minutes.

Bolan pulled his hat brim low, his arms folded across his chest, feigning fatigue. The proprietor showed no interest in him but a lot in the woman. Once again her gift for gab served them in good stead. She smiled and joked, and as soon as Bolan pulled out, imparted what she had learned.

''He was a friendly cuss. He guessed I'm of Japanese descent, and mentioned how he doesn't see many foreigners out this way so it was a treat for him to serve us. He also told me that yesterday morning a convoy of flatbed trucks crammed with soldiers stopped to refuel. The soldiers weren't very friendly.''

''Did he see the missiles?''

''He tried to look under the canvas, but the soldiers became angry and shooed him away. Warned him that if he tried to do it again, they would shoot him.'' A blank expression came over her once more and she sagged against the seat.

''You were saying before we stopped?'' Bolan prompted when she gave no sign of going on.

''You'll think it's silly.''

''Try me.''

Tanaka faced him. ''I care for you, Mike Belasko. Really, truly care. From the day we met, there's been

something special about you. A quality I can't define.
I've thought about you a lot since then, every day, in
fact, and dreamed of getting to know you better.''

"I'd say you have," Bolan said, trying to lighten her
mood.

"That's just it. I haven't. All I've done is throw
myself at you." She tenderly touched his wrist. "Don't
get me wrong. It was everything I'd hoped it would
be. I've never been happier than I was when you took
me in your arms.''

"You have a strange way of showing it.''

"Hear me out. I was floating on air. Yeah, I know
it sounds corny, like a teenager, as you put it. But I
can't help how I felt." She bit her lower lip. "Afterward, when we were lying there in each other's arms,
I kept waiting for you to say that you care for me as
much as I care for you.''

Bolan's grip on the steering wheel tightened.

"That's when it hit me. I'd made an utter fool of
myself. I all but ripped off your clothes, yet you never
once came right out and told me how you feel about
me. Oh, I can sense you care. But now it's dawned on
me you might not care as much as I care for you. That
this is one-sided.''

He opened his mouth to speak.

"Wait. Please. I'm not done." Her lips compressed
into a thin line. "I know you're not the kind of man
who wears his emotions on his sleeve. You keep all
your feelings bottled up, so admitting you care might
not come easy. I can live with that." She took a deep
breath. "What I can't live with is the thought that the
greatest day of my life might be no more than a one-
night stand to you.''

"It was much more than that," Bolan confessed. But

he refused to deceive her. "I won't come right out and say I love you because I'd be lying. Love is like trust. It has to be earned, and that takes time. Whether we'll have that time remains to be seen. Once this is over, I'll be heading back to the U.S., and I honestly can't say if we'll ever set eyes on each other again." There. He had been as honest as he could.

Tanaka was silent for several moments. "In my head I know it's unreasonable to ask for any more than that, but in my heart I crave a lot more. I want to go away with you when this is done. Just the two of us, somewhere the world can't intrude."

"That's not possible."

"Don't you ever take time off?" she asked. "Aren't you entitled to a vacation now and again?"

What could he say? Bolan wondered. That he seldom stopped to smell the roses because he was too busy pruning the thorns? That his ongoing battle against the piranhas of the world came before all else? That he had sacrificed everything—family, friends, a future, in order to wage an unending war? "It's been a while since I had any time to myself," he compromised.

"In other words, I shouldn't get my hopes up," she said bitterly.

"All we can do is take life one day at a time and hope for the best," Bolan responded.

She grew quiet and didn't speak for hours. About two in the afternoon, he let her spell him at the wheel.

Bolan gave a lot of thought to concocting an excuse to get her out of harm's way. In the state she was in, she would get herself killed. But short of ordering her to the American Embassy in Beijing, his hands were tied.

By evening they were well into a new mountain range. The road became narrower and more treacherous. Towns and villages were farther and farther apart.

Bolan drove until midnight, averaging twenty miles per hour over the speed limit. They had a lot of time and distance to make up if they were to overtake the convoy before another day went by, as he planned.

Tanaka had slept the past four hours. She was still moody and didn't say a word when he pulled over, walked around to the passenger side and opened the door for her.

"Ready to switch?" Bolan said. Overhead the heavens blazed with a myriad of stars. The air smelled of pine, mixed with the dank scent of rich earth.

Nodding, she slid out. She took a step, then suddenly whirled and gripped him by the shoulders with an intensity that surprised him. "I can't stand it anymore, Mike. I need to know. I didn't make a complete fool of myself, did I? Please. Be honest."

"You could never do that, Kerri. You're a generous-hearted and loving person."

Tanaka mustered a halfhearted grin. "When I fall, I fall hard. I give of myself with all my heart. Is that so wrong?"

"It is if you let it turn you into a basket case." Bolan smiled. "We'll talk about this later, okay?"

They settled into a routine. Four hours of driving, four hours of rest. They ate on the road, Tanaka buying whatever they needed. At each stop she asked about the convoy. Invariably whoever she spoke to remembered it.

By all indications they were gaining. The road climbed continuously, and the steep grades, Bolan reasoned, were slowing the big rigs. Towering peaks reared on all sides, mantled by ivory crowns of snow. Spectacular gorges, sheer bluffs and swift-flowing rivers testified to the wildness of the region.

It was early evening when a faded roadside sign caught Tanaka's eyes. "There's a small town just up ahead."

"We'll stop for gas," Bolan said. They were running low again, and he would hate to be stranded with so much at stake.

She had a notepad on one knee and her map on the other and was scribbling in a notepad. "If my calculations are correct, we should overtake General Tsanghsien by noon tomorrow."

Bolan hoped so. His secret fear was that the general would launch the PPS-1s before they caught up.

"It's strange there hasn't been anything more on the news about Hakka Island," Tanaka remarked, fiddling with the radio. "Nothing about General Tsanghsien, either. Do you suppose the government has imposed a news blackout?"

"They might if they suspected he was up to no good."

Around the next bend was a quaint hamlet nestled in the crook of a narrow valley bisected by a picturesque stream. They crossed an arched stone bridge and bore left onto a wide square dominated by a three-story pagoda caked with the dust of decades.

Men and women lounged at ease. Children scampered about at play. But only until Bolan braked at the pump and Tanaka climbed out. Then everyone stopped what they were doing and stared.

An old man shuffled toward them from a small store, his clothes as seamed as his features. He smiled, as friendly as could be, yet Bolan noticed his eyes nervously dart toward a nearby building.

Tanaka was fishing money from her pocket and hadn't seen it. She gestured at the pump and asked him to fill their tank.

Bolan saw a frightened girl run to her mother, saw a man urgently usher a family down a side street. Undoing two of the buttons on his shirt, he slipped his hand underneath and palmed the Beretta.

More villagers were starting to fade away, but they stopped when a stocky man with close-cropped hair strode from a doorway and motioned. He wore the same kind of clothes they did, but there was something in his bearing and manner that set him apart. Their fear of him was almost thick enough to be cut with a knife.

Bolan scanned the buildings. A face vanished from a window in the one the old man had glanced at. He looked into the rearview mirror and spied the front bumper of a vehicle jutting from behind the pagoda.

Bending toward the passenger side, Bolan tried to get Tanaka's attention without being too obvious. She was chatting away, as usual. The old man was smiling, but it was forced and wooden.

Since she wouldn't look his way, Bolan reached out the window and tugged on her shirt. "Make it fast," he whispered when she ducked her head inside. "Something isn't right."

"You're telling me," she whispered. "This old geezer is as talkative as a clam. Do you want me to have him stop so we can take off?"

"No, we need the fuel," Bolan said. Without it they might as well be on foot. "Be ready to jump in if I give a yell."

As Bolan straightened, he peered into the rearview

mirror and spied a soldier crouched beside a hedge to the right of the pagoda. One of General Tsanghsien's men, he suspected. He began to unlimber the 93-R, then saw that the soldier wasn't about to attack. The man was spying on them, his SMG pointed at the ground.

The numbers on the pump scrolled with frustrating slowness. At last they clinked to a stop and the old man replaced the nozzle. He bowed politely as he accepted the money Tanaka offered, and trotted toward the store as if he couldn't get out of there fast enough.

Bolan jerked the key, shifted into first and punched the gas pedal before Tanaka had the passenger door closed. They shot across the square like a cannonball.

An army jeep leaped from behind the pagoda. The soldier by the hedge rushed over and hopped in. So did another from inside the building the old man had glanced at. That left the soldier in civilian clothes, who cast them off as he ran to the center of the square.

Bolan took a corner on two wheels. Within seconds the narrow mouth of a side street yawned on the left and he whipped into it, their tires squealing. His door almost scraped a wall as he roared along a row of homes and cut sharply around the last.

"Look out!" Tanaka warned.

A chicken coop, of all things, had materialized before them. Bolan stomped on the brake pedal but for an instant thought they would crash anyway. Instead, they came to a halt inches from a wire fence that surrounded the coop.

"I hope you know what you're doing," Tanaka said, twisting to grab her M-16. "If they cut us off, there's no other way out."

Bolan threw the shift into neutral, jumped out and

ran to the corner in time to see the four soldiers flash by. Racing back, he ground the gears into reverse and sped after them. They were taking the west road out of the village, unaware the hunters had become the hunted.

His companion chuckled. "If you ever decide to give up killing people for a living, you should become a race-car driver."

Bolan was trying to make sense of the situation. "Why did the general leave those four men here?" He voiced the question uppermost on his mind.

"Maybe we're close to Tsanghsien's stronghold. Maybe the village is an outpost."

"Or maybe he knew we were coming and left a welcoming committee," Bolan said.

"How could he? Not even Mr. Brognola knows where we are at this point."

"Let's ask the soldiers," Bolan said, and drove faster. He would rather avoid a confrontation, but if General Tsanghsien was on to them, they needed to know.

Twilight was falling. Darkening shadows cast by steep slopes and sheer cliffs dappled the roadway. Sinuous curves gave Bolan no inkling of what lay beyond each new turn. At the end of the valley a switchback climbed toward an upland bench. They were midway to the top when he glimpsed the army jeep speeding up over the rim.

The crest was two thousand feet above the valley floor. But it was only a stepping-stone to a much higher plateau several miles to the west, a foreboding rampart of jagged mountains, the geologic gateway to the Tibetan Plateau and—many leagues distant—the mighty Himalayas.

"Magnificent!" Tanaka exclaimed.

Bolan scoured the bench for the other vehicle. A quarter of a mile off, it was wheeling in a U-turn, its headlights piercing the gloom. The soldiers had finally realized they had been outfoxed and were heading back.

Applying the brakes, Bolan brought the Jeep to a stop in the middle of the road. He snatched his M-16 and slid out, leaving the engine running.

"What are you up to now?" Tanaka inquired, emulating his example.

"Ever hear of the Trojan horse?" Bolan rejoined as he led her into thick undergrowth. Lying flat, he tucked his cheek to the rifle.

"You sure know how to treat a girl to a fun time. High-speed chases. Firefights. Being shot to ribbons by helicopter gunships. There's never a dull moment."

"You can always put in for desk work," Bolan mentioned.

"And spend the rest of my life bored to tears? Thank you, no. I'd go nuts."

An engine growled and the army vehicle streaked around a curve. Its headlights illuminated their Jeep, and the driver came to a screeching stop.

The man on the passenger side slid out, worked the bolt of an SMG and cautiously advanced.

Bolan wanted all four in the open but the other three didn't take the bait. "We need a couple of them alive," he whispered. "Don't shoot to kill unless you have to."

The next moment the driver climbed out to cover his companion. He said something, and the first man stopped cold.

Tanaka leaned closer. "The driver just reminded the

other one that General Tsanghsien wants to take the tall American alive. He must mean you.''

So the general *did* know they were coming, Bolan thought. But how? Through a leak at Brognola's end? Through an intelligence network of the general's own? Or was it simply a hunch? After all, the general was shrewd enough to realize the U.S. government wouldn't rest until the PPS-1s were found. Bolan put the issue aside for later consideration and sighted down his M-16 at the driver. ''Shout for them to drop their weapons and raise their hands.''

Tanaka complied. The two soldiers swung toward them, and for several moments the tableau was frozen as the pair decided whether they were going to comply. It was the driver who made up his mind first and extended his SMG. Bolan sent a burst into the man's legs and he crumpled, screaming in torment.

The soldier nearest them was just as pigheaded. He squeezed off several rounds before Tanaka's return fire punched him backward.

Over in the jeep, the soldiers in the back were scrabbling to clamber out. They had to squeeze between the front seats and the door, and that slowed them down. When the first one popped out, Bolan cored him through the ribs.

The last soldier wasn't as reckless as his companions. He dived flat and rolled toward the brush on the far side, firing as he rolled.

Bolan embraced the earth as dirt kicked up inches from his head. The last man was good. When he looked up the soldier had melted into the undergrowth. ''Watch the others,'' he whispered. ''I'm going after him.''

The Executioner crawled to the right, past the army

jeep and the driver, who was thrashing and moaning, his hands clamped to the holes in his thighs, his fingers and his uniform stained red.

Bolan had yet to spot the last soldier. A wide tree trunk provided the temporary haven he needed to rise into a crouch. Then, his legs churning, he raced across the road. Apparently he took the soldier unaware because no gunfire resulted.

Dropping onto his belly in the shadow of a thicket, Bolan strained his ears for the slightest sound and his eyes for the slightest movement. The deepening darkness handicapped him. After waiting a suitable interval, he crabbed eastward, pausing every few yards to survey the terrain. He circled the spot where the last solider had gone to ground but failed to find him.

The guy was a pro.

The three wounded men still lay where they had fallen, the driver groaning and quaking, another in a fetal position.

Bolan inched to a pine and rose slowly. For over two minutes he stood stock-still but couldn't pinpoint his quarry. He bent to find a rock he could toss. It was an old trick, but sometimes the oldest ones worked best.

Then an astounding thing happened.

Kerri Tanaka walked into the open, right out into the glare of headlights. The last soldier couldn't ask for a better target. And to compound her folly, she called out, "Mike! Where are you?"

Bolan wasn't about to answer and give his location away. He was stupefied by her stupidity until he realized her hands were empty and a shadowy shape had attached itself to her back. He brought up the M-16 but couldn't get a clear shot.

"Mike, I'm sorry! He came up behind me! He says if you don't show yourself, he'll kill me." She thrust her chin out defiantly. "But don't you dare, you hear me? The mission is more important. Take this bastard out and don't worry about me."

Bolan stealthily crept to the right to outflank them, but he had only gone three steps when Tanaka's left arm was brutally wrenched back and she involuntarily cried out.

"He says you have ten seconds!"

The Executioner remembered the driver telling the other soldier that General Tsanghsien wanted him alive.

"When he shoots me, nail him!" the woman yelled, then smothered a scream as her arm was savagely twisted even farther.

"Tell him I'm coming out!" Bolan shouted. "Tell him I won't try anything!"

"No! Don't do it. I'm not worth it."

Bolan was already moving toward them. Elevating his arms, he held the M-16 overhead and slowly stepped from the trees. He saw part of the soldier's swarthy face over Tanaka's shoulder.

She spoke in Chinese. Without warning, the man flung his foot in front of her and shoved, hurling her to the ground. The barrel of his weapon was trained on Tanaka, not on Bolan. He growled angrily in Chinese.

"He wants you to toss the M-16 behind you, take three steps forward and kneel." She was on her side in the dust, rubbing her left shoulder. "He says not to try anything. That if you so much as twitch wrong, I'll die."

Bolan did as he had been instructed. He tensed,

thinking the soldier would move in close to frisk him, but the man once again demonstrated he was no fool.

"You're to take off your shirt," Tanaka said, relaying the command. "You're to do it one button at a time, using one hand and one hand only. You're to slide the sleeves off slowly and let it fall behind you, not in front of you. Any quick moves and he'll put a bullet in my brain."

Once more Bolan did as he had been told. Out of the corner of his left eye he noticed the driver had stopped thrashing and sat up.

A smirk lit their captor's features when he saw the Beretta and the Desert Eagle, and he barked at Tanaka.

"He says you're to throw them to your left. Use your thumb and forefinger, nothing else."

The barrel pointing at her never wavered. Frowning, Bolan got rid of both pistols exactly as he had been instructed.

"Now you're to lie on your stomach and not move," Tanaka said. "He wants me to cut strips from your shirt and tie you. What do I do?"

"Whatever he wants," Bolan said. The driver was pointing an SMG at them. No matter what their general wanted, Bolan wouldn't put it past either soldier to open fire if he or Tanaka resisted.

"Are you sure?"

"Just do it."

The soldier who had caught the woman produced a penknife and tossed it to her. Reluctantly she opened it, retrieved his shirt and, with a lot of effort, sliced off several strips. Under the watchful glares of the two Chinese, she bound Bolan's wrists behind his back, then moved to one side.

Their captor snarled at her, and Tanaka lay face-down. Exercising extreme caution, he sidled around the warrior and verified Bolan's wrists were secure by yanking on the strips. Satisfied, he picked up another and spoke to the driver, who fixed Tanaka in the SMG's sights. The threat was transparent.

In under a minute she was bound, too. The soldier moved in front of them, smug now that they were at his mercy.

"He says we should thank him," Tanaka translated.

"For what?" Bolan asked.

"For a few more days of life. Once he turns us over to General Tsanghsien, we're as good as dead."

CHAPTER FIFTEEN

The soldier who had taken them prisoner was a sergeant named Ergun. He did what he could for the driver and the man Bolan had shot in the ribs and hoisted both into the army vehicle. The fourth man was dead. The sergeant dragged him over and carefully placed him in the rear.

Tanaka translated everything they said.

Sergeant Ergun directed the two wounded men to return to the village to be doctored while he went on ahead. He gazed after them until their taillights disappeared. Chortling, he slapped his leg and crowed, "Fate has smiled on me. Now the honor will be mine and mine alone. The general will be greatly pleased and reward me handsomely."

Unslinging his rifle, Ergun gathered up the Beretta, the Desert Eagle and the two M-16s, and carried the hardware to their Jeep. He wedged the Beretta under his belt but dumped the rest on the back seat. Then, switching on the Jeep's headlights, he covered his prisoners.

"Stand and walk toward me. Keep well apart and do not attempt to run off. You will never make it."

Bolan was told to climb in on the passenger side. Tanaka was guided at gunpoint to the driver's seat.

Drawing the Beretta, Ergun jammed it against her temple and eased in past her. He leaned his rifle against the side and untied her with his other hand. "You will drive, woman," he directed. "You will go as fast as I tell you and stop when I tell you. Never forget you are expendable. The general is only interested in your tall friend." He nodded at the Executioner.

Bolan hadn't uttered a peep in protest or done anything to antagonize the noncom. But he hadn't let his guard down. Sooner or later the sergeant would make a mistake, and he would be ready.

Tanaka pulled out, the Beretta's muzzle a finger's width from the back of her head. "This is all my fault," she said to Bolan. "He caught me by surprise. I was so concerned about you I didn't think to look behind me."

"It could have happened to anyone."

"You're just saying that. If I'd kept my mind on what we were doing, I might have spotted him before he jumped me." She frowned. "You were right. It's a mistake to mix business and personal affairs in our line of work."

Sergeant Ergun spit a few words at them.

"He doesn't want us to talk unless we have his consent," Tanaka translated. "Otherwise he'll make us regret it."

For half an hour no one said a word. The wall of mountains swelled, seeming to climb to the very stars.

The sergeant leaned forward, peered up through the windshield and uttered a few comments that Tanaka repeated. "He says we'll reach the pass into Tsanghsien Province by one in the morning. From there it's a seven-and-a-half-hour drive to the general's ancestral home on the lake."

"What lake?" Bolan asked.

Tanaka translated Ergun's reply word for word. The answer was illuminating. "Tsanghsien Lake, of course. The fortress on the bluff overlooking it was built over a thousand years ago and is a monument to the greatness of the Tsanghsien line."

"It sounds like you think highly of the general," Bolan remarked, fishing for more information.

"As well I should," the sergeant said through Tanaka. "Soon he will bring the Western powers to their knees. Once they fall, the other countries of the world will follow. A new era will begin. China's era. The planet will be ours to do with as we please."

Bolan had the impression the noncom was parroting statements Tsanghsien had made. "The whole planet? Your general doesn't think small, does he?"

Sergeant Ergun sat back and lowered the Beretta a fraction as Tanaka translated. "General Tsanghsien is a genius. Only he could devise the grand plan that will soon bring us victory. Only he could carry it out."

"Do all the soldiers under his command feel the same?" Bolan quizzed. The man's esteem for Tsanghsien bordered on fanaticism.

"Without question. We were handpicked by the general himself. Only those who hate the West as much as he does and want to see America and her allies in ruins passed muster."

The general's very own storm troopers, Bolan thought. An army within an army, as it were.

"Stealing the missiles was only the first step. Once the Russians arrive and the nuclear warheads are installed, the final countdown begins. In thirty-six hours it will all be over."

Trying to sound casual so the sergeant wouldn't realize he had slipped up, Bolan had Tanaka say, "The general is in league with Russians? I'm surprised he likes them any better than he likes the U.S."

"He doesn't," Sergeant Ergun told her. "Russians are crude pigs who possess no honor. I have heard General Tsanghsien say as much many times. But the Black Tiger has the warheads the general needs."

"Where is your general getting the money to pay for them?" Bolan asked.

Sergeant Ergun laughed. "Who says he will, American?"

Bolan was relieved to hear the missiles hadn't been fitted with nukes yet, but thirty-six hours wasn't a lot of time. Not when he had to escape the noncom's clutches, reach Tsanghsien's fortress, stop the warheads from changing hands *and* destroy the PPS-1s.

Now that Sergeant Ergun was more at ease, he wouldn't shut up. "I am honored to be part of the general's undertaking," he said through Tanaka. "Soon, very soon, China will do what no other country in history ever has. She will rule the world."

"You're deceiving yourself," Bolan said. "If we don't stop you, your own government will."

"Who is deceiving whom? Our government pretends to be friends with the West, but we both know they're not sincere. When General Tsanghsien offers them America on a platter, they will be all too happy to go along."

Bolan was willing to concede Ergun was probably right. Which made it all the more crucial he stop the general before it reached that stage.

The grade was so steep Tanaka was continually downshifting to regain speed. Bolan figured it had taken the flatbed trucks over a day to get from the village to the pass, and if that was the case, the trucks weren't all that far ahead. He turned in his seat just enough to be able to watch Ergun without Ergun catching on.

The sergeant still had the Beretta pointed at Tanaka, but his hand had drooped onto the top of her seat. The barrel was slanted toward her spine rather than at the back of her head.

She said something to him and held off translating until Ergun's long-winded reply ended. "I wanted to know how he could be a party to mass destruction," she related. "I asked him how he could live with himself knowing he helped kill millions of innocent men, women and children."

"What did he say?"

"That there are no innocents. Everyone born under America's flag is tainted from birth with the evil of capitalism. The deaths of those the missiles kill are for the greater good of all humankind." She negotiated a hairpin curve. "He compared it to culling weak and unfit cattle. Once America has been destroyed, the rest of the world will be better off." She swore under her breath. "So much for appealing to his humanity."

Sergeant Ergun hissed at her and she fell quiet.

Bolan had noticed something. When she took the curve, centrifugal force has pushed all three of them to one side. The sergeant's gun hand rotated a few degrees, just enough for the barrel to point at the floor, not at the driver. Should that occur again, it would be the opening he needed.

The road, though, was climbing straight toward the summit through a phalanx of high rock walls split by ravines and drop-offs.

Bolan braced his feet against the floor under the

dash. He needed leverage for what he had in mind. Looking at Tanaka, he laughed loudly as if he were making a joke, and said, "Take the next bend we come to as fast as you can. And be ready to help me." He'd need her assistance to pull it off. With his hands bound, he wouldn't be able to take the sergeant out with one or two blows.

Ergun snapped at Tanaka and she answered, then relayed, "He demanded to know what you just said. I told him you were laughing at the irony of life. At being caught by a lowly sergeant."

Ergun didn't appreciate the insult and was glaring at Bolan.

"Do whatever you have to," she continued. "Don't hold back on my account like you did earlier when Ergun took me prisoner. My life means nothing compared to the millions at stake if General Tsanghsien carries out his insane plan. I knew when I signed on with Mr. Brognola that one day I might have to sacrifice myself in the line of duty. It comes with the job."

That it did, Bolan agreed. But her willingness was still commendable. Her affection for him aside, she was a courageous, bright and dedicated young woman. Most men would give their eyeteeth to have a woman like her care for them.

Sergeant Ergun had more to say.

"He hopes the general will permit him to witness your execution," she translated. "The general can be quite inventive. One time he hung a man by his ankles from the battlements and let him dangle until he rotted. Another enemy was buried up to his neck next to an anthill. But Sergeant Ergun's favorite was the time the general staked a man out, poured gasoline on him and lit him on fire. The man screamed and screamed."

"A regular sadist," Bolan said, nodding at the sergeant.

Ergun bent toward Tanaka and whispered, then cackled with glee.

"What now?" Bolan prodded when she didn't pass it on.

"He was just saying I have a lot to look forward to. The general has a fondness for beautiful women. If I grovel and whine and please him in bed, Tsanghsien might let me live a while. If I refuse, he'll give me to his troops to do with as they please, as he's done to several others." She paused, her face hardening. "The soldiers pulled a train on them. They were raped by sixty or seventy men in a row. Most bled to death internally."

"Destroying the missiles isn't enough," Bolan said gravely. "We can't leave without eliminating the general."

"Nailing that son of a bitch is my top priority," Tanaka vowed, and frowned. "You know, I keep forgetting America isn't the world."

"How so?"

"In America we have laws to deal with animals like General Tsanghsien. By and large it's a safe place to live. People can follow their dreams and go about their lives in peace. But that's not the case in much of the rest of the world, where human life is held so cheap. Where women can be raped by a company of soldiers and not one of them thinks it's wrong."

"The evils men do are legion," Bolan said with a weariness born of his long struggle. "The human capacity for wickedness knows no bounds. Fortunately there are enough decent people in the world to hold it at bay. But the balance is precarious."

"Is that why you do what you do? To help stem the tide?"

"I do what I do because unless there are good men willing to stand up to those who hold human life so cheaply, then no one, anywhere, is truly safe." Bolan could tell her more. How he had seen the dark side of human nature in all its many perversions and cruelties. How he had known men who wallowed in it like pigs in a pigpen. How he had dedicated himself to resisting the tidal wave of vice and violence by any means necessary. But just then Sergeant Ergun ordered them to be quiet.

It appeared the road would climb straight forever.

Glancing back out his window, Bolan spied points of light far, far below. The lights of the village, as tiny as the stars themselves.

Tanaka coughed a little too loudly, as if to get his attention, and worked the shift.

Another bend was revealed in the glow of their headlights. Bolan tensed and lowered his left shoulder as the Jeep gained speed. It was doing forty-five when Tanaka sped into the inside of the curve and hurtled out the other side as if flung by a slingshot.

Once again centrifugal force pushed them sideways, but not hard enough. Sergeant Ergun's hand didn't move. The barrel of the Beretta was still pointed at her nape.

Bolan looked at her and gave a slight shake of his head. They needed to wait until another, sharper, bend came along. But Tanaka decided not to wait. She suddenly spun the wheel to the left, sloughing the Jeep sideways.

The Executioner was nearly pitched from his seat. He saw Ergun slide five or six inches, saw his gun hand slip off the top of Tanaka's seat. Instantly he thrust outward with both legs and slammed into Ergun, his shoulder smashing against the noncom's sternum. At the same time he brought his forehead crashing down onto Ergun's face. Not once, not twice, but three times, and at the third blow Ergun's nose crunched and he roared in pain.

For a moment Bolan had the upper hand but only for a moment. Unable to use his arms, he was unable to ward off a flurry of punches Ergun rained on him, punches that battered him backward, giving the man room to point the Beretta at him.

Bolan tried to scramble to his knees, but he couldn't possibly reach the noncom before Ergun fired.

Both of them were taken off guard when the Jeep lurched to an abrupt stop. Ergun was thrown against the back of the seat. His shot went wild. Bolan wound up half on the floor, unable to rise.

Again the Chinese pointed the Beretta. His nose had been mashed flat and blood smeared his mouth and chin. Rumbling deep in his chest, like a mad dog about to pounce, he began to curl his finger around the trigger.

From where Bolan lay, he couldn't see Tanaka. But he heard her say something that caused Ergun to glance at her, and he saw her hand cleave the air like a sword. Her fingers as rigid as nails, she slashed Ergun across the throat. There was another, muted crunch.

The sergeant jerked back, scarlet froth gushing from his lips. Wheezing and gasping, he clutched at his throat. His face clouded, darkening to a deep purple, and the tip of his tongue protruded from his mouth. He started to flop about, then stopped, gripped the Beretta with both hands, and swung it toward Tanaka. His arms were shaking as if he were throwing a fit, but he was determined to kill her before he died.

Bolan twisted and arced his right leg up and around. His heel caught Ergun under the chin, smashing him against the seat, just as the Beretta belched. The slug intended for Tanaka spanged into the roof. Ergun slumped, but Bolan kicked him two more times for good measure.

Broken teeth and red spittle dribbled over the soldier's chin as he sank onto his side and was still.

"Are you all right?" she asked anxiously, grabbing Bolan by the front of his shirt and pulling him high enough to sit.

"Just fine. That was quick thinking on your part." Bolan turned his bound wrists toward her. "Untie me. We have a lot to do."

"I was scared to death. I thought that shot hit you," she said, gently stroking his cheek. Tears moistened her eyes, and she trembled.

Until that moment Bolan hadn't fully appreciated how deeply she cared. She loved him, genuinely loved him, and it pierced him to his core. He had tended to think of her affection as no more than the misguided caring of a woman too young to know what true love was, but now he realized he had been wrong. She cared for him with every fiber of her being. Small wonder, then, she had been so upset at how aloof he was after they made love. But he thought he was doing her a favor by refusing to become more involved. It could never work out, not in a million years. He would never give up the War Everlasting, and she could never be happy with a man who was never there for her.

She found Ergun's penknife, opened it and sliced at

the cloth strips. "Strange," she said softly, glancing at the noncom.

"What is?"

"Remember how violence always bothers me? It didn't this time. I actually liked killing him. He deserved it. Him and all his kind."

The strips fell from Bolan's forearms, and he rubbed his sore wrists. "Be careful you don't get carried away. Liking to kill for killing's sake lowers us to the same level as them."

He gripped the limp form of Sergeant Ergun by the arm. Sliding out, he hauled the noncom to the edge of the road, to the brink of a cliff hundreds of feet high. He squatted and went through the dead man's pockets. They contained a thin billfold with money and Ergun's military ID card. That was it.

A hard push sent the soldier tumbling over the edge. Bolan rose and watched as the body careened off the cliff on its way to the bottom.

Tanaka had switched seats and was now on the passenger side. She had rearmed herself with the Mustang and propped her M-16 between her legs.

Bolan reclaimed the Beretta, then the Desert Eagle. "We're going into a hot zone," he said, tossing her blacksuit into her lap. "No more civvies." His own blacksuit in hand, he hurriedly stripped to his underwear.

A brisk wind pricked Bolan's skin as he once again girded for war. He checked all the pockets and pouches, insuring everything he needed was there. Sinking into the driver's seat, he inserted a fresh magazine into his M-16 and fed a grenade into the grenade launcher. He was as ready as he'd ever be.

Tanaka hopped in and threw her Chinese garments into the back seat.

Bolan worked the stick shift. The Jeep gained speed slowly, but soon they were rolling along twice as fast as before, wending ever higher into the remote mountains.

An hour went by. Two hours. Out of the blue Tanaka asked, "Do you think Mr. Brognola would let me do what you do?"

"Don't even think it," Bolan said. "I wouldn't wish my life on anyone."

"But there must be others like you. Men and women who work for the government in the same capacity?"

Bolan thought of Phoenix Force and Able Team. "A few," he acknowledged. "But you're better off settling down in the suburbs somewhere with a doting husband and couple of kids."

"How about a dog, a cat and a goldfish while I'm at it?" Tanaka dripped sarcasm. "Did you ever stop to think that maybe I want something different? That maybe married life isn't for me?"

Bolan would be the first to admit it was her decision, but it wasn't the kind a person made on the spur of the moment. "I'm just suggesting you might want to give it a lot of thought."

Over the course of the next forty-five minutes, fatigue continually nipped at Bolan, but he resisted. Tanaka tried to find a station on the radio, with no luck. All that came over the speaker was static. They were too deep in the mountains, cut off from civilization and all of its trappings.

Then the Jeep whipped around a curve, and high above them lights appeared. Bolan thought they were vehicles at first, but as the minutes passed and the lights stayed in the same place, it became obvious they weren't. The smart thing for him to do was kill the Jeep's headlights, but trying to navigate the road's treacherous twists and turns in the black of night was certain suicide.

Tanaka had spotted them, too. "Lanterns, you think?"

"Remember that pass the sergeant mentioned?" Bolan said. "My guess is an outpost manned by some of General Tsanghsien's troops."

"They must have seen us by now," she said. "There's no way we can take them by surprise."

"Where there's a will, there's a way," Bolan quoted the old cliché. "Put your map away and strap on your fanny pack. We're about to hoof it." Grabbing his large black pouch from off the rear seat, he draped it over his left shoulder. He had enough C-4 left to rig three charges, and something told him he would need all three before they were done.

The steepest grade yet rose ahead of them, and the Jeep's transmission protested the abuse. In a short while the lights above came into sharp focus some two hundred yards off. They were spotlights. Two were mounted on guard towers on either side of the road. Two more were on buildings bordering the road. Several vehicles were parked close by, and a dozen uniformed figures were in evidence.

"We'll never be able to fight our way through that many," Tanaka stated.

"We won't try." Bolan brought the Jeep to a halt with its headlights angled to the right, and turned off the engine. Setting the emergency brake, he stepped out but left the door open and the headlights on.

Tanaka quickly joined him. "Mind if I ask what you have up your sleeve this time?"

"It's called divide and conquer," Bolan answered. Placing his hand on the horn, he pressed it three times. The clarion blare echoed off the stony heights, drawing the soldiers to the middle of the road, where they stood and stared, trying to figure out what was going on.

"Stick with me," Bolan said. She glued herself to his heels as he ran to the left side of the road, then sprinted directly toward the pass.

One of the soldiers began gesturing and shouting at the others. An officer, no doubt, and half the men rushed to a truck and piled in, two in the cab, the rest in a canvas-topped bed. It wheeled from the parking area and came speeding down the mountain toward the Jeep.

"Down!" Bolan ordered, flinging himself behind a boulder. Tanaka landed beside him seconds before the truck's headlights splashed over them. He peered out, waiting for the truck to go by. The moment it did, he was up and running toward the pass again. When next he looked back, the truck had braked at an angle and the soldiers had jumped out and were approaching the Jeep with their weapons poised for action. When they saw no one was inside, they spread out, searching. He ran on, until he was forty yards from the guard towers.

Tanaka was breathing heavily but she had kept up. "What now?" she whispered.

"We introduce ourselves," Bolan said, raising the M-16 to his shoulder.

CHAPTER SIXTEEN

The officer was pacing back and forth. Six soldiers at attention behind him were awaiting orders. In the guard towers were two more troopers manning Type 67 heavy machine guns.

The Executioner stalked closer, using the shadows and random boulders to their best advantage. When he was near enough, he aimed the grenade launcher at the top of the tower on his side of the road, and let fly. A buckshot grenade looped into the guard box, landing with a thud. One of the soldiers saw it and screamed a warning. Both men tried to scramble down the ladder, but the grenade went off before they took two steps. What was left of their ruptured bodies rained to the ground with the other debris.

The officer and the half-dozen men with him did what anyone else would have done—they spun toward the tower.

That gave Bolan the few seconds he needed to feed another grenade into the launcher and trigger it. This one struck the ground dead center between the officer and the enlisted men. They whirled to scatter, but just like their buddies in the tower they were caught in the blast radius. Those not slain instantly were left in limp shreds.

The two Chinese in the tower on the other side of the road were galvanized into action. They didn't know exactly where Bolan was but they had a fair idea, and now they brought their machine gun to bear. Thanks to a cyclic rate of over six hundred rounds a minute, the Type 67 spewed lead hot and furious.

Bolan sprang toward a large boulder and flattened just as rounds thudded into the earth on both sides of it and whined off the top. He checked on Tanaka and saw she had also gained cover in time.

There was a lot of shouting by the Jeep. The soldiers were piling back into the truck to rush to the aid of those at the pass.

Delving into his mesh pouch, Bolan selected an armor-piercing antipersonnel grenade. He loaded it, then raised the sight leaf. The elevation scale consisted of five lines spaced equally apart, with the index line on the left. Adjusting it one increment moved the impact point of the grenade approximately thirty feet at that range.

Bolan fired just as the truck completed a U-turn and was gaining speed. The grenade was right on target. It smashed through the windshield into the cab, and the next moment the front end lifted off the ground as a blinding flash seared the night. Out of control, engulfed in flames, the vehicle skidded to the right, toward the precipice. Shrieks and wails from the men in the back echoed eerily as the truck sailed over the rim. The crump of impact was a long time coming.

The men in the second guard tower had momentarily stopped firing, overcome with horror at the fate of their friends. But now they resumed spraying lead with a vengeance, chewing up the ground for yards around Bolan and Tanaka. Sentiment had made them reckless, one of the worst mistakes anyone could make in combat. They fired and fired until the machine gun clicked dry, then bent to feed more ammo in.

Rising, Bolan loaded another grenade on the run. He crossed the road, angling the M-16 upward. One of the soldiers spotted him and pointed. They had reloaded the machine gun and now swung the barrel toward him. But he fired first, the explosion reducing the box to scrap metal and the soldiers to bits and pieces of flesh and gore.

Silence descended. Two of the spotlights had been knocked out, leaving much of the pass in darkness.

Tanaka ran to the Executioner's side and gazed around her in astonishment. "Dear God in heaven," she said in awe. "They didn't stand a prayer."

A door to one of the buildings flew open, and out barreled several more soldiers in various stages of dress. They had been asleep, and in their befuddled state they barely got off a round before the warrior cut them in half with several short, controlled bursts.

"Get the Jeep," Bolan commanded. As the woman dashed off, he ran to the doorway and peeked in. Rows of empty bunks took up most of the space, some neatly made, others rumpled and in disarray. No more soldiers were inside.

Bolan moved to the second building, a small office. It held nothing of interest except a map on the west wall, an old, yellowed hand-drawn map of what had to be Tsanghsien Province. Removing the tacks that held it in place, he rolled it up and exited.

Two more vehicles were close by, both trucks. Both had keys in the ignition, but Bolan didn't intend to use either. They were too slow, too ponderous. He was only interested in how much gas they had, roughly half a tank in each.

Hoping to siphon some into the Jeep, Bolan hastened to the back of the first truck. He needed a hose or a siphon kit but he found something much better—two spare gas cans, full to the brim. Shouldering the M-16, he clutched a can in each hand and walked to the road just as Tanaka braked to a halt in front of him.

"Need a lift, sailor?"

"I need you to see if there are any gas cans in the second truck," Bolan said. "If there are, pour some in both cabs and inside the buildings, then set them on fire."

"Won't the flames be seen for miles?"

"That's the general idea," Bolan answered. More soldiers would be sent to investigate, and the more that came, the fewer he had to deal with on his run to the fortress. Uncapping a can, he filled the Jeep's tank, then placed both spare containers on the floor behind the front passenger seat.

It took another minute for Tanaka to splash enough gas in the barracks. Backing out, she lit a lighter and touched it to a puddle on the floor. Flames whooshed and spread in a crackling sheet. She sped to the office, then to the trucks, setting each ablaze in turn.

She climbed into the Jeep, and the tires crunched on the asphalt as Bolan stomped on the gas. The pass was another fifty yards beyond, a natural gap in a rock wall, the opening wide enough for two lanes of traffic. Bolan looked back as they came to the summit. Flames were shooting skyward dozens of feet into the air and spreading rapidly.

Bolan drove at a dangerous pace, taking curves so sharply his companion had to grip the dashboard to keep from being slammed against her door. When they came to a straight stretch, she switched on her flashlight and unrolled the map to study it.

"If this thing is accurate, there are three villages between Tsanghsien Pass and the fortress, which is called the Heart of Tsanghsien and is located on the north shore of Tsanghsien Lake." She tapped a spot marked with a conspicuous dot. "On the south shore is another village or town. It's hard to tell how big it is since whoever made this map neglected to note its size."

"Are there other military installations we need to worry about?"

"None are shown. But this is an old map. At a guess, I'd say it was sketched maybe seventy or eighty years ago. And nothing has been added since."

Bolan was now in the dark in more ways than one. There might be more outposts somewhere ahead, or an entire base, and he wouldn't know it until he was right on top of them.

"Wait a minute. Here's something." Tanaka bent until her nose nearly touched the paper. "Someone scribbled a few lines at the bottom. Distances between various points. The lake is 258 miles from the east pass, 493 from the west pass." She straightened. "From the look of things, the entire province is surrounded by mountains that are miles high. The two passes are the only way in or out."

Bolan glanced to the south at the ring of towering peaks. The general's homeland was an ideal stronghold. With a few hundred men and the right armament, the general could hold out indefinitely if the Chinese government ever tried to take him into custody.

"We might end up trapped," Tanaka commented.

"Think positive," Bolan said.

"Okay. Let me rephrase it. We could end up being hunted down by a couple of battalions of fanatics led by a madman intent on conquering the world, with no means of contacting the outside world for help."

"You call that positive?"

HE WAS HOME.

A sense of deep inner contentment came over General Soong Tsanghsien whenever he returned to the fortress that had been his family's ancestral home for more generations than most countries on Earth had existed. The Heart of Tsanghsien was literally that, the heart and soul of the ancient and venerable Tsanghsien line.

Now, buffeted by stiff winds as he stood on the battlements hundreds of feet above Tsanghsien Lake, General Tsanghsien gazed out over his domain and thought of his many illustrious forebears, warriors of renown, just as he was.

In 1600 B.C. the first Tsanghsien warlord had carved out a minor empire within China herself. It was later absorbed into the Shang Dynasty, in which the warlord's heirs held prominent posts.

In 210 B.C. another Tsanghsien warlord rose to the rank of supreme military commander and led the army on several successful campaigns against barbarian invaders.

During the late 1200s, when Mongol hordes overran China, the only province to withstand them was Tsanghsien Province. For months the Mongols tried to force the two passes but were unable to use their cavalry or their archers effectively. Finally Kublai Khan agreed to allow Tsanghsien Province autonomy in exchange for a pledge of loyalty to the Mongols as long as they ruled the country.

Later, when the Manchus rose to power, a special unit from Tsanghsien served as imperial guardsmen and was instrumental in putting down several minor rebellions. By then the name Tsanghsien had become synonymous with "warrior." Over subsequent generations many of her sons were awarded high positions in all branches of the military.

World War II brought severe setbacks. The Tsanghsiens fiercely resisted the Japanese. They were at the forefront of China's efforts to repulse the invaders, but many lost their lives. By 1945 only three descendants of the original warlord were left, and of those, one left no heirs and another perished in a freak automobile accident.

That left only Soong's grandfather, whose only son, Soong's father, was born and raised in their home province and later went to Peking, where he rose to the rank of colonel. For a Tsanghsien, so paltry an accomplishment was a cause for shame. Soong himself held little respect for the man who sired him, and had only visited his father's grave once in the fifteen years since his father died.

Now General Tsanghsien was the last of his line. The last of the warlords. He had no wife, no children. He had been too busy fostering his career. But once things settled down, once he had broken the backs of the vile capitalists and elevated China to her rightful place in the hierarchy of nations, he would see to fathering an heir to carry on the Tsanghsien name after he was gone.

Boots scraped behind him, but the general didn't turn. Only one person was permitted to interrupt his meditation. "Yes, Colonel Chen? I trust it is important."

"Sir, you asked to be advised as soon as we heard from the Black Tiger. We have just received radio confirmation. He will arrive by dawn."

"Excellent. You will take immediate possession of the warheads. Escort them and Comrade Pechora to the missile center. He is to begin work immediately. His crew has twenty-four hours to convert the PPS-1s. Not a minute more."

When the colonel didn't leave right away, the general knew there was more news. "What else?"

"Sir, we have a report from Lieutenant Jinzhou at the garrison at Subei. A sentry roused him from bed to report the pass was glowing. Lieutenant Jinzhou thinks it is on fire."

"Have you contacted Captain Xiangfen at the pass itself?"

"We've tried, sir, but he doesn't answer. I took the liberty of instructing Lieutenant Jinzhou to take his men and see what happened."

"He will find Captain Xiangfen and all his men dead, and the buildings burned to the ground," the general stated.

"The American again, sir?"

"Who else? He has followed me halfway across China, overcoming every obstacle." The general smiled. "Magnificent! We must arrange a suitable reception for my worthy adversary. You will permit him to enter the fortress before capturing him."

"Forgive me, sir, but is that wise? Wherever this American goes, he leaves destruction and death. I can secret fifty men outside the tunnel, and when he shows up, we will riddle him with bullets before he can take one step from his vehicle.''

"Slay him from ambush? I should say not. We have nothing to fear. Did not the great Sun Tzu say, 'He who waits for his enemy to come to him is at ease?' And again, 'Leaders versed in war bring their enemies to the field of battle and are not lured there by them.' '' Tsanghsien paused. "I look forward to meeting this American, Colonel. The man who deprives me of the honor will live to regret it.''

"In that case, sir, I will have the guards withdraw so he can enter unmolested.''

The general wheeled. "There are times, Colonel Chen, when you worry me. You will do no such thing. If you pull the guards, the American will know it is a trap.''

"But some of them might lose their lives if I don't, sir.''

"To catch a mouse, one must expect to lose a little cheese," the general responded. "It is auspicious, is it not, that the warheads and the American will both arrive on the same day?'' He rubbed his hands together in eager anticipation. "I can hardly wait.''

Washington, D.C.

THE JUSTICE BUILDING was empty except for Hal Brognola and a few agents working late. He had left his door open, and when he heard the click of high heels in the reception area he closed the file he had been reading and rose to greet his guest.

Abigail Harkness's spindly frame was buried in the folds of a knee-length fur coat. Her dyed hair had been done up in a bun, and she looked fifteen years younger than she actually was. "I was about to go out on a night on the town with my husband when I received your message," she said without ceremony. "I trust it's as important as you made it sound."

Brognola gestured at a chair. "I assure you it won't be a waste of your time."

Harkness perched on the edge of the seat, her leather purse in her lap. Her expression was haughty, almost challenging. "I'm listening."

Rather than confront her directly, Brognola tried a roundabout approach. "You must like your job as a deputy director of communications at the White House."

"It has its perks," Harkness said, smiling, but the smile didn't reach her eyes. "I've met every president in the past twenty years. And I enjoy tapping into the pulse of the world as part of the most sophisticated communications network on the planet."

Brognola didn't mention that the setup at Stony Man Farm was every bit as sophisticated, if not more so. "Yes, it must be nice to have access to all that classified information. And to be able to send encrypted messages to anywhere in the world at a moment's notice."

"Your pleasantries have a point, I suppose?" Harkness said.

"Just that a person in your position could get word of an impending weapons test to anyone, anywhere, with little risk of being caught."

Her pinched features became more so. "There's a saying, Mr. Brognola, that's older than I am. Quit beating around the bush."

"Very well, Abigail. I believe you're a traitor to the

United States government. I believe you sold classified intel to a buyer in China.''

Harkness accepted the accusation coolly. ''And you base this ridiculous assumption on what, exactly?''

Brognola was impressed by her calm bearing. She was either innocent, or she was as arrogant as they came. ''For starters, we've uncovered part of a message sent from the White House through a series of proxy servers to a Chinese army post outside Beijing three days before the helicopter attack on the USS *Hampton*. The message contained the latitude and longitude of where the ship would be when the missiles were launched.''

''Oh, my,'' Harkness said in mock fear, putting a hand to her cheek. ''Did it have my signature on it?''

''Granted, any one of over eighty people could have sent it,'' Brognola admitted, ''but there's more.''

''I can't wait.''

''The message was sent in Chinese. And I've learned that before you went to work at the White House, you specialized in Chinese-U.S. relations. That you are, in fact, quite fluent in the language.''

''So now it's a crime to be bilingual?'' Harkness rebutted, and grinned. ''Yes, I speak Chinese like a native. But really, Mr. Brognola. All this is circumstantial at best. I expected better of a man of your sterling reputation.''

''Then how about this. A clerk at the naval yard distinctly remembers someone answering your description waltzed into his office waving a White House ID and demanding to see the design schematics on the *Hampton*. Claimed it was a matter of national security.''

''Oh, my. Now you have me.'' Harkness's grin widened. "Did the clerk happen to get any of this on video? Or is all you have to go on a vague description? And did he actually see the woman take schematics from his office?"

Brognola had hoped to loosen her tongue by presenting enough incriminating information, but she had deftly thrown it back in his face and pointed out the legal flaws in his case, to boot. "No on both counts. The time frame fits, though. It happened weeks ago, about the time Admiral Thomas chose the *Hampton* to be the test vessel and sent a message to the White House to that effect."

"So now you hope to convict me based on a time frame?" Harkness rose. "What a monumental waste of my time. If you really had something concrete, you wouldn't sit there making such silly accusations. You'd have me arrested." Leaning on his desk, she looked him in the eyes. "And just so there is no misunderstanding, I've never sold a single secret to the Chinese or anyone else."

"What, you gave away the intel?" It was Brognola's turn to laugh. Her sincerity was undeniable, but he was positive she was the one he was after. "You know you're guilty, and I know you're guilty, and before I'm through I'll prove it."

"Ah. But guilty of what?" Harkness said, and bundled herself into her fur. "Now if you'll excuse me, my dunderhead of a husband is waiting in our limo out front. We have a dinner date with the secretary of transportation and his wife." She walked briskly to the doorway.

"Mrs. Harkness?" Brognola said.

"Call me Abigail, please," she said, stopping in the

doorway. "What is it now? Am I wearing a sign on my backs that says I'm A Spy. Kick Me?"

"Over the course of my career, I've dealt with traitors, drug lords, gunrunners, Mafia Dons and crazed loons of every kind. And do you know what?"

"Not one of them was as clever as they thought they were." Harkness took the words right out of his mouth.

"Something like that, yes."

She gave a little wave. "Toodles, Hal." She took another step, then glanced back. "I can call you Hal, can't I, now that we're on a first-name basis?"

"It's only a matter of time."

"Don't take forever, Hal. I'm sixty-four. Based on an average life expectancy, I'll be lucky to live another decade." Blowing him a kiss, Harkness departed.

Brognola stared after her. He considered having her brought back and grilled but decided it would be a waste of time. She'd never crack. Not a tough old bird like her. He reviewed their conversation, marveling at how composed she had been. How she had refuted all his evidence. How she had bragged about being fluent in Chinese. "Yes, I speak Chinese like a native." Those had been her exact words.

His brow puckering, Brognola reached for the telephone. The only way someone spoke a foreign language like a native was if that person had lived in the country where the language was used. Punching a certain number, he mentally crossed his fingers.

China

BELASKO CARED for her.

Kerri Tanaka had realized it for certain when she was taken prisoner by Sergeant Ergun. He had surren-

dered to spare her life. He had been willing to give his
own life to save hers. What greater proof did she need?

She could see affection in those piercing blue eyes
of his when he looked at her sometimes. Her fondest
desire had come true, and her heart was near to bursting
from happiness.

Her knight in skinsuit armor was also pleased at how
well she had handled herself. He had come right out
and said so. She aimed to continue impressing him, to
prove she was worthy of being his partner not just on
one mission, but on many others in the future. She
wanted to see him again and would do whatever it took
to persuade him to pay another visit.

One way, Tanaka thought, was to show she was
more like him than he imagined. He still hadn't revealed his exact status with the government, or exactly
how he was connected to Hal Brognola. But she had
gleaned enough to guess he wasn't an ordinary federal
agent. In her opinion he was what the French called a
"cleaner," someone who went around cleaning up
messes others made—by whatever means necessary. If
she could show she had what it took to do the job he
did, he might be more likely to want to get to know
her better.

Another positive note was that now they had established she wasn't looking to marry and settle down, he
seemed to be much more at ease. He actually smiled
now and then, and he hadn't objected a while ago when
she reached over and stroked his hand.

All things considered, she told herself, things were
looking up. She glanced at him again, at his rugged,
chiseled features and his eyes. Oh, those eyes. There
was something about them. When he looked at her, she
had the feeling he was looking right through her. He

had a presence about him unlike any man she'd ever met. It did things to her, stirred her deep inside.

Tanaka wasn't about to tell him she had every intention of becoming a permanent fixture in his life. How, she couldn't say. They would go their separate ways when the mission was over, but that wouldn't be the end of it. She would find a way to be with him again, even if it meant transferring back to the States and ingratiating herself with Mr. Brognola.

Throughout her whole life, Kerri Tanaka had been able to get pretty much anything she wanted. Part of it had to do with the discipline her father instilled in her. But mainly she succeeded because she refused to accept failure. When she set her mind on something, she went after it with every particle of her being.

And she had set her mind on Belasko.

They were flying down the winding road at a breathless rate. Dawn was still a couple of hours off. Tanaka hadn't slept since the previous afternoon, but she wasn't all that tired. Excitement had a lot to do with it. She practically tingled at the thought of their impending clash with General Tsanghsien. The odds seemed so hopeless it would be a miracle if either of them got out alive.

She told herself she had to have confidence in Belasko. Miracles were his stock in trade. If anyone could get them out alive, it was him.

"Look for a spot to pull off the road," he abruptly announced.

"Is something wrong?" she asked.

He pointed at approaching headlights a mile below. "Reinforcements are on their way."

CHAPTER SEVENTEEN

The Executioner preferred to avoid General Tsanghsien's underlings except when he was left with no option. He had a limited supply of ammo and explosives, and it wouldn't do to squander them before he reached the fortress. So when he spotted the row of headlights, his first thought was to find cover.

The terrain had changed. Gone were the sheer cliffs and rocky ravines. Arid, almost desertlike land stretched into the darkness, littered by countless boulders of all shapes and sizes. So many boulders lined the road that finding an opening wide enough for the Jeep posed a problem until Kerri Tanaka jabbed a finger and exclaimed, "There!"

Killing their headlights, Bolan braked and crawled between boulders as big as log cabins. Pulling around the one on the left, he switched off the ignition and got out. Tanaka shadowed him as he moved partway back around it and hunkered at the base.

They could hear the trucks growling uphill like so many angry beasts. Three of them, and each, the Executioner suspected, was packed with soldiers. Since there hadn't been time for troops to be sent all the way from the fortress, he speculated there had to be a garrison somewhere between the pass and the lake. The nearest village, possibly.

"Do we let them go by?" Tanaka asked.

"You're learning," Bolan said.

"I have a good teacher."

Bolan had noticed her gaze adoringly at him several times in the past few hours, and now she did it again. He narrowed his gaze. She was letting her affection distract her, a potentially fatal mistake. "Are you up for this?" he asked.

She blinked. "Why wouldn't I be? I'm looking forward to showing you what I'm capable of."

"All I want is for you to come out of this alive," Bolan said. "To do that you need to always be on your toes."

"I won't let you down. I promise."

The trucks were grinding gears to cope with the steep grade. Bolan inched forward, his left hand on the grenade launcher. The men in the cab of the lead truck were bound to have seen the Jeep's headlights, and they would be wondering where it had gone. If they stopped to hunt for it, a few well-placed grenades would nullify the threat. But he only had eight left and might need them later on.

As Bolan lay there, waiting, he thought about the firefight at the pass. Tanaka seemed to think it had been a great feat to fight their way through, but there hadn't been all that many soldiers. Which had struck him as peculiar.

Military logic dictated General Tsanghsien should do all in his power to safeguard the two entry points into Tsanghsien Province. By Sergeant Ergun's own admission, the general knew a "tall American" was after the missiles, and the general had left Ergun and the others at the village to trail him when he showed up.

It made no sense, though, for the general to order the sergeant not to harm him. Why was Tsanghsien going to such extraordinary lengths to make it easy for him to reach the fortress? He was responsible for the destruction of the depot at Hakka Island. He was to blame for the deaths of scores of loyal soldiers. By rights the general should want him dead.

Bright beams suddenly washed over the asphalt. Bolan crabbed backward and tucked the M-16 to his side seconds before the first truck rumbled into view, lumbering by like an elephant. The driver was staring off up the road and never slowed. The same with the driver of the next, and the third.

Rising, Bolan lost no time getting into the Jeep and carefully backing out. He left the lights off until they had gone several hundred yards and then brought the speedometer to seventy to make up for lost time.

The land grew level. Two miles from the bottom of the range was a small village called Subei. They reached it just at the break of dawn, a sleepy, dusty collection of huts and hovels. Only a few people were abroad, tending goats and other livestock kept in rickety pens. West of the village were several olive-drab buildings surrounded by a fence. The gate was closed and padlocked, and there wasn't a sign of life anywhere.

"Now we know where those trucks came from," Bolan commented.

Vegetation was sparse, mainly scrub trees and dry grass. The earth had a reddish hue, as if dyed in blood, and reddish dust was constantly whipped by the wind. Dust devils were a frequent sight.

Bolan saw Tanaka yawn and suggested she get some sleep.

"You need it more than I do," she said. "Why don't I take the wheel and wake you in a couple of hours?"

Bolan declined. Two hours wouldn't make much of a difference. He was accustomed to going lengthy spells without rest. She wasn't.

Tanaka leaned her temple against her door and closed her eyes. "All right. I'll try. But I'm telling you now, I won't be able to doze off. I'm too keyed up."

Five minutes later she was dead to the world. Bolan watched her lips flutter with every breath, and grinned. She was a feisty one but she had a lot to learn. Her confidence was more than offset by her naïveté. Given a couple of years, she might mature into a first-rate operative, provided she lived that long.

The monotonous scenery and the drone of the engine combined to leaden Bolan's eyelids. He had to struggle to stay awake. All he needed to do was hold out another four hours. By noon they'd reach the vicinity of Tsanghsien's lair, and since a frontal assault in broad daylight was out of the question, he planned to sleep until sunset, then penetrate the fortress. They still had twenty-four hours or so until the general launched the PPS-1s. It wasn't a lot, but Bolan felt they could spare a few hours for him to recharge his batteries for the final conflict.

Figures appeared ahead at the side of the road. The Executioner tensed, but they were only a middle-aged man and woman in baggy hillmen garb leading a string of goats toward Subei. They smiled, as friendly as country folk everywhere.

The next village was Baima, a larger version of Subei—more huts, more livestock and more people.

Rustic, hardy souls who barely eked a living from the land but were content with their Spartan lot in life. The road skirted Baima on the north, and a group of children saw fit to scamper over to it and wave and laugh, as if the Jeep going by were the greatest thing that had happened to them all day.

To Bolan, it was ironic. The same land that produced such simple people of the earth had also produced a madman like Soong Tsanghsien.

Traffic was nonexistent. Between Subei and the third village, Tohom, Bolan didn't meet up with a single car or truck, not even a military vehicle. It, too, was peculiar. Whether their absence was normal, or whether the general had banned traffic to permit him to reach the fortress unmolested, was impossible to say.

Eventually the road forked. One branch bore to the south end of a huge lake glistening in the distance, toward a modern town complete with four- and five-story buildings and a fair amount of visible traffic. The other fork angled to the north end of the lake, toward an enormous bluff, or mesa. Atop it was the Heart of Tsanghsien, a giant fortress formidable even from that distance.

A sedan appeared, coming from the direction of the city. Bolan stayed where he was, waiting to see what would happen. A man and woman in modern civilian clothes went by without a glance, heading east.

As Bolan turned right, Tanaka shifted, sat up and rubbed her eyes in confusion. "Where are we? How long was I out?" She squinted at the sun. "It's pretty near noon! Why did you let me sleep so long?"

"You needed the rest," Bolan said. The other reason was so she would be able to stay awake when it was his turn to nap.

"It's not fair to you," Tanaka grumbled. She shook herself and started to yawn, but her mouth froze half open as she set eyes on the bluff. "Tsanghsien Lake! And the general's fortress! We're almost there."

"Another twenty miles would be my guess," Bolan said.

She consulted the map. "Twenty-three, to be exact. Half an hour, forty minutes, tops." She didn't exactly sound elated.

"We're not going in until dark," Bolan stated, putting her anxiety to rest. "I need some sleep, too, or I'll be next to worthless."

The landscape had undergone a dramatic change. More and more vegetation had sprouted the closer they drew to the lake. Grassland initially, then low hills lush with thickets and tall brush, and now mile after mile of dense woodland bordering Lake Tsanghsien itself.

There were also more people. Out in the grassland Bolan had occasionally seen shepherds grazing flocks. The hills had been dotted by scattered homesteads overrun by livestock. Now modern homes were the rule, dwellings akin to those in China's most modern cities. The people who owned them apparently worked in the town at the south end of the lake, and commuted.

"Look at all those tall buildings!" Tanaka exclaimed as they climbed a hill. She had shifted in her seat and was gazing out the back window. "It must be the province's leading urban center."

Bolan had been looking for sign of a military installation. Unless the troops who manned the fortress were billeted there, the general had to have a base nearby for logistical support. There was no mention of a base on the map, but it was old and had never been updated. Which made him wonder why it had been

hanging in the HQ at the east pass until he realized the
general might not want to display a map that revealed
crucial intel. He hadn't thought to search the office for
a newer version.

Four miles farther on, the road curved to the northwest. On the right the trees thinned, and Bolan pulled
off and threaded through them for a good hundred
yards. Under the canopy of a leafy giant, he braked and
killed the engine. "We'll stay here until sunset."
Stiffly climbing out, he stretched.

Sparkling shafts of sunlight filtered through the
branches. In nearby trees birds warbled merrily.

Smiling, Tanaka commented, "What a romantic setting."

"Don't even think it," Bolan said. Striding to a
grassy parcel, he sank onto his back, placed the M-16
within quick reach and laced his fingers behind his
head.

Tanaka strolled over, an undeniable gleam in her
eyes. "A half hour is all I'm asking. It will help you
sleep like a baby."

"You're shameless," Bolan said, not entirely in jest.
"But the answer is still no." He had given in to her
once, but at the time they hadn't been in any immediate
danger. This was different. They were deep in enemy
territory, and in seven or eight hours would be involved
in the firefight of their lives.

"Where you're concerned, I guess I am. It's only
because I know each minute I spend with you is precious. You'll be leaving for the States as soon as we
wrap this up. Who knows when I'll see you again?"

"Kerri…" Bolan warned. Closing his eyes, he
willed himself to relax.

"We'll play this by the book, then. But don't think

I'm discouraged. Quite the opposite. In time you'll see I'm as persistent as they come."

Bolan offered no reply, but he wasn't so sure he liked the sound of that. She was so young, so naive and much too pushy. She had yet to learn affection between two people should be nurtured with great care. The women he had loved most in his life were those he had slowly grown to care for over a period of time.

Tanaka sank to the ground close to him. "Get your beauty sleep, then. I'll keep watch. If I see or hear anything, I'll wake you right away."

"Be sure you do," Bolan said.

The Executioner drifted to sleep and dreamed he was on a fog-shrouded hill, armed with an M-60. From out of the fog floated shuffling noises broken by bestial snarls and hisses. A pale shape in tattered clothes hove out of the gloom, shambling on stick legs, its fingers clawed, thin lips drawn back over pointed teeth. Behind it was another, and another. Zombies, a legion of them, stalking up the hill toward him.

In his dream Bolan opened fire, mowing the front ranks down. But for every creature he slew, two more took its place. He fired and fired, expending thousands of rounds of ammo, and still the undead snuffled toward him, scrambling over the piled heaps of their dead.

The wall of bodies grew until it was fifteen feet high, yet wave after wave crested the top. Bolan fought with maniacal energy but he couldn't stop them. Cold iron hands fell on his shoulders, on his arms. He started to fight them tooth and nail, and suddenly he was awake, caked with sweat, Tanaka's hand on his shoulder.

"Are you okay? You were tossing and turning something fierce."

Rubbing his eyes, Bolan sat up. The sun was starting to sink below the western horizon. He had slept the afternoon away, but it felt as if he'd only dozed off a couple of minutes ago. "I'm fine," he answered, clearing his head with a shake.

Bolan wasn't one of those people who looked for deep meaning in every dream and nightmare. He erased them from his memory as soon as he awakened, and through force of will never thought about them again. To do otherwise was to court trouble, as many a veteran had learned to his profound regret.

Rising, Bolan moved out from under the tree. Far to the north the top of the bluff was bathed in russet hues. The ancient fortress, with its massive stone walls and slanted, many-tiered roofs, was silhouetted against a cloudless sky.

"Nothing much happened while you were out," his companion reported. "A few cars and trucks went by out on the road. Once I thought I heard someone yelling off to the southwest. But it was so far off I couldn't make out what they were saying."

"Time to get ready," Bolan said. From a pocket in his webbing, he removed a packet of combat cosmetics and proceeded to smear some on his cheeks, forehead and chin. He passed it to Tanaka, who pulled out a compact and flipped it open so she could view her handiwork in the mirror.

"Our primary objective are the PPS-1s," Bolan reiterated as she worked. "We have to destroy them by any means possible. Once that's done, my secondary goal is to locate and eliminate General Soong Tsangh-sien."

"Don't you mean 'our' secondary goal?"

"We're not under specific orders to terminate him,"

Bolan reminded her. "As soon as the missiles are disposed of, I'd like for you to make yourself scarce. I can handle it from then on."

"You want me to bail out on you?" Tanaka shook her head.

"The decision to go after the general is mine and mine alone. He's too great a threat to the security of the United States to be allowed to live."

"I couldn't agree more, which is why I'm tagging along to the finish."

Bolan tried one more time. "As a personal favor to me, let me go after the general alone."

She pretended she hadn't heard.

Right then and there, Bolan made up his mind what he was going to do, but he didn't let on. After she gave back the packet, he climbed into the Jeep. The lower third of the sun was gone, and the shadows were lengthening.

"'Into the valley of death rode the six hundred—'" Tanaka quoted as he cranked the engine over. "Oh, wait. It's just the two of us."

Looking at her then, at her earnest smile and youthful innocence, Bolan almost regretted his decision. But it wasn't enough to change his mind. He had her best interests at heart, whether she would agree or not. He drove toward the road, taking his time, needing the sun to set well before he reached fortress.

Tanaka was apprehensive, but she masked her worry with humor. "What do you suppose the State Department will tell my parents if we don't make it out alive? 'Mr. and Mrs. Tanaka, your daughter lost her life when she and the Shadow Man took it on themselves to invade China?'"

"Who?" Bolan said.

"Oh. Sorry. That's my pet nickname for you. The Shadow Man, because you live in a world of shadows, of deceit and death."

Bolan thought it highly appropriate.

Tanaka slid her M-16 between her legs. "Knowing our government, the Feds will fib and tell my parents I choked on a rice ball."

As the Jeep neared the roadway, Bolan slowed to confirm no vehicles were approaching, then he sped up and wheeled northward.

She was talkative. "They won't fool my father, though. He has some idea of what I really do. I never told him about Mr. Brognola, but he knows I do work I can't tell him about, and that some of it is dangerous."

The road climbed to the top of another hill, and from the top Bolan had an unobstructed view of Tsanghsien Lake. Fishing boats and other craft plied its turquoise surface. The water, he saw, lapped at the very base of the high bluff on which the fortress rested. No one could reach the Heart of Tsanghsien from that side unless he or she scaled sheer cliffs hundreds of feet high.

"I wonder if the road goes clear to the top?" Tanaka was also studying the bluff. "There are bound to be plenty of guards. Maybe an electrified fence and dogs."

"I'll find a way up."

"Don't you mean 'we'?"

It wasn't long before the sun vacated the heavens and stars took its place. Dozens of artificial stars blazed in the fortress and at different points both on top of the bluff and below it.

"It's lit up like a Christmas tree," Tanaka observed.

"If we disable the power line, maybe we could sneak in right under their noses."

"They'll have generators for backup," Bolan guessed. The general was too crafty a warrior to overlook something so basic. "And if the line is cut, they'll sound an alarm."

"How do we know they're not already on alert? They know about the pass. You realize, of course, that what we're doing is crazy? It's like trying to infiltrate a hornet's nest after the hornets have been stirred up."

Or, as Bolan liked to think of it, sowing the seeds of confusion to weaken an enemy's defenses. Although General Tsanghsien was expecting him, the general didn't know when he'd strike. That alone gave him an edge.

They encountered fewer and fewer homes. Over ten miles were covered without incident, then Bolan whipped around a curve and beheld what he had known had to be close by all along. Fifteen to twenty acres were devoted to a small military base. Hemmed by a high fence, it consisted of four long barracks, an HQ, an infirmary and a motor pool. Activity was light, and only two sentries were on duty at the main gate.

Most of the troops, Bolan imagined, were up in the fortress guarding the PPS-1s. As he drew abreast of the sentries, they stopped chatting to stare. He had slid lower in his seat when he spotted them, and as he went by he looked the other way. Tanaka, though, leaned across him, her bosom brushing his face, and waved cheerily as if she and the sentries were best friends.

"What do you think you're doing?"

"We don't want them phoning ahead, do we?" Tanaka said. "In the dark I can pass for a Chinese. Maybe they'll think we have a legitimate reason to be here."

A check of the rearview mirror showed the pair hadn't budged. Bolan also saw something else. A troop transport was parked between two of the barracks, and soldiers were filing up onto it. There was every chance it was bound for the fortress, and if so, he could exploit that to his advantage. But he didn't have much time to act.

Speeding up, Bolan held to over eighty miles per hour until they were approximately two miles from the bluff. From afar it had looked to be several hundred feet high, but now it towered to the clouds, as tall as the Empire State Building, if not taller, a massive monolith of solid rock, impregnable, invincible. Atop it, like a crown atop a craggy monarch, sat the imposing fortress, every window and portal aglow.

"I hope you can sprout wings and fly," Tanaka cracked, "because I don't see any other way up there."

Bolan once again needed a place to turn off. When one materialized on the left, he spun the wheel, catching the woman off guard. She gripped her seat and glanced at him quizzically.

"We're going to hoof it the rest of the way?"

"Not quite." Bolan stopped in a starlit glade and turned off the lights but not the engine. "Get out. I have something to show you." She did as he requested, and while her back was turned he reached into the back seat and gathered up the cloth strips Ergun had used to bind their wrists. Holding the strips where she couldn't see them, he walked toward her.

"So what is it?" Tanaka asked. She had her M-16 over her shoulder and stood with her hands on her shapely hips.

In response, Bolan tackled her, bearing her to the ground so quickly she had no chance to resist. He tried not to be too rough as he grabbed her left wrist, flipped her onto her stomach, and yanked both arms behind her. To pin her down he placed a knee on her lower back. She was too bewildered to resist until she felt the strips being wrapped around her wrists, then she heaved upward, seeking to buck him off.

"No! What is this?"

Ignoring her, Bolan tied a double knot, then bound her ankles. Tanaka kicked and wriggled and tried to roll away but he was too strong. In a minute the deed was done and he slid off. "I'm sorry."

"Like hell you are!" she fumed. "You have no right! I'm under orders from Mr. Brognola!"

Bolan relieved her of her dagger and tossed it into the weeds. "I figure it will take you most of the night to free yourself. By then it will all be over, one way or another." Holding the last of the strips in both hands, he lowered it to her mouth to gag her.

"One question!" she cried, nearly in tears. "Why are you doing this? I'm entitled to know!"

Bolan bent and lightly kissed her forehead. "I don't want you hurt," he said, and applied the gag. The truth was, he honestly didn't know if he would make it out of the Heart of Tsanghsien alive.

CHAPTER EIGHTEEN

General Soong Tsanghsien was in the communications room high atop his family's ancestral fortress when the door was thrown open and in strode the man feared throughout Europe and much of Asia as the Black Tiger.

Alexi Igra Smolensk was a brute accustomed to getting his own way. From under beetling brows he glared at the general, the jagged scar on his left cheek red with anger. He wore a tailored suit that seemed out of place on his hulking frame, and when he thrust a finger at the general, his bulging muscles rippled. "What is the meaning of this outrage?" he demanded.

General Tsanghsien handed the message he had been studying to Colonel Chen and pivoted to face his irate guest. "Which specific outrage are you referring to, Alexi?" he asked in impeccable Russian. "The world is so full of them—"

"Don't bandy words with me," Smolensk declared. Behind him were six of the twenty bodyguards he had brought along, husky, nervous men in dark suits and sunglasses. "You know very well what I am talking about."

"Would it be the rest of your money?" General Tsanghsien asked.

"What else?" Alexi Smolensk exploded. A communications specialist blundered into his path, and he rudely shoved the man aside. "I have been here nearly twelve hours and I have yet to be paid."

"I thought I made it clear to you that you would be paid as soon as our transaction was completed?"

"What are you trying to pull?" Smolensk snapped. "Our deal concluded when I delivered the warheads. I have fulfilled my end of the bargain. Now you will fulfill your end, or you will not like the consequences."

"Was that a threat?" the general asked, smiling at the childishness of it. "I sincerely hope not. You have twenty men at your disposal, twenty-five if you count the crew of your aircraft and Pechora. I, on the other hand, have three hundred seasoned troops. So I ask you, which of us will least like the consequences?"

Alexi Smolensk was an ugly man. He became even uglier when enraged. But he contained his legendary temper and spit, "Now who is threatening whom? Just be warned, General. I have taken steps to insure against treachery."

"The Russian army will invade China?" the general asked facetiously.

"Scoff all you want. But as you well know, two of my cousins are my seconds in command. They have vowed to avenge me should anything go wrong."

"Avenge you how?" Tsanghsien said. "By putting out a contract on my life?" He made a show of pondering the possibility. "I suppose there would be a marginal chance of success. They can afford to hire the very best."

"Damn right they can," Smolensk said smugly. "Now, where is my money? One million for each warhead. You paid two million in advance. That leaves twenty-three million payable on delivery.''

"Not quite," the general disagreed. "Our arrangement also included the provision that your specialist, Pechora, would oversee the conversion of the PPS-1s. And as I understand it, they won't be done until late tonight.'' He paused. "*That* is when you will receive what is due you.''

Glowering, Smolensk took a step but caught himself when soldiers lining the walls gripped their SMGs. His bodyguards moved to protect him, reaching under their jackets, and for tense moments the outcome hung in the balance.

"Put yourself in my place," the general said, breaking the tension. "The warheads alone are of little use to me. They must be fitted to the missiles. I specifically requested that provision and you willingly agreed. From my perspective, our deal isn't done until your expert verifies the missiles are ready to be launched.''

"Yes, I did agree," Smolensk reluctantly conceded. "But I would at least like to see the money. In fact, I insist on it.''

Tsanghsien's thin lips pinched together. "Are you implying I have conspired to cheat you?''

"Of course not," Smolensk said, his expression hinting otherwise. "But you have kept me dangling long enough. As a common courtesy you should be willing to extend a gesture of good faith.''

"Very well. I can see it is pointless to expect you to wait until the conversion is complete.'' Turning to Colonel Chen, the general said, "Escort our guests to the banquet hall by way of the launch bay so our esteemed visitor can ask Pechora how much longer it will be before the work is finished. I will join you in the banquet hall in due course, and we will put an end to this matter."

The colonel moved toward the doorway. "If you will be so good as to follow me, sir," he said to Smolensk.

The Black Tiger scowled. He didn't like it, didn't like it one bit, but he rotated and stormed off, his bodyguards forming a living wall around him.

Tsanghsien moved to a console and stabbed a button on an intercom. "Sergeant Yatsen?"

"Sir?" the noncom's crisp response came back.

"You will take forty men to the banquet hall and deploy according to our conversation this morning. Do not do anything until I arrive."

"Understood, sir."

The general left the com center. He walked down a long corridor and up a flight of stone stairs to his personal quarters. Once inside, he went straight to a bank of video monitors on the far wall and activated them. Various rooms and hallways were displayed. He saw Yatsen quick-stepping at the head of forty soldiers, each armed with a Type 64 silenced machine gun. He also saw the colonel leading Alexi Smolensk into the gigantic bay where the PPS-1s were being prepared.

Tsanghsien had installed the monitors long ago. As Sun Tzu taught, spying was as essential to warfare as arms and ammunition. To Tsanghsien's way of thinking, that applied to a leader's own men, as well as the enemy's. He loved the feeling of godlike power it gave him to sit there for hours on end and eavesdrop. Of all his staff, only Chen knew cameras had been secretly placed throughout the fortress, concealed in the very walls.

Pechora, the technical wizard, was hard at work on

the third PPS-1. At a hail from his employer, he stepped down from the gantry.

Smolensk draped an arm across his underling and guided him out of earshot of Chen and everyone else.

Tweaking a dial, the general adjusted the gain on the omnidirectional microphone. The Black Tiger's guttural Russian blared from the speakers.

"I do not trust these stinking Chinese. Tsanghsien is up to something. How soon before the missiles are converted?"

"By two in the morning, three at the very latest," Pechora answered. "What has the general done?"

"The bastard hasn't paid me yet. He's dragging his heels. I can't believe he would try to double-cross me, but he's so egotistical he might think he can get away with it."

"What do you want me to do?" Pechora asked. "Delay the conversions?"

Smolensk's apish face contorted in displeasure. "No. That would give him even more of an excuse to hold off paying. Finish early, if you can, so we can get the hell out of here that much sooner."

"I'll try my best," the wizard said, "but it is slow going. All the instructions I give the Chinese must go through an interpreter. They are competent enough workers, but they are slow."

"They can't help it," Smolensk said. "Being slow-witted runs in their veins." He clapped Pechora on the back. "Keep at it. I will return later to see how things are going."

The general glanced at the monitor to the banquet hall. Yatsen and the forty soldiers had entered and dispersed around the immense chamber. At a command from the sergeant, the soldiers ducked behind ceiling-high tapestries that loosely covered all four walls. He pressed another button, and the camera angle changed. It showed the soldiers taking up positions where the tapestries overlapped so they would be ready to burst out at the prearranged signal.

It wasn't long afterward that Chen led Smolensk's party into the hall. The Black Tiger sat at the head of the table, his twenty bodyguards sinking into chairs on either side. Several admired the tapestries but none thought to look behind them.

"Simpletons," the general declared, and rose. Excitement welled as he made his way along several hallways. It was possible, he thought, that Alexi Smolensk would pose more of a challenge than he anticipated. When he entered the banquet hall, many of the bodyguards stiffened and grew wary, as well they should. Not that it would do them any good.

"About time," Smolensk grumbled. "But I see you didn't bring the money."

"There was no need," the general said, stopping.

"Why would that be?" Smolensk demanded.

"Because I never intended to pay you." He clapped his hands. At his signal, the forty soldiers sprang from concealment and forty silenced machined guns coughed in unison. A hailstorm of hot lead bored into the bodyguards from all directions before they could think to bring their pistols into play. Bodies sprawled over chairs, over the table, over the floor. In seconds it was over.

The only Russian left alive was Smolensk, who leaped to his feet, his mouth working in impotent fury.

"You brought this on yourself," the general said, moving toward him. "Greed blinded you to reality.

Where did you think I could get my hands on twenty-three million dollars?''

"You told me you could!'' Smolensk bellowed. "And you had no problem acquiring the two million you paid me in advance!''

"No problem?'' General Tsanghsien laughed. "I'm a Communist, not a capitalist. If you knew all the trouble I had to go to, the deals I had to strike—'' He halted several strides from his incensed guest.

"The advance money was just to lure me here?'' Smolensk finally grasped the truth, or most of it. Balling his big fists, he declared, "You'll get yours! When I fail to return to Russia, my cousins will put a bounty on your head.''

The general had saved the best for last. "Not unless they can do so from beyond the grave. Burian and Rurik died three hours ago in a bomb blast at their favorite restaurant in Novosibirsk. You know, the one they ate at every day. Rather careless of them to be so predictable, but that's how these things go.''

"Burian and Rurik?'' Defeat drained the color from Smolensk face. "Finish it, then!'' he snarled. "Have your gnats to kill me as they did my men.''

"Wouldn't you rather have what the American calls a sporting chance?''

"How do you mean?''

"I have given orders to my men not to harm you if you make it from this room alive.''

Smolensk glanced toward the corridor. "What is the catch?''

The general adopted a bow-and-arrow stance, his left hand in a tiger claw, his right in a dragon fist. "All you have to do is make it past me.''

"That's all?'' Smolensk sounded contemptuous.

"I have offered a similar opportunity to others. Not one has ever succeeded." Tsanghsien watched the Russian's ferret eyes, and when they involuntarily narrowed he rose on the instep of his right foot and hardened his right fist. The attack was swift and savage, as brutish as the man who sprang at him. Smolensk delivered a right uppercut that would have shattered his jaw and crushed his teeth had it connected, but a flick of the general's right wrist deflected it.

Instantly Smolensk speared a knee at Tsanghsien's groin. The general shifted enough to absorb the brunt of the blow on his thigh, then arced his dragon fist downward. A strangled grunt resulted as Smolensk clutched his manhood.

Gracefully pivoting, Tsanghsien executed a high kick. The point of contact was a fraction below the Russian's sternum. Smolensk staggered, his face reddening again but not from anger.

Suddenly springing into the air, the general wrapped a steely arm around Smolensk's bull neck, placed the heel of his other hand against the base of the Black Tiger's head and wrenched.

The crack was loud enough for everyone present to hear.

"How disappointing." The general stood over the body and frowned. "He posed no challenge at all."

"There's always the American, sir," Chen stated.

"Yes," the general said with relish. "There is always the American."

THE EXECUTIONER NEVER needlessly put his life in peril. Not if he could help it. Years of combat experience had instilled a battle savvy far beyond that of most men. From it he had learned that tactics were the key to winning any conflict. Strategy won more battles than sheer numbers or force of arms ever could.

He was a master tactician. He seldom went up against an enemy without a plan. As conditions changed, he adapted, adjusted, modified his plan to achieve his goal.

The latest mission was no exception. Bolan had hurt Kerri's feelings by leaving her behind, but it was necessary. As skilled an operative as she was, she had never been in combat and knew next to nothing about warfare. She was too green, too untested, and would only get herself killed. So he had done what needed doing.

Now Bolan had to move on to the next step, penetrating the fortress. He ran to the Jeep and raced back onto the road. The troop transport had not yet caught up, but he could see its headlights to the south.

Bolan barreled northward, increasing his lead. When he was a quarter mile from the bluff, he tramped on the brake and brought the Jeep to a stop on the left side of the road. Leaving it running and the lights on, he threw both doors open, then gathered his gear and sprinted to the right, into the brush. He slung the M-16 across his back, secured the pouch containing the C-4 under his left arm and made certain every pocket in his blacksuit was sealed.

The throaty purr of the truck was the Executioner's cue to hug the soil. It grew louder, and soon the transport chugged around the last bend. The driver slowed the moment he saw the Jeep. An officer on the passenger side gestured, and the truck rattled to a stop. They looked around, and when they didn't see anyone, they climbed down, the officer drawing his pistol. In the back, some of the soldiers leaned out to see what was going on.

Everyone's attention was on the vehicle on the left side of the road. No one was looking at the right side.

Doubled over, Bolan darted to the transport and rolled under it. Careful not to touch the hot exhaust pipe, he crabbed to a cross brace and wrapped his forearms around it. He jammed his feet into a gap in the undercarriage and waited.

The officer was chattering up a storm. He had the driver move the Jeep to the side of the road and turn off the engine. At his order, four soldiers jumped from the transport, hastened forward and snapped to attention. The officer gave them instructions and they took up positions around Bolan's vehicle. Chances were, they had to stay there and stand guard until someone was sent from the citadel.

Finally the officer and the driver climbed back into the truck. It gave a sharp lurch as it kicked into gear.

Bolan held on tight, his legs locked. His back was only six inches above the asphalt, and he crooked his neck to keep watch for dips and ruts. The roar of the engine drowned out all other sounds. Every now and then the front tires dislodged pebbles that pelted him on the head and shoulders but did no real harm.

Several curves brought them to a hill. On the other side the roadway flared with light, and for hundreds of feet they paralleled a fence. Beyond it Bolan glimpsed the base of the bluff, a wall of weathered rock laced by occasional clefts. He nearly lost his hold when the truck abruptly jagged to the left.

The driver had brought the transport to a stop in front of a wide metal gate. A guard shack was just inside. Bolan saw a pair of polished boots come over.

The guard and the officer exchanged a few words, and the truck was permitted to enter.

Bolan figured they would park somewhere and the soldiers would continue on foot, but that wasn't the case. The driver bore straight toward the bluff, gaining speed rapidly. A crash seemed imminent. Puzzled, Bolan slackened his grip enough to lower himself a few inches so he could see what lay ahead.

A two-lane tunnel had been carved out of the solid rock. Overhead fluorescent lights bathed the troop transport as the driver drove up into it. The sides were sheer and smooth, and the tunnel had a dank, musty odor. Bolan also noticed something else. Machine-gun emplacements stood in wide nooks spaced at regular intervals. Anyone foolhardy enough to try to assault the fortress through the tunnel had to run a gauntlet of withering firepower.

The transport looped around a series of S-turns reminiscent of those in a parking garage, always climbing higher. To maintain speed the driver constantly shifted.

Bolan lost track of time, but it had to be a full five minutes after they entered the tunnel that it widened and the transport rumbled into a parking garage, a mammoth cavern lined by rows and rows of parked trucks and jeeps.

Slowing, the driver wheeled into a space between a couple of other trucks. The officer jumped down and commenced barking orders. The troops spilled out of the bed. They lined up in formation. Then, at another command, they doubled-timed it toward a nearby door.

Bolan slowly sank onto the cool rock floor but didn't crawl out from under the vehicle until the last of the soldiers was gone and the door banged shut. Snaking to the right, he slowly rose, his ears pricked. The cavern was as still as a tomb. He moved toward the door, but he had only a few steps when the driver of the transport came strolling around the front of the truck.

The man's eyes widened to the size of walnuts. Crying out, he stabbed for a pistol in a flapped holster on his left hip.

Bolan took a single bound forward and stroked the butt of the M-16 against the soldier's skull. He caved like an accordion. Drawing the Beretta, Bolan threaded the suppressor onto the barrel, pressed the muzzle against the man's head and stroked the trigger twice. To insure the body wasn't found any time soon, he rolled it under the troop transport.

The Executioner slipped the Beretta back into his shoulder holster and padded to the door. He was about to open it when he heard voices, growing louder by the second. Backpedaling, he ran to the nearest troop transport, dropped onto his back and wriggled under it. The door banged open and he saw several pairs of booted feet come through the doorway. He thought they were after him, but they walked to the next row over.

Exercising exquisite caution, Bolan levered himself out and rose slowly. The soldiers were climbing into a military jeep. They gave no indication they thought anything was wrong. He stood stock-still as the vehicle purred into the tunnel and dipped from sight.

Dog-trotting to the metal door, Bolan put an ear to it but didn't hear a sound this time. Gingerly he turned the handle and cracked it open. A well-lit corridor led off in both directions. He poked his head out but saw no one.

Which way to go? Bolan wondered. It made sense that if the general intended to launch the PPS-1s, it would be done from somewhere high in the fortress.

Heading upward seemed a good bet, so in search of stairs or an elevator he turned right. The corridor ran straight for a score of yards, then jogged to the left. He came to an unmarked door and tried the latch. It was a utility closet filled with buckets and mops and cleaning supplies. He started to step back out, then heard approaching footsteps. Pressing against the jamb, he pulled the door inward but left it open a crack.

Six soldiers marched past, SMGs and rifles over their shoulders.

Once their footsteps faded, Bolan hurried on. The place was crawling with troops. He had to find the missiles before he was discovered. Once an alarm was sounded, extra men would be assigned to protect the PPS-1s and reaching them would be next to impossible.

Lady Luck smiled on him. The next door opened onto a stairwell. Leaning over the rail, Bolan gazed upward. Twenty or thirty landings above, the upper reaches were lost in gloom. He started up, taking the steps two at a stride, pacing himself so he wouldn't tire himself out. On the doors to each landing were Chinese characters Tanaka could have translated, but the warrior wasn't sorry he'd left her behind. He had done the right thing, whether she agreed or not.

At the tenth landing a change occurred. The solid rock surface gave way to ancient walls of brick and stone, walls that had been erected before the birth of China itself, vestiges of a bygone era when warlords ruled the land.

Bolan had reached the bowels of the fortress. He continued to climb, expecting at any moment to run into more soldiers, and sure enough, boots clomped several floors above. Springing to the next landing, he inched the door open. He was at the end of a brightly lit hallway. It was empty, but he heard people talking farther down.

Catfooting to the first room, Bolan peeked in. A slate blackboard bore writing in Chinese. Under it was a desk facing half a dozen rows of chairs. A briefing room, maybe. He remained there long enough for whoever was descending the stairwell to go by, then resumed climbing.

The big question for Bolan now was how high should he go? Searching the entire fortress would take days, and he had mere hours. Exactly how many was hard to say. It might be as many as six; it might be a lot less. There was no way of telling if the timetable mentioned by Sergeant Ergun was accurate.

Bolan elected to go to the very top, then work his way down level by level. If his hunch was correct, he'd find the missiles in relatively little time.

The warrior climbed past ten more landings. Past fifteen. At the next he paused. He thought he'd heard something. Far below shadows moved. More soldiers, possibly, but they posed no threat.

Only a few levels were left. Bolan was a few steps shy of the next when the landing door opened and out strolled five Chinese wearing white smocks. Ducking low, he grabbed for the Beretta. He needn't have worried. They never spotted him. They were too wrapped up in a discussion they were having, and they went up the stairwell, away from him.

Bolan rated it unlikely the five were doctors. Computer personnel, maybe, or technicians of some sort, and in that case, they might lead him right where he needed to go. He silently ghosted their footsteps to the third level from the top. After they strolled off down the hall, he mentally counted to ten and scouted it out.

They were just going through a doorway about forty feet off.

Bolan raced to the same door. Judging by the hubbub on the other side, he'd hit pay dirt. One glimpse was sufficient to confirm it.

An enormous launch bay had been constructed of reinforced metal plating to withstand extremes of heat and force. At the moment the center of the bay was occupied by horizontal missile gantries, which were pointed at an opening as large as a football field on the far side. Workers were swarming over them like bees in a hive, engaged in a variety of tasks. Most were Chinese. The exception was a bearded Caucasian in a suit.

To the right of the bay was the launch control room. Visible through thick plate glass were state-of-the-art computers and sophisticated electronic equipment manned by more specialists in white coats.

Bolan slid his third-to-last packet of C-4 from the black pouch and knelt to the right of the door. Working swiftly, he rigged it at the base of the wall, then pulled the transmitter from his pocket and ran to the stairwell. Before feeding in the code, he took a few seconds to replace the armor-piercing grenade in the M-203 with a smoke grenade. At last he was ready.

The warrior touched a finger to the transmit button.

All hell was about to break loose.

CHAPTER NINETEEN

Georgetown

Hal Brognola wanted to do this one himself.

Trailed by four Justice Department agents, Brognola stalked up a cobblestoned walkway to the front door of the Harkness mansion. He gripped a large silver knocker in the shape of a gargoyle's head and pounded it several times. A butler answered. Brognola flashed his ID and showed the warrant. "We're here to see Mrs. Harkness."

"I'm afraid she's not in at the moment, sir, but Mr. Harkness is. Would you care to speak to him?"

Brognola entered a lavish foyer. "Where did Mrs. Harkness go?" he asked skeptically. The four agents had been watching the mansion for hours, and to the best of their knowledge both the husband and wife were at home.

Someone else answered. "My wife left over an hour ago and wouldn't say where she was going or how long she would be gone." Striding down a flight of marble stairs toward them was a stately older gentleman in a suit that cost more than most people earned in a month. "I'm Harold Harkness. You wouldn't be Mr. Brognola, would you?"

"Your wife mentioned me?" Brognola asked as the man offered his hand.

"It's the strangest thing," Harold said. "Before she left, she told me you would be by, and she asked me to show you something."

Brognola was totally perplexed. He glanced at his agents. "Check the mansion anyway. Every room. Every closet."

As they hustled off, he said to Harold, "You'll have to forgive my suspicious nature. My people had the front and back covered, so I don't see how your wife could have slipped out without them knowing." Especially when the entire estate was surrounded by an eight-foot-high wall.

"Were they watching the side gate, too?"

"Side gate?" Brognola repeated, a sinking sensation in his gut.

"In the east wall. It's so overgrown by ivy, you'd miss it unless you knew exactly where to look." Harold pivoted. "Follow me to the study."

Still wary of a trick, Brognola asked, "You're not the least bit curious about why I'm here?"

"I'd imagine it involves Abigail and her mysterious absences. There have been a lot of them of late." Harold slowed and pointed at a portrait of his wife. The artist had captured her abrasive, aloof personality in the flinty flash of her eyes and the haughty tilt of her head. "My Abby has always been secretive. From the day we met, she refused to discuss her past. It was taboo. The few times I tried to bring it up, she turned on me like a wildcat."

"Did you know she spent time in China?"

Harold nodded. "She told me that much. She was

with the diplomatic corps for several years, I believe, and was attached to the embassy in Peking.''

"She purged her record of any mention of it," Brognola disclosed. "But she couldn't purge every State Department file." A little digging on his part had been enough to unearth the information.

One of Brognola's agents had gone even one better. A year ago Abigail Harkness had taken a vacation. She'd told everyone she was going to take a tour of the Mediterranean, but she'd actually booked a flight to Hong Kong. The agent had traced the hotel she stayed at and learned General Soong Tsanghsien spent three days there on the very same floor.

Brognola still found it incredible. A woman like Harkness, a woman who had everything, who had married into money and had a prestigious job at the White House, had turned traitor. The thing he couldn't figure out was her motive. Money wasn't a factor; Harold was worth five million, not counting his real-estate holdings.

"Here we are," Harold said, opening a door that had been polished to a sheen. Bookshelves lined three of the four walls. Against the fourth stood a giant entertainment center, including a wide-screen TV that took up half the wall.

Harold walked over and took a videocassette from a shelf. "This is the one she wanted me to play. I have no idea what's on it, but she said I might find it interesting, as well." He inserted it into a VCR. "If it's okay with you, that is?"

"I have no objection." Brognola tried to think of why the woman had gone to the trouble. To justify her treachery? To taunt them?

An image filled the screen. Abigail Harkness was

seated in a plush chair. She stared straight into the camera with that arrogant glare of hers, and smiled thinly. "There are things that need to be said. Since I don't have any desire to say them from behind bars, I'm recording this to set the record straight."

"She filmed this upstairs in our drawing room," Harold said. "I recognize that chair. We purchased it in Sweden."

Harkness sat back and folded her slender hands. "I'm not without my resources, Mr. Brognola. I know you've been snooping into my past. By now you've learned I lived in China for three years, and you no doubt think you have it all figured out. But you couldn't be more wrong."

Brognola moved closer. Her composure, as always, was extraordinary. He was beginning to believe nothing ever fazed her.

"You undoubtedly think I've betrayed my country," she said. "That I sold out and passed on sensitive intel to a certain party in China. Well, I admit to passing on the intelligence, but it wasn't for gain or power or any of the usual trite reasons."

"Oh, my," Harold said.

"To understand, you must travel back into my past, to when I was a minor functionary at the embassy in Peking." The woman was silent a bit. "I was young and guileless and not overly attractive, so when a handsome Chinese colonel showed an interest in me, I was flattered. We met at a social function. One thing led to another and I became pregnant with his child."

Brognola didn't see where her revelation was leading, but there had to be a point to it.

"I loved him," she said with no trace of emotion. "I thought he loved me. But when our child was two,

I learned he had struck up a relationship with me under orders from his commander. He was a spy, you see, and I was a prime source of information.''

Harold was hanging on every word. ''My poor darling.''

''I wanted nothing more to do with him and put in for a transfer. He didn't care if I left, but he insisted on keeping our child. His government took an active role, insisting the child's interests were better served by a Chinese upbringing. I appealed to our government, but they turned their back on me. In the interests of U.S.-Chinese relations, the child was taken from me and turned over to the father. Political expediency deprived me of my offspring.''

''I never knew she had a child,'' Harold remarked. He glanced at Brognola. ''Did she say whether it was a boy or a girl?''

''She didn't—'' Brognola began, and suddenly he knew. Suddenly he understood why Abigail Harkness had done what she did. It hit him with the impact of a sledgehammer, and he took a step back, shocked beyond measure. ''My God!'' he blurted.

Harkness had gone on. ''The colonel's name, Mr. Brognola, was Huan Tsanghsien. Our son's name is Soong Tsanghsien. When I told you I hadn't sold a single secret to the Chinese, I was being truthful. I didn't sell my son anything. I gladly, and freely, passed on the intel he needed.''

''She did what?'' Harold asked in confusion.

''You see, Mr. Brognola, my son and I have kept in touch over the years. We are a lot alike, he and I. Oh, we're at different ends of the political spectrum, but he's grown into a fine man, someone any mother would be proud of.''

Brognola's mind was racing with the implications.

"I know, I know," she said. "You still can't quite comprehend it. A mother's love is one thing. Bringing the U.S. to its knees is quite another." She stopped, her cool exterior evaporating under the blazing heat of raw hatred. "But it's the least our government deserves. I've never forgotten how I was treated. I've never forgiven them for taking my son away, for prying him from my arms as I screamed and cried and begged them not to." The woman was scarlet from her neck to her hairline. "Consider this payback, Mr. Brognola. My son has given me the chance to repay the country that turned its back on me in the most spectacular fashion possible. How could I refuse?"

Brognola had to find a phone, had to place a call to the White House.

Harkness's hand rose toward the camcorder, then stopped. "Oh. Harold. I almost forgot. If you're viewing this, our marriage, such as it is, is over. I suggest you invest in a fallout shelter and stockpile enough provisions to last a year. Don't worry about me. Depending on if my son's contingency plan goes into effect or not, I'll be leaving for China in either a few days or a couple of weeks to spend the rest of my days with him."

The video ended and the screen dissolved into erratic black-and-white squiggles.

Hal Brognola didn't see it. He was already halfway out the door.

China

GIVEN HOW CLOSE the stairwell was to the launch bay, the Executioner felt it wise to hunker and hold on to the rail. He pressed the transmit button, and a tremendous explosion resounded. The landing shook, the door vibrating on its hinges. Before the echoes died, he leaped to the hallway and raced to the launch bay. There hadn't been enough C-4 to do much damage, but there had been enough to accomplish his purpose, which was to sow panic and confusion.

A broad, jagged hole existed where none had been before. As Bolan leaped through the opening into the bay, amid a swirling blanket of dust and smoke, shouts and fearful cries broke out. From a pocket in his webbing he pulled the first of three smoke grenades he had brought along, jerked the pin and tossed the bomb toward the missiles. He threw the second grenade to the right of the first, the last grenade to the left.

Bolan didn't have much time. The smoke grenades would spew thick white smoke for up to two and a half minutes. How long the resultant cloud would screen him depended on how long it took the bay's exhaust vents to disperse it. He figured he had five to six minutes at the very most.

Plunging into the smoke, Bolan nearly collided with workers in white coats hastening toward the corridor. He glimpsed others on both sides. A general exodus was in full swing, all the technicians rushing to presumed safety. He let them go by. None were armed, and most were coughing and sputtering and rubbing their eyes. They had made the mistake of inhaling too deeply. The trick to getting through the smoke was to do as he was doing—to move in a crouch, breath shallowly and keep both eyelids slitted.

Somewhere overhead a Klaxon began blaring. It wouldn't be long, the Executioner reflected, before soldiers rushed to the scene.

More technicians staggered by. One pointed at Bolan and yelled but kept on going. He quickened his pace, casting about in the acrid soup for the PPS-1s. Suddenly a gantry materialized, and Bolan moved to a short ladder that brought him to a catwalk. Hurrying forward along the missile to the nose cone, he looked for a panel near the stabilizing fins. It was exactly where Brognola had said it would be.

Before he departed the States, Bolan had sat down with the big Fed and gone over a design schematic so he could find and remove the access panel, if need be. Now, removing a screwdriver from a pouch, he unfastened four large screws and jimmied the seal. Under the cover, in a special titanium-alloy housing, was the missile's brain, the onboard computer that guided and armed the PPS-1.

Bolan had memorized the code he needed. It wasn't complicated, but the sequence had to be exact. He stabbed the keys. One by one the proper numbers and letters flashed on a digital readout. When a green light began blinking, he knew the missile was programmed and ready to go. He quickly replaced the panel and screwed it down.

Running to the ladder, Bolan descended and moved toward where he thought the next gantry should be. Smoke tingled his nose and made him want to cough, but he resisted the impulse. The Klaxon was still blaring. Over toward the corridor, men were yelling back and forth.

Another giant shape loomed. Bolan roved to the right, found the ladder and soon had the second access panel removed. As he set it down and bent over the control pad, the Klaxon stopped shrieking. Seconds later the shouting ceased. In the unnerving silence that ensued, the low whir of exhaust fans warned him he was running out of time. Whitish tendrils were spiraling toward the ceiling at a rapid rate.

Bolan used the same code as before, in the same sequence. The scientists who designed the plasma-propulsion missile had assured Hal Brognola the code would override all previous programming, and that once initiated, it couldn't be overridden by anyone else. Finished, he put the cover back on and secured it. As he sped back along the catwalk, he checked his watch.

The scrape of footsteps alerted Bolan he wasn't alone. Instead of climbing down, he jumped. He had only taken a few strides toward the next gantry when the roiling cloud parted, revealing dozens of soldiers who instantly swung their rifles and SMGs toward him. He clutched at the M-16 but froze when a tall Chinese stepped forward and addressed him in accent-free English.

"I wouldn't, were I you. You've come so far, surmounted so many obstacles, it would be a shame to needlessly perish."

Bolan had never seen a photograph of General Soong Tsanghsien. He had never been provided with a description by Brognola; the Feds didn't have one. But he knew as sure as he was standing there that the tall Chinese with the ramrod posture and intensely intelligent eyes was the madman who wanted to embroil the world in a bloodbath that would make both world wars pale by comparison. All he had to do was level the M-16 and fire, and the madman would die. But there was no guarantee he could do it before the soldiers cut him down, and that gave him pause.

"I've been looking forward to meeting you," the

general said. "Hand over your weapons, and I'll grant you half an hour more of life."

Bolan studied the soldiers. They were as tightly strung as piano wire, their trigger fingers curled, just waiting for an excuse to open fire.

"Your sacrifice would be in vain," Tsanghsien said. "Even if you slay me, it won't stop the missiles from being launched."

Half an hour more of life was better than none. Bolan slowly extended his rifle. A soldier snatched it. Another relieved him of the Beretta, the Desert Eagle and his pouch.

General Tsanghsien was smiling, at ease, acting as if they were long-lost friends. "This is a treat. It's so rare to meet a man of your quality. The feats you performed at Hokkaido and on Hakka Island, to say nothing of the ease with which you destroyed my garrison at the pass, have demonstrated how extraordinary you are."

"And you're not upset?" Bolan asked, thinking the man couldn't possibly be sincere.

"At what? Hakka Island was a government facility, not mine. I regret the loss of my men, but they were soldiers. Dying is part of their job, as you Americans might say." The general chuckled. "Besides, what has all your effort accomplished? I still have the PPS-1s. My plan is still being carried out, right on schedule. Soon the missiles will be ready to launch, and there isn't a thing you can do about it."

Bolan didn't let on he already had. Or that he had less than fifteen minutes to get out of there.

"I suppose it would be silly to ask you to tell me a little about yourself?" the general said. "Your name, your background, where you're from?"

"That's not going to happen," Bolan said. The request was ridiculous.

The general shrugged. "More's the pity. I'm a student of human nature, and I would very much like to know what molded you into the man you are. The great Sun Tzu once wrote, 'When you know the enemy and know yourself, you are invincible.'" He paused. "With the resources your government has as its disposal, I'd imagine you've learned all sorts of facts about me. Except perhaps the most important."

Since the general was being so open Bolan saw no harm in asking, "What would that be?" He saw more soldiers fanning out around the bay's perimeter, sixty or seventy or better.

"Something no one else in China knows. I disposed of all those who did." Tsanghsien scanned those present. "Let's see. You killed Sergeant Ergun. And the only other man in my command who speaks English isn't here. So it's safe to share my little secret." He came closer. "We have more in common than you suspect."

"I doubt that," Bolan said.

"Isn't your mother American?"

"What does that have to do with anything?"

"So is mine."

The warrior stared.

"Surprised, yes? Except for my height and my eyes, no one would know it to look at me." He bobbed his chin toward the control room and motioned for Bolan to accompany him. "But it's true. The country I hate most, the country I want to grind into the dust, is the same country that spawned me." He chortled. "The absurdity of life never ceases to amaze me."

"Is your mother still alive?" Bolan asked.

"Very much so, yes." Undeniable fondness crept into the general's tone. "She's a remarkable woman. Your government separated us when I was young and denied her the right to rear me. But she defied them. She married into money, I believe the expression goes, and used her wealth to seek me out and contact me. We've met secretly over a dozen times, once for over a month. She thinks very highly of me."

"Would she think so highly if she knew what you were up to?"

"Who do you think has been instrumental in my success?" the general rejoined. "If not for her, I never could have stolen the plasma missiles. She hates your government almost as much as I do. After what they did, she would as soon see your countrymen burn in hell. Those were her exact words."

The soldiers covering Bolan were right on his heels, their weapons steady in their hands. One wrong twitch and he would pay.

The general surveyed the launch bay. "Impressive, is it not? The upper third of my fortress has been fully modernized. Much of the material, I admit, was obtained by rerouting shipments intended for government installations—"

"You stole it, in other words," Bolan said.

"For the greater good of my country and the world," the general said by way of justifying the thievery. "It took years to accomplish. But soon, very soon, all the time and energy I've expended will pay off."

Bolan gazed off across the bay and noticed something he should have noticed sooner. "There are only four PPS-1s. Where's the fifth?"

"Being shipped elsewhere," the general said. "I am what you Americans would call a poor loser. So I put a contingency plan into effect in case my plan is thwarted.''

"What kind of plan?" Bolan probed.

"Suffice it to say that if I die, so will some important people in your country.''

A whole new problem confronted Bolan. The fifth PPS-1 could end up anywhere in the world and be launched at any target. Tracking it down in time posed a major challenge "Did you have it fitted with nuclear warheads before you sent it off?" he asked, dreading the answer.

"Of course. It was the first one converted. By itself it's not enough to destroy the U.S. But it will insure lasting fame for the Tsanghsien name.''

The technicians were returning. Among them was the bearded Caucasian, who spotted the general and hastened over.

Bolan wasn't fluent in Russian, but he knew it when he heard it, and he was impressed when Tsanghsien engaged the man in a short discussion. That made three languages the general spoke. Who knew how many more?

Switching to English, the general said, "Allow me to introduce Ivan Pechora. He has been overseeing the conversion and he has just given me wonderful news. The PPS-1s are about ready to launch.''

Bolan glanced at the gantries. Two of the four were more ready than Tsanghsien realized. Trying not to be obvious, he checked his watch. Twelve minutes and counting.

"How auspicious," the general stated. "You're the one person who might have stopped me, and you've arrived at this most momentous of moments. Perhaps it would be fitting to keep you on hand to witness the destruction of everything you hold dear." He moved toward the control-room door. "I was going to amuse myself by slaying you in hand-to-hand combat, but it can wait."

Bolan had to stall by any means he could. If the Chinese tried to feed target coordinates into the missiles he had tampered with, they would discover something was wrong. Clutching at a verbal straw, he called out, "Is that the real reason? Or are you afraid you can't beat me?"

Tsanghsien glanced back. "Really, now. I expected better of you. So childish a ploy is beneath a man of your caliber." He took a few more steps.

"Go on, then," Bolan said. "I can't stop you from murdering millions of innocent people, but I can avenge them by killing you afterward."

The general halted, then turned slowly. His features had undergone a change. Gone was the friendliness, the cheerful smile. In its place was simmering resentment. "The supreme moment of my life, and you seek to spoil it with your pettiness? I thought you were a true warrior, like myself, but I've misjudged you."

"A true warrior never refuses a challenge," Bolan said. Which might have been true in times past, in the Middle Ages or during the days of the samurai, when a man's honor mattered above all else. Few in the modern world, though, lived by the old creed. Bolan was gambling Soong Tsanghsien was one of them; the general was a throwback to the warlords of yesteryear.

Two men approached, another officer and a noncom. The general addressed the former and handed his pistol to the latter.

Bolan noticed a ripple of excitement flow through the soldiers. They whispered to one another and relayed word to their companions along the walls and to the workers in the white coats.

The general stalked toward him like a tiger sizing up its prey. "My mother once told me of another Americanism. How does it go again?" He snapped his fingers. "Oh, yes. Be careful what you wish for. You might just get it." His hands behind his back, he began to slowly circle Bolan. "I refuse to have the greatest day of my life ruined. I'll dispose of you first, then send the missiles on their way."

"What if I win?" the warrior asked. Eleven minutes remained until the PSS-1s he had programmed blasted off.

The corners of Tsanghsien's mouth twitched. "I suppose there's a slight chance you might prevail." He barked at his troops, who lowered their weapons. "I've told them no one is to shoot, no one is to harm you, no matter what the outcome." He added a few statements for the benefit of the junior officer. "If I lose, Colonel Chen, there, will see to it you are driven to the east pass and given your freedom."

"You expect me to believe he'll do it?" Bolan said.

"I take that as an insult. My men have taken an oath to follow my orders without question."

"Would they be loyal if they knew about your mother?" Bolan was still stalling, trying to work out in his mind how to accomplish what he had to without getting himself killed.

"Therein lies another sweet irony. The genes I inherited from an American have helped me greatly in my quest to destroy America. My green eyes, my size, they're taken as a sign of divine favor. To my followers, I have become the hope of China incarnate."

"If I kill you, will they agree to turn the PPS-1s over to my government?"

The general chortled. "Be serious. Colonel Chen will carry on in my place. Your capitalistic cesspool of a country must still be destroyed." He sank into a horse stance. "Now, then. Are you prepared to die?"

CHAPTER TWENTY

The Executioner had come prepared for almost any contingency. If he couldn't destroy the missiles by any other means, he had been supplied with a code that programmed the PPS-1s to destroy themselves. The boomerang code, the experts dubbed it. Once entered into a PPS-1's onboard computer, the missile traveled a specified distance, then returned to the spot it was launched from.

Two variables entered into the equation; Bolan decided when the missiles were fired and how far they traveled. He had set the computers so the plasma engines would ignite fifteen minutes after he entered the codes, giving him time to slip away. But now he had been taken prisoner. He would die along with everyone else in the bay unless he could get out of there in time.

The code Bolan had been given wasn't supposed to detonate the warheads on impact. If it did, if something went wrong and the nukes went up, it wouldn't matter how far he ran. He would be vaporized along with the fortress.

Now, as General Soong Tsanghsien pumped his arms in a series of practice strikes, Bolan said to delay the other's attack, ''What about your mother? How do you know she won't be caught in the blasts or the fall-out?''

Tsanghsien paused. "Credit me with a modicum of intelligence. She's already safe in Canada." Gliding forward, he swiveled his feet in a manner that maintained his balance and stance. "I'll be sure to relay your concern when I see her."

Less than ten minutes to go, Bolan saw as he raised his clenched fists. Trying to run for cover would be pointless. He'd be mowed down before he went three yards. But it might be possible to use the general's arrogance to his benefit. All he had to do was stay alive long enough.

Then, in a whirlwind blur, General Tsanghsien sprang. Always on the offensive, he used his hands, his arms, his legs, his feet in a nonstop barrage of battering blows, never letting up for an instant.

Retreating under the onslaught, Bolan blocked and countered. Most of the punches and kicks were absorbed by his forearms and his legs, but a spinning kick and a crane strike both pierced his guard, sparking sharp pain. He wanted to give the impression it was all he could do to hold his own and in that he succeeded because Tsanghsien abruptly stopped in indignation.

"What are you trying to pull?"

"I don't know what you mean," Bolan said, playing ignorant, rubbing a sore spot on his ribs where the other's iron fingers had grazed them.

"You are the best America has to offer, yet you fight like a raw recruit. Any one of my men could defeat you. It's almost enough to make me think you are unworthy of my personal attention."

"Maybe I'm not." Bolan was sixty feet from the hole the C-4 had created, but it might as well be a mile.

"Again you insult my intellect," the general said. "You are much more lethal than you pretend to be, or you wouldn't have made it to Tsanghsien Province." His eyes narrowed. "You're up to something, American."

Bolan had to remember he wasn't dealing with a rank amateur. Whatever else Soong Tsanghsien might be, he had an exceptionally high IQ, perhaps genius level.

"For a reason I have yet to fathom, you're holding back," the general said. "Perhaps you didn't believe me when I said my men won't kill you if you win. Perhaps you have another motive. Whatever the case—" he assumed a scissors stance "—as of this moment you'll stop holding back or I'll cripple you, then kill you by slow degrees."

And with that, the general threw himself at the warrior with redoubled ferocity, his hands and feet flying in deadly cadence—crane strikes, tiger-claw attacks, leopard-paw thrusts, high kicks, low kicks, sweep kicks. He never slackened, never slowed, raining blow after blow after blow, doing all in his considerable degree of skill to break through the warrior's guard and deliver a killing stroke.

For Bolan's part, he was severely hampered by wanting to get close to the corridor before time ran out. He blocked. He countered. He ducked. He dodged. Every now and again he flicked a fist or a boot, just often enough, hopefully, to convince his adversary he was trying his utmost.

While Bolan lacked the general's long training in the martial arts, his combat savvy and instincts more than made up for it. He was able to hold his own, which seemed to anger his foe. In the frenzied swirl of heated combat, he lost track of the time, so when the general stopped and stepped back, he was surprised to see less than eight minutes were left.

"Better, but still not good enough." Tsanghsien made talons of his fingers. "Time to end this farce." He surged forward, relentless, unstoppable.

Bolan retreated, blocking strikes as fast as they were thrown. Taking a risk, he glanced toward the corridor to gauge how far it was and paid for his mistake when a granite foot nearly took his head off. His legs swept out from under him and he smashed onto his back. He struggled to get back up but dizziness assailed him and his muscles wouldn't cooperate. A vague shape solidified. His throat was caught in the grip of a vise and he was partially hoisted off the floor.

"And so it ends," the general declared. "You lasted longer than most, but you're nowhere near my equal."

Bolan's vision crystallized. Tsanghsien's sneering visage was inches from his face. In reflex he slammed his knee into the general's groin and was rewarded with a strangled grunt. The vise on his throat slackened, and he drove his knee up a second time. Tsanghsien staggered back, giving him the room he needed to push erect and deliver an uppercut that rocked the general on his heels. Bolan whipped into a high spin kick, his foot connecting with the tip of Tsanghsien's chin. Suddenly it was the general who was on his back, and Bolan moved in to end the fight.

The rasp of a bolt being thrown brought the warrior to a halt. One of the soldiers had taken aim with an SMG. He braced for the sensation of slugs tearing into his flesh, but Colonel Chen shouted an order and the soldier lowered his weapon.

No one else moved as the general rose onto his elbows, blood trickling from a corner of his mouth.

The hole made by the C-4 was now only twenty-five feet away, and Bolan was tempted to make a run for it.

Just then the general spit and rose slowly. "I was wrong about you, American. You aren't a true warrior. You have no honor. You have no dignity."

Bolan glanced at the PPS-1s. "Why? Because I do whatever it takes to win?"

The general wiped a sleeve across his mouth, stared at the scarlet smear and scowled. "You resorted to the refuge of the weak. You're not the man I thought you to be. You deserve no special treatment. I'll have you executed where you stand and be done with you."

"Go ahead," Bolan said. "But I'll die knowing I've won."

"You're delusional."

"Am I?" Bolan pointed at the gantries. "What do you think I was doing to the missiles when you showed up?"

Furrows lined the general's forehead. "I assumed you were planting explosives to blow them up, but Colonel Chen checked and found none."

Bolan hoped the experts had been right when they claimed the code he had entered couldn't be overridden or erased. "No, I was reprogramming the PPS-1s. In about five minutes your fortress is going to come crashing down around your ears." Or go up in a mushroom cloud, Bolan thought, if the experts were wrong about the warheads.

General Tsanghsien whirled toward the onlookers and snarled at the Russian, Pechora, who dashed to the gantries. As luck would have it, he picked the first missile Bolan had reset and climbed up.

The warrior tilted his wrist so he could glance at his watch without anyone noticing. It took the Russian twenty-three seconds to reach the nose cone, another forty to search for a screwdriver and over a minute to remove the screws and take off the cover. Pechora leaned down, examined the display and called out to the general.

"You entered a launch sequence?"

Bolan said nothing.

Pechora stabbed the keys, trying to override the code. When he failed, he swore, hollered to Tsanghsien and bent to try again.

"He says you didn't arm the warheads. What are you up to, American?"

By Bolan's reckoning under three minutes remained.

"Why would you do such thing?" The general was thinking out loud. "What purpose does it serve to launch the missiles but not arm them?" He smacked his hands together. "I know what you're up to! You want to dispose of them without endangering the lives of innocents. What target did you choose? Off in the Pacific Ocean somewhere? Or maybe the Great Lakes so your Navy can recover them without too much difficulty?"

Bolan inched backward.

"You think you've beaten me but you haven't," Tsanghsien said. "I'll have the Russian switch off the onboard computers. The missiles aren't going anywhere." He yelled instructions to Ivan Pechora.

A logical step, Bolan agreed, but doomed not to work. The computer would refuse all new commands, including a command to shut down. His watch told him they had two minutes and thirty-seven seconds until the plasma engines ignited.

"I'm glad I didn't kill you before," the general told him. "You must die slowly, in terrible agony. I personally will rip out your fingernails one at a time. Then your toenails and your teeth."

Now it was two minutes and twenty-seven seconds. Bolan glanced behind him to insure no one was blocking his way.

The Russian tried the same procedure over and over, and it wouldn't work. Whatever he said next caused the general to glower like a mad bull about to charge.

"You will tell me how to override the code you fed in," Tsanghsien demanded. Marching to the noncom, he reclaimed his pistol, turned, and pointed it at Bolan's groin. "I'll count to ten. If you haven't told me what I want to know by then, I will shoot you once every five seconds until you do." He paused. "One!"

Bolan let the madman count. Every second that elapsed was a second nearer to ending the threat of a nuclear holocaust of unimaginable magnitude.

"Two!"

Ivan Pechora turned toward them. Beads of perspiration dotted his brow, and he appeared tremendously nervous.

The general stopped counting to listen to what the Russian was saying. "He thinks the missiles are set to launch soon. Is he correct?"

In one minute and eleven seconds, but Bolan wasn't going to admit it. To his left stood the soldier who had taken the Beretta and Desert Eagle, and he turned slightly to be that much closer when the time came.

"Answer me this instant," Tsanghsien said, cocking his pistol.

"Answer which question?" Bolan jousted for precious time. "Where the missiles are targeted? Why I didn't arm the warheads? Or how soon they'll launch?"

"All three."

"I didn't activate the warheads because I don't want the nukes to go off," Bolan said. In under a minute he would find out if they would nor not. If the experts had miscalculated, he would go out in a literal blaze of glory.

"The target?"

"You were right a while ago," Bolan said. "I picked a spot where innocent lives won't be lost." The lives of the general and his fanatical followers were another matter entirely. Every last one deserved to be eliminated.

"I knew it," Tsanghsien gloated. "How soon?"

"Soon."

"How can I stop them, then?"

"There is no way to stop them," Bolan said. "The code I entered is tamperproof. Nothing you do can prevent the Tsanghsien line from coming to an end."

"My line from—?" General Tsanghsien went rigid and glared at the gantries in rising rage. "You didn't!"

"Yes, I did." Bolan held his watch up to his chest. "Ten. Nine. Eight. Seven—"

Tsanghsien's soldiers didn't speak English, but they realized something dire was about to occur and they worriedly glanced from their leader to the missiles and back again.

For a few seconds no one paid any attention to Bolan, and he capitalized by lunging at the man with the Beretta and the Desert Eagle and wrenching both from the private's grasp. Spinning on the balls of his feet,

Bolan sprinted toward the corridor. Someone shouted, and lead sizzled past his ear. To make it harder for them to hit him, he zigzagged, but no one else fired. Instead, a tremendous roar shook the bay, a roar of deafening proportions, a roar like that of an erupting volcano.

Bolan shot a look over his shoulder and saw all eyes were on the two PPS-1s. Their plasma engines had ignited and were glowing red. Soldiers and technicians alike had started to back away in transparent fear. Ivan Pechora was clinging to the catwalk, barely able to stay on his feet because the entire gantry was shaking so violently.

The warrior covered another five yards and dived into a forward roll. He knifed through the hole in the wall and up onto one knee. Blistering heat struck him as he faced around.

All were running for their lives. It was every person for himself, soldiers and workers shoving one another in their haste to flee. Technicians spilling from the control room were swept up in the headlong flight. Some people tripped and were trampled.

Bolan saw no sign of General Tsanghsien, but he did spot Colonel Chen vainly striving to stem the terror-struck tide.

Impossibly the roar swelled louder, attaining a shattering crescendo that obliterated the screams of the Chinese and brought whole sections of the ceiling crashing down on their heads. Fractures laced the walls, and the superheated floor behind the two PPS-1s began to buckle and crack.

It was but a prelude. The missile on the right tore from its gantry and hurtled out the far end of the bay. Ivan Pechora's wail was cut short as the plasma engine incinerated him to mere ashes. A heartbeat later the second missile streaked out into the night, its gantry tumbling end over end in a twisted heap of tangled metal.

Most of the soldiers and workers slowed or stopped in the mistaken belief the worst was over. How wrong they were.

Bolan rose and tried to run. He had programmed the PPS-1s to fly a thousand miles due south and execute an elliptical flight path that would bring them back to the exact point they were launched from. A thousand miles seemed like a lot, but at the astounding speed the PPS-1s were capable of, in excess of thirty thousand miles per hour, they returned two seconds after they were launched.

Bolan had taken only one step when the missiles slammed into the bay with the devastating power of twin juggernauts. It was a miracle neither reached the corridor. One struck the floor and ricocheted like a giant bullet up into the ceiling, while the other slammed into the side. Most of the Chinese were bowled over by the explosions, which shook the entire fortress.

It all happened in the blink of an eye. Before the soldiers and techs could rise, a fiery whirlwind of hellish magnitude engulfed a majority of them in an inferno. Only those closest to the corridor were spared. The flames also engulfed the other two PPS-1s, which blew like giant sticks of dynamite.

Bolan was pitched onto his stomach. He pushed against the floor to stand but slipped, which was just as well. Searing sheets of fire narrowly missed his head. Keeping low, he crawled toward the landing. The smell of burned flesh saturated his nostrils until he slid into the stairwell and shoved the landing door shut.

As Bolan rose, the Klaxons began anew. He started down, wreathed by wisps of smoke wafting from a ventilation vent. He'd lost the M-16 and his pouch, but he could get by without them. The important thing was that he'd destroyed the PPS-1s—and, apparently, Soong Tsanghsien along with them.

The warrior leaped three steps at a time, his goal to reach the parking garage and help himself to a vehicle before everyone else realized the gravity of the crisis and decided to escape.

The clang of a door brought Bolan to a stop. A cluster of men in uniforms and white smocks barreled up the stairs. To avoid a confrontation, he ducked into the next corridor, and regretted it. Four soldiers were rushing toward the stairwell. On spotting him they grabbed for their hardware, but he already had the Beretta and the Desert Eagle in his hands and they died without getting off a shot.

Bolan wished the Klaxons would stop. He couldn't hear much over their racket. But by pressing an ear to the landing door, he heard the heavy tread of boots pounding upward. When the last had gone by, he resumed his flight.

At the next landing were two more soldiers. One had a Type 68 assault rifle, the other a Type 64 silenced machine gun. Both reacted by leveling their weapons, but they were slow on the trigger. A round from the Beretta cored the skull of the man with the rifle at the same moment a slug from the Desert Eagle drilled a hole through the sternum of the man with the SMG.

Bolan needed more firepower. He shoved both pistols into their respective holsters and snatched up the Type 64 silenced machine gun. The soldier who had carried it wore a web belt crammed with spare magazines and ammo, which Bolan appropriated.

Better armed, Bolan moved on. The next landing was empty but not the second. As he neared it, the door was flung wide and out rushed five more soldiers. They looked up, into the muzzle of the SMG, and tried to drop him before he dropped them. In a tight, controlled burst he chopped them down like so many saplings and vaulted over their twitching bodies.

Bolan didn't much like the idea of having to fight his way clear to the garage. There had to be elevators somewhere, but searching for them would take valuable time. What he needed was a disguise.

Feet spanged on the metal steps below. A lone technician in a baggy white coat was climbing toward him. The man had his collar pulled high and his head hunched low. He didn't realize the warrior was there until they were about to collide. Then he glanced up and jumped back, flourishing a Mustang in a two-handed grip.

Not until then did Bolan realize the "man" wasn't a man at all.

"You!" Kerri Tanaka blurted. Her M-16 was under her coat, the sling over her left shoulder.

"You shouldn't have come," Bolan said. Grasping her elbow, he whirled her around and tried to move on.

Tanaka dug in her heels, bringing them to a halt. "Is that the thanks I get for wanting to help even after what you did to me?"

"Not now," Bolan said, hauling her lower by sheer strength.

"Do you have any idea how hurt I was?" Tanaka went on anyway. "You betrayed my trust. You left me there all alone. Helpless. Defenseless.'' She jerked from his grasp. ''It took me almost an hour to crawl to my dagger and cut myself loose.''

Bolan was trying to listen for soldiers above the raucous caterwauling of the Klaxons and her carping. ''We'll discuss this later.''

''There's nothing to discuss. What you did was unforgivable. I could have been killed.''

''I was going to free you when I got back,'' Bolan said, hoping that would appease her.

''*If* you got back, you mean!'' Now the woman seized his arm and spun him. ''For all you know, I could have laid there for days. Or General Tsanghsien's men might have found me.'' In her fury she hiked a fist to hit him. ''You had no right!''

Bolan made no attempt to defend himself. He had to defuse her temper while they still had a slim chance of making it out alive. ''I did what I thought was best. If that's not good enough, we can settle up once we're in the clear.''

''You're damn straight that's not—'' Tanaka began, and suddenly shoved him against the rail and leveled the Mustang.

For a second Bolan thought she was aiming at him. But her attention was on something lower down. He twisted as she fired and saw a soldier's face burst like an overripe melon. Behind him were others, half a dozen strung out in a row, the nearest about to return fire with an assault rifle.

Bolan was quicker. Crimson geysers spewed from the man's chest, and he tottered back into his companions, knocking two of them over. The Executioner didn't let up on the trigger. He emptied the magazine, stitching holes in torsos, in craniums, in limbs.

Tanaka emptied the Mustang, as well, and when they were done the steps were littered with bodies convulsing in the throes of death.

Bolan ejected the spent magazine, slapped in a full one and skirted spreading puddles of scarlet to reach the next landing. He tried the door. The hallway was deserted. "I need something to wear over my blacksuit," he announced. A hat would help, too, if he could find one, but no disguise could hide his height.

"I found the coat I'm wearing in a closet," Tanaka said. She wasn't quite finished reloading the Mustang.

A door on the right seemed as likely a place to look as anywhere. Bolan opened it, and was suddenly face-to-face with four men in civilian garb, more technicians or computer personnel who were on their way out. Pointing the machine gun at them, he said to Tanaka, "Tell them to do as I say and they won't be hurt."

She was never given the chance.

Uttering a harsh cry, one of the men leaped at Bolan. Not wildly or recklessly but smoothly and agilely, arcing high and sweeping his right foot in a crescent kick. Bolan squeezed off a round but it missed. The man's foot connected with the 64's barrel, ripping the SMG from his fingers. He speared a hand for the Beretta, but the worker was on him like a pit bull on an intruder. He blocked a knife-hand chop to the throat, then skipped to the left to avoid a kick to the knee.

The other workers took their cue from the martial artist. They surged from the room, one to help the man fighting Bolan, the others toward Tanaka.

Bolan didn't care if they were civilians. They were trying to kill him and he responded in kind. He had no reason to hold back, as he did in his fight with the general. So when his first attacker performed a scissors kick, he sidestepped and rammed a fist into the man's gut. When the man doubled over, Bolan wrapped an arm around the man's neck and wrenched with all his might.

The crack of the spine breaking gave the second tech pause. The guy watched his friend fall lifeless to the floor. A smart man would have fled, but this one flew at the warrior in a frenzy.

Pivoting, Bolan lanced his knuckles into the tech's ribs. He felt two or three crack. The man howled but didn't give up, so Bolan punched him full in the throat. Wheezing and spitting blood, the tech fell against the wall. He was dead before he stopped moving, his eyes wide in shock.

Bolan spun to help Tanaka, but she required no assistance. One of her opponents was down, motionless, and the second had just been on the receiving end of a spin kick that sent teeth sailing from the man's mouth and the man crashing against the wall.

"Let's keep going," Bolan said, bending to retrieve the machine gun. As his hand wrapped around the stock, something came sliding along the floor toward them from the direction of the stairwell.

It was a grenade.

CHAPTER TWENTY-ONE

The Executioner reacted without thinking. He sprang toward the grenade, not away from it, snagged it while it was in motion, and like a major-league pitcher throwing a hardball, he hurled it toward the stairwell. Without breaking stride, he spun, wrapped his arm around Tanaka's waist and propelled them toward the room the four technicians had been in. They cleared the jamb and sprawled onto the floor as the grenade detonated, the wall shielding them from the shrapnel.

The blast was punctuated by screams of anguish. Dust and bits of debris flew past the doorway.

For a moment Bolan and Kerri were nose to nose, their bodies flush. "Are you all right?" he asked.

"What do you care?" she responded stiffly, and pushed up.

Rising, Bolan peered out. The door to the landing was a shambles, and wisps of smoke were issuing from the stairwell. Molding the machine gun's stock to his shoulder, he moved toward it to finish off any soldiers who were left. The closer he grew, the more his nose tingled to an acrid odor reminiscent of burning charcoal. He found out why when he peeked past the shattered jamb.

Several uniformed figures—or what was left of

them—lay scattered on the severely damaged landing. But the odor didn't come from them. Nor did the wisps of smoke. Looking up, Bolan discovered the upper levels of the fortress were ablaze. Streams of fire gushed into the stairwell, flames so hot they reduced the stairs to molten slag. And the flames were spreading at an astounding speed.

Voices warned Bolan dozens of men were climbing toward him. Backing into the corridor, he ran to Tanaka. "We're cut off. We have to find another way down. Let's see where this hallway leads."

Forty feet farther was a junction. The left branch was a dead end, but at the far end of the right fork was a bank of elevators. Nudging his companion, Bolan jogged toward them and almost ran into a technician who blundered from a room directly in his path. A stroke of the SMG's barrel dropped the tech to the floor.

All three elevators were in use. Tanaka stabbed the buttons and stared in frustration at the position indicator, which showed one of the cars was ten stories above them and the other two cars at various levels below. "Come on! Come on!"

"Wait for one to stop," Bolan said.

Seconds later the car that was rising did just that. She pressed the down button and didn't release it. She yipped for joy when the blinking indicators light showed it was descending toward them. "We can take it down to the garage, swipe a vehicle and kiss this place goodbye!"

The light slowed as if the car were about to stop five floors above. It flashed a few times, then the car sank toward them twice as rapidly. A harsh metallic screech sounded and it grated to a stop.

The door began to hiss open. Bolan saw smoke curling from under the frame and he flung himself at Tanaka, pushing her against the wall a millisecond before searing flames whooshed from the car and nearly singed his clothes and hair. Another second and the shaft resounded to a grinding noise and the car shot like a fiery meteor toward the bowels of the fortress.

The warrior edged to the brink. The car was still dropping, the cables burned through. He glanced up. The upper third of the shaft was on fire. As yet the flames hadn't spread to the other two shafts but it wouldn't be long before they did.

The woman stepped to his side. "My God! We've got to go back and use the stairs."

"And fight our way down twenty floors?"

"What else can we do?" she asked.

At that moment the elevator on the left pinged and the door opened. Bolan moved toward it only to stop cold at the sight of three soldiers. They gawked, then sought to bring their SMGs into play. He stroked the Type 64's trigger, the chug of its autofire chorused by the sound of slugs tearing into soft flesh and the tinny noise those same slugs made as they exploded out the backs of the Chinese and into the walls.

"Help me," Bolan said, gripping a body to drag it out.

From down the corridor rose upraised voices and the heavy pounding of many feet. Others had the same idea they did.

Bolan reached for the second body and tossed it on top of the first. Tanaka had taken care of the third and was nervously eyeing the elevator.

"Are you sure it's safe?"

Bolan was spared from having to persuade her by a

mad stampede of Chinese military and civilians who stormed around the junction and let out with screams of outrage. Tanaka promptly leaped into the car, and he was quick to follow suit. She hit the down button, but the door wouldn't close fast enough. Several soldiers opened fire with rifles and pistols. Bolan shouldered her aside and sprayed lead to keep the throng back. Two men fell, another clutched his chest and the rest hesitated, unwilling to invite oblivion.

The door finally thudded shut and the car descended. Tanaka gazed apprehensively overhead, voicing the question that was uppermost on the warrior's mind, too. "What if the fire burns through the cables before we reach the bottom?"

Tense, awful moments ensued. They passed the next level, and another. At the third the car came to a stop. Five people were waiting to enter, technicians who took one look at the machine gun Bolan held and backed off with their hands raised.

The car continued down. Tanaka stomped a foot in impatience, then snapped irritably at him, "How can you stand there so calmly?"

Bolan shrugged. He had resigned himself to the inevitable a long time ago. In the line of work he had chosen, the odds of living to a ripe old age were next to nil. It wasn't a question of "if" it happened; it was a question of "when." Worrying about it was useless. He took each day as it came, and if he was alive to greet the next dawn, so much the better.

The car descended smoothly.

As level after level glowed brightly on the control panel and nothing happened, Tanaka began to relax. They were seven stories from the bottom when she grinned self-consciously and said, ''I guess I'm a worrywart, huh?''

Suddenly the car lurched. Bolan kept his balance by thrusting a hand against the side, but his companion was thrown toward the rear. A few seconds later a horrendous grating noise echoed from above and the car slowed to a crawl.

''The fire has reached our shaft!'' Tanaka guessed. ''We need to get out of here before the cables give way!'' She lunged at the control panel and pressed the button for the seventh floor. The car slowed even more, but to her dismay it didn't stop. It sank past the floor and on toward the next. ''What do we do?''

Bolan rose onto his toes and placed a palm against the roof. It was warm to the touch. He stepped to the control panel, watching the indicator light intently. When they were almost to the next level he speared a finger at the red emergency button.

Again the car lurched. Bolan was slammed against the wall, and Tanaka was hurled onto her hands and knees. For a few seconds it seemed the car was going to keep on going, then it tilted slightly and abruptly ceased moving.

Bolan hit the button to open the door, but it had no effect.

''We're trapped!''

''Maybe not,'' Bolan said, and drew a Ka-bar from a boot sheath. He inserted the tip into the middle of the door where the two halves joined and wriggled the blade. The crack widened a hair. By carefully levering the hilt from side to side, he enlarged the gap to where he could grip the inner edge of each half. Then he tried to force the door all the way open. The muscles on his shoulders and neck bulged, but the best he could do was separate the doors about eighteen inches.

Tanaka dropped onto her hands and knees and bent her neck to scan the corridor. "The coast looks clear."

"You go first," Bolan suggested. One of them had to insure the door didn't slide shut.

She didn't argue. Lying on her belly, she wriggled partway through the opening, lithely twisted and pushed against the door. Her legs slid out and she did an acrobatic flip, landing in a crouch. Raising the M-16, she said, "Your turn. I'll cover you."

The warrior let go of the two halves of the door to see if they would slide shut. They didn't, and after replacing the knife in its sheath, he laid on his side and lowered the machine gun as far as his arm would allow, then let it fall. As he turned and slipped his legs through the opening, the car groaned like a person in misery. He tensed when the doors moved a fraction, but they still stayed open. He started to shimmy through as Tanaka had done and was as far as his chest when the car unexpectedly shuddered and an earsplitting grinding noise foretold worse was yet to come.

"Get out of there!" Tanaka cried.

The brakes gave way and the car began to drop. Bolan experienced the sensation of falling and saw the bottom of the frame rushing toward his face. He shoved outward. For an instant he thought he would be mangled beyond recognition. Then his shoulder struck the floor and the car flashed past, wailing like a banshee.

"You almost bought the farm."

To Bolan it wasn't worth mentioning. To him close calls were as routine as breathing, and he dismissed them from his mind the moment they were over. "We have six floors to go," he said, turning to pick up the

64. He didn't like the idea of using the stairwell, but it was the only option left them.

"Hold it." Tanaka was staring at a sign above a door a few yards from the elevators. "That signs says To The Docks," she translated. "Think it's another way down?"

"Only one way to find out." Bolan pulled on the handle. A narrow spiral staircase wound into dank depths. Part of the original fortress, the stairs were stone, the walls a mix of stone and old mortar. Pale starlight filtered through slits high in the walls but wasn't enough to alleviate the gloom. Bolan padded downward and presently detected the smell of water.

"Do you think we can reach the garage this way?" Tanaka asked. "We have to hurry or pretty soon there won't be any cars or trucks left. A mass exodus must be under way."

Bolan was thinking more along the lines of a boat. Escaping across the lake would be easier than escaping by land. It surprised him no one else was trying to reach the docks, but maybe most had been trapped on the upper levels. He passed another door and realized he couldn't hear the Klaxons anymore. He couldn't hear anything, in fact, other than their own footfalls. After the clamor up above the deep quiet seemed unnatural.

"Look there!" Tanaka said, jabbing a thumb at the wall.

It glistened with moisture. Through the next slit wafted the rhythmic lapping of waves. Bolan wondered how it was the sound reached them five stories above-ground. In a few yards he had his answer. The stairs curved to the right and ended at a pair of broad metal doors, one of which hung open. On the other side, bathed in the glow of bright floodlights, were three long docks. A freighter and several small boats were at berth.

They weren't five stories up. They were at ground level. The stairs continued down into subterranean levels.

Creeping to the doorway, Bolan noticed the light outside was flickering and dancing as if alive. Wary not to expose himself to potential hostile fire, he leaned out far enough to glance at the rocky ramparts high above.

The warrior had been mistaken. There weren't any floodlights. The base of the bluff was being lit up by a spectacular pyrotechnic display on top of it. The Heart of Tsanghsien was burning. Flames leaping into the sky had turned the stronghold into a giant torch. Roaring columns of fire lit up the bluff and the lake for hundreds of yards around as if it were daylight.

Movement on the freighter gave away the presence of its crew. They had lined the forward rail, mesmerized by the conflagration.

Bolan saw no one on the nearest boat, a low-slung outboard built for speed. Crooking a finger at Tanaka, he moved into the open, relying on the freighter crew's preoccupation with the raging firestorm to permit him to reach the boat unnoticed. But he had hardly gone three steps when someone on the ship shouted in alarm. He thought they had been spotted, but a sailor was gesturing at the sky.

Out of the night fell dozens of pieces of burning debris. Sizzling like bacon in a frying pan, they landed in the lake, sputtered and were extinguished. They were merely droplets before the storm, a harbinger of descending doom. A huge section of the fortress was about to break away and would plummet toward the docks at any moment.

"Into the boat!" Bolan hollered, running flat out.

The men on the freighter had awakened to their peril and were rushing to man their posts. Some started to raise the anchor. Others were making for the wheelhouse to get the ship under way before she shared the fortress's fate.

Bolan jumped into the speedboat. "Cast off!" he commanded, hurrying to the control console. The keys weren't there. Squatting, he drew his knife. The two wires he needed were attached to the underside of the ignition. He cut them off, swiftly stripped the plastic sheath and the insulation to expose the stranded wires and touched one hot wire to the other. Sparks flew as the motor sputtered and growled and rose in volume to a throaty purr. Bolan glanced at Tanaka to see if she had cast off the line and saw her riveted in place, staring upward. "Cast off!" he repeated, and when she didn't move, he darted over to do it himself.

"We're dead!" she breathed as he reached her side.

The warrior bent his head back.

Amid fiery showers of blazing brands, the upper third of the fortress was crumbling away from the rest, dissolving in slow motion like the top of a hill in the grip of a mudslide. The flames had eaten at the beams and timbers that shored up the walls and ceilings, and now the ancient structure was breaking apart at the seams, like a dwelling devoured by termites. A seething mass of wreckage was at the core.

Bolan unwound the rope and flung it aside. Tanaka still hadn't moved as he turned and raced to the controls. A push on the throttle sent the speedboat surging forward. They might not make it. The fireball was streaking toward them like a comet, complete with a flaming tail.

The sailors on the freighter were frantically raising her heavy anchor and throwing the lines down. A gangplank was being hurriedly detached.

At that juncture a squad of soldiers appeared. They spied the speedboat and commenced firing in furious abandon, oblivious to the peril swooping from on high.

"Get down!" Bolan yelled at Tanaka. But she stood there like a zombie, unable to tear her gaze off the fireball.

A slug whined off the console. Others smacked against the transom dangerously near the outboard.

Bolan shoved the throttle all the way open. Like a Thoroughbred responding to a tug on the reins, the speedboat nearly leaped out of the water. A fine spray dampened his face. The starboard side was too close to the dock, but Bolan was more concerned about their lives than a few dings and scrapes.

Tanaka screamed.

The fireball seemed to fill the sky, a glowing mountain that eclipsed the stars. The roar of its passage was the roar of a volcano amplified a thousand times, a roar so tremendous it drowned out the outboard and the fading notes of the woman's scream.

Heat blistered Bolan's head, shoulders and back as he bent over the wheel. He didn't look up again because it would waste seconds better spent putting as much distance as they could between themselves and imminent destruction. The speedboat came to the end of the dock and he spun the wheel too far, too hard, slewing the aft end in a wide crescent. Compensating, he straightened the boat and shot toward the center of

Tsanghsien Lake. They covered twenty yards, forty, fifty.

A hand fell on his shoulder. Tanaka clung to him, her eyes laced with unbridled fear. "We're going to die."

Bolan held the throttle down. They raced another sixty feet. When her fingernails bit into his skin, he glanced back.

The colossal caldron of flame slammed into the docks with the impact of a bomb. Soldiers and boats alike disappeared under its gargantuan bulk. Half the freighter was shorn asunder; the other half was instantly set ablaze. Sailors combusted like matches, several diving into the lake in a vain bid to save themselves.

The impact generated a wave of stupendous size. Displaced by the wreckage, the water swelled up into a frothing onrushing wall fifteen feet high. It swamped what was left of the docks and capsized what was left of the freighter.

Bolan still had the speedboat's throttle full open, but the wave swept toward them as if they were standing still. He pulled Tanaka closer and looped his other arm around the wheel. In a span of seconds the wave overtook them, towering over their low craft, a watery fist about to smash it to bits.

"Hold on!" Bolan shouted to be heard above the bedlam of sibilant hiss of the water and the snarl of the outboard. He took a deep breath to fill his lungs with air and felt Tanaka trembling uncontrollably.

The wave curled. Bolan swung the woman against the console and shielded her with his own body. Suddenly the aft end of the speedboat canted upward. He thought they were going to flip over, but the boat was caught on the wave's shoulder and they were borne along like deadwood caught in surf. For hundreds of feet they were pushed headlong across the lake. Gradually the size and force of the wave diminished and the speedboat leveled off.

Bolan moved Tanaka to one side so he could concentrate on steering. Her eyes were shut and her hands were clenched, her nails digging into her palms. He looked at the bluff and beheld a sight to rival the spectacle at Hakka Island.

The Heart of Tsanghsien was a gigantic bonfire, ablaze from end to end, the upper half gone or in fiery ruins, the lower half being rocked by explosions and spurts of flame that shot in all directions. Loud rumblings issued from the subterranean levels, and the sheer stone walls shook as if in the grip of an earthquake. The docks were gone. The section of the freighter still afloat soon wouldn't be.

Over on the highway a line of vehicles raced southward.

Bolan saw no other boats in their vicinity. They had made it out alive and unscathed, and no one was after them. He turned due west and asked, "Are you all right?"

"I was scared."

"Who wouldn't have been?"

She opened her eyes. They were brimming with tears. "You don't understand. I was so scared I couldn't think—I couldn't move. I was paralyzed."

"So were a lot of others, I'd imagine." Bolan spied a light in the sky circling over the north end Tsanghsien Lake.

"Not you. You never froze up, never acted the least

bit afraid. You were calm and professional the whole time.''

"I'm used to it," Bolan said. The light banked down low and started flying in their general direction. It was too soon to be certain, but it appeared to be on an intercept course.

Overcome by misery, Tanaka failed to notice. "How can anyone become used to something like that?" She nodded toward the nightmare scene of devastation and death. "I doubt I could if I lived to be a hundred." Slumping against the console, she said forlornly, "I care for you. I thought maybe the two of us would work well together, but I was wrong. I'm not up to it. I'm not in your league."

"We'll talk about it later," Bolan stated. The aircraft was definitely zeroing in on them. A patrol plane, he figured. It would force them to stop or else blow them out of the water.

"There's nothing to talk about," Tanaka said, tears trickling down her cheeks. "I see that now. I could never do what you do."

Above the growl of their outboard rose the sound of much more powerful engines. The aircraft was a lot larger than the single running light had led the warrior to believe.

"I was deluding myself," she continued. "I thought we were just right for each other. I thought you were the man of my dreams."

"You did?" Bolan didn't take his gaze off the aircraft. He couldn't determine what kind it was, but odds were it was a war bird and packed enough firepower to sink a destroyer.

"I was going to ask Mr. Brognola for a transfer to

the States,'' she disclosed. "I was going to do whatever it took to make you mine."

Like a bat out of the night, the aircraft flew directly over the speedboat. It was so low Bolan could have hit it with a rock if he'd had one. The plane bore no markings, no insignia. But he did observe pontoons, the earmark of an amphibian.

At last Tanaka shook off her melancholy and stood up straight. "What now? The general has his own private air force, too?"

"If it opens up on us, we won't last ten seconds," Bolan said. "Can you swim?"

"Like a fish."

"So can I, but if we have to jump for it we might be in the water a long time. Search for life vests. They'll help keep us afloat without too much effort."

Nodding, Tanaka opened a compartment along the starboard gunwale and sorted through the contents. "A rope, a can of motor oil and a small toolbox. That's all."

"Try another one." Bolan rearmed himself with the Type 64 SMG. It wouldn't be much use against a war bird the size of the amphibian, but it had to do.

The aircraft had banked again. This time it swooped toward them head-on from the west, so low the pontoons skimmed the surface.

"They're landing," Bolan said, and brought the speedboat to a stop. He could aim better standing still. Sighting on the cockpit, he waited for the plane to come within range.

The pilot brought it in with extreme skill and precision. It set down lightly, coasted to within forty feet of their boat and swung broadside. A four-prop job with a broad, blunt nose, its fuselage was painted black.

"You can stop searching," Bolan told Tanaka, and lowered the machine gun.

"Aren't we putting up a fight?"

"There's no need." Bolan had recognized the amphibian. "It's one of ours."

Soon the bay door lowered, revealing a lanky figure in a blue flight suit. "Howdy, folks," Jack Grimaldi hailed them. "Care for a lift, or would you rather thumb it back to the U.S.?"

Bolan revved the outboard and brought the boat alongside the aircraft. On either side of Grimaldi was a hardman in a blacksuit, both armed with M-16s fitted with night-vision scopes. "I thought Hal had decided it was too risky to send you in."

"You know how fickle the big guy is," his friend said, and bent, extending a hand toward Tanaka. "Ladies first." A man in black helped pull her up.

"How did you know it was us in the boat?" Bolan asked as he was boosted on board.

Grimaldi patted the amphibian. "This baby is packed with more state-of-the-art surveillance gear than a Russian embassy. I might ask the big guy to give it to me for Christmas."

"Get us out of here," Bolan said. "I need to get in touch with Hal and get back to the States as quickly as possible." Somehow they had to stop General Tsanghsien's contingency plan from being carried out.

"What about you, missy?" Grimaldi said to Tanaka. "Want me to arrange to take you back with us?"

Her face was cloaked in shadow. "No. Drop me off in Japan. It's where I belong."

EPILOGUE

The Executioner drove north along Interstate 5 toward the U.S.-Canadian border. He wore the same clothes he had worn on his last visit and was driving the same modified four-door Chevy sedan provided by the Feds. At the point of entry he pulled into the same lane and was approached by the same examiner.

"Good afternoon, sir." The young Canadian glanced into the back seat at the poles and tackle. "I remember you. Back for more fishing, eh?"

"There's no such thing as too much," Bolan said, showing the phony car registration, birth certificate and proof of insurance.

"I hope you catch a big one."

"I'm hoping to catch at least two," Bolan said, and was waved on. He followed the same route into Vancouver, and at the third exit he took Cambie Street north and crossed the span over False Creek. He rode around Lost Lagoon and into Stanley Park. As he had done on his last visit he went over Lions Gate Bridge and turned right on Marine Drive.

Lions Heights was quiet at that hour. A few kids were playing in their yards, but it was suppertime, and most families were indoors.

Bolan's features hardened as he drove past the front

gate to Carl Merrill's estate. His hand slid under his jacket and curled around the Beretta, but he didn't draw it. Soon, though. Very soon.

The warrior continued around to the rear of the estate and pulled off the road at the same spot he had pulled off before. Concealing the car in the cluster of trees, he shut off the engine and sat back.

Brognola had come through again. The Feds had tracked the shipment of a large crate from the Chinese port of Qingdao to an import firm in Vancouver, a company owned by Carl Merrill's. Luck had been a factor in that a transmission between the captain of the vessel and one of Merrill's lieutenants had been intercepted off Hawaii.

Bolan checked his watch, slid a cellular phone from his pocket and tapped in a number. It was answered on the third ring. "I'm in position. Are we still good to go?"

"They're all yours," Brognola said. "I'll make the call."

Bolan pressed the off button. Unknown to Merrill, the freighter had been intercepted twelve miles out and the PPS-1 had been removed from the crate and replaced with scrap metal. Under guard, the crew was permitted to bring the vessel into port. Canadian authorities had agreed not to release the crate from customs until they received a call from Brognola, which he was placing at that very moment.

The warrior drew the Beretta, threaded a suppressor onto the barrel and placed the pistol on his lap. Unbidden, thoughts of Kerri Tanaka pricked his conscience. He remembered their bittersweet parting at Yokota Air Force Base, how she had hugged him until he pried her loose and the sorrow in her eyes as he walked off.

Bolan felt sorry for her. She had learned a hard lesson about herself, and about life. He was confident she would recover and one day find a man better suited to give her the love she deserved. In time she'd forget about him, or at least be able to think about him without breaking into tears.

To take his mind off her, Bolan reviewed the new intel the Feds had turned up. Or, rather, the Canadians had, and then kindly passed it on to interested agencies south of the border.

Merrill had lied. He'd been involved with smuggling long before the Di Stefano brothers came along. He hadn't dabbled in drugs, but he had his dirty fingers into every other illicit traffic known to man and operated an extensive pipeline from all parts of the world. Luigi and Gino Di Stefano had recognized a good thing when they saw it and muscled in to use Merrill's network for the distribution of their heroin.

According to new information, Merrill smuggled in everything from historical artifacts to human organs. Anything and everything anyone wanted, he obtained for the right price.

Canadian officials had caught on when they apprehended one of Merrill's couriers trying to smuggle a human heart into the country. It seemed a wealthy individual in need of a transplant had grown tired of waiting and arranged to have one smuggled into Canada. The courier had talked to reduce his sentence, and Canadian authorities had been all set to close Merrill down when Brognola contacted them about the crate.

The sun was almost gone.

Bolan got out, the Beretta in hand, and walked to the brick wall. He pulled himself up, paused long enough to verify the coast was clear, then dropped to the other side. No guards were patrolling the grounds, nor were any near the main house. Their absence didn't surprise him. With the truck due soon, Merrill probably had all his hired guns out front.

The heart-shaped pool shimmered undisturbed. Few lights were on in the house, but the long garage was lit up like a birthday cake and its wide door hung open. Merrill's collection of vintage cars had been driven out and parked near the fountain to make room for the special delivery.

A hedge screened Bolan until he was almost to the house. He sprinted the last twenty yards to the back door and without hesitation entered. A plush hall took him past the kitchen and the living room. Both were empty. He passed a stairwell but heard no sounds from upstairs. It appeared Merrill had given the staff and the lovely ladies the night off. Which made sense. He wouldn't want anyone to become unduly curious.

What had surprised Bolan was learning Merrill planned to have the crate brought to the estate. A wiretap had turned up that little gem. The only conclusion Brognola could reach was that Merrill considered the PPS-1 too important to be shunted to a warehouse.

The front door was bordered by strips of colored glass. Bolan peered through one and saw Merrill and eight underlings by the front gate, awaiting delivery. Two more men were in the garage, along with someone Bolan couldn't see but whose shadow was etched on the opposite wall. He knew who it was. She had been staying at Merrill's for the past two days.

Headlights heralded the arrival of a diesel truck hauling a flatbed covered with canvas. It seemed as out of place in ritzy Lions Heights as a Rolls-Royce would in a trailer park. Merrill barked at his men, who scrambled to open the gate and closed it the instant the truck came through.

The driver looped the cab toward the fountain and braked, then threw the semi into reverse, grinding gears when he did. Poking his head out his window, he slowly backed the flatbed toward the garage.

Merrill and his men were on the other side, their view of the house blocked by the big rig.

Bolan opened the front door and walked toward the cab. The driver was looking the other way and never saw him. Hopping onto the step, Bolan gripped the door handle. The passenger-side window was down, which expedited things nicely. "I have a question for you," he said.

"Shit!" the driver blurted, and spun. He was a beefy slab of muscle with a handlebar mustache and beetling brows. "Who the hell are you? What do you want?"

"You're one of Carl Merrill's men, aren't you?"

"Yeah. What of it?"

"I just wanted to be sure," Bolan answered, and shot him between the eyes. The rumble of the diesel smothered the cough of the Beretta, and he hopped back down with none of the bodyguards aware anything was wrong.

"Harry? What are you waiting for?" Merrill shouted from over near the garage. "Back it in!"

Bolan walked around the front of the cab. He saw the driver slump against the seat, and evidently the man's foot slipped off the clutch because suddenly the truck lurched backward and the tail end of the flatbed almost smashed into the garage.

"Harry!" Merrill fumed. "Watch what the hell you're doing!"

The engine coughed a few times and died. Bolan

stepped past the cab and fell into a combat crouch, catching the guards flat-footed. With practiced precision he put a slug through three of them. The rest galvanized to life and he ducked behind the cab to avoid a swarm of lead. When they stopped firing, he popped out again and downed two more.

Merrill was throwing a fit. "Into the garage! Get in the garage! We'll hold him off while I call for help!"

Bolan ejected the magazine and slipped it into a pocket. Replacing it with a full one, he moved toward the rear. The back tires were only a dozen feet from the garage, and he crouched beside them to target the opposition.

Merrill and his would-be protectors were too far in to spot, except for a solitary gunner who was slinking toward the control box to lower the door.

The warrior took aim. At the same split second the gunner detected him and elevated a Smith & Wesson pistol. The Executioner fired first and had one less triggerman to deal with.

Bending, he saw the stout legs of a second man but not the man's whole body. So he dipped lower yet, seeking a better angle.

From the farthermost recesses of the garage Carl Merrill yelled, "Hey! You out there! Who are you? Why are you doing this?"

Bolan spied a chest attached to the stout legs. Fixing a bead on the sternum, he squeezed off two shots.

As the bodyguard fell, he smashed against a tool rack and tore it loose. The racket the tools made when they spilled onto the concrete floor dwarfed whatever slight sound Bolan made as he sprinted to the near corner of the garage.

The smuggler had only two guards left, and he was

growing desperate. "Let's talk about this! What do you say? Did the Mob send you? I can pay double whatever they're paying."

Sinking onto a knee, Bolan caught sight of a shadow on the opposite wall. He held both arms straight out, swiveled at the hips and snapped off a shot. The gunner creeping toward him never had a prayer.

Now Merrill was down to one bodyguard—and the person who had arranged with Merrill to have the crate smuggled in.

"Listen to me, mister! I can make you rich! All you have to do is agree to let me live! Let's talk it over!"

Bolan let the Beretta do his talking. Throwing himself into the open, onto his side, he nailed the last bodyguard with a round to the cheek.

"Don't shoot!" Merrill wailed, throwing his arms into the air. "I'm unarmed!"

As if it made a difference.

Warily rising, Bolan was amazed at how calm the woman was. She had on a full-length fur coat and a diamond bracelet that sparkled in the fluorescent light. In her left hand was a leather purse. Her right hand was in the folds of her coat.

"You!" Merrill bleated.

"I told you I'd be back if you had lied," Bolan reminded him.

To the woman he said, "Abigail Harkness, I take it?"

As coolly as if she were on a receiving line at a formal ball, Soong Tsanghsien's mother smiled and responded, "You have the advantage of me, sir. I have no idea who you are. Unless—" She scrutinized him intently. "Brognola sent you, didn't he?"

Merrill's confusion was almost comical. "Who the hell is Brognola? How's he figure into this?"

"He's the power behind the throne," Harkness replied.

"Huh?" Merrill swore luridly. "Lady, I never understand half of what you say. Are you telling me Brognola works for the queen of England? And this big guy here is a British secret agent?"

She sighed and looked at Bolan. "Do you know why the world is in the deplorable state it is? I do. We have a surplus of simpletons. They're everywhere, breeding like rabbits, and fouling every country on the globe with their rank stupidity."

"Who are you calling stupid, you old hag?" Merrill declared. "I'll have you know I've done quite well for myself."

"Mr. Merrill," Harkness said wearily, "for two days straight I've had to endure your asininity, and my patience is at an end." She bestowed another smile on the warrior. "Would you be a dear and put him out of my misery?"

Merrill still didn't get it. "What? You think he's going to kill me just like that?" He snapped his fingers.

"Why do you think I'm here?" Bolan said, and shot him.

The smuggler was punched against a workbench. His legs upended and so did the bench, and he landed on his back with gray matter oozing from a new cavity in his temple.

Bolan trained the Beretta on Abigail Harkness, who didn't bat an eyelid.

"It's my turn now, I presume?"

"Brognola asked me to give you a choice. He'd like for you to turn yourself in."

She smirked. "Why? To submit to a media circus of epic proportions? To endure a public trial and life in prison with no chance of parole? I think not. Now that my son's contingency plan has failed, I intend to travel to China and live out the rest of my days by his side."

"You're forgetting something," Bolan said, wagging the Beretta.

"Young man, I never forget a thing," Harkness replied. She raised her hand from the folds of her fur coat. In it was a grenade, and the pin had already been pulled. "I understand the time-delay fuse on this particular model is only four seconds and the blast radius is forty-five feet. Can you cover that much distance in that amount of time? I know I couldn't."

"I can't let you leave."

She stepped toward him. "You can't stop me. Not unless you want to die along with me."

"You would be throwing your life away," Bolan said. Hoping to shock her into surrendering, he broke the bad news. "Your son is dead. I was there. I know."

To the warrior's amazement the woman laughed. "That was you? My, you do get around. But I'm afraid you're mistaken a second time. Soong is very much alive. I talked to him on the phone not three hours ago." She took another step.

Bolan stood his ground. "Tsanghsien made it out of the fortress alive?"

"Very much so, but he's badly burned, I understand." Harkness took two more strides, the grenade in front of her, ready to let go if he fired. "What a small world we live in. He'd asked me to do some digging and find out who destroyed his ancestral home, and here you are!"

"He'll never find me," Bolan said.

"Never underestimate my pride and joy," she

crowed. "He'll be coming for you, mister. It might be a month from now, it might be a year, but he'll track you down. When he does, he's going to make you suffer as he's suffered. He's going to destroy whatever you value most in this world, and then he'll destroy you." She advanced several more yards as she spoke.

"I won't hold my breath."

Harkness shrugged. "It's your funeral."

Bolan had let her get close enough. Now he leaped. He clamped his left hand onto her fingers to prevent her from releasing the grenade while simultaneously slamming the Beretta against her forehead. She collapsed, the heavy fur coat cushioning her fall, and he carefully relieved her of the grenade.

In the distance sirens howled. It was time for the warrior to leave. His job was done. The Canadian authorities would take Harkness into custody and turn her over to the American Feds. As for General Soong Tsanghsien, time would tell whether he would make good on his threat.

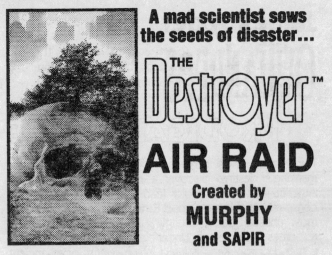

James Axler

OUTLANDERS®

PRODIGAL CHALICE

The warriors, who dare to expose the deadly truth of mankind's destiny, discover a new gateway in Central America—one that could lead them deeper into the conspiracy that has doomed Earth. Here they encounter a most unusual baron struggling to control the vast oil resources of the region. Uncertain if this charismatic leader is friend or foe, Kane is lured into a search for an ancient relic of mythic proportions that may promise a better future…or plunge humanity back into the dark ages.

In the Outlands,
the shocking truth is humanity's last hope.

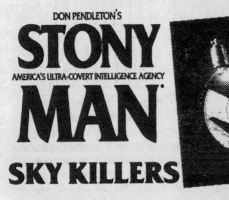

JAMES AXLER

DEATH LANDS®

Breakthrough

Deathlands is a living hell, but there is someplace worse: a parallel Earth where the atomic mega-cull never happened. Now, this otherworld Earth is in its final death throes. Yet, for an elite few, the reality portal offers a new frontier of raw energy, and expendable slaves—a bastion of power for Dredda Otis Trask. Her invasion force has turned the ruins of Salt Lake City into the deadly mining grounds of a grotesque new order—one that lies in wait for Ryan and his companions.

In the Deathlands, danger lurks beyond the imagination.

Available in March 2002
at your favorite retail outlet.